IS IMMORT...

It is if it can only be achieved by feeding on the lifeblood of others to survive. But vampires, once feared as evil incarnate, have in modern times come to assume a less terrifying role. Not all of these beings of the night are evil, not all are seductive purveyors of death. Here is your chance to meet both those who walk the night in search of human prey and those who haunt the shadows, hunting down beings far more dangerous than themselves in such imaginative tales as:

"Origin of a Species"—Can a homicide detective on an archaeological dig in Turkey solve a millennia-old murder mystery?

"The Night of Their Lives"—Was she an angel of mercy . . . or on a far darker mission?

"Night Tidings"—Even a priest might form an unholy alliance to clear the name of a woman who could no longer defend herself. . . .

VAMPIRE
DETECTIVES

VAMPIRE DETECTIVES

EDITED BY
Martin H. Greenberg

DAW BOOKS, INC.

DONALD A. WOLLHEIM, FOUNDER

375 Hudson Street, New York, NY 10014

ELIZABETH R. WOLLHEIM
SHEILA E. GILBERT
PUBLISHERS

ACKNOWLEDGMENTS

Introduction © 1995 by Ed Gorman.
Vampire Dollars © 1995 by William F. Nolan.
This Town Ain't Big Enough © 1995 by Tanya Huff.
Girl's Night Out © 1995 by Kathe Koja and
   Barry N. Malzberg.
Home Comforts © 1995 by Peter Crowther.
Origin of A Species © 1995 by J. N. Williamson.
Fangs © 1995 by Douglas Borton.
The Night of Their Lives © 1995 by Max Allan Collins.
Night Tidings © 1995 by Gary Alan Ruse.
God-Less Men © 1995 by James Kisner.
No Blood for a Vampire © 1995 by Edward D. Hoch.
The Count's Mailbox © 1995 by William Sanders.
Tom Rudolph's Last Tape © 1995 by John Maclay.
The Turning © 1995 by Jack Ketchum.
You'll Catch Your Death © 1995 by P. N. Elrod.
Shell Game © 1995 by John Lutz.
The Secret © 1995 by Barbara Paul.
Blind Pig on North Halsted © 1995 by
   Wayne Allen Sallee.
Phil the Vampire © 1995 by Richard Laymon.
Undercover © 1995 by Nancy Holder.

CONTENTS

INTRODUCTION
by
Ed Gorman

Poe got it right. The human spirit is divided by two conflicting needs: The need for the fantastic and the need for the rational.

The theme of vampire detective neatly combines these needs.

Consider for a moment the vampire, creature of dark night and even darker myth. And the detective, the ultimate expression of science seeking rational explanation for irrational acts.

Poe was the first writer to combine these two elements. One need say nothing more than "The Murders In The Rue Morgue" to let modern readers know where this form of fiction first began.

In this book, you'll find the descendants of Poe, and a century-and-a-half of variations on the themes he first gave us.

By now, of course, the vampire has become the all-purpose ghoul: he (or) she can be sinister, funny, sad, sexy, or (as in Klaus Kinksi's remake of "Nosferatu") a creature of great and melancholy lyricism.

You'll find all these tones and moods in the stories that follow, tales that emphasize in equal parts the fantastic and the rational, just as Mr. Poe suggested so long ago.

VAMPIRE DOLLARS
by
William F. Nolan

Just as I rang the bell, I heard a scream. Followed by another. Piercing, blood-chilling screams from inside the house. Somebody was in real trouble. Should I try to smash my way inside? Or call 911? The door looked massive, solid as a boulder. I'd probably dislocate my shoulder. Better to go for some law.

I was halfway back to my car when the door opened behind me and a woman's voice called out. "Mr. Challis? Where are you running off to?"

I happen to be a connoisseur of horror movies, especially vampire films, and the voice was familiar. It belonged to Sandra Steele, Hollywood's one-time "Queen of Horror." A legend. In the same league with Bogart and Elvis and Marilyn Monroe. Only Sandra was still very much alive.

I walked back to the house. She looked exactly like I'd expected. Pale, thin-wristed, dressed entirely in black, with deep, heavy-lidded dark eyes. A silver batpin (appropriate) held her thick hair in a French roll. She extended a long-fingered hand with curving, red-lacquered nails. Like the hand of Fu Manchu.

I shook it. "Hi," I said.

"I'm pleased you're here, Mr. Challis," she told me in her velvet vampire's voice.

"What was all the screaming about?"

She smiled thinly, beckoning me inside. "I'll show you."

The house was like a museum. Posters from all of her films. Framed death masks. Mannequins lining the hallway dressed in the costumes she'd worn in a variety of blood-sucking epics.

We entered the library. Above the stone fireplace, a large oil painting dominated the room. Of Sandra, as the Queen Vampire, standing above an open grave, arms spread wide, her black cape extended like huge batwings. A video was running without sound on her VCR. I recognized it. *The Devil Bat's Daughter*. A classic.

She picked up the remote control, pressed a button, and the film reversed. Then she stopped it, hit "play," and turned up the sound. Screams. Loud and blood-chilling. Onscreen, Sandra had her fangs buried in the neck of a terrified young virgin.

"I'm hopelessly sentimental," she told me. "Replaying my early films is like visiting old friends. And I tend to turn up the volume. I barely heard the door chime."

I nodded, feeling a little silly. Mistaking canned screams for the real thing. Dumb.

She killed the VCR. "Would you like a drink, Mr. Challis?"

"My brother drinks in the afternoon," I told her. "I usually wait till the sun goes down."

"Your brother is quite a famous detective," she said. "Frankly, I was attempting to hire him, but they gave me your number."

"That's because Bart's out of the game. I've taken over for him. It's the *Nick* Challis Agency now."

"I see." She waved me to a sofa with pillows big enough to smother a horse. I settled into them.

"That film you were watching. Wasn't that one of Karloff's last?"

"Indeed it was. Boris played the role of my depraved father. A demon bat. At the end they drove a stake through his chest and burned him into ash. He was a dear, dear man." She sat down next to me. "Are you familiar with my career?"

"Sure. I'm a big fan of yours."

"Then you are aware that I retired from the screen five years ago?"

I nodded. "In 1988, right after the death of David DuPlain."

"David directed all of my best films. I did not wish to continue without him." She sighed. "These days I try to keep busy with investments ... real estate."

"Helped, no doubt, when your daddy left you a flock of office buildings on Wilshire."

"Ah, yes . . . my father was very generous in his will." She gave me another thin smile. "You *do* know a lot about me."

"Famous people are easy to find out about," I said. I leaned toward her. "I understand you want me to find your daughter?"

"Yes. Janet's been gone for almost a month. I've had no word from her and I'm very concerned."

"She live here with you?"

"She's always lived with me. She refused to attend college, or seek any kind of job. Janet has depended on me for everything."

"You don't like her much, do you?"

"We never got along. She's always been a very difficult child."

I walked over to a hand-crafted cherrywood bookcase, picked up a framed photo. "This her?"

"Yes. It was taken out by the pool."

The color shot revealed a lush-figured redhead in a black thong. "Some child," I said. "How old?"

"Janet turned twenty-three last month. We had a terrible argument on her birthday."

"What about?"

"About a man she's been seeing. Lee Snowden. A very unsavory individual. A television actor who's mostly unemployed."

"You think she's with him now?"

"That's exactly what I think. And I want you to find them."

"Why?" I put the photo back on the shelf. "If your daughter wants to live with a loser, that's her business."

Sandra gave me a penetrating look, the same intense look I'd seen so many times on the screen. "I just want to find out where she is. To satisfy myself that nothing unfortunate has happened to her." She got up from the sofa and walked over to a French window. "Once I know for a certainty that she's with Snowden, I shall dismiss her from my thoughts. She can throw away her life as she pleases."

"So I find Snowden and if your daughter's with him, that's it. End of case."

"Precisely."

I picked up the pool photo, slipped it out of its silver frame. "I'll need this."

"Take it."

"I'll also need a retainer."

She walked over to an antique roll-top desk, fished out an envelope and handed it to me. "Find her, Mr. Challis."

I glanced at the check inside the envelope. "Sure," I said.

And left the Vampire Queen's castle.

Later that afternoon. I was in the office in Studio City when my partner walked in. Mike Cahill. A muscular ex-cop from St. Louis who works out regularly with guys like Schwarzenegger at Gold's Gym in Santa Monica. In the year he'd been with me I'd learned that Mike was a good man. Tough and smart. And great at snooping out dirt when dirt was needed.

I told him about my meeting with Sandra. "I want you to dig up everything you can find on film director David DuPlain."

"Guy's dead," said Mike, running the edge of a fore-finger along his upper lip. "Somebody shot him. What else is there to know?"

"Just dig," I said.

"What's DuPlain got to do with the missing girl?"

I shrugged. "Maybe nothing."

"So I'll dig," said Mike.

The blonde receptionist at the Actor's Guild was a knockout, obviously a Madonna wannabe, putting in her time until she was discovered. She gave me a smile with a lot of teeth in it. "Help you?"

"I'm with Pacific Pictures," I told her. "We're trying to locate an actor named Lee Snowden. I believe he's a Guild member."

The blonde punched computer keys. "His membership's expired."

"Is there an agent listed for him?"

"Hal Bickelman. I can give you his number."

"I'd appreciate it."

She scribbled on a sheet of notepaper, handing it to

me with another toothy smile. "You ever need a blonde in your pictures, I'm available."

"I'll bet you are," I said.

And I was out of there.

.   The Bickelman All-Star Talent Agency on little Santa Monica, just west of Century City, was on the top floor of an outdated, three-story, weathered-brick building built to collapse in earthquakes. The reception room stank of stale tobacco smoke, which figured when I got ushered in to see the Big Man.

Hal Bickelman was lounging back in a worn, cracked-leather chair with a lit cigar buried in one cheek. Cheap suit (when every other agent in town was wearing designer jeans), cheap office, and cheap cigar (when nobody besides George Burns was smoking them anymore). He looked like a leftover cliché from the 50s.

When I gave him my phony cover story and told him who I was looking for, he made a grunting noise and shook his head.

"Believe me, you don't want this guy," he told me. "Lee's got no class. Hell, he stiffed me my ten per cent on the last job I got him. That's why we parted company."

"Know where he is now?"

He ignored my question, having more to say about his ex-client. "Physically, Lee just didn't light up the screen. No inner glow. All the big ones, they got that. An inner glow."

"I still need to find him." I laid a folded twenty on Hal's desk.

He scooped it up like a pelican goes for fish. "When I knew him, he lived in Culver City. Little bungalow on one of the streets behind what used to be MGM. But he moved. I lost track of him till yesterday."

"What happened yesterday?"

"Guy I know tells me he saw Lee at a mobile home park in Venice. Near one of the canals. That help?"

"It helps."

I started to go when he waved his fuming cigar at me. "You find Lee, you might remind him he owes me."

"Yeah, I might," I said.

I needed fresh air.

* * *

I picked up Mike outside the office and we headed for Venice in my Honda Civic. As we drove, he filled me in on David DuPlain. I wanted to know how he died.

"A .38 slug in the chest. The cops put it together. According to the report, DuPlain comes home late one night while his house is being robbed. The robber shoots him. They never found the murder gun or the guy who did it."

"Anybody else at the house that night?"

"Negative. DuPlain was alone. He'd separated from his wife and she was in Chicago."

"Sandra Steele never made another picture after he died," I said. "Could be they had a thing going."

Mike rubbed his neck. "Could be. But if so, they sure kept it under wraps."

"Uh-huh," I said, pulling the Honda into the gravel yard of Pacific Vista Mobile Home Estates, a grand name for a depressing piece of real estate. A scatter of old mobile homes parked on a raw-dirt lot surrounded by a sagging slat fence.

We got out and walked to an outdated single-wide with a cracked-plastic OFFICE sign nailed above the aluminum screen door. I rang the bell and could hear it hiccough inside. "Anybody here?"

A rail-thin woman with a face like unbaked bread opened the screen. "You want a space here, you've come at exactly the right time. We have several fine vacancies and I can offer you our best introductory rate: one free month's rent on sign-in, another free month if you take a year's lease. We've got full, paid utilities and I can—"

"Lee Snowden," I said, breaking into her practiced spiel. "Does he rent here?"

She frowned. "Not for long. If he doesn't pay what he owes me by the end of the week, I'm going to kick his rosy red butt off my property." She made a hissing sound. "Big TV actor! A big *nothing* if you ask me."

I cut into her bullshit again. "Which space?"

"Number six. The beige with the brown shutters near the fence."

"Got a girl in there with him?" asked Mike.

She arched a bony shoulder. "How would I know?

They come and they go. Could have a goddamn *harem* in there for all I care. Just tell him to pay up or he's out."

We walked back to the car. "You stay here," I told Mike. "I'll handle this solo."

"Hard to believe Sandra Steele's daughter would shack up here with a lowlife like Snowden."

"Love is blind, Michael," I said, heading for number six.

A dented, burnt-orange '87 Chevy pickup was parked behind the beige double-wide. Probably belonged to Snowden.

The electric bell was hanging by a single wire, so I banged on the door. It was opened by a big, slab-muscled guy who needed a shave. Shirtless and hairy as an ape. He hadn't bothered to zip the fly on his threadbare Levis and he *wasn't* smiling.

"Who the fuck are you?"

"Hiram Bixby," I told him. "Of Bixby Life—the insurance company with the policy that leaves you with an inner glow. This week we have a special on—"

"Get lost," he growled. "I don't want any friggin' life insurance."

Then I heard a female voice from inside. "Who is it, Lee?"

A red-haired young woman in purple slacks and a black tank top appeared at the door, looking pale and rumpled. Janet Steele.

"Some creep selling insurance," said Snowden.

He started to shut the door, but I blocked it with my foot.

"Perhaps, if I could just talk for a moment to the lady of the house . . ."

Snowden was steaming. "You're lookin' for a broken foot, asshole. Didn't I tell you to get lost?"

"Sure you did," I said, and drove my right fist into his red face, a solid blow which sent him crashing backward onto the floor. Out cold.

Janet was in shock. "Why . . . why did you hit him?"

I shrugged. "Seemed like the thing to do."

I walked back to Mike at the car.

"How'd it go?"

"Peachy," I said.

"Was she with him?"

"Yep. Just like Mama said."

We got into the Honda and I started the engine.

"So," said Mike, "you phone in your report and it's over."

"Maybe," I said, gunning out of the lot. "And maybe pigs fly."

Back at the office I phoned Sandra Steele, telling her I'd found her daughter with Snowden, giving her their address in Venice. She told me she was satisfied with my work. Was her check enough to cover my fees?

"More than enough," I said. "But there's just one other thing I'm curious about. Were you and David DuPlain having an affair?"

That's when she slammed down the phone. The only answer I got was a dial tone.

Mike was on the office couch, riffling through the latest *Playboy.* "What'd she say?"

"She didn't. But it's pretty clear they were hitting the sheets together. Which makes me wonder if Davey boy was really shot by a burglar."

"What are you gonna do?" Mike asked. He was holding the centerfold upside down and grinning.

"Next move's up to the Vampire Queen. I'd guess she has a special reason for wanting that address."

"So?"

"So I want you to stake out Snowden's mobile home. See what happens."

"What do you *expect* to happen?"

"Hey, who knows? Maybe it'll turn into a pumpkin at midnight."

While Mike was on stakeout that night, I rented a half-dozen of Sandra Steele's classic films and, with a supply of 7-Up and Cape Cod cheese popcorn, I settled in for my own vampire film festival. There was something disturbing about the lady, something that I couldn't put a label on; I hoped that if I studied her films I might be able to discover what was bugging me.

Halfway through *Blood Sisters* the phone rang and I killed the sound. It was nearly midnight and I'd been glued to the TV screen for nearly four hours.

"Yeah?" I said into the receiver.

"Nick, it's me—and I got some hot news for you."
Mike sounded agitated.

"Fill me in."

"Snowden and the girl left, so I trailed along to see
where they went. It was a movie. A crime thing with
Mel Gibson. I waited until it was over and they came
out. They stopped at an all-night coffee shop for some
burgers and—"

"So far your news is ice cold," I told him. "When
does it heat up?"

"I'm coming to the good part. When they got back
home, it turns out somebody'd been there. I crawled up
close so I could see through the window. A royal rip-
up, like a tornado had come through. But whoever did
the job missed what they were looking for."

"How do you know that?"

"Because I saw Snowden pull apart a section of air
vent and take out a small package. Seemed real relieved
it was still there."

"Did he open the package?"

"Naw, just put it back in the vent."

"Go home. Hit the sack. We'll talk more about this
tomorrow."

"Yeah, I could use some z's," said Mike.

We hung up.

When I unlocked the door to my office the next morning, Lee Snowden shouldered in roughly behind me,
kicking the door shut. His jaw was set and he had a
silver-plated Browning automatic in his right hand.

"And a good morning to you," I said.

"When you showed up yesterday with that phony insurance story I thought I'd seen you before. And I was
right. You were in the *Times* about three months ago
when you saved that black kid."

"Since when do actors point real guns at people?" I
asked him. I was trying to be cool, but the palms of my
hands were sweating.

"You made a big mistake trashing my place last night,
Challis. A real big mistake."

"It wasn't me."

He ignored that one. "But you didn't find what you were looking for, did you?"

"And what would that be?"

"What the bitch sent you to get." He was crazy-eyed with anger.

"Put down the gun and we can talk."

"I don't think so, pal. I owe you one."

He leaned forward to smash the barrel across my skull. I went down, taking a chair with me. I blinked up at him from the floor, half-conscious, my words slurred: "You'd better lay off, Snowden. You might get me mad."

He chuckled. "You got balls, I'll give you that." He steadied the gun on me. "I could put you away for good."

"I don't think you really want to, Lee. Wouldn't be a very smart move."

He lowered the automatic, stowed it in his windbreaker. "You get the message. Stay out of my life."

After he was gone, I sat on the floor, patting at my bleeding scalp with tentative fingers. I hate the sight of blood.

Especially my own.

Sandra was in her pool, taking an afternoon dip, when I walked up to her. Out of her shapeless black dress, and wearing a yellow designer swimsuit, she'd lost her vampire menace. But she was still too skinny and the bright sunlight wasn't kind to her wrinkles.

"Mr. Challis! What a surprise."

"Life's full of 'em," I said.

She climbed out of the pool and slipped into a terry cloth robe. We sat down at a white enameled table under a pastel-striped umbrella.

"You must have come through the gate. I thought I'd locked it."

"You did. I *un*locked it."

She began toweling her hair. "Doesn't that qualify as trespassing?"

"That's something I'm sure you know a lot about."

Her eyes darkened. "What's that supposed to mean?"

"It means I don't like playing finger man. In particular, I don't like getting cold-cocked with a gun by a low-life who thinks I'm still working for you."

"Did Lee Snowden assault you?"

"*After* accusing me of a break-and-enter job. Claimed I was looking for something, but he didn't say what."

She shook her head. "I don't understand any of it."

I gave her a hard look. "I think you understand *all* of it. You knew that Janet was living with Snowden, but you didn't know *where*. So you paid me to find the address."

"But why would I—"

"So you could break in when he wasn't there and search for something you wanted. But you didn't find it." I leaned back in the patio chair. "Snowden figured you sent me to look for it and massaged my skull with a Browning automatic."

She stood up. "I know you don't drink in the afternoon, Mr. Challis, but right now *I* could use one."

I followed her through the sliding-glass door to the wet bar in the game room. She fixed herself a Scotch on the rocks and we sat down again.

"I'm sorry you got hurt," she told me. "I didn't expect Lee to get violent. At least, not with you."

"Then ... you *did* go through his place?"

She nodded.

"Looking for what?"

"I can't tell you that."

"Then maybe you'd like to tell the cops."

She put her glass down so hard the Scotch splashed on the bar. "Why are you treating me this way? I paid you more than enough for finding Janet."

"I don't like being jerked around. You weren't straight with me."

"I was as straight with you as I could afford to be. You're not involved in this. There are ... factors ... that you know nothing about."

"Connected to the death of David DuPlain?"

Her eyes told me how angry she was getting. "I want you to leave now. And if you tell the police that I broke into Snowden's mobile home, I'll deny it. My word against yours."

I stood up, pushing back the bar stool. "This isn't for the cops—not yet. But you're wrong about my not being involved." I touched the lump on my head. "As of now, whether you like it or not, I'm *very* involved."

And I left her there.

I spent the rest of the afternoon at the Academy of Motion Pictures Arts and Sciences Library, reading material on David DuPlain. I was certain, at a gut level, that he was connected with the item Sandra had tried to take away from Snowden. Of course, if I'd known what that item was, it would have made things a lot easier.

I'd kept Mike on stakeout at the mobile home park and late that night I got another call from him.

"They skipped," he told me.

"When?"

"Dunno exactly. I got hungry. I mean, I was *starving*— so I drove over to Denny's for a grilled cheese and a Coke. When I got back, they were gone. I'm real sorry, Nick."

"That makes two of us." I sighed. "How come you're so sure they're gone?"

"Their unit was empty. The door was open. I looked inside and they'd taken all their clothes. I tried the vent to see if the package was still there, but—naturally—it wasn't." He hesitated. "Sorry I let 'em slip by me."

"Hey, you're only human. Besides, I've got a hunch we'll be running into Snowden and the girl again before long. Whatever game Lee's playing, it isn't over."

The next day, instead of going to the office in Studio City, I drove straight into Burbank, to the Warner's lot. I knew the gate guard, and he gave me a big good-morning smile.

"They shooting that new detective show on Stage Eleven?" I asked him.

The guard nodded. "That's right."

"Okay," I said, "I'm going over and have a talk with Ted Steele. Personal matter."

The guard waved me through the gate.

I'd read about the new TV show in the *Hollywood Reporter*. It was being produced for cable as one of the fall season's leads and Ted Steele was exec producer. He was Sandra Steele's first husband. She'd kept his name when she became a star. He was also Janet's father.

I parked my Honda behind the production stage and entered through a side door. They were between setups and I spotted Steele in a huddle with the star of the series, Rick Rutherford, a blond hunk with capped teeth and muscles to spare. He played private detective "Johnny Pride," which explained the show's title, *Pride of L.A.* Cute. They love cute titles in TV-land.

When Rutherford was called offstage for a costume change, I walked up to Ted Steele. "I'd like to talk to you, Mr. Steele."

"Not now," he said, checking the next scene in his copy of the script. He had it in a dark maroon leather binder with his name scrolled into the leather.

"It's important," I said. "About your ex-wife."

His head swung up and he fixed his eyes on mine. "I don't give a damn about what's happening to Sandra."

"Not even if she's being blackmailed by the creep your daughter is shacking up with?"

"Who are you?"

"Name's Challis. I'm a private investigator. A for-real one."

"How do you know that Sandra is being black-mailed?"

"I don't. Just an educated guess. All I know for *sure* is that she was desperate enough to break into Lee Snowden's place looking for something he has." I let that sink in, then said: "He worked for you, didn't he?"

Steele nodded. He had a strong face, with sharply-chiseled features, and I could see he'd been quite handsome in his younger years. "Snowden did some bits in a couple of my shows when I was with Three Star. That's when my daughter met him." His voice softened. "I'm sorry to hear they're living together."

"I take it you don't care for him?"

"I never trusted Snowden. There was an element of sleaze in his nature. But that didn't seem to bother Janet." He ran a slow hand along the edge of his script. "I had the feeling he'd do anything for money."

"Including blackmail?"

"It fits."

"Did your ex-wife have an affair with David DuPlain?"

He gave me a heated glare. "Why do you ask such a question?"

"I happen to believe DuPlain's death is tied into this. The police never caught the shooter who killed him. I think maybe Sandra knows who did it."

"That's ridiculous. DuPlain was killed by a burglar who was robbing his home. Sandra wasn't there that night."

"But she *was* sleeping with him, wasn't she? Which is why you divorced her."

Before he could respond, a harried-looking little man padded up with a set design sheet to be signed off. Steele scribbled his signature on the sheet and the little man padded away.

Steele turned to me, a defeated expression clouding his face. "Funny . . . how you can stop loving somebody," he said slowly. "We'd had a good marriage up to then . . . until she got involved with DuPlain. She became obsessed with him. Then she began drinking heavily. The situation became intolerable, so I ended it."

"What about Janet?" I asked. "What did she think of DuPlain?"

"We haven't discussed him. But then Janet has never confided in me. In many ways, we're like strangers."

"Where was Sandra on the night DuPlain was shot?"

"At a film premiere, with Janet. They went together."

"Was she drinking that night?"

He lowered his head, like a bull facing the sword; wounded, yet defiant. "She drank *every* night. Still does, I suppose. But you'd never know it. Sandra can hold her liquor. Up to a point, that is. One minute she'll seem okay, the next she's passed out. That's the way it hits her."

"I'd like to know if you—"

"I have work to do, Mr. Challis. We're a day behind schedule on this show, and I've no time for your conversation."

"Just two more questions: Do you know what Snowden has that Sandra wants so desperately?"

"I have no idea."

"And did you know your daughter was living with Snowden?"

"No—but Janet's an easy mark. I told her to stay clear of him, but she wouldn't listen."

"Thanks for your honesty, Mr. Steele."

"Funny ... how a thing can ... just stop ... suddenly be over." I could read the pain in his eyes. "I never thought I'd stop loving Sandra. Never."

I didn't have anything to say to that.

I'd left Burbank and was on Ventura, heading for Studio City, when I noticed a burnt-orange Chevy pickup pulling up fast behind me. Snowden.

He meant trouble, I had no doubt of that. I swerved the Honda into a wide asphalt parking lot next to a boarded-up (LOST OUR LEASE!) furniture store—and went for the .38 I kept taped under the dash.

The Chevy roared into the lot and slammed to a tire-squealing stop. Three men were in it, with Snowden at the wheel. He'd brought along two of his pals, one short, one tall, both chunky and snake-mean. They got out of the pickup and started toward me.

I hesitated, my hand on the gun. Better leave it. Maybe I could talk my way out of this. Gunwork wasn't my style. I eased back, opened the driver's door and stepped out to meet them.

"I warned you, Challis. I told you to stay out of my life." Snowden's hands were fisted, his legs braced like a bulldog.

"Sorry, but I don't operate according to your instructions."

"You were at Warner's, talking to Steele. About *me*, right?"

"Your name came up in the conversation." I nodded toward his two pals. "I see you've brought your army with you."

Snowden grinned. "A man needs friends he can count on in this cold world."

It was time to quit stalling. I knew they were seconds away from attacking me. At least I could take the initiative.

"Hello, boys," I said to the two beefheads. "Allow me to introduce myself."

And I buried my right fist in the tall one's stomach. When he doubled over with a startled grunt, I shin-kicked the little guy and snapped back his jaw with a short left hook.

Snowden was on me by then, wrestling me to the asphalt and applying a stranglehold. I managed to break the hold and drive an elbow into his face, but before I could follow up, I felt my head explode. The tall guy had used a leather sap on me.

I was on my hands and knees, spitting blood, when I heard Snowden's voice above me. "Let's give him something to remember us by."

That's when the short guy kicked me in the ribs. I toppled over like a felled ox.

Suddenly, in the proverbial nick of time, my guardian angel arrived. In his CJ-5 hardtop Jeep.

"The party's over," Mike Cahill announced behind his twelve-gauge short-barrel. It was double cocked and ready for action.

They backed off fast. Only a mental case argues with a loaded sawed-off.

"Another time, Challis," said Snowden, waving his goons back to the Chevy. By the time I was able to stand up, they were gone.

"How'd you find me?" I asked Mike.

"I happened to spot Snowden's pickup on Ventura and started following him, but I got stopped by a red light. When the light changed, he'd disappeared. I knew he *had* to be in this area. Took me a while to find him, though—and you."

"Yeah, well, if you hadn't, I'd be on a stretcher headed for the emergency ward. Those boys were just getting started."

Mike chuckled. "You *do* tend to get people upset."

I leaned back against the fender of Cahill's Jeep, rubbing my head. "It's a bad habit of mine."

"I got some news," said Mike. "About DuPlain."

"What about him?"

"One of my contacts, Sid Haining, came through with some inside info. Sid used to work for DuPlain, as his gardener, and he knows a lot."

"Like?"

"Like you were right on your hunch about our boy

getting off with Sandra. But, at the same time, he was also playing around with somebody else."

"Who?"

"Sid doesn't know her name, but he heard DuPlain on the phone talking sweet to her a couple of times. Sandra used to be with DuPlain right at his house, but this other one he'd see elsewhere. Maybe at a motel."

"I'd better talk to Ed Russo," I said. "He might have something we don't."

"Want me with you?"

"No, I want you on another stakeout."

"So who do I watch?"

"The Vampire Queen," I told him. "Keep an eye on her place. See who goes in or out. Follow her when she leaves. She's still got to deal with Snowden on whatever's between them."

I climbed stiffly into the Honda. I felt pretty rocky, but I'd lucked out. No ribs were broken.

"Why are we doing all this?" Mike asked. "Nobody's paying us."

I grinned. "We're pursuing truth and justice."

"Bullshit!"

"Okay, then, let's just say I don't like being worked over twice in the same week by a prime scumbag like Snowden. I want to nail him, but I want it legal."

I put the Honda in gear and drove out of the lot.

I had one hell of a headache.

When I walked into Lieutenant Eddie Russo's office at Beverly Hills Homicide, he was using paper hinges to fit Laurel and Hardy stamps into an emerald-green album on his desk.

"Hot on the trail of crime, I see."

"It's lunch," he growled. "I'm entitled."

"Everybody needs a hobby," I said, easing onto his brown vinyl couch.

"Want some vodka?" he asked.

"No, but I could use a couple of aspirins."

"I'm not running a drug store," he said, pouring himself a shot from a liter of Absolut. He lifted the white paper cup and drained it in a gulp. "I'm not supposed to have this stuff in the office."

"Believe me, Eddie, only your liver cares."

I'd saved his life once in a Westwood bank shootout. We were pals.

Russo leaned back in his swivel chair. "So what's up?"

"I need to see your file on David DuPlain."

"The film director," he grunted, getting to his feet. "Wait here."

I waited. He returned with a manila folder, tossing it into my lap. "Enjoy."

I scanned the material while he went back to his stamps. Nothing new.

"What are you after, Nick?"

"Something to help prove DuPlain's death wasn't what it seemed."

"You won't find it. Why not buy things the way they went down? Mr. D. was shot by a house thief. Plain and simple."

"Yeah, too plain and too simple."

"Happens all the time. Guy gets home, sees his place being robbed, and tries to play hero. Ends up eating a bullet."

"I think there's more."

"That's your trouble, you can never let things be. You chew away at every case the way a dog works a bone."

"That's why people hire me."

"And who's hiring you to poke around in a five-year-old murder case?"

"I've hired myself."

He looked amused. "Is that smart business?"

"It's *my* business." I got up, laid the folder on his desk. "Thanks for the look-see."

I walked to the door.

"You turn up any killers, I'd appreciate hearing."

"Count on it," I said.

That night, at nine, Mike phoned, telling me he was calling from a convenience store about a mile from Sandra's house. "She's got a meeting set up with Snowden."

"When?"

"At ten. I was close to the house and overheard the conversation. You called it on the blackmail angle. She told him she had 'the rest of the cash ready.' Then she warned him that he'd 'better have it for her this time,' and that this was 'the last payment.' And she called him Lee."

"Obviously, she's trying to buy back whatever Snowden's been using to blackmail her with," I said.

"That package he had in the vent."

"That's gotta be it," I said. "Do you know where they're going to meet?"

"Some road away from the main drag. I didn't get a name, but she told Snowden 'I know the road. I can be there by ten.' And that's everything, Nick."

"It's enough," I said. "You head back to the stakeout point and I'll meet you there. We'll follow her in the Honda." And I rang off.

It was going to be an exciting night.

I got over to Sandra's in twenty minutes, pulling in behind Cahill's parked Jeep. He locked the door and walked toward the Honda, looking like a kid going to a party. He was carrying his sawed-off.

"Leave the shotgun in the Jeep," I told him. "I don't want that thing with us. We might be tempted to use it."

"But Nick, those guys will have—"

"We're there to observe, not engage in some hairy-ass firefight. *Leave* the sawed-off."

He took it back, locked it in the Jeep, then joined me. We could see Sandra's heavy iron entry gate from where we sat.

"She still in there?"

"Sure is." Mike checked his watch. "But she's due out any time now."

Within minutes the gate swung back and Sandra's white Caddie Seville purred out, heading off into the darkness. She was driving.

The road she'd mentioned was the dirt section of Mulholland Drive at the western end of the San Fernando Valley. I followed the Cad as it took a hard left off the pavement onto the roughly-pitted gravel. Just before making the turn, I killed my lights. Dangerous, but necessary. Otherwise, she'd have spotted us behind her—the only two cars on this solitary section of Mulholland.

The road was a wash of inked blackness and bumpy

as hell. Ahead of us: the glowing taillights of the Cad, a
moving white ghost in the dark.

"Talk about spooky," said Mike. "This is *real* vampire country."

"But tonight the bloodsucking comes from Snowden."

In the near distance a pair of headlights blinked three
times: on-off, on-off, on-off. The Cad replied with the
same pattern.

"That's our boy," said Mike. "Better pull off before
he spots us."

I eased the Honda to the far edge of the road, cutting
the engine. The heavy night sounds of crickets swelled
around us.

The two cars rolled slowly toward one another like
questing animals, their tires grinding against the gravel,
lights probing the road. Sandra stopped her car fifty feet
short of the pickup. The Chevy's door opened and Snowden got out, joined by his two beefcake pals. Sandra
stepped out to meet them.

The four headlights carved a circle of brightness from
the shrouding dark. Snowden waved his goons back and
walked up to Sandra, illuminated in the powdery cone
of light.

"You bring the money?" he asked her.

"I said I would." She held out a roll of bills. "Now
give me what I came for."

Snowden took the cash, flipped through it in a quick
count. Satisfied, he put the money away in his coat.

"I said *give* it to me!" Sandra's voice was strident.

"Sure," said Snowden, handing her a small brown
string-tied package. She ripped it open.

Mike leaned toward me. "Can you make out what
it is?"

"A gun," I said. "Looks like a .38 short-barrel."

That's when one of Snowden's boys spotted us. The
tall one. "She was followed!" he yelled.

Snowden shaded his eyes to look, snapping out a
curse. "It's Challis!"

He jerked a .45 from his belt while his goons ran for
their automatic weapons in the pickup. Snowden got off
one round before I was able to start the Honda's engine.

"We gonna take 'em?" asked Mike.

"Are you *nuts*?" I gasped, slewing the Honda around in the dirt. "We're gonna get the hell out of here."

By now Snowden's troops had opened up on us. I floored the pedal and we shot forward, bashing over the road dips. Lee and his boys piled into the Chevy and blasted off after us.

The chase was short but nerve-racking. When the Chevy had closed to within shooting distance, and bullets were clanging metal behind us, I grabbed the .38 from below the dash and shoved it toward Mike. "See if you can take out their headlights."

Cahill leaned from the passenger window and squeezed off three fast rounds. He missed the lights, but one of his bullets splintered the Chevy's front window and the pickup slid violently into a stand of boulders flanking the road.

In my rearview mirror I got a last look at the wrecked truck, tumbleweeds exploding around it from the force of the crash.

And that ended the night's activity.

Early the next morning I was outside Sandra Steele's locked gate, speaking to her through the gate's communication box.

"It's Nick Challis," I said. "We need to talk."

"I've been expecting you," she told me.

The gate slid silently back on its oiled runners. I drove in and parked under the portico just outside the entrance. Her front door was open. The Vampire Queen was standing there with a drink in her hand, waiting for me.

We went inside. To the library. Where I sat down while she freshened her drink at a portable bar. All without any conversation.

Finally, she said: "Why did you follow me last night?"

"I was curious."

"And you saw what Lee gave me?"

"A gun," I said.

"*This* one." She turned to face me, the .38 in her right hand. "I can't let you spoil everything now."

"I don't think you want another dead body on your hands, do you?"

"So you figured it out?"

"DuPlain didn't come home to face an armed burglar. You were with him that night—after the film premiere—and that .38 you're holding is the gun that killed him."

She sat down on the edge of an antique velvet chair, facing me, keeping the gun between us. She looked pale and shaken and her eyes were haunted. "Yes, this *is* the gun . . . and . . . I shot David with it."

"And when Lee Snowden got his hands on it, he had the bright idea of blackmailing you. Threatened to turn the gun over to the law if you didn't kick through."

She nodded, then eased back into the chair. "I don't want to kill you, Mr. Challis." She allowed the .38 to slip from her hand. It thumped on the rug.

I relaxed—but there was still a lot to be said. "You got fed up paying and sent me to find Snowden so you could try and *steal* the gun back. But that didn't work."

"Lee knew I was getting desperate," she said, her voice dulled, mechanical. "He agreed to a return last night, for a final payment."

"How did he get the gun in the first place?"

"Janet—she was there that night—she promised me—after I'd killed David—that she'd destroy it."

"Then why didn't she?"

"I don't *know* why. She was terribly frightened and upset. Somehow Lee discovered that she'd kept the gun. He couldn't get another acting job and needed money. . . ."

"And he knew you could supply it."

She nodded. "Janet admitted to me she was staying with Lee only out of fear. He *beats* her."

"Tell me about the night of the murder . . . everything you remember."

"Will you turn me over to the police?"

"What I will or won't do is wide open right now." I looked steadily at her. "Tell me about the murder."

She stood up, began pacing the room.

"We'd been fighting all that evening, David and I, saying really bitter, horrible things to one another."

"What was the fight about?"

"He was involved with another woman. I didn't know who, but I was jealous and angry." She hesitated, drawing in a deep breath. "We were both drinking that night, me more than David. I was trying to numb the pain."

"And the gun?"

"It was David's. He carried it for protection in the glove compartment of his car."

"How did you get it?"

"I don't remember. There are a lot of things about that night I don't remember." She stopped suddenly, hands shaking. "I need another drink."

"Okay," I said.

She made herself a Scotch and water. It drained some of the tension from her. She sat down again, fixing her dark eyes on mine.

"After I ... shot David ... I ... blacked out. When I came to, I was still holding the gun. Janet had seen it all, and she was terrified."

"And so the two of you faked a robbery?"

"Yes. We broke the sunroom window from the garden and took the silver ... some jewelry ... to make it look like a thief had been there."

She drew in another long breath. Her head was down, her voice a low mumble. "Then we left David lying there in the living room. The blood had pooled around his body. There was so much ... so *much* blood. ..."

I didn't phone the cops. I wasn't sure of anything yet.

That night I had bad dreams.

Blood dreams.

Mike was in Chicago that weekend, running down some important leads on another of our cases. I was alone at my desk, completing some long-overdue (and seemingly endless) government forms, and trying not to think about vampire queens or murdered film directors. If what Sandra told me was true, I was guilty of not reporting what she'd said to the police. Technically, I was shielding a murderer. But somehow. ...

That's when Janet Steele walked into the office, wearing a mint green and white outfit that neatly set off her red hair. But her makeup was smeared and she looked frightened and uncertain.

"Mr. Challis ... do you remember me?"

"Sure," I said. "From the trailer. Only we weren't introduced that day. But I *do* know who you are, Miss Steele."

"Ms.," she said automatically.

"Ms.," I agreed. I nodded toward a scoop-backed chrome chair near my desk and she took it, but her posture was anything but relaxed.

"I came about Lee," she said.

"Did you know he tried to kill me?"

"I'm not surprised. He's insane." She looked out the window, trying to maintain emotional control. "I finally got up enough courage to leave him. But ... I'm still very afraid of him."

"Where is he now?"

"I don't know."

"Why did you come to me?"

"To thank you."

"*Thank* me?"

"For not turning in my mother to the police. She had a very special reason for killing David DuPlain."

"Jealousy?"

Janet shook her head. "No. *Hatred.* Over what he'd done to me. It just kept building inside her until she ... did what she did."

Janet was twisting a small white purse in her hands as she talked. This wasn't easy for her.

"What did DuPlain do to you?"

She met my eyes, but her lower lip was trembling. "He ... he *raped* me. When I was fifteen."

I walked around the desk to take the chair next to her. "How did it happen?"

"I've never told anyone else."

"Tell *me.* I think you need to."

Her voice was strained but forceful—as if talking about what happened gave her an inner strength.

"It was on my fifteenth birthday. Mom and David ... they were both drinking and they offered me some champagne. You know, to celebrate. I felt ... all grown up ... like a *woman.* So I drank the champagne ... a lot of champagne. ..."

"Then what?"

"We were at David's house. When I got dizzy, he carried me up to the bedroom. He laid me on the bed and then he ... he. ..."

Tears glittered in her eyes.

"When did your mother find out?"

"I told her the next day. And I remember what she

said, and the cold way she said it. She told me: 'I'll kill David for this.' "

"Why did she wait three years to do it?"

"Because she also *loved* David. They had this crazy love-hate thing going between them."

"Your mother said you were present on the night of the shooting."

"Yes. We'd come back from a movie premiere and she wanted to stop at David's place. They began to argue and he said he was going to leave her—for this other woman. It all came together— she hated what he'd done to me, and now she was losing him to someone else. She was very drunk. I saw her stagger outside to his car for the gun. When she came back, she was carrying it."

"Did he try to take it away from her?"

"Yes. They struggled over it and ... and I saw her shoot him. In the chest. Then she blacked out. She still had the gun in her hand."

"What kept you from getting rid of it afterward?"

"I don't honestly know. I *meant* to, but ... after that awful night ... I just couldn't bring myself to touch it again."

"How did Snowden get it?"

"From me. He found out I had it and he ... just took it."

"And you let him?"

"I thought I *loved* Lee. He seemed to understand what I'd been through—and he promised he'd get rid of it for me. Instead ... he used it to blackmail my mother."

She began to cough, an emotional reaction. I brought her a paper cup of water from the office cooler.

"Why didn't you leave him a lot sooner?"

"I was afraid to. He said if I ever left him, he'd kill me. He's a very violent man."

"Could you find him again?"

"I know some of his friends. I think I could."

"Then do it. Pretend you're going back to him, then let me know where he is. I'll come for him."

My own rage was building inside me. This thug ... rapist ... blackmailer ... had to be put out of action.

And I'd just elected myself to do the job.

*   *   *

It took her less than thirty-six hours to find him. My apartment phone rang just before ten p.m. the following night. It was Janet.

"I'm with him now," she said.

"Can you talk?"

"Yes. He's in the front part of the house, watching TV."

"Did you have any trouble with him?"

"No. He was real glad I came back. But he warned me again about leaving. He's as violent as ever."

"All right. Give me the address."

The house was on Ridgecrest and belonged to a pal of his. I asked if anyone else was at the house.

"No, just me and him."

"What about those two goons he's been traveling with?"

"They split for San Francisco after that road thing the other night. Afraid of the cops."

"Okay, hang tight. I'll be there in half an hour."

Ridgecrest is one of those twisty little streets winding up from Laurel Canyon. The house I wanted was a wood-and-stone single story at the top of the ridge. I pulled the Honda to a stop, checked the load in my .38, and headed for Lee Snowden.

I didn't know exactly what I intended to do with him or to him—I'd play it by ear. But he *had* to go down.

I approached the house through a curtain of heavy brush. The crickets were in full harmony and a sickle moon painted the ground with pale silver.

Suddenly, a beam of bright light hit me, and I brought up the .38, my heart pounding.

"Nick! It's me."

Janet was on the narrow stone porch with a large flashlight in her hand.

"I thought it was you," she said, "but I had to be sure."

"Better shut up," I warned her as I reached the porch. "He'll hear us."

"No." The word was flat, emotionless. "Lee can't hear anything. He's dead."

She was right. Snowden was sprawled on the polished

oak floor, on his back, arms extended. His eyes were open, but there was no pulse. It was a head shot, very little blood; he'd died instantly.

I stood up from the body. "You do it?"

"No," she said. "After I phoned you, Mom showed up. She was crazy drunk and she had the gun she'd used on David. She called Lee a 'blackmailing son of a bitch' and shot him. Then she drove off. She didn't say a word to me. It was as if I didn't exist."

I phoned Eddie Russo, giving him the address. I didn't tell him who did it. Or that I wouldn't be there when he arrived.

I had business with the Vampire Queen. And I took Janet with me.

When we reached Sandra's gate, I simply picked the lock, as I'd done once before, and the gate slid open for us. Picking locks is an art every private detective should cultivate.

The house was totally dark when we rolled up to it in the Honda.

"This has to be a surprise visit," I said. "Can we get inside without letting her know we're here?"

"I still have a house key," Janet said. She fished it out of her purse.

"Use it," I told her.

We got in quietly. So far, so good. I was here to find some final answers. Confronting Sandra was necessary if the tangled strings of this case were to unwind.

The interior of the house was menacing. Under the thin beam of my pocket flash the bloody posters and death masks seemed to watch our silent passage.

"Where is she?" I asked in a low whisper.

"In her bedroom, upstairs."

"Shoots somebody, then just goes calmly home to bed. Not likely," I said.

I walked to a wall switch and turned on the lights.

Janet looked startled. "Why did you do that?"

"Because your mama isn't here," I said. "My guess is she's probably out of the state by now."

"But why would she leave?"

"Maybe she was afraid you'd testify against her in

court. About seeing her shoot DuPlain ... and now Snowden."

She stared at me. "But I'd *never* do that to my mother. I want to protect her. There's a lot about her that you don't know."

We were in the hall just outside the library and I walked in, switching on the lights.

"Then you'd better tell me." I sat down on the sofa. "I'm ready to listen."

"What I'm going to say is going to sound totally bizarre."

"Try me."

Janet walked over to the large oil painting of her mother above the fireplace. "It's real," she said.

"What do you mean?"

"I mean that she's one of them. The Undead."

I grinned broadly at that. "You're telling me that Sandra Steele is—"

"—a vampire."

"Hey now, I've heard some wild stories, but—"

"Let me finish. You want the complete truth ... I'm giving it to you."

I eased back on the sofa. "Go ahead."

"Just before Mother met David DuPlain, she toured Europe. She'd always been drawn to the offbeat, to anything strange or unusual. She would always seek out the ... dark places. In Europe she found a special kind of darkness. She was infected there."

"Infected?"

"With the disease of the Undead. When she returned to the States, she'd changed."

"Into a vampire?"

"Not in the traditional sense. Not the kind from the movies she played, or from books. She didn't need to sleep in a coffin or avoid sunlight. Nothing like that. But she *did* need human blood."

I sighed. "Okay, I'm going along with this. So just how did she get this human blood?"

"David DuPlain arranged it. He saw to it that she was ... *fed*. That was the real bond between them. He supplied her with fresh blood."

"From where?"

"I never found out. From hospitals maybe, or blood banks. Stolen or bought. I don't know."

"Is that it, then?"

"There's not much more. After Mother shot David— for what he'd done to me—she couldn't go on with her career. Her blood supply had been cut off. She couldn't function normally."

"How could she function at all?"

"By getting blood from the black market. It can be done. But it was barely enough to keep her alive. That's why she lost so much weight."

"Well," I said, standing up to stretch. "That's quite a fairy tale."

"It's all true," she said quietly.

"I see the story a bit differently. Shall I give you *my* version?"

"I don't know what you—"

I guided her to a chair. "Sit down and listen."

"All right."

"First of all, your mother didn't shoot David DuPlain. *You* did."

She clenched her fists. "But you *know* that isn't true! Mother admitted to you that she shot David."

"She also told me she was so drunk that night she couldn't remember much of anything. She blacked out— a habit of hers when she drank too much. While she was out, you shot DuPlain, then put the gun in her hand. When she came to, you told her *she'd* done it, and she believed you."

"Why would I kill David?"

"You were afraid of losing him. Afraid he'd go back to your mother. She told me that DuPlain was involved with another woman. That woman was you."

"But he *raped* me! Why would I—"

"I think it was the other way around. You seduced him, then got into a heavy love affair with him. You never had any intention of ditching the murder gun. Not as long as you could use it to blackmail your mother. You and Snowden—with you pulling all the strings."

"Then why did I come to you?"

"To get rid of Snowden. You showed up at the office with that 'I'm afraid he'll kill me' act, then set things up so I'd go out to his place and find him dead. And, once again, your dear mama was the patsy."

"How do you know she didn't shoot Lee?"

"Because my guess is she'd left town. You told Sandra I was going to turn her in to the cops and warned her to get the hell away before they grabbed her. Then you take me out here to her empty house and come up with this wacky vampire yarn." I grinned at her. "Did you *really* think I'd buy it?"

That's when she stood up and shot me. In the right leg. A flesh wound that bled all over the library floor but wasn't all that serious.

Before she could get off another round I managed to wrestle the gun away from her and call Eddie Russo.

We found the Vampire Queen's white Caddie Seville parked in the back garage. But there was no trace of Sandra.

Nobody ever saw her again. Maybe she killed herself, thinking there was no other way out.

Or maybe she turned herself into a bat and flapped away in the night.

Go figure.

THIS TOWN AIN'T BIG ENOUGH
by
Tanya Huff

"Ow! Vicki, be careful!"

"Sorry. Sometimes I forget how sharp they are."

"Terrific." He wove his fingers through her hair and pulled just hard enough to make his point. "Don't."

"Don't what?" She grinned up at him, teeth gleaming ivory in the moonlight spilling across the bed. "Don't forget or don't . . ."

The sudden demand of the telephone for attention buried the last of her question.

Detective-Sergeant Michael Celluci sighed. "Hold that thought," he said, rolled over, and reached for the phone. "Celluci."

"Fifty-two division just called. They've found a body down at Richmond and Peter they think we might want to have a look at."

"Dave, it's . . ." He squinted at the clock. ". . . one twenty-nine in the a.m. and I'm off duty."

On the other end of the line, his partner, theoretically off duty as well, refused to take the hint. "Ask me who the stiff is?"

Celluci sighed again. "Who's the stiff?"

"Mac Eisler."

"Shit."

"Funny, that's exactly what I said." Nothing in Dave Graham's voice indicated he appreciated the joke. "I'll be there in ten."

"Make it fifteen."

"You in the middle of something?"

Celluci watched as Vicki sat up and glared at him. "I was."

"Welcome to the wonderful world of law enforcement."

Vicki's hand shot out and caught Celluci's wrist before he could heave the phone across the room. "Who's Mac Eisler?" she asked as, scowling, he dropped the receiver back in its cradle and swung his legs off the bed.

"You heard that?"

"I can hear the beating of your heart, the movement of your blood, the song of your life." She scratched the back of her leg with one bare foot. "I should think I can overhear a lousy phone conversation."

"Eisler's a pimp." Celluci reached for the light switch, changed his mind, and began pulling on his clothes. Given the full moon riding just outside the window, it wasn't exactly dark and given Vicki's sensitivity to bright light, not to mention her temper, he figured it was safer to cope. "We're pretty sure he offed one of his girls a couple of weeks ago."

Vicki scooped her shirt up off the floor. "Irene MacDonald?"

"What? You overheard that, too?"

"I get around. How sure's pretty sure?"

"Personally positive. But we had nothing solid to hold him on."

"And now he's dead." Skimming her jeans up over her hips, she dipped her brows in a parody of deep thought. "Golly, I wonder if there's a connection."

"Golly yourself," Celluci snarled. "You're not coming with me."

"Did I ask?"

"I recognized the tone of voice. I know you, Vicki. I knew you when you were a cop, I knew you when you were a P.I. and I don't care how much you've changed physically, I know you now you're a . . . a . . ."

"Vampire." Her pale eyes seemed more silver than gray. "You can say it, Mike. It won't hurt my feelings. Bloodsucker. Nightwalker. Creature of Darkness."

"Pain in the butt." Carefully avoiding her gaze, he shrugged into his shoulder holster and slipped a jacket on over it. "This is police business, Vicki, stay out of it. Please." He didn't wait for a response but crossed the shadows to the bedroom door. Then he paused, one foot over the threshold. "I doubt I'll be back by dawn. Don't wait up."

Vicki Nelson, ex of the Metropolitan Toronto Police Force, ex private investigator, recent vampire, decided to let him go. If he could joke about the change, he accepted it. And besides, it was always more fun to make him pay for smart-ass remarks when he least expected it.

She watched from the darkness as Celluci climbed into Dave Graham's car. Then, with the taillights disappearing in the distance, she dug out his spare set of car keys and proceeded to leave tangled entrails of Highway Traffic Act strewn from Downsview to the heart of Toronto.

It took no supernatural ability to find the scene of the crime. What with the police, the press, and the morbidly curious, the area seethed with people. Vicki slipped past the constable stationed at the far end of the alley and followed the paths of shadow until she stood just outside the circle of police around the body.

Mac Eisler had been a somewhat attractive, not very tall, white male Caucasian. Eschewing the traditional clothing excesses of his profession, he was dressed simply in designer jeans and an olive-green raw silk jacket. At the moment, he wasn't looking his best. A pair of rusty nails had been shoved through each manicured hand, securing his body upright across the back entrance of a trendy restaurant. Although the pointed toes of his tooled leather cowboy boots indented the wood of the door, Eisler's head had been turned completely around so that he stared, in apparent astonishment, out into the alley.

The smell of death fought with the stink of urine and garbage. Vicki frowned. There was another scent, a pungent predator scent that raised the hair on the back of her neck and drew her lips up off her teeth. Surprised by the strength of her reaction, she stepped silently into a deeper patch of night lest she give herself away.

"Why the hell would I have a comment?"

Preoccupied with an inexplicable rage, she hadn't heard Celluci arrive until he greeted the press. Shifting position slightly, she watched as he and his partner moved in off the street and got their first look at the body.

"Jesus H. Christ."

"On crutches," agreed the younger of the two detectives already on the scene.

"Who found him?"

"Dishwasher, coming out with the trash. He was obviously meant to be found; they nailed the bastard right across the door."

"The kitchen's on the other side and no one heard hammering?"

"I'll go you one better than that. Look at the rust on the head of those nails—they haven't *been* hammered."

"What? Someone just pushed the nails through Eisler's hands and into solid wood?"

"Looks like."

Celluci snorted. "You trying to tell me that Superman's gone bad?"

Under the cover of their laughter, Vicki bent and picked up a piece of planking. There were four holes in the unbroken end and two remaining three-inch spikes. She pulled a spike out of the wood and pressed it into the wall of the building by her side. A smut of rust marked the ball of her thumb, but the nail looked no different.

She remembered the scent.

Vampire.

". . . unable to come to the phone. Please leave a message after the long beep."

"Henry? It's Vicki. If you're there, pick up." She stared across the dark kitchen, twisting the phone cord between her fingers. "Come on, Fitzroy, I don't care what you're doing, this is important." Why wasn't he home writing? Or chewing on Tony. Or something. "Look, Henry, I need some information. There's another one of, of us, hunting my territory and I don't know what I should do. I know what I want to do . . ." The rage remained, interlaced with the knowledge of *another*. ". . . but I'm new at this bloodsucking undead stuff, maybe I'm overreacting. Call me. I'm still at Mike's."

She hung up and sighed. Vampires didn't share territory. Which was why Henry had stayed in Vancouver and she'd come back to Toronto.

Well, all right, it's not the only reason I came back. She tossed Celluci's spare car keys into the drawer in the phone table and wondered if she should write him a note to explain the mysterious emptying of his gas tank. "Nah. He's a detective, let him figure it out."

Sunrise was at five twelve. Vicki didn't need a clock to tell her that it was almost time. She could feel the sun stroking the edges of her awareness.

"It's like that final instant, just before someone hits you from behind, when you know it's going to happen, but you can't do a damn thing about it." She crossed her arms on Celluci's chest and pillowed her head on them, adding, *"Only it lasts longer."*

"And this happens every morning?"

"Just before dawn."

"And you're going to live forever?"

"That's what they tell me."

Celluci snorted. "You can have it."

Although Celluci had offered to light-proof one of the two unused bedrooms, Vicki had been uneasy about the concept. At four and a half centuries, maybe Henry Fitzroy could afford to be blase about immolation, but Vicki still found the whole idea terrifying and had no intention of being both helpless and exposed. Anyone could walk into a bedroom.

No one would accidentally walk into an enclosed ply-wood box, covered in a blackout curtain, at the far end of a five-foot-high crawl space—but just to be on the safe side, Vicki dropped two by fours into iron brackets over the entrance. Folded nearly in half, she hurried to her sanctuary, feeling the sun drawing closer, closer. Somehow she resisted the urge to turn.

"There's nothing behind me," she muttered, awkwardly stripping off her clothes. Her heart slamming against her ribs, she crawled under the front flap of the box, latched it behind her, and squirmed into her sleeping bag, stretched out ready for dawn.

"Jesus H. Christ, Vicki," Celluci had said squatting at one end while she'd wrestled the twin bed mattress inside. *"At least a coffin would have a bit of historical dignity."*

"You know where I can get one?"

"I'm not having a coffin in my basement."

"Then quit flapping your mouth."

She wondered, as she lay there waiting for oblivion, where the *other* was. Did they feel the same near panic knowing that they had no control over the hours from dawn to dusk? Or had they, like Henry, come to accept the daily death that governed an immortal life? There should, she supposed, be a sense of kinship between them, but all she could feel was a possessive fury. No one hunted in *her* territory.

"Pleasant dreams," she said as the sun teetered on the edge of the horizon. "And when I find you, you're toast."

Celluci had been and gone by the time the darkness returned. The note he'd left about the car was profane and to the point. Vicki added a couple of words he'd missed and stuck it under a refrigerator magnet in case he got home before she did.

She'd pick up the scent and follow it, the hunter becoming the hunted and, by dawn, the streets would be hers again.

The yellow police tape still stretched across the mouth of the alley. Vicki ignored it. Wrapping the night around her like a cloak, she stood outside the restaurant door and sifted the air.

Apparently, a pimp crucified over the fire exit hadn't been enough to close the place and Tex Mex had nearly obliterated the scent of a death not yet twenty-four hours old. Instead of the predator, all she could smell was fajitas.

"Goddamn it," she muttered, stepping closer and sniffing the wood. "How the hell am I supposed to find ... ?"

She sensed his life the moment before he spoke.

"What are you doing?"

Vicki sighed and turned. "I'm sniffing the door frame. What's it look like I'm doing?"

"Let me be more specific," Celluci snarled. "What are you doing *here*?"

"I'm looking for the person who offed Mac Eisler," Vicki began. She wasn't sure how much more explanation she was willing to offer.

"No, you're not. You are not a cop. You aren't even

a P.I. anymore. And how the hell am I going to explain you if Dave sees you?"

Her eyes narrowed. "You don't have to explain me, Mike."

"Yeah? He thinks you're in Vancouver."

"Tell him I came back."

"And do I tell him that you spend your days in a box in my basement? And that you combust in sunlight? And what do I tell him about your eyes?"

Vicki's hand rose to push at the bridge of her glasses but her fingers touched only air. The retinitis pigmentosa that had forced her from the Metro Police and denied her the night had been reversed when Henry'd changed her. The darkness held no secrets from her now. "Tell him they got better."

"RP doesn't get better."

"Mine did."

"Vicki, I know what you're doing." He dragged both hands up through his hair. "You've done it before. You had to quit the force. You were half-blind. So what? Your life may have changed, but you were still going to prove that you were "Victory" Nelson. And it wasn't enough to be a private investigator. You threw yourself into stupidly dangerous situations just to prove you were still who you wanted to be. And now your life has changed again and you're playing the same game."

She could hear his heart pounding, see a vein pulsing framed in the white vee of his open collar, feel the blood surging just below the surface in reach of her teeth. The Hunger rose and she had to use every bit of control Henry had taught her to force it back down. This wasn't about that.

Since she'd returned to Toronto, she'd been drifting; feeding, hunting, relearning the night, relearning her relationship with Michael Celluci. The early morning phone call had crystallized a subconscious discontent and, as Celluci pointed out, there was really only one thing she knew how to do.

Part of his diatribe was based on concern. After all their years together playing cops and lovers, she knew how he thought; if something as basic as sunlight could kill her, what else waited to strike her down. It was only human nature for him to want to protect the people he loved—for him to want to protect her.

But that was only the basis for *part* of the diatribe.

"You can't have been happy with me lazing around your house. I can't cook and I don't do windows." She stepped toward him. "I should think you'd be thrilled that I'm finding my feet again."

"Vicki."

"I wonder," she mused, holding tight to the Hunger, "how you'd feel about me being involved in this if it wasn't your case. I am, after all, better equipped to hunt the night than, oh, detective-sergeants."

"Vicki . . ." Her name had become a nearly inarticulate growl.

She leaned forward until her lips brushed his ear. "Bet you I solve this one first." Then she was gone, moving into shadow too quickly for mortal eyes to track.

"Who you talking to, Mike?" Dave Graham glanced around the empty alley. "I thought I heard . . ." Then he caught sight of the expression on his partner's face. "Never mind."

Vicki couldn't remember the last time she felt so alive. *Which, as I'm now a card-carrying member of the blood-sucking undead, makes for an interesting feeling.* She strode down Queen Street West, almost intoxicated by the lives surrounding her, fully aware of crowds parting to let her through and the admiring glances that traced her path. A connection had been made between her old life and her new one.

"You must surrender the day," Henry had told her, *"but you need not surrender anything else."*

"So what you're trying to tell me," she'd snarled, *"is that we're just normal people who drink blood?"*

Henry had smiled. *"How many* normal *people do you know?"*

She hated it when he answered a question with a question, but now she recognized his point. Honesty forced her to admit that Celluci had a point as well. She did need to prove to herself that she was still herself. She always had. The more things changed, the more they stayed the same.

"Well, now we've got that settled—" She looked

around for a place to sit and think. In her old life, that would have meant a donut shop or the window seat in a cheap restaurant and as many cups of coffee as it took. In this new life, being enclosed with humanity did not encourage contemplation. Besides, coffee, a major component of the old equation, made her violently ill, a fact she deeply resented.

A few years back, CITY TV, a local Toronto station, had renovated a deco building on the corner of Queen and John. They'd done a beautiful job and the six-story, white building with its ornately molded modern windows, had become a focal point of the neighborhood. Vicki slid into the narrow walkway that separated it from its more down-at-the-heels neighbor and swarmed up what effectively amounted to a staircase for one of her kind.

When she reached the roof a few seconds later, she perched on one crenelated corner and looked out over the downtown core. These were her streets; not Celluci's and not some out-of-town bloodsucker's. It was time she took them back. She grinned and fought the urge to strike a dramatic pose.

All things considered, it wasn't likely that the Metropolitan Toronto Police Department—in the person of Detective-Sergeant Michael Celluci—would be willing to share information. Briefly, she regretted issuing the challenge, then she shrugged it off. As Henry said, the night was too long for regrets.

She sat and watched the crowds jostling about on the sidewalks below, clumps of color indicating tourists among the Queen Street regulars. On a Friday night in August, this was the place to be as the Toronto artistic community rubbed elbows with wanna-bes and never-woulds.

Vicki frowned. Mac Eisler had been killed before midnight on a Thursday night in an area that never completely slept. Someone had to have seen or heard something. Something they probably didn't believe and were busy denying. Murder was one thing, creatures of the night were something else again.

"Now then," she murmured, "where would a person like that—and considering the time of day we're assum-

ing a regular not a tourist—where would that person
be tonight?"

She found him in the third bar she checked, tucked
back in a corner, trying desperately to get drunk, and
failing. His eyes darted from side to side, both hands
were locked around his glass, and his body language
screamed *I'm dealing with some bad shit here, leave me
alone.*

Vicki sat down beside him and for an instant let the
Hunter show. His reaction was everything she could
have hoped for.

He stared at her, frozen in terror, his mouth working
but no sound coming out.

"Breathe," she suggested.

The ragged intake of air did little to calm him, but it
did break the paralysis. He shoved his chair back from
the table and started to stand.

Vicki closed her fingers around his wrist. "Stay."

He swallowed and sat down again.

His skin was so hot it nearly burned and she could
feel his pulse beating against it like a small wild creature
struggling to be free. The Hunger clawed at her and her
own breathing became a little ragged. "What's your
name?"

"Ph ... Phil."

She caught his gaze with hers and held it. "You saw
something last night."

"Yes." Stretched almost to the breaking point, he
began to tremble.

"Do you live around here?"

"Yes."

Vicki stood and pulled him to his feet, her tone half
command-half caress. "Take me there. We have to talk."

Phil stared at her. "Talk?"

She could barely hear the question over the call of his
blood. "Well, talk first."

*"It was a woman. Dressed all in black. Hair like a
thousand strands of shadow, skin like snow, eyes like
black ice. She chuckled, deep in her throat, when she saw
me and licked her lips. They were painfully red. Then she
vanished, so quickly that she left an image on the night.*

"Did you see what she was doing?"

"No. But then, she didn't have be doing anything to be terrifying. I've spent the last twenty-four hours feeling like I met my death."

Phil had turned out to be a bit of a poet. *And* a bit of an athlete. All in all, Vicki considered their time together well spent. Working carefully after he fell asleep, she took away his memory of her and muted the meeting in the alley. It was the least she could do for him.

Description sounds like someone escaped from a Hammer film; The Bride of Dracula Kills a Pimp.

She paused, key in the lock, and cocked her head. Celluci was home, she could feel his life and if she listened very hard, she could hear the regular rhythm of breathing that told her he was asleep. Hardly surprising as it was only three hours to dawn.

There was no reason to wake him as she had no intention of sharing what she'd discovered and no need to feed, but after a long, hot shower, she found herself standing at the door of his room. And then at the side of his bed.

Mike Celluci was thirty-seven. There were strands of gray in his hair and although sleep had smoothed out many of the lines, the deeper creases around his eyes remained. He would grow older. In time, he would die. What would she do then?

She lifted the sheet and tucked herself up close to his side. He sighed and without completely waking scooped her closer still.

"Hair's wet," he muttered.

Vicki twisted, reached up, and brushed the long curl back off his forehead. "I had a shower."

"Where'd you leave the towel?"

"In a sopping pile on the floor."

Celluci grunted inarticulately and surrendered to sleep again.

Vicki smiled and kissed his eyelids. "I love you, too."

She stayed beside him until the threat of sunrise drove her away.

"Irene MacDonald."

Vicki lay in the darkness and stared unseeing up at the plywood. The sun was down and she was free to leave her sanctuary, but she remained a moment longer, turning over the name that had been on her tongue when she woke. She remembered facetiously wondering if the deaths of Irene MacDonald and her pimp were connected.

Irene had been found beaten nearly to death in the bathroom of her apartment. She'd died two hours later in the hospital.

Celluci said that he was personally certain Mac Eisler was responsible. That was good enough for Vicki.

Eisler could've been unlucky enough to run into a vampire who fed on terror as well as blood—Vicki had tasted terror once or twice during her first year when the Hunger occasionally slipped from her control and she knew how addictive it could be—or he could've been killed in revenge for Irene.

Vicki could think of one sure way to find out.

"Brandon? It's Vicki Nelson."

"Victoria?" Surprise lifted most of the Oxford accent off Dr. Brandon Singh's voice. "I thought you'd relocated to British Columbia."

"Yeah, well, I came back."

"I suppose that might account for the improvement over the last month or so in a certain detective we both know."

She couldn't resist asking. "Was he really bad while I was gone?"

Brandon laughed. "He was unbearable and, as you know, I am able to bear a great deal. So, are you still in the same line of work?"

"Yes, I am." Yes, she was. God, it felt good. "Are you still the Assistant Coroner?"

"Yes, I am. As I think I can safely assume you didn't call me, at home, long after office hours, just to inform me that you're back on the job, what do you want?"

Vicki winced. "I was wondering if you'd had a look at Mac Eisler."

"Yes, Victoria, I have. And I'm wondering why you can't call me during regular business hours. You must know how much I enjoy discussing autopsies in front of my children."

"Oh, God, I'm sorry, Brandon, but it's important."

"Yes. It always is." His tone was so dry it crumbled.

"But since you've already interrupted my evening, try to keep my part of the conversation to a simple yes or no."

"Did you do a blood volume check on Eisler?"

"Yes."

"Was there any missing?"

"No. Fortunately, in spite of the trauma to the neck, the integrity of the blood vessels had not been breached."

So much for yes or no; she knew he couldn't keep to it. "You've been a big help, Brandon, thanks."

"I'd say *any time,* but you'd likely hold me to it." He hung up abruptly.

Vicki replaced the receiver and frowned. She—the *other*—hadn't fed. The odds moved in favor of Eisler killed because he murdered Irene.

"Well, if it isn't Andrew P." Vicki leaned back against the black Trans Am and adjusted the pair of nonprescription glasses she'd picked up just after sunset. With her hair brushed off her face and the window-glass lenses in front of her eyes, she didn't look much different than she had a year ago. Until she smiled.

The pimp stopped dead in his tracks, bluster fading before he could get the first obscenity out. He swallowed, audibly. "Nelson. I heard you were gone."

Listening to his heart race, Vicki's smile broadened. "I came back. I need some information. I need the name of one of Eisler's other girls."

"I don't know." Unable to look away, he started to shake. "I didn't have anything to do with him. I don't remember."

Vicki straightened and took a slow step toward him. "Try, Andrew."

There was a sudden smell of urine and a darkening stain down the front of the pimp's cotton drawstring pants. "Uh, D ... D ... Debbie Ho. That's all I can remember. Really."

"And she works?"

"Middle of the track." His tongue tripped over the words in the rush to spit them at her. "Jarvis and Carlton."

"Thank you." Sweeping a hand toward his car, Vicki stepped aside.

He dove past her and into the driver's seat, jabbing the key into the ignition. The powerful engine roared to life and with one last panicked look into the shadows, he screamed out of the driveway, ground his way through three gear changes, and hit eighty before he reached the corner.

The two cops, quietly sitting in the parking lot of the donut shop on that same corner, hit their siren and took off after him.

Vicki slipped the glasses into the inner pocket of the tweed jacket she'd borrowed from Celluci's closet and grinned. "To paraphrase a certain adolescent crime-fighting amphibian, I *love* being a vampire."

"I need to talk to you Debbie."

The young woman started and whirled around, glaring suspiciously at Vicki. "You a cop?"

Vicki sighed. "Not any more." Apparently, it was easier to hide the vampire than the detective. "I'm a private investigator and I want to ask you some questions about Irene MacDonald."

"If you're looking for the shithead who killed her, you're too late. Someone already found him."

"And that's who I'm looking for."

"Why?" Debbie shifted her weight to one hip.

"Maybe I want to give him a medal."

The hooker's laugh held little humor. "You got that right. Mac got everything he deserved."

"Did Irene ever do women?"

Debbie snorted. "Not for free," she said pointedly.

Vicki handed her a twenty.

"Yeah, sometimes. It's safer, medically, you know?"

Editing out Phil's more ornate phrases, Vicki repeated his description of the woman in the alley.

Debbie snorted again. "Who the hell looks at their faces?"

"You'd remember this one if you saw her. She's . . ." Vicki weighed and discarded several possibilities and finally settled on, ". . . powerful."

"Powerful." Debbie hesitated, frowned, and continued in a rush. "There was this person Irene was seeing a lot but she wasn't charging. That's one of the things that set Mac off, not that the shithead needed much encouragement. We knew it was gonna happen, I mean we've all felt Mac's temper, but Irene wouldn't stop. She said that just being with this person was a high better than drugs. I guess it could've been a woman. And since she was sort of the reason Irene died, well, I know they used to meet in this bar on Queen West. Why are you hissing?"

"Hissing?" Vicki quickly yanked a mask of composure down over her rage. The other hadn't come into her territory only to kill Eisler—she was definitely hunting it. "I'm not hissing. I'm just having a little trouble breathing."

"Yeah, tell me about it." Debbie waved a hand ending in three-inch scarlet nails at the traffic on Jarvis. "You should try standing here sucking carbon monoxide all night."

In another mood, Vicki might have reapplied the verb to a different object, but she was still too angry. "Do you know which bar?"

"What, now I'm her social director? No, I don't know which bar." Apparently they'd come to the end of the information twenty dollars could buy as Debbie turned her attention to a prospective client in a gray sedan. The interview was clearly over.

Vicki sucked the humid air past her teeth. There weren't that many bars on Queen West. Last night she'd found Phil in one. Tonight; who knew.

Now that she knew enough to search for it, minute traces of the other predator hung in the air—diffused and scattered by the paths of prey. With so many lives masking the trail, it would be impossible to track her. Vicki snarled. A pair of teenagers, noses pierced, heads shaved, and Doc Martens laced to the knee, decided against asking for change and hastily crossed the street.

It was Saturday night, minutes to Sunday. The bars would be closing soon. If the *other* was hunting, she would have already chosen her prey.

I wish Henry had called back. Maybe over the centuries they've—we've—evolved ways to deal with this. Maybe we're supposed to talk first. Maybe it's considered bad manners to rip her face off and feed it to her if she doesn't agree to leave.

Standing in the shadow of a recessed storefront, just beyond the edge of the artificial safety the streetlight offered to the children of the sun, she extended her senses the way she'd been taught and touched death within the maelstrom of life.

She found Phil, moments later, lying in yet another of the alleys that serviced the business of the day and provided a safe haven for the darker business of the night. His body was still warm, but his heart had stopped beating and his blood no longer sang. Vicki touched the tiny, nearly closed wound she'd made in his wrist the night before and then the fresh wound in the bend of his elbow. She didn't know how he had died, but she knew who had done it. He stank of the *other*.

Vicki no longer cared what was traditionally "done" in these instances. There would be no talking. No negotiating. It had gone one life beyond that.

"I rather thought that if I killed him you'd come and save me the trouble of tracking you down. And here you are, charging in without taking the slightest of precautions." Her voice was low, not so much threatening as in itself a threat. "You're hunting in my territory, child."

Still kneeling by Phil's side, Vicki lifted her head. Ten feet away, only her face and hands clearly visible, the other vampire stood. Without thinking—unable to think clearly through the red rage that shrieked for release— Vicki launched herself at the snow-white column of throat, finger hooked to talons, teeth bared.

The Beast Henry had spent a year teaching her to control, was loose. She felt herself lost in its raw power and she reveled in it.

The *other* made no move until the last possible second then she lithely twisted and slammed Vicki to one side.

Pain eventually brought reason back. Vicki lay panting in the fetid damp at the base of a dumpster, one eye swollen shut, a gash across her forehead still sluggishly bleeding. Her right arm was broken.

"You're strong," the other told her, a contemptuous gaze pinning her to the ground. "In another hundred years you might have stood a chance. But you're an infant. A child. You haven't the experience to control what you are. This will be your only warning. Get out of my territory. If we meet again, I *will* kill you."

Vicki sagged against the inside of the door and tried to lift her arm. During the two and a half hours it had taken her to get back to Celluci's house, the bone had begun to set. By tomorrow night, provided she fed in the hours remaining until dawn, she should be able to use it.

"Vicki?"

She started. Although she'd known he was home, she'd assumed—without checking—that because of the hour he'd be asleep. She squinted as the hall light came on and wondered, listening to him pad down the stairs in bare feet, whether she had the energy to make it into the basement bathroom before he saw her.

He came into the kitchen, tying his bathrobe belt around him, and flicked on the overhead light. "We need to talk," he said grimly as the shadows that might have hidden her fled. "Jesus H. Christ. What the hell happened to you?"

"Nothing much." Eyes squinted nearly shut, Vicki gingerly probed the swelling on her forehead. "You should see the other guy."

Without speaking, Celluci reached over and hit the play button on the telephone answering machine.

"Vicki? Henry. If someone's hunting your territory, whatever you do, don't challenge. Do you hear me? *Don't* challenge. You can't win. They're going to be older, able to overcome the instinctive rage and remain in full command of their power. If you won't surrender the territory ..." The sigh the tape played back gave a clear opinion of how likely he thought that was to occur. "... you're going to have to negotiate. If you can agree on boundaries, there's no reason why you can't share the city." His voice suddenly belonged again to the lover she'd lost with the change. "Call me, please, before you do anything."

It was the only message on the tape.

"Why," Celluci asked as it rewound, his gaze taking in the cuts and the bruising and the filth, "do I get the impression that it's "the other guy" Fitzroy's talking about?"

Vicki tried to shrug. Her shoulders refused to cooperate. "It's my city, Mike. It always has been. I'm going to take it back."

He stared at her for a long moment then he shook his head. "You heard what Henry said. You can't win. You haven't been ... what you are, long enough. It's only been fourteen months."

"I know." The rich scent of his life prodded the Hunger and she moved to put a little distance between them.

He closed it up again. "Come on." Laying his hand in the center of her back, he steered her toward the stairs. *Put it aside for now,* his tone told her. *We'll argue about it later.* "You need a bath."

"I need ..."

"I know. But you need a bath first. I just changed the sheets."

The darkness wakes us all in different ways, Henry had told her. *We were all human once and we carried our differences through the change.*

For Vicki, it was like the flicking of a switch; one moment she wasn't, the next she was. This time, when she returned from the little death of the day, an idea returned with her.

Four-hundred-and-fifty-odd years a vampire, Henry had been seventeen when he changed. The *other* had walked the night for perhaps as long—her gaze had carried the weight of several lifetimes—but her physical appearance suggested that her mortal life had lasted even less time than Henry's had. Vicki allowed that it made sense. Disaster may have precipitated *her* change, but passion was the usual cause.

And no one does that kind of never-say-die passion like a teenager.

It would be difficult for either Henry or the other to imagine a response that came out of a mortal rather than a vampiric experience. They'd both had centuries of the latter and not enough of the former to count.

Vicki had been only fourteen months a vampire, but she'd been human thirty-two years when Henry'd saved her by drawing her to his blood to feed. During those thirty-two years, she'd been nine years a cop—two accelerated promotions, three citations, and the best arrest record on the force.

There was no chance of negotiation.

She couldn't win if she fought.

She'd be damned if she'd flee.

"Besides . . ." For all she realized where her strength had to lie, Vicki's expression held no humanity. ". . . she owes me for Phil."

Celluci had left her a note on the fridge.

Does this have anything to do with Mac Eisler?

Vicki stared at it for a moment then scribbled her answer underneath.

Not anymore.

It took three weeks to find where the *other* spent her days. Vicki used old contacts where she could and made new ones where she had to. Any modern Van Helsing could have done the same.

For the next three weeks, Vicki hired someone to watch the *other* come and go, giving reinforced instructions to stay in the car with the windows closed and the air-conditioning running. Life had an infinite number of variations, but one piece of machinery smelled pretty much like any other. It irritated her that she couldn't sit stakeout herself, but the information she needed would've kept her out after sunrise.

"How the hell did you burn your hand?"

Vicki continued to smear ointment over the blister. Unlike the injuries she'd taken in the alley, this would heal slowly and painfully. "Accident in a tanning salon."

"That's not funny."

She picked up the roll of gauze from the counter. "You're losing your sense of humor, Mike."

Celluci snorted and handed her the scissors. "I never had one."

"Mike, I wanted to warn you, I won't be back by sunrise."

Celluci turned slowly, the TV dinner he'd just taken from the microwave held in both hands. "What do you mean?"

She read the fear in his voice and lifted the edge of the tray so that the gravy didn't pour out and over his shoes. "I mean I'll be spending the day somewhere else."

"Where?"

"I can't tell you."

"Why? Never mind." He raised a hand as her eyes narrowed. "Don't tell me. I don't want to know. You're going after that other vampire aren't you? The one Fitzroy told you to leave alone."

"I thought you didn't want to know."

"I already know," he grunted. "I can read you like a book. With large type. And pictures."

Vicki pulled the tray from his grip and set it on the counter. "She's killed two people. Eisler was a scumbag who may have deserved it, but the other ..."

"Other?" Celluci exploded. "Jesus H. Christ, Vicki, in case you've forgotten, murder's against the law! Who the hell painted a big vee on your long johns and made you the vampire vigilante?"

"Don't you remember?" Vicki snapped. "You were there. I didn't make this decision, Mike. You and Henry made it for me. You'd just better learn to live with it." She fought her way back to calm. "Look, you can't stop her, but I can. I know that galls, but that's the way it is."

They glared at each other, toe to toe. Finally Celluci looked away.

"I can't stop you, can I?" he asked bitterly. "I'm only human after all."

"Don't sell yourself short," Vicki snarled. "You're quintessentially human. If you want to stop me, you face me and ask me not to go and *then* you remember it every time *you* go into a situation that could get your ass shot off."

After a long moment, he swallowed, lifted his head, and met her eyes. "Don't die. I thought I lost you once and I'm not strong enough to go through that again."

"Are you asking me not to go?"

He snorted. "I'm asking you to be careful. Not that you ever listen."

She took a step forward and rested her head against his shoulder, wrapping herself in the beating of his heart. "This time, I'm listening."

*   *   *

The studios in the converted warehouse on King Street were not supposed to be live-in. A good seventy-five percent of the tenants ignored that. The studio Vicki wanted was at the back on the third floor. The heavy steel door—an obvious upgrade by the occupant—had been secured by the best lock money could buy.

New senses and old skills got through it in record time.

Vicki pushed open the door with her foot and began carrying boxes inside. She had a lot to do before dawn.

"She goes out every night between ten and eleven, then she comes home every morning between four and five. You could set your watch by her."

Vicki handed him an envelope.

He looked inside, thumbed through the money, then grinned up at her. "Pleasure doing business for you. Any time you need my services, you know where to call."

"Forget it," she told him.

And he did.

Because she expected her, Vicki knew the moment the *other* entered the building. The Beast stirred and she tightened her grip on it. To lose control now would be disaster.

She heard the elevator, then footsteps in the hall.

"You know I'm in here," she said silently, *"and you know you can take me. Be overconfident, believe I'm a fool, and walk right in."*

"I thought you were smarter than this." The *other* stepped into the apartment, then casually turned to lock the door. "I told you when I saw you again I'd kill you."

Vicki shrugged, the motion masking her fight to remain calm. "Don't you even want to know why I'm here?"

"I assume you've come to negotiate." She raised ivory hands and released thick, black hair from its bindings. "We went past that when you attacked me." Crossing the room, she preened before a large ornate mirror that dominated one wall of the studio.

"I attacked you because you murdered Phil."

"Was that his name?" The other laughed. The sound had razored edges. "I didn't bother to ask it."

"Before you murdered him."

"Murdered? You *are* a child. They are prey, we are predators—their deaths are ours if we desire them. You'd have learned that in time." She turned, the patina of civilization stripped away. "Too bad you haven't any time left."

Vicki snarled but somehow managed to stop herself from attacking. Years of training whispered, *Not yet*. She had to stay exactly where she was.

"Oh, yes." The sibilants flayed the air between them. "I almost forgot. You wanted me to ask you why you came. Very well. Why?"

Given the address and the reason, Celluci could've come to the studio during the day and slammed a stake through the *other's* heart. The vampire's strongest protection, would be of no use against him. Mike Celluci believed in vampires.

"I came," Vicki told her, "because some things you have to do yourself."

The wire ran up the wall, tucked beside the surface-mounted cable of a cheap renovation, and disappeared into the shadows that clung to a ceiling sixteen feet from the floor. The switch had been stapled down beside her foot. A tiny motion, too small to evoke attack, flipped it.

Vicki had realized from the beginning that there were a number of problems with her plan. The first involved placement. Every living space included an area where the occupant felt secure—a favorite chair, a window ... a mirror. The second problem was how to mask what she'd done. While the *other* would not be able to sense the various bits of wiring and equipment, she'd be fully aware of Vicki's scent *on* the wiring and equipment. Only if Vicki remained in the studio, could that smaller trace be lost in the larger.

The third problem was directly connected with the second. Given that Vicki had to remain, how was she to survive?

Attached to the ceiling by sheer brute strength, positioned so that they shone directly down into the space in front of the mirror, were a double bank of lights cannibalized from a tanning bed. The sun held a double menace for the vampire—its return to the sky brought complete vulnerability and its rays burned.

Henry had a round scar on the back of one hand from too close an encounter with the sun. When her burn healed, Vicki would have a matching one from a deliberate encounter with an imitation.

The *other* screamed as the lights came on, the sound pure rage and so inhuman that those who heard it would have to deny it for sanity's sake.

Vicki dove forward, ripped the heavy brocade off the back of the couch, and burrowed frantically into its depths. Even that instant of light had bathed her skin in flame and she moaned as, for a moment, the searing pain became all she was. After a time, when it grew no worse, she managed to open her eyes.

The light couldn't reach her, but neither could she reach the switch to turn it off. She could see it, three feet away, just beyond the shadow of the couch. She shifted her weight and a line of blister rose across one leg. Biting back a shriek, she curled into a fetal position, realizing her refuge was not entirely secure.

Okay, genius, now what?

Moving very, very carefully, Vicki wrapped her hand around the one by two that braced the lower edge of the couch. From the tension running along it, she suspected that breaking it off would result in at least a partial collapse of the piece of furniture.

And if it goes, I very well may go with it.

And then she heard the sound of something dragging itself across the floor.

Oh, shit! She's not dead!

The wood broke, the couch began to fall in on itself, and Vicki, realizing that luck would have a large part to play in her survival, smacked the switch and rolled clear in the same motion.

The room plunged into darkness.

Vicki froze as her eyes slowly readjusted to the night. Which was when she finally became conscious of the smell. It had been there all along, but her senses had refused to acknowledge it until they had to.

Sunlight burned.

Vicki gagged.

The dragging sound continued.

The hell with this! She didn't have time to wait for her eyes to repair the damage they'd obviously taken. She needed to see *now*. Fortunately, although it hadn't seemed fortunate at the time, she'd learned to maneuver without sight.

She threw herself across the room.

The light switch was where they always were, to the right of the door.

The thing on the floor pushed itself up on fingerless hands and glared at her out of the blackened ruin of a face. Laboriously it turned, hate radiating off it in palpable waves and began to pull itself toward her again.

Vicki stepped forward to meet it.

While the part of her that remembered being human writhed in revulsion, she wrapped her hands around its skull and twisted it in a full circle. The spine snapped. Another full twist and what was left of the head came off in her hands.

She'd been human for thirty-two years, but she'd been fourteen months a vampire.

"No one hunts in *my* territory," she snarled as the *other* crumbled to dust.

She limped over to the wall and pulled the plug supplying power to the lights. Later, she'd remove them completely—the whole concept of sunlamps gave her the creeps.

When she turned, she was facing the mirror.

The woman who stared out at her through bloodshot eyes, exposed skin blistered and red, was a hunter. Always had been really. The question became, who was she to hunt?

Vicki smiled. Before the sun drove her to use her inherited sanctuary, she had a few quick phone calls to make. The first to Celluci; she owed him the knowledge that she'd survived the night. The second to Henry for much the same reason.

The third call would be to the eight hundred line that covered the classifieds of Toronto's largest alternative newspaper. This ad was going to be a little different than the one she'd placed upon leaving the force. Back then, she'd been incredibly depressed about leaving a job she loved for a life she saw as only marginally useful. This time, she had no regrets.

Victory Nelson, Investigator: Otherwordly Crimes a Specialty.

GIRL'S NIGHT OUT
by
Kathe Koja and
Barry N. Malzberg

Annie: Thirty-six years old and already her breasts had begun to sag, accept the truth: faint erotic droop now that in ten years, five, would be less appetizing and more ominously maternal, then urged by gravity into the pendulous collapse of the old. Soft shelf of flesh behind the high-buttoned shirt, not a place to cry in climax now but a place to merely cry, fall to the woes, the sheer brutality of her city. Around Annie's waist the slightest roll of fat, still mere pudge, but she did not believe in exercising, working out, had passed the physical when she came on duty at twenty-five and that was the end of that. Plenty of working out on the job, she thought; what a job. Up and down the corridors of the city, pad out, looking for knowledge, one by one the secrets of the city disclosed—unwillingly, unwillingly—to her.

Marvin: the cop's boyfriend. Oh, God, poor Annie, thirty-six and forty-two and they were *boyfriend* and *girlfriend,* what kinds of names were those for what they did, for what they were to one another? Sucking it up and putting it back, night after week after night again and the name for what they did could be as cute (*playing house, hide the salami*) as the boyfriend-girlfriend business. Marvin, half-bald and with his own spreading pudge, Marvin who had recently opened a CopyCopy franchise with borrowed money, most of it hers, had all kinds of names for her job, for what she did. "It's all shit," he told her, arm crooked about her shoulder, her head uncomfortable on his chest (which bore at times a resemblance to hers: but no use pointing that out), "just

shit, just lies and more lies. They lie to you, you lie to
the lieutenant, the lieutenant lies to the chief who lies
to the mayor. Who lies to the people. Who lie to you.
Get it?''

Well, yes, she supposed she did get it. "Thank you for
pointing that out," Annie said. Her back was aching
again; she shifted against the sheets, squirmed for comfort, tried to stay out of the wet spot which always
seemed to be on her side of the bed. "Now you can
explain what's so noble about running a copy place."
With my money, she thought, *and about five hundred
from the bank.* "At least I'm trying to make a contribution, trying to extend—"

"Trying to *what*? Extend, lady, was that what I
heard?" He leaned toward her, his gaze keen and persuasive, persuasive Marvin, casting back like CopyCopy
refractory images of himself, little shades of Marvin on
the wall, reproductions of Marvin in her vision: infinitely
reproducible, eternally dead. —Well, maybe that was too
harsh; you couldn't have this much energy, this much
assurance and be dead, could you? "Make a difference,"
he said, and smiled in the way that he would only *after*
he had gotten himself off, a don't-care, no-excuses smile.
"Is that why you became a cop? A *detective,* excuse me,
I don't mean to forget the promotion, is that why? What
are you detecting these days, anyway? Kids who go off
on one another in alleyways? Fathers who do things
broadside to their daughters, nickel and dime window
thieves hustling crap down back alleys? Oh, that's a
major contribution to society, isn't it. Of course we don't
talk much about the job," he said, "you aren't exactly
forthcoming. Which is okay by me, but if you're talking
about difference, Annie, what exactly is the point? All
you're trying to do is solve what can't be solved; a pen-
sion can't be worth this."

It makes a difference to me, she wanted to say to this
one example of the Marvins who lay beside her in the
bed, but instead she said nothing, turning again in his
loose grasp to face away from him, face the wall: bare
wall, bare space for Marvin after that second divorce,
three years ago and still no pictures, posters, nothing on
his walls but a CopyCopy calendar with the old franchis-
er's name obliterated and his markered in. The least he

could do was make up some calendars of his own. The
least he could do was be halfway decent to her, she
had been screwing him for five years, even before that
miserable divorce, had put up with his crying and com-
plaints; the least he could do was shut up, that would
have been a decent thing under the circumstances but
they never did, did they?

"Now what are you doing?" he said. "Busy, busy, always on the move, can't let it lie, detective, can't rest can
you? But what now for God's sake, it's after midnight."

"I'm going home," she said. "I'm going home, there's
work to do."

"Annie, come on, what the hell work could you have
to do? at this hour?" *You're lying,* his gaze said, intense
and subtle that gaze and he could muster more intensity,
more sheer *eroticism* for argument than he could ever
manage in fucking when the eyes, open only intermit-
tently, said (and not to her but to the silent refracted
self, the self inside): *come on, come on, get it over with
now, I have to finish, have to get it done,* oh the wives
had loved it, hadn't they? Well, maybe. No accounting
for taste or the power of misguided pity and anyway
with Marvin getting it over with fast was a blessing.
"You're lying to me, Annie," he said. "You, too. See
what I mean? All in a circle and little Annie out there
in the alleys taking notes, but you ought to break the
chain; or would that make too much of a difference?"

"No," she said, "as a matter of fact I'm not lying. I've
got paperwork." Her panty hose were loose and baggy;
she did not put them on. Buttoning her shirt, off-duty
shirt that looked after all like the on-duty attire, uniform, uniform, no private place for Annie. *I have to go
detect some paperwork, Marvin, that's what I have to do.
I have to get away from you,* she almost said but let it
go, said it instead with her gaze at the bare walls, past
the bare walls into the bare space of their time together:
boyfriend and girlfriend, sorrow and waste, Annie and
Marvin and the wet spot always on her side. *I have to
go someplace where I don't think about you,* she thought,
where I can't think about you. Good-bye. "Good-bye,"
she said, standing, looking for her shoes. "Be in touch.
Don't be a stranger."

"Annie," the man who had taken her money without

giving her a note because if two people were close
enough to make love they should not let paper come
between them (and she had fallen for that, had let herself fall), "Annie, this is stupid. We don't have to talk,
we don't have to sleep either if you don't want, we could
just watch TV or something. Or if you're not satisfied
down there, I could try to—"

"I can sleep at home," she said, "or watch TV or do
that other thing myself without help. All right?" and to
the door, out the door and, *What a sweetheart,* she
thought, *what a wonderful generous guy. If I'm not satisfied down there, he'll help me.* No perp had ever made
her a better or more sincere offer. The closed door was
silent and she realized she had left her gloves inside.
Screw it, she thought, *I'll get them next time, or buy some
downtown if it's cold tomorrow.* Brown gloves with furry
white lining, like the whores wear, the whores beckoning
imperious as traffic cops to the patrollers downtown. In
her early years she had worked entrapment detail a few
times, been a whore with furry gloves on the winter
streets, had tricked the tricks right into her circle: the
best of the detail, even with the cold. She had always
had a talent for connecting fast and she had—so young
then—loved to hear the johns whimper with terror and
sudden, stunning knowledge as the uniforms arrived. All
the bullshit, all the come-ons and the hey-babys gone,
gone, down the drain, all their smiles to silence as she
sat and stroked her gloved hands against her knees: waiting as they did for the uniforms, waiting with a pleased
and pleasant smile.

It was brutal outside, the cold hurt, the air small sliv-
ering knives in her harsh, uneven respiration; hard to
breathe; *cold inside,* cold Annie now cold as a corpse,
as a body in the street. She could no longer remember
the first dead person she had ever seen—that was a
myth, about never forgetting the first one—but she did
remember the dead whore she found frozen in a bus stop
shelter, sheltered from nothing, eyes open and hands in
her pockets; she had had no gloves either, nothing to
keep her warm. That, too, had been in the first year,
when she was still riding patrol, riding with men who
disdained or actively hated her or tried to come on to
her all at the same time; until after the hearings and

more bad publicity, it was apparently not all right to harass policewomen (although calling them "cunt" or "bitch" was not specifically harassment, it was all the same sort of good-natured hazing all the new officers had to put up with, and you were a bitch, a cunt anyway if you complained). So first-year Annie, still passionate, had argued with the dead whore's pimp at the morgue, too new to understand his display of decency by responding to her call, came in but that was as far as he had been willing to take it. She had tried to shame him into at least taking custody of the body, at least giving the body her proper name.

"She's listed as a Jane Doe, Bobby," she had said, her back aching, her eyes burning. "For God's sake, the least you can do is give us her real name for the death certificate. She had *your* name in her pocket, that's why I called you. You must owe her something for that."

Pettishly, pulling on his gloves, expensive leather driving gloves: "I don't fucking *know* her real name, all right?" They give themselves names and are gone, and Jane Doe the whore was buried, buried in the frozen ground but being frozen herself probably didn't mind too much, did she? Did she? Or was that another lie and was the afterlife a CopyCopy franchise *too* and you just kept on feeling everything just as you had before, the same stuff infinitely replicated, again and again and again *and* again, all the way down to dust? Merciful, unfeeling dust but who knew even then? There were no takers, no statements from the opposition here.

So: away, now, from Marvin, driving one-handed, the other in her pocket but cold, still so cold and her bed back there was cold, too, the sheets austere and pale green: pictures of the forest on her walls, the forest in autumn, Bambi's lair in early spring. When Annie was a little girl, she had wanted to be a botanist. Study plants: play with flowers. Growing things. Did the plants feel what it was like to grow, roots moving slow as death itself underground? And did they feel the coming of the cold, when they shriveled in winter, when they fell into the darkness, did they know what was happening?

Herself under blankets later, cold and cold, two sleeping pills and she did not remember passing the cusp, going into the darkness, did not remember when the alarm she had routinely set rang, and rang, and rang, ejecting her if only temporarily from that darkness, startling her, starting her, beginning the next of Annie's days.

Which lurched ahead, no meaning, even on the new night shift she tried to keep her days full, tried not to make of herself an invalid, striking at sleep against the day, against the drawn shades: she read, she watched television, she thought of her life, she thought of essences and chronology draining in her sterile, functional little civil servant's apartment. Of course no call from Marvin, no call *to* Marvin, to hell with Marvin and his wet spots and his certainty of lives, and she took herself out to dinner, a late dinner for the midnight shift. Bloomington was a college town, but one could hardly infer this from the bleak restaurant and its neighborhood and the hard, lost people who sat one by one or in pairs in the dining room or at the bar and did not say anything to her and little more to each other. *Here it is,* she thought, *this is it, this is life,* and a man laughed, watching the waitress walk away he laughed, and said something to the woman with whom he shared the table; who did not laugh in return but made the brief smile of the unwilling accomplice; what had the man said? Nice ass? What's the blue plate special and do you come with it? It was the kind of thing Marvin would have said.

After the restaurant, it was still too early to check into work, but Annie did not want to go home, did not know exactly what she wanted (had she ever?) and so drove the old car around Bloomington's downtown and then to the university, barren and vacant now, the exuberant children done in perhaps by weather, colder still tonight. She rubbed at the windshield with her ungloved palm, the defroster working only in small clear islands leaving the larger, clotted patches of white. Cold fingers on cold glass, it had been stupid not to go back for her gloves, but nothing, *nothing* was going to put her back into contact with Marvin unless he called first, he could keep the gloves, he could keep the loan, too, could stiff her for seventy-five hundred dollars; it was worth it not to feel that she had *bought* this terrible man for that amount.

New shift: still only the second week. Midnight was all the same, they told her, she would adapt. She shrugged, did not particularly care, day or night, night and day what did it mater? Marvin was right on that issue: everything was a circle, lie up, lie down, lie all around and: It's not for long, they told her, just a routine reassignment to balance off staff levels, wait until after the election and the pressure will come off, which as Marvin could have told her was another lie; but she did not need Marvin to figure that one out any more than she needed Marvin to have an orgasm; and it had been a long time, hadn't it, Miss Eagle-Eye, Miss Marple, Miss Tracer of Lost Knowledge? Had been a long, long time, not that Marvin had noticed or—and here was some measure of her plunge—*she* had taken account of it, until now. You burrowed deep into the blanket of your life, the coverlet and the folds covered you, inside and outside ceasing to contrast, differentiation gone forever and wasn't she too young to be having thoughts like this? No, she guessed, having them proved evidently she was not.

Her night was quiet: reports on a high school hanging (and weren't they surprised to find the girl dangling in the faculty bathroom, stretched out and blue at the end of a rope; a pregnancy? AIDS? lost love? Seventeen; who knew) which appeared to be suicide; a mutual husband-and-wife asphyxiation when the Medicare benefits had run out, chronic nephritis the dry-eyed son had said in his statement, they would have gone broke paying the bills (and her insane urge to pat his hand, say, *This way is better, isn't it?* just to see him, just to see his face; funny how you could always, always tell the bastards; like Marvin: two words and you knew); a few problems with the chronic prostitution at the south end which had picked up apparently in the long, continuing absence of Miss Eagle-eye, she supposed. When the cat's away. Or something. Cold sifting air beneath the desk, the broken space heater squatting miserable as a pet beside her ankles, her only pet and companion in the room: thin staff at night, most of them cruising, warmer in the squad cars than in here. Paperwork: that was the lie that was no lie. Working her way through it, the pile deep as a pile of leaves, some botanist: signing her name over and over, *Annie, Annie, Annie, Annie* here and here and here. When her shift ended, she shuffled outside,

hands in pockets to her car: and saw the color, bright
scarf, something, hanging from the dumpster.

Of course, she had to look against her sudden cool
revulsion, that was her profession, it was nothing, but
she had to look: who throws away a brand-new scarf?
Across the parking lot, cold inside and out and inside
the dumpster, pillowed with trash, frozen garbage and
broken boxes and half of a busted crate, dead rats: and
a dead woman, curled like a fetus, one end of the scarf
still soft, gripping her neck.

Another Jane Doe, another whore maybe, too, but it
was hard to tell: she was almost too pretty to be a whore,
too clean-looking, too expensive-looking. Long dark
hair, model's pallor, very pretty this one and her clothes
were pretty too, as pretty as she was dead. Annie
gasped, the impact of the dead woman, the sight of the
dead woman, and each was the same, the same as the
first time, as the last time: and with the sick feeling of
replication she reached toward the dead, pretty woman
in the dumpster, the absolute pallor of those features
locking that face into the remoteness, the falsely gentle
artifice of portraiture and in her exposed pectoral, Annie
could now see the small fissure, the cradling stamp of
blood which told the story and the bullet somewhere
within the skin, smashed toward the bone. Reaching to
touch her, to confirm the mortality of the ruin there
before she went back inside to report this, begin the
tedious motions of official discovery which would keep
her there for hours, hours and hours and maybe longer
than that, reaching toward the corpse she felt in the
instant of touch, the moment of communion that dead
hand and the leap, the instant spring of the cold as if on
tendrils, little tendrils and strings of cold grasping her,
and in that grasp and spring the pressure, small squeezing pressure of that hand on her own and, *She's alive,
this one is alive,* as the whickering cold passed through
her wrist, pulsing with the rhythm of life and the moving
eyes of the corpse, woman now, rolling in slow arctic
motion as the pressure of cold fingers, tendrils, strings
became enormous, hard enough to bruise.

As Annie dragged her hand free, as she stumbled back
toward the building only fifty yards away: *She's alive.*
Get help, get a doctor, and still stumbling in cold as-

tonishment that they did not respond to her screams, only stared at her as she fell deadweight on the crash bar, as she cried out her knowledge, until she became aware that all of this was strangling in her throat, she had made no sound at all: and then in the language of panic, of gesture her swooping arm: *Hurry!* and then they moved, uncertain, but they moved and *"Get her to a hospital,"* she said that aloud, she was sure she had heard herself speak: her own voice but lower, higher, something, different, as if the cold regained, metal box and tin like a coffin, a body in garbage had gifted her with her own true voice: not the burble of shock, not the blank laconic accent of the law, the streets, the criminal justice system but her own true voice, calling, testifying, directing as: *Yes* in the dumpster, *yes* in the scarf and movement, *yes,* as they returned from the parking lot, the cold to summon the white wagon, the paramedics, as they turned to her as if to listen to what her new voice had to say.

St. Luke's, the statue just to the left of the heavy red EMERGENCY sign: apostle and healer and the staff had offered Annie no real resistance. "This is a criminal investigation," she could have said. "I must have access," but no one said much of anything, no challenge, no confrontation as she walked into and then cleared Sylvia's room: "We are entitled to privacy during questioning," she could have said, or, simply: "Finders keepers," but it was unnecessary. They responded to her without heat, they left her and the woman alone: Sylvia.

Sylvia, that was the woman's name, one of the first things she had said when she returned to a consciousness roped in running plastic, tubes in and out, veins and nostrils but no identification, only a halting and then stammering line of questions: her name was Sylvia and she did not know what she was doing here. What had happened? What had happened to her? She remembered nothing but the screams near the dumpster and then her slow arc toward light; she did not know from where she had come or what all of this meant; she knew her name, that she had been lying badly hurt yet somehow untouched, some cold and central part of her inviolate and without pain.

Lying there, morgue-beautiful still with her gown and her tubes, upper lip dry against her teeth and she reached out to Annie, grasped her again in that cold tendentious fashion, the little tendrils now with faint blood-heat and in the breathing silence created by this touch she and Annie looked at one another for a long time, blood past pallor in that face now, the swimming aura of life and implication. "I don't remember," Sylvia said, "I don't know what happened. I saw light, and then you were touching me. I don't remember anything before. My name is Sylvia; I don't know where I live or who I am. I only know that somehow I deserve to be here."

Her gown, blue printed high and modest around that throat and with her free hand Annie reached, gently tugged it down, lower, to stare at the place where the hole had been: and could not know its presence.

"I deserve to be here," Sylvia said again.

"No," Annie said, squeezing the hand she held, "don't say that. Someone hurt you: that was wrong. It wasn't your fault, do you understand? Someone *shot* you, Sylvia, I saw it, I saw the wound—" and Annie touched it, touched the place where the hole had been "—and it *wasn't your fault."*

"No one hurt me," Sylvia said; incredibly she was smiling, dry lip across dry teeth, flesh against smooth enamel; "they just don't understand," she said. She put her hand atop Annie's hand, the one at her gown; their other hands were still connected. "They thought I was one thing," she said, "but I was really something else."

Annie said nothing; felt as if in amazement that cold vitality, that feeling of blood beneath the skin; how smooth Sylvia's hands were. The terrible wound already closing over when the attendants had begun to load her onto the stretcher, and in its place the smooth, smooth skin.

"What do you think?" Sylvia said.

Annie's hands without motion; the tubes going in and out. A little light above the bed began to blink, red and out, red and out.

Marvin: and it was she who called him after all, called him from her apartment, from the pale end of the morn-

ing after the dark had gone. Crouched on the chair, arms
stiff somehow as if she could still feel those tendrils, that
cold: "She's an amnesiac," Annie said, holding the
phone to her mouth as if Marvin were there beside her,
or on the other end of the world and only this instrument could make bearable any conversation they might
share. "She doesn't remember anything. Who shot her,
how she might have gotten there, anything."

"Why haven't you called?" he said. "That was some
way you walked out last week, I never saw you act that
way before. I don't know who you think you are or what
you're doing but that's not the kind of thing you should
do, I won't be—"

"She just doesn't know," Annie said. "Don't you get
it? But it isn't her fault; none of it is. I told her that, I
said, Sylvia, it's not your—"

"Listen, Annie, I don't know what the hell you're talking about and I can't stay on the phone all day, I'm
busy. I have a business to run down here, there's people
in the shop and I don't have time for this. You just be
over tonight, I should be back around midnight, and if
I'm not, you wait for me. You understand? Annie, are
you listening?"

She smelled dust; she smelled her whole life around
her, bereft of conscious odor, of sweat or burning, of
gasoline or cosmetics or blood. Dust, everywhere, dust
on the phone as she put it down, dust on the coffee
table, dust in the air. None of the rooms contained real
color, beige walls, brown carpets: only the testament of
muted greens, bedsheets and calendar, her closet filled
with businesslike clothing, her shoes in tired piles, brown
and black. Sylvia was an amnesiac; it was not and never
could be her fault.

At the hospital it was easy, easy: how could they stop
this? how declare it was not feasible? Sylvia was sane,
she was healthy (*the closed wound, the open door*) and
there was no way, no way whatsoever Annie knew that
they could keep Sylvia in the hospital or prevent her
from staying with the detective who had found her. She
was amnesiac, certainly, but as certainly competent to
make decisions; her condition left her both vulnerable
and closed off, nowhere else for her to go, nowhere else
where she might have been taken, no one else hovering

on the perimeters of her life; all of it easier than Annie
could have imagined, first the thought, then the circum-
vention, then the plan working itself with a kind of un-
coiling ease which confirmed everything which Marvin
had said to her that night: lies, it was all lies, she lied to
the staff who lied to headquarters who lied to the chief
who lied to the press by denying it all and soon enough
Annie, in a kind of thrall she could not have imagined,
would be sitting in her rooms with Sylvia, just the two
of them in a kind of confidentiality which Annie had
intimated but never known, guessed without experienc-
ing, longed for without identifying. And then Sylvia
would, from the very vacancy of her history, begin telling
all her secrets, one by one by one while Annie, detecting, would be absorbing those secrets in a kind of
attention and rigor she could not have imagined she
would possess. *"She was dead,"* she could have told
them. *"She had no vitals when I found her in that dumpster,"* but somewhere between the cold and the rescuing
ambulance those tendrils, those pointing streaks had become warmth, a strange, clinging warmth which rose
through Sylvia and arced into Annie, together now
through the process of circumstance into what had become an absolute. Looking at Sylvia dressing now in
Annie's own clothes, chosen with care, carried to the
hospital, Annie could see not so much the woman herself, either dumpster corpse or restored simulacrum of
that corpse later, but something else: she saw replica-
tions of herself, CopyCopies, layers upon layers of An-
nies which were being sent back to her through those
same tendrils which first had carried the cold, then the
warmth: Annie's blouse and blue jeans, Annie's socks
and shoes, Annie's silence and silent acceptance: but
why reject for Sylvia that which she seemed—through
her job, her wretched relations with Marvin—to have
accepted for herself? Annie's old ski jacket, zippered
against the cold; smooth hands, bare as Annie's were
bare. In the car Sylvia said nothing, sat gazing calmly out
the window, watching Bloomington pass by; the heater
wheezed and blew dust, warm air into their faces; in the
apartment the dust settled, and was still.

Neither of them asked the obvious questions: *Why am
I here? Who are you? Where do you come from?* Sylvia

sat quietly, looking out the window, gazing past the
blinds; Annie went back to work. When she came home,
Sylvia was still in the chair; she might not have moved
once; she was still wearing the blouse, the jeans, the
shoes. Slowly Annie approached her, set down her
purse, pulled off her coat. Slowly she sat beside her, sat
on the floor as Sylvia turned slightly in the chair so that
Annie was almost touching, was closer still. Annie's head
against Sylvia's knee; silence between them, detective
and victim, woman and woman.

"Are you a prostitute?" Annie said.

Sylvia shrugged. "I suppose," she said. "I suppose I
could have been. You're a policewoman," she said, "a
detective; aren't you?"

"Yes," Annie said.

They sat for a long time that way. Annie could feel
her own blood, moving through her body, moving
through the silent chambers of her heart, whisk of ventri-
cle, stutter of motion. Inside Sylvia's body everything
was still, its inner noises denied by that greater silence,
the envelope of flesh, not of mystery but memory: the
body, and how it hurts: the body and how it heals. Replication, and disaster; flesh, and blood.

"Men like me," Sylvia said, smiling her dry-lipped
smile. "They like me a lot. But they're never as smart
as they think they are, or should be."

"I don't understand," Annie said, "I don't understand
anything. I know this man—" and stopped. Sylvia
waited. Annie leaned her head against Sylvia's knee,
pressed it there strongly, the denim of the jeans
strangely cool against her face. She said nothing; Sylvia
said nothing. Both were waiting. Finally Annie said,
without moving, barely moving her lips, "Why?" That
was the question which it seemed she had wanted from
the first to ask, but trapped within her own restraint, her
panic and dismay could not: an absurd solemnity and
shyness which piece by piece Sylvia, her nearness, her
silence, had stripped from her: "Why are they like that?
What do they think they are? What do they want of us?
Or is it really us they want," she could have asked, "or
the casting image which they seek, some huge, idealized
image of themselves tossed up and over the screen of
orgasm, some answer to a question they are too self-

absorbed to ask? What is it, what do they want from
us?'' and she had never conceived that she would even
be asking such questions, conditional or otherwise, of
anyone, let alone an amnesiac shooting victim yanked
first from a dumpster and then a hospital bed. She had
not even known that these questions were important to
her or that it was possible to frame them, but now she
knew nothing else, was nothing but a swirl of disorder
and pain around those seeking questions and it was possible to wonder, memory in mind of that smooth, vacant
place on Sylvia's body, the hole that was not a hole, if
Sylvia had any kind of objective reality or had merely
appeared in response to Annie's questions, Annie's
needs, a need pasted together of the shards of her own
confused insight and Marvin's contempt, of her midnight
shift and her *own* contempt for what she had become:
through her fault, her silent and grievous fault.

"Sylvia," she said, leaning harder into that knee, that
bone, that stalk of flesh, no tendrils now but the smooth,
desperate connection established in the cleaving silence.
"Please," she said, "tell me. Who else can I ask? Who
else can you tell? I need this, Sylvia," she said, "it's just
us and I need to know."

"Yes," Sylvia said, looking at her: and the two of them
seemed to conjoin, conflate in the agony of Annie's
need: "yes," she said, "I'll tell you, I'll tell you all about
them, I'll tell you what they are and what *we* are too.
I'll teach you: and then I'll show you what to do." Lustrous eyes, and the slow, dreamy caress of her breath,
so soft it stirred no dust, woke no echoes, displaced no
memories or agonies of same: the silence of the apartment, the feel of denim, the arc of defiance, submission,
those looping strophes in the light.

The phone: and she called him, of course she called
him, they would not speak otherwise for why should *he*
call *her*? "Marvin," she said when he answered, Copy-
Copy loud, loud behind him, "Marvin, I want you to
meet someone, Sylvia, she's my new friend, I want you
to come and see us together, we've been busy, but now
I want you to come."

"Is that right?" Marvin said, "you want me to come
calling? After you ignore me, you don't call for a week,

two weeks, and you expect me to come when you call? Forget it, Annie," he said, "just forget it. If I have any time later on this week, *I'll* call *you*, but otherwise you can just forget—"

and Sylvia in the corner, winking. "You don't have to take that," she said by her posture, the curve of her lips, "he's nothing to you, you never have to listen to anything like that from him again."

"No," Annie said, "no, Marvin, I don't think you understand, I don't think you understand your position and while we're talking, Marvin, where's that seventy-five hundred you borrowed?"

Silence. The sounds of replication, of one and another, and another, and another. "Listen here," Marvin said, although more quietly, "listen, Annie, we don't need—"

"You didn't even give me a note," Annie said, gazing at Sylvia who gazed back at her, "so I guess I'll have to take it out of you personally instead of looking for the courts to do it, and I will, I will, you have no idea how sure I am about this." He said nothing over the phone, seemed to be breathing, shaking his head, the sound of teeth, then clicking. "I want you to come over here, Marvin," Annie said, "I have my rights too, this cuts both ways."

"I'm busy," he said, "I'm busy down here. This is a job you know."

and Sylvia laughed, the sound of her laughter present somehow through the wire, through the made connection and

Marvin said, "Now look here—" and Annie said, "No, no, *you* look. As soon as you close, you come down, you come over here," and put the phone down, determined, smashing the connection, smashing Marvin, and then looking over at Sylvia. "Was that all right?" she wanted to say, "did I do it the right way?" But she did not say that because there was no need to say it, Sylvia gave her the answer unbidden, streams of further laughter and then she flung the phone high in the air, watched it hit the wall, then bounce to floor, and Annie said, "It was always that easy, wasn't it? It was never that much of a problem, anytime we wanted we could have done this?"

"Yes," Sylvia said, "yes, we could have done it, they lie helpless to us, to our touch." In her tone, her voice their utter fragility, their vulnerable posturing, their torment: and the laughter again. Annie laughing harder now and all of their sounds gathering, the crash of the dumpster, clatter of the ambulance, whicker and clash of the copy machines, dim sounds of sirens or solicitation: all of it present, all of it just.

Later: Marvin: but not too much later, he had closed the store early, had perhaps responded to something in Annie's voice. Marvin: Marvin in the room, coming through the door with his own key, looking at Annie and then at Sylvia, at them together in confusion and then with a slow, gathering attention which might have been apprehension.

"What is this?" he said, "what's going on? Is this what you wanted me to see?" And Annie, smiling, came upon him.

"Go ahead," Sylvia said in the darkness, the deep shadows concealing her, taking her from the frame of vision, no reference in the room. "Go ahead: do this. I've taught you what they are," Sylvia said, "and now you know exactly what to do."

Oh, the luster of Sylvia's eyes and the slow, dreamy caress of her assent, the imparted knowledge between them fire, and she came toward Marvin. Astonished, he retreated, one step, two: "Annie," he said, *"Annie,"* and she came closer again, he was against the wall, hammered against the wall in the way that she had been pressed against the bed, as indifferently, as carelessly he had fucked her and, "Here," Annie said, "here's what you want," and oh, *oh* that slow connection, the arc of defiance, submission, the looping strophes; the thin and greedily suspired little rivulets of blood, taking in the blood as she took him in against all of the circumstances, the loops and strangled lines of her new necessities.

Sylvia, laughing in the dark.

"Is this what you wanted? Is *this* what you wanted?"

"Oh, yes, oh, yes," she said, gasping with the flow, more and more and she felt herself beginning to suffocate, closure of the breath, closure of the wound and fought to breathe even as she would not release that connection, oh, no, *oh,* no: no release, no closure, the fullness of the fluid, the fullness of her stink, the keening and the roaring and the wheedling, greedy, gulping little sounds of her ingestion; oh, yes. Oh, Marvin, and all of the Marvins, a hundred copied Marvins plunging beneath Annie ascendant, her history calamitously restored: in state, in passion, in frieze atop her prey, that broken man beneath restored now as well, pure as an original and Annie atop whispering, "I am Sylvia I am Sylvia I am Sylvia," detecting no longer, prostituting nothing but the attitudes of those feeble copies left behind now, drained empty now, dusty-dry in silence on the floor: "I *am* Sylvia," she said, mouth sore, throat heavy with what lay inside her, the squared confines of the dumpster as deep and icy as the replicating night.

HOME COMFORTS
by
Peter Crowther

The sign comes up on our right. *Merrydale,* it says, *4 miles.*

I look across at Melanie, her face set to the wind-screen and bathed a faint green in the dashboard light. Her mouth moves around, saying nothing in particular, just chewing syllables. Quiet.

The turning comes up quicker than I expected in the gloom and I almost miss it, spinning the wheel into the gravel and earth at the side of the road, watching the headlights wash across trees and earth and the last far-off gleams of the sun going down. Rain washes the windows and runs down in thick rivulets that the single wiper can't easily clear. For a second I think we're going to get stuck, but the wheels, skidding noisily just the one time, catch on something solid and the old Dodge jumps back onto the road. Now we can see a tree-lined lane in front of us, stretching down a hill. No streetlights. No noise. No signs of life.

Never any signs of life.

"Maybe here, honey," I whisper to Melanie, placing a hand that she once recognized gently on her knee. "Maybe this is the place." I put the hand back onto the steering wheel. There had been no response to it.

We start down the lane.

A few minutes later we roll onto a main street that must have once looked like something out of a *Saturday Evening Post* cover. Now it looks as lost and forlorn as we must look, drifting into town through the mud and the rain, our bellies empty of food, eyes empty of warmth, minds empty of compassion.

I check the gas gauge. It's low.

"Gonna have to get some gas, honey," I tell Melanie, though I know she isn't listening. I snatch a sideways glance and see her head making those staccato movements as she checks the storefronts and the barn doors, and we roll on down the road to what looks like it might be, or maybe once was, the Merrydale town center.

Up ahead there's the remnants of a picket fence surrounding a square of overgrown grass. Behind the square is a wooden walkway, its slats sticking up into the nighttime sky, and a general store, a barber shop and a couple of others I can't make out. The windows are smashed in, a couple of them boarded over and the wood pulled open. The darkness behind the wood is absolute. A pure color. Complete black.

Round back of the square, to the left, I see a Texaco sign swinging in the wind. In my head I hear its rusty whine, like a baby left too long by itself, all hoarse and cried out, died up of tears and passion. I pull off the main drag, into the shade of the buildings, and the rain seems to ease off. I drive around the square and now I see the garage. There's an old DeSoto, tires flat, windows smashed, parked half in and half out the station window where once a kid, or maybe some old guy who'd spent his whole life in Merrydale, would sit listening to the ball game or the Wednesday night fight or rap music, watching, and waiting for cars and customers.

Suddenly the rain seems more insistent, wetter, relentless. The night looks darker and colder and even less hopeful. But we left hope, Melanie and me, a long way and a long time back.

I park the Dodge and get out. As I open the door, Melanie grabs my arm and shakes her head, groaning. She points into the back seat. "It's okay, honey, it's okay," I tell her. "I'm just gonna see if there's any gas in those pumps, is all." But no, she won't have it. She hangs onto my jacket, fingers white, eyes wide and staring. I tell her okay, and I reach in back for a couple of the stakes. Lift the old strapped hammer and shrug it over my head and my right shoulder so it sits around me like a gun. And I step out into Merrydale.

The wind is whistling and the rain coming down in intermittent sheets. A few steps away from the car and I'm soaked.

The pumps are smashed up, the nozzles removed and cast across the forecourt. I walk over to the DeSoto, look inside. There's a mummified body on the back seat. It's a woman. She doesn't have any eyes, just black, staring sockets. Her clothes are pulled up and her scrawny breasts exposed . . . her pants are down, legs pulled wide apart. For a second I think maybe I saw something move down there . . . something small with a long tail . . . but I convince myself it's just the clouds across the moon making shadows. Something I don't want to feel turns around inside me, calls to me to let me know it's still there. I take a look back at my car. Melanie is hunched forward in her seat, nose against the windscreen, watching me through the rain. I smile and shrug, walk away from the DeSoto to the pumps.

On closer inspection I see that I might be able to put one of them back together. I glance around to make sure I'm still okay and then crouch down, lay the wooden stakes on the pavement, pick up the nozzle, and heft it to the pump. It just needs screwing in again. I do that.

Melanie knocks on the windscreen. She's telling me to get the stakes. I wave and she stops knocking. Then I pick up the stakes and jam them inside my jacket pocket. The pump gun lever seems to be stuck, so I give it a tap with the hammer to free it up. I give it a gentle squeeze and nothing happens. Squeeze it some more. Still nothing. I curse my stupidity. No electricity. Just before I wrench the nozzle back out again, I see the crank-bolt on the side of the pump. Of course! There had to be a way to get the gas moving manually in such an out-of-the-way place. I look around on the floor for something to use, but there isn't anything. I lay the nozzle down and walk back to the Dodge.

Melanie leans over and lifts the catch. I pull the door open and crouch down beside the car. "Honey," I say, real soft and slow, so she won't start to panic on me, "I'm gonna go into the filling station, get a wrench or something to crank up some gas."

She shakes her head.

I reach over and take her small white hand in mine, stroke it once or twice. "Melanie, honey, we *need* gasoline. I have to try. Now you just sit tight right here and

I'll be back before you know it." She blinks at me like she doesn't believe it. For a second I see how much she looks like her mother. How much she looks like my beloved Mary. But her memory seems tainted now.

I stand up and slam the door, turn my back on them, on Melanie and Mary. Walk over to the office.

Most of the glass is gone, littered across the inside of the room. In back there's a sign saying *Washroom,* but I ignore the privacy it promises. Near the counter is a comic book stand, no comic books in it, and a book rack with no books. Down on the floor I see a dog-eared paperback all puffed out with water damage. I pick it up and read the cover. It shows a baseball and a bat. *Gone To Glory.* Guy called Robert Irving or Irvine . . . I can't make it out. Something about it being "a moroni traveler mystery." I toss it back onto the floor and slide across the counter to where the pump controls lay covered in dust and dirt.

From the other side of the counter I can see the Dodge. I give a wave to Melanie, but she isn't looking my way. I see her profile. Watch her 11 years turn into 34 years, see her face turn from a girl into a woman. I jerk my hands up to my face and jam fingers into my eyes, stop the thoughts.

It would be so easy to just walk out of the office, walk out of the filling station, take it on the lam from beautiful, downtown Merrydale and hightail it up to the interstate, catch a ride on a truck heading for St. Louis or maybe Kansas City, chew the fat with one of the good-ol'-boy truck-drivin' boys while we listen to some sounds on his radio or shout back yells and thoughts at the voices that come over the CB . . . and, outside, the night speeds by us and he offers me some of his sandwiches and maybe a slug of Lone Star beer he's had cooling in the box beneath his seat. And he pulls his old steam whistle that honks into the darkness, lets everyone know we're alive . . . and we're comin'!

I take the hands away.

There are no trucks on the Interstate. There are no sounds on the radio, no voices on the CB, no ham on rye and no cold beers. There're just a few survivors and a few drinkers. Guy back in Racktown, little place due south of Columbus, had told me that there weren't too

many drinkers left, he figured. He hadn't seen one in
more than a year. That maybe it was all over now and
it's time to rebuild.

*I tell Melanie what the guy said. "Now ain't that just
the best news you've heard all year?" I ask her. But she
doesn't respond. Guy watches her and then asks me if
she's okay. "Sure she's okay," I tell him. "Sure she's
okay." And Melanie just stares ahead, past the old man,
watching the road out of Racktown across the state of
Ohio and into Indiana, next stop Indianapolis and, after
that, Springfield, Illinois and, after that . . .*

Melanie can see me now. I wave at her and she waves
back at me. The wave looks strange, woodenlike.

The old guy's voice comes back into my head.

*"So what's wrong with her, then?" he says. "She your
daughter?" I nod back to him and smile, proudlike.
"Yep," I tell him. "So what's wrong with her?" he asks
me again.*

"She's been hurt." I tell him.

*"Hurt?" he asks. "Yeah," I tell him. "Drinker got her."
I say it real low so that Melanie can't hear me too well.
"Back home, Macon, guy got her in the house and . . ."
I let my voice trail and let him figure the rest. "That's
what we're doin' now, her and me," I tell him. "Trackin'
that bastard down."*

He shakes his head in my memory.

*"Look," I say to him. And I reach over to pull Melan-
ie's scarf down from her neck. They're still there, on her
neck, the bruises. Both sides. "Skin ain't broke," the old
guy says. "No," I agree, "and that right there is the one
almighty blessing." And I pull up the scarf again. Melanie
doesn't move, she just stares at the road. "But she got
broke in other places," I tell him sadly. As if on cue,
Melanie clasps her hands on her lap and draws her knees
tight together.*

"Trackin' him down, you say?"

*"Right in one," I say. I take a sip of the lemonade he's
given us. It tastes like I always figured champagne would
taste, little bubbles tickling my face as I drink.*

"Like a detective on an old TV show," he says.

I grunt, thinking back to television shows.

*"You got any idea which way he's headin'?" he says.
I shake my head.*

The old guy nods. "Happened back in Georgia, you say?"

"I say."

"Long ways," he says.

I nod in agreement and look up at the sun, squinting.

"Long ways for such fresh-lookin' bruises," he mutters, and shakes his head, giving Melanie the once-over, looking down at her tiny, clasped hands. "Funny," he carries on, "I ain't never heard of a drinker doin' that."

Pretty soon after that we got back inside the Dodge, Melanie and me, and we rode on out of Racktown.

Melanie has settled some now, I see, my mind coming back to the filling station office. Now that she can see me.

I try to cast my mind back to before the sickness, before the "drinking" plague ... the plague made that AIDS thing seem like a summer cold. It's like a dream to me now.

And I think back to Mary. In my mind I watch her getting sick. Lord knows where she got it from, or who gave it to her. She just got it. I think back to how we kept her locked up during the nighttime, when it was dark, and she was thirsty, thinking maybe it would just wear itself out, the sickness, like a fever. And how, during the daylight hours, we kept her safe and warm and dark. She had lost all recollection of who she was early on, become just like an animal. And Melanie and me we fed her the occasional animal I caught out in the woods. Let her drink to her heart's content.

But old man Snapes caught on to how he never saw Mary during the day. I told him she was sick with the flu—there was one going around at the time, which was a big help. But after a while most everyone else who'd caught it was getting better and Mary still didn't make an appearance.

I shake my head at the memory, but it's all churned up now and I have to run it through.

I think back to the night when they came for her. Old man Snapes and Corley Waters and a couple of boys I hadn't seen before. Knocked on the door, large as life, like they were making a social call, and then pushed past me and Melanie with their stakes and their hammers.

"Where is she, Jake?" Corley Waters shouts. I don't

*say anything, just grab hold of Melanie and glance at the
bedroom door. They see the bolts, of course. And they
go in, close the door behind them.*

But we heard it, Melanie and me. We heard every
thud and every scream.

*A few minutes later, they drag her out in a sheet, blood
all over it, and a few of the stakes are still in her. "You
shoulda told us, Jake," old man Snapes says to me. His
eyes look sad and tired as they look everywhere but right
at me. "Woulda been easier."*

And then they left, leaving the house quiet and still.

*Melanie doesn't say a word. She just walks to the bed-
room door and pulls it closed, pushes the bolts home.*

Somewhere behind me I hear a noise.

I spin around and stare into the gloom.

Back away from the counter, the office lets onto a
corridor with a door at the end. The noise came from
in there. I glance back outside and wave at Melanie. She
gives me that dull wave again, like a puppet, someone
working her strings.

I creep slowly away from the window, into the corridor and towards the door. I hear it again, softer this
time.

My hand is shaking as it reaches out for the handle,
tests it, and finds it moves. I turn it all the way and push
gently. As it opens, I can hear more noises now. Seems
there was a whole lot of little sounds but, with the door
closed, I could only hear the heavier ones. I get my head
up against it and look inside.

It's light in there. The light is coming from a candle
that flickers in the little breezes and drafts that find their
way into the back room. It's a storage room . . . or was
once. There's a whole line of shelving made out of metal
scaffolding. On the shelves are a load of boxes and
clothes, some hanging there on hangers. The room is
done out like a home. On the floor, in front of the candle, a man is cleaning something. It's an animal. Looks
like he's preparing something to eat. I can't make out
what it is but I see a tail. Then I know why the woman's
been left in the DeSoto. Bait.

Next to the man a woman is lying across some blankets and carpets. They're about 30 years old, maybe
younger.

I watch the man.

I see him smile at the woman.

He smiles at her the way I used to smile at Mary.

He smiles at her the way I tried to smile at Melanie that first time, back in Macon. When I pushed her down and held her hands and made believe she was Mary. When I told her I needed some home comforts. Man can't get by without home comforts, I told her. That was when she stopped talking to me. When she stopped saying anything at all.

I pull the hammer off my shoulder and push the door open wide. It slams against some of the shelving right behind it and I march into the room. The man looks up at me, but I walk straight to the woman. She's making to get up, but the hammer catches her in the face and she falls right back down. I swing the hammer high and bring it down right into the face ... that face that took the man's smiles. It bursts like a watermelon. The woman lies still.

"J–Jane?" the man says, making it a question. He knows there's no chance he'll get an answer from that pulp, but he just has to ask. For a second I feel a little sympathy. For a second. But I have other things to think about.

I reach down and grab the man's shirtfront, hoist him to his feet. As I drag him out of that back room, he's shouting back over his shoulder to the woman. Then he's shouting at me, asking me what I'm doing, telling me he isn't a drinker. He uses God's name a lot, and Jesus', too. But they don't have any place in this. They don't have any place in anything any more. I don't say anything.

I drag him through the office and out into the night. My blood's pumping inside me and I feel something uncurling inside my pants.

Melanie gets out of the Dodge.

"I got him, honey," I shout to her. "Daddy's got the bastard what messed with you."

"What ... what the hell are you—"

"Shut the fuck up," I tell him, smacking him across his face with my free arm, letting the hammer drop to the forecourt where its clattering echoes a while and then fades away.

Melanie is out of the Dodge now and leaning against the hood. Her eyes are wide and expectant, her hands are rubbing themselves together.

I lift the man and toss him onto the hood, pull a stake out of my pocket. He holds his hands up in the air, covering his chest, pulling his knees up like a baby. He's shouting at me, but I don't hear. The thing in my pants is screaming now. I hold the stake over his chest and Melanie hands me the hammer. "Thanks, honey," I say to her and she smiles at me one of those special smiles.

"Jesus Christ," the man shouts, trying to grab my arm. But he just isn't strong enough.

"Is he the one, honey?" I ask her, ask her the way I've asked her all the other times.

She nods, quickly, emphatically . . . like she's nodded to me on all of those same times.

"I never seen her bef—"

The hammer comes down on the stake and drives it into the man's chest, stopping him in mid-sentence. The blood spurts like an oil-gusher. When I lift my hand from him he stays right where he is, jerking his belly up and down, not saying anything, and I figure the stake has gone right through into the Dodge's hood. I pull out another stake and hand it to Melanie. She holds it over his left hand side and I hit it squarely. The man is still now.

"He's dead," I tell Melanie, exhausted. "I killed him for you, honey. He can't hurt you no more."

Melanie takes my hand and squeezes it tight. The way she's done it after all of the others. The way she did after the boy in South Carolina and the old man in Racktown. Like after the youngster in Raleigh and the young feller in Charleston.

She squeezes and leads me around the Dodge to the back seat, pulls open the door. I get inside first, sweeping all of the wooden stakes onto the floor. Before she climbs in after me, Melanie helps me with my pants.

When we're through, I ask her, "Are you sure he was the one, Melanie honey? Do you think we could've made a mistake?"

Melanie frowns and looks down at her hands, pulls her dress over herself. Then she nods.

"Then he's still out there," I say to her, "the bastard."

Within an hour I've found a wrench and gotten some gasoline out of the old pump. Our luck is in.

With the sun starting to show across the hills, we leave Merrydale for points north.

As we pull onto the deserted freeway, I think back to what that old man said, back in Racktown. About how maybe I was like a detective in one of the old television shows.

Watching the road trailing into the distance I half imagine I hear end-credits music drifting across the blacktop and the roof of my old Dodge. At my side, Melanie stares out of the side window . . . like she's hoping to see something different to what we've just passed by.

I pat her on the knee, but she doesn't respond . . . just gives out a little shiver.

After a few hours, a sign comes up on our right. *Hannibal,* it says, *28 miles.*

I look across at Melanie, her face set to the windscreen. Her mouth moves around, saying nothing in particular, just chewing syllables.

Quiet.

ORIGIN OF A SPECIES
by
J. N. Williamson

When Erwin Parrish decided to go to Turkey to get a look at the dead body, it was (in a way) a busman's holiday.

After all, Parrish had been a homicide detective for most of the 23 years he'd spent on the force. He had seen enough corpses to make anyone gag, if the effect of looking at them had been cumulative, and he didn't even have any reason to think that the one in Turkey was the victim of foul play.

But Erwin, at 48, had never seen one that was more than 3,000 years old.

For nearly as long as Detective Parrish could remember, his consuming hobby had been archaeology. Even as a stolid, square-built, crewcut-headed boy of eight or nine, Erwin had been peculiarly fascinated by the origin of things—"things" from people and their ways to the communities in which they lived and their worlds at the particular times they'd been alive. It was as if he had needed to get at the heart of things, trace the happenstance of life to its roots in order to learn why the person or persons and their artifacts had even existed.

But because the folks with whom Erwin happened to grow up were poor and uneducated, no one thought to steer him toward archaeology till his grades were far too ordinary to earn him a college scholarship. By then, anyway, he had decided to become a police officer. Without knowing why, it had seemed like the thing to do.

So as a young cop riding in a prowl car—looking just the same except for growing up and adding a drooping mustache to munch on whenever he needed to keep his

mouth shut—Erwin had settled for letting his oldest fas-
cination become his primary reason for getting up each
day and doing his work well so he could go home again
and read. There, for decades, he had spent his free time
studying the exploits of other men who went on uncovering the secrets of the past—men whom Erwin Parrish
came to believe were little better informed than he.

It might have been enough except he also got married
two years out of the academy and fathered two sons.

Once, several years ago when Parrish was making a
genuine effort to save the marriage, he'd gone to a psychologist named Travis Goodnight, and the man suggested Erwin's avocational interests absorbed him the
way they did because his unconscious mind wanted to
know the origins of his personal problems, needed for
him to explore his own past.

Chewing on the fringes of his sandy mustache, Parrish
had mulled over his "personal problems." Never once
had he laid a finger on anyone in his family, but Carmen
had claimed for years that he "hungered" to batter her
and the boys. She was convinced he was a powderkeg
that had wanted to go off since she met him, that he got
sullen and spent a lot of time by himself because police
work demanded self-discipline and his marriage man-
dated it, so silence and study were the only ways he had
to keep from turning into a psycho or something.

Well, he'd pushed those notions around in his mind,
even wondered if he had decided to be in law enforcement just so he'd learn to keep a lid on his temper and
had gotten into homicide for some sort of vicarious goddamned thrill. Except the truth of the matter was that
he hadn't ever wanted to belt Carmen until she got those
weird ideas in her own head.

And the problem with what Doctor Goodnight suggested about his unconscious needing for him to explore
his past was that it was sheer crap. "See," he told the
shrink, "I've dug archaeology since long before I even
saw my wife." The pun about "digging" archaeology was
an old quip meant to deflect the curiosity of people who
found his hobby strange.

"I didn't mean the problems in your marriage," Goodnight had explained. "I meant those personal problems
you've sensed in your own mind ever since you were a

small boy. Everybody has their own kind—but you made no waves for your parents, didn't join the Scouts or go out for basketball, or turn into a brain. You began to study the origins of things in the past at a time when most boys think anything that happened a month ago is old stuff. I'm only suggesting that the majority of people doesn't look for the answers to questions nobody has asked, especially while they are children." Goodnight added softly, "Not unless they're screen questions for the real things people can't yet ask themselves."

Erwin had dutifully pondered the doctor's observations for a week. During that seven days Carmen conspicuously attempted to keep their late-teenage sons away from him, made Parrish sleep on the couch, and the cop abused no one—except for a recruit in his squad who came very close to losing some valuable evidence.

When he returned to Goodnight's office at the appointed hour of the appointed day, he took his seat across the desk from the psychologist rather quickly. "Doc," Parrish began, "let me ask you some questions for a change. I've really hoped I could hold my family together, but it just isn't happening. So is archaeology a good hobby for me, or not? Does it help me stay nonviolent, or is the whole thing going to go off in me like a bomb someday?"

Although Goodnight was a lot younger, he was smart enough not to ask what Erwin thought. Instead, he made some remarks Parrish would not forget. "I'm not even an amateur archaeologist, Detective, but think about this: You're around murdered people all the time in your job. Then—ostensibly for relaxation and pleasure—you yearn to go to digs where you hope to find ... dead things." He almost smiled. "Dead things such as people. I wonder, Erwin, if it isn't just possible that you're a homicide detective twenty-four hours a day whether in fact or in your oldest dreams."

"I suppose that's possible," Erwin had said with a grunt.

And Goodnight responded by spreading his hands on his desk and practically beaming at him. "Then how can you hope to find yourself in a normal family relationship when the members of your family are *alive*?"

Parrish had stood then and turned expressionlessly

toward the office door. "My problem got solved for me in the last twenty-four hours, Doc," he said. "My oldest boy announced his engagement and plans to get married next month, and my other son moved in with the love of his life—a kid named Kevin. Right after that, my wife threw me out. I'd recommend Carmen come to see you, because I think she needs a hell of a lot of help, but I wouldn't do that to a nice young psychologist with a vivid imagination and a family of his own. You haven't got enough insurance to protect you when a woman like Carmen gets *her* imagination going!"

That had ended Parrish's counseling sessions, but the neurotic suspicions Carmen had voiced continued to occur to him as time passed and his family was supposed to begin becoming just a memory. He sought to cheer himself up by reminding himself that, living alone now, the powderkeg Carmen had believed to be inside him would never go off at anybody he loved. Goodnight's points about his unusual choice of a hobby and the notion that he was a detective of homicide—of death—on a full-time basis depressed him a while and he wondered repeatedly if there might be anything to the many lousy things people kept saying about him.

For three years or more after the divorce was final, Erwin worked as many hours as he could. When he wasn't investigating a possible homicide or one that was indisputably that, he was boning up—he scarcely recognized the pun—until an important realization dawned on him one afternoon at a death scene: he liked archaeology now one hell of a lot more than he did police work, and he probably always had.

Not only that, Parrish perceived, he was good, *damn* good—as knowledgeable as most kids fresh out of a university course! Everything about the vast subject intrigued him, from anthropology and philology to paleography and sheer history. No more than a couple of hundred years old as a social science, archaeology studied the past through identification of the material remains of human cultures—but also through interpretation. As much as anything, that was surely the element he had taken from his lifelong passion to his law enforcement career. In homicide detection, too, you had to discover all the facts, then be skilled enough to interpret what you had in front of you. In addition, a detective wound up feeling like he was cock of the walk when he'd solved a case. Erwin could only imagine how successful a man would feel when he dug up something at an archaeological site that no one else had ever seen.

But he knew that when the archaeologist did it—and when he *proved* his theories about the dig and its products—the guy was showered with both praise and envy. A police officer who did the same thing might have to watch *his* find, the felon, parade straight out of the courtroom when everybody in the place knew the cop was right!

The trouble was both disciplines required fieldwork. You had to be there as soon as you could get to the scene, and you had to keep it clean, unsullied. Everything about both kinds of investigation demanded painstaking procedure, enormous care. Just as it was in homicide, an archaeologist had to study the artifacts around a bag of dead bones, the weapons and tools, if any, the clothing, and the condition of absolutely everything. Schliemann, Evans, Woolley, and Carter had made the discipline a systematized science in the nineteenth century, taught other archaeologists that even a *midden*—a refuse pile, maybe human droppings—held huge amounts of significance. Cultivated seeds led to the unearthing of more data; what a skeleton was wearing and how the man had died were sources of additional clues.

Parrish spent all of four regret-filled years bemoaning the loss of his marriage and his failure, as a boy, to pursue his primary interest in life until—pushing fortynine years of age—he came across a little filler item in his daily newspaper.

Though it wasn't remotely as ancient as the amazing "Iceman" unearthed early in the nineties, a startlingly well-preserved male body had been found on a mountain in eastern Turkey. Parrish read that the remains were revealed when a number of boulders were unexpectedly dislodged and sent down the slopes of Mount Ararat. Clad in a full-length hooded robe and sandals—all in good repair—the corpse discussed in the newspaper was particularly interesting because, ten days after its discovery, radioisotopes and other forms of dating failed to establish the fellow's age. All anyone on the scene was willing to say now was that "reasonable estimates placed his period as thirty-five hundred to five thousand years ago, possibly longer," and that "additional tests are bound to bring us a closer fix." The last line of the piece mentioned that the body was damaged in the area of the chest cavity, and the heart seemed to be the only organ that had been damaged.

Erwin tried to make himself lay the newspaper aside and leave for work on time, but he kept rereading the article, all the knowledge he had crammed into his head setting off buzzers. Maybe the general public didn't know it, but, while no dating system devised could establish the birthdate of any corpse (including that of someone who perished a week ago), modern science was outstanding in dealing with periods only several hundred years ago. Fifteen hundred years, "possibly longer," was much too large a gap. Not only that, determining the age of remains no older than five thousand years should not represent any kind of imposing problem.

Parrish folded the newspaper carefully so that the filler piece showed clearly and, shaking his head, made himself rise. The thought passing through his mind that moment came to him as unbidden as any of his recent birthdays: *A far-out explanation for the trouble they're having with this guy would be that he was old as Methuselah when something or someone killed him.*

Erwin turned in the direction of where Carmen would be sitting if this was their home, instead of his lonely apartment, and they were still together. He knew about that aspect of the past—how rumors still existed that a race of men in that part of the world had lived to incredible ages—because of his ex-wife. When she had begun making sounds about getting fed up with him and how he seldom seemed to notice her, Parrish had tried to get religion, too. He'd taken to attending church with her on Sundays, even accepted the Bible the minister offered him.

Then he had made the mistake of reading it, from scratch—"mistake" because the Good Book had gotten interesting to Parrish and further distanced him from Carmen.

Because a good archaeologist was not only a detective

at heart but an historian, Erwin had rediscovered something he'd forgotten while he was reading Genesis: A lot of the Bible needed to be taken on faith, but from a certain point in the Old Testament forward, it was just about as reliable a work on ancient history as any book a man could find. People who weren't religious—which Erwin wasn't—forgot that. They even preferred to ignore the fact that the yen for recording anything for posterity—the actual compulsion to *write*—was first motivated by religious beliefs and feelings. Why, Johann Gutenberg's first volume off the press in 1450 was a Bible!

So because Erwin was a man who was mesmerized by the origins of things, he had gotten so fired up about the story of Noah—not only the parts concerning the Flood, but the recorded ages of men before and after it—that he'd immediately gone back to tuning Carmen out! He hadn't wanted or meant to, he'd even tried to share what he learned with her. Facts, though, even those that were easy enough to understand and had to do with the lives of every creature on earth today, just weren't Carmen's thing. Sometimes Parrish had believed she just liked sitting in a pew dressed in her Sunday best, relaxing.

Erwin realized with a start that the reason he was so worked up over today's newspaper story was that the dead guy discovered in eastern Turkey was lying on the same mountain where Noah's ark was supposed to have come to rest after the Flood finally stopped. He certainly didn't imagine the old boy was Noah and definitely didn't believe he'd been hundreds of years of age when he died, but everything about the find intrigued Parrish immediately. Hell, there hadn't even been a dig—the corpse in the hood and robe had simply popped into view!

On his way to the 32nd Street station that morning he suddenly remembered he had enough accumulated leave time to fly across the world and go into the field while the Mount Ararat Man—the press named him that—was still an archaeological process as much as an event. Sure, it would set him back a bundle—but who did he have to spend money on now anyway? The boys were grown, on their own. His settlement with Carmen had let her take the house and ninety percent of the furnishings in exchange for paying no alimony. If Parrish wanted to blow his small savings plus all the leave money he hadn't taken on the adventure of his lifetime, there was nothing to stop him—

And nobody, basically, to mourn him if he fell off the damn mountain!

So before he could change his mind, Erwin told Chief Middleton that afternoon that he'd be using all his vacation time in one big chunk, then booked a flight for Ankara. He was sweating freely when he was done, but he felt free, too—free, and younger than he'd felt in thirty years! And if the department found a way to suspend him for such an abrupt action, shit on it, he had his twenty in, he could retire tomorrow if they pushed too hard!

During the four days before he caught the big bird, Parrish had a lot to do, including the renewal of his passport and getting his shots. He also placed a long-distance phone call to a Turkish policeman he knew named Gus—short for Augustos—Ekin. The two law men had met when Gus was in the country to facilitate the extradition of a Turkish national, and they'd liked each other. Cops tended to hang together closely and Erwin figured his acquaintance might cut a little red tape, point him in the right direction, and put him on the slopes of Ararat more quickly than if Parrish wandered off on his own. Ekin said he'd be happy to do anything he could.

Ararat was a dormant volcanic mountain, but it hadn't erupted since 1840, Erwin found when he set out, feverishly, to learn as much as possible about the site of discovery. It had two peaks rising above thirteen thousand feet, seven miles apart, and the fact that oxygen starvation was entirely possible at the summit provided part of the reason why even modern explorers had not been able to sustain a search for the ark of Noah. Other reasons included the instability of the slopes because of snow and occasional unexpected avalanches of rock.

But Mount Ararat Man, the newspapers had reported, had been a considerate fellow. Whether he'd lost his life from falling boulders or his remains had rolled down the slope for unaccountable reasons, the body had been found fewer than 300 feet from the foot of the mountain.

Almost, Erwin mused while he was packing, *as if he finally* wanted *to be seen—buried, maybe.*

But he had to be careful about drawing assumptions of that sort, pretending to be "interpreting" the facts when he had almost no data to interpret. Even if the dead man he was hopeful of examining had been born only 3,000 years ago, 99 percent of today's customs and most modern beliefs were newer than that, largely unknown to a human being whose life might have preceded the Flood. Burial rites had been changing throughout history and they also varied from country to country—and Turkey was bounded by the Black Sea, nations of the old U.S.S.R., Iran, Iraq, Syria, the Mediterranean, Greece, and Bulgaria. The Euphrates and Tigris Rivers rose in the east, for God's sake!

And the Armenians called Mount Ararat, Parrish remembered with something akin to a wondering shudder, "*the Mother of the World.*"

Finally aboard the plane flying him away to the excellent adventure of his life—to southeast Europe and its bristling interface with Asia Minor—Parrish recalled the carefully detailed story of Noah from the Bible Carmen's clergyman had given him. Folks used Methusaleh as a synonym for astonishing longevity, but he had been only one of many whose reported lifespans exceeded those of any modern man or woman. Noah himself was supposedly five hundred plus when he begat Sham, Ham, and Japheth, and most of the males who were cited as living prior to the Flood were said to have been around for centuries: Seth, Adam's son, for nine hundred and twelve years; Mahalaleel made it to eight hundred and ninety-five; Methusaleh to age nine hundred and sixty-nine; and Noah's father, Lamech, lived to be seven hundred and seventy-seven. Of those mentioned in Chapter five of *Genesis,* only Enoch didn't surpass 365 at which point it says, unaccountably, "And Enoch walked with God: and he was not; for God took him."

Of course, Parrish reflected, everyone but fundamentalists usually poked fun at longevity of that kind. Erwin could see why; he just collected the data. Yet the curious thing about the Bible was that its authors usually got things like Ararat itself right and, in recent times, archaeological digs with some regularity had been uncovering city-states located right where the Bible claimed they were. Like the man on Mount Ararat today, they had only been covered—buried—by time.

Critics and "analysts" were the same whatever the field of inquiry, Parrish thought. One of the factors that had hooked him on *Genesis* was the way it indicated a *clean distinction* between the period of time before the Flood, and after it. Before passing along instruction to Noah, God said (in *6:3*), "My spirit shall not always strive with man, for that he also is flesh: yet his days shall be as an hundred and twenty years." By the time Noah's sons were grown and, after the tower of Babel was unwisely constructed, people were scattered abroad "upon the face of all the earth," human beings were living shorter and shorter lives. As early as Chapter 11 of *Genesis,* Nahor survived only to one hundred and nineteen.

The detective ate the meal he was brought by a handsome uniformed woman and perversely wished they still allowed smoking on airplanes—perversely because giving up cigarettes was one of the things he'd long since done to try to please Carmen and keep the marriage going. Man's days would be "an hundred and twenty years." Last month on TV Parrish was watching some talk show and he had heard several modern-day experts on life expectancy say there was no reason in the world the human body shouldn't be expected to last for one hundred and twenty years. The longer Erwin lived, it seemed, the more often he heard things tentatively confirmed that so-called experts had derided in his childhood!

So what had happened to change everything for people starting with the "generations of Noah," and did that have anything to do with the first archaeological site Erwin Parrish had ever seen in person? Right after the Almighty's new statement about the longevity of humankind there was a marvelous combination of words that had thrilled and also chilled him every time he'd read them—"There were giants in the earth in those days"—words Parrish doubted that any professional archaeologist believed for a minute. "Giant" was from the Greek *gigas,* he'd learned, but that told him shit. What had it meant when some unknown translator, hundreds of years ago, had tried to convey a matter of importance: afterward, after all, the Flood seemed to have wiped out everything but Noah, his family, and the mated sampling of life on the planet, then human longevity had been cut to a fraction of what it supposedly was! Was it possible "giant" was originally connected to a different sort of person entirely, or, alternately, to the passage of time when there was no such thing as a decent printed calendar? Anyone who knew how to read could see in *Genesis 6:1-4* a distinction being made between offspring and descendants of the offspring "of the sons of God and the daughters of men," or the part about "when man began to multiply . . . and daughters were born unto them."

Almost as if the "daughters" hadn't previously been born to them.

Or, Parrish thought, as if "daughters of men" did not have the same origin as "the sons of God." But what the hell could that mean?

Unless there were not only "giants" on earth, but more than *one kind* of women.

Erwin checked his watch, closed the Carmen-inspired copy of the Bible, and settled back to nap. He was disgusted with himself. For most of his 48 years he'd longed just to be present at an active dig, but he'd never seen anything more wonderful up close than a few touring mummies and a handful of tiny bones from a bird that had lived during the Cro-Magnon period, a lousy twelve to thirty thousand years ago. By archaeological reckoning, that was about the time of the Kennedy administration! Yet here he was on the verge of fulfilling his oldest desire and he was more interested in a bunch of Biblical curiosities any real scientist would dismiss.

Gus Ekin proved to be as likable and pleasant a man as Parrish's memory insisted, but shockingly older. The very next day after Erwin's plane finally touched down on Turkish soil, they were in a Jeep leaving Ankara and headed toward the eastern coast when Erwin realized that 14 years had flown the coop since the other lawman visited America. Now the white-maned, dark-skinned man with the sparkling black eyes was a semi-retired chief who appeared overjoyed to be of service to his colleague from the United States.

Parrish tried again to thank Ekin for easing his way through customs, then entertaining him at his home. "I have enough *otorite,* what you call 'clout,'" Gus said from behind the steering wheel, "to get you many places, even taken you directly to any of Turkey's many borders. I also have acquaintance with certain Iranian and also Iraqi border guards, but I do not think you shall care to meet them—or the Syrian patrols, who tend to dislike the Turkish as well as Americans."

"I'm only interested in the mountain," Erwin told him, "and the dead man they found on it." It occurred to him his remark might sound a trifle brusque and he managed an apologetic smile. "Apart from old friends, of course."

Lighting another of his endless, foul-smelling cigarettes, Gus grinned back. He had a disconcerting habit of raising his hands from the wheel whenever he turned to regard Parrish. "United States people put a high *fiyat* on friendliness. In this part of the world, at this point in history, there are few friendships and fewer people still who wish to see the Ararat Man. It is probably because of this that I have the good news for you."

"You know someone in government who can clear it for me to see the dig?" Erwin asked eagerly.

"Better yet, I know Professor Dag," Gus replied proudly, "the archaeologist who is representing Turkish rights to this find."

"Gus, you're amazing!" Parrish exclaimed.

"Maybe so! He's agreed to permit you to view the remains—pardon the universal police language, eh?— this night and all of tomorrow." Gus negotiated an especially complex curve in the improbable-looking highway speeding them through the countryside. "You see that it is only *maybe* I am so amazing, Erwin. Dag did not welcome you to his party for a longer period than that."

Parrish leaned back against the passenger seat and munched on the fringes of his mustache. "I don't know whether to jump up and down with joy because you've got me on the slope or to cry because—"

"Because you came so far for one day and one-half," Ekin finished for him. "Thank me many times, and jump perhaps once, my friend, because Dag did not wish an amateur there at all. It seems there is more to the Mount Ararat Man than the press has been told. I had to tell him you're the American who helped me return a *fine insan*—a bad man—to our nation, where he was executed."

"I wondered what you people did with that bastard," said Parrish.

"What is often done to the killers in this part of the world," Gus said. Then he lifted his steering hand to watch Erwin's reaction. "You may find it amusing to know what the professor Dag's name means in our tongue. Maybe, my *dost,* it shall explain why you share a common interest."

" 'Dag' has some meaning?" Erwin said. "What is it?"

"It means 'mountain.' " Gus replied, and laughed so heartily Parrish was afraid he might tip the Jeep over.

But Professor Dag, in person, reminded Erwin more of a molehill when the two met at the foot of Mount Ararat. Aging and small enough to have been called "petite" if he'd been a female, Dag was perfunctory in greeting Parrish, then waving for the American to follow him. There were several muttered syllables that might even have added up to sentences, but either the professor did not speak English or he did not choose to.

For an instant Parrish, wearing a parka that now felt too heavy for the late spring day—he had decided to take warmer apparel thousands of miles from home on the theory that he could always take it off—stared longingly after the departing Ekin who was both helper and translator. Gus had said he'd be back for Erwin tomorrow night, then left with a cheery wave. It was the first time in years Parrish could recall being alone in an unfamiliar place and being mildly frightened by it.

Then he turned to find Professor Dag, and Erwin's eyes and head rose as he stared up at the twin peaks of the Hittites' Ararat high above him.

Mother of the World, thought Erwin. There were higher mountains—many of them—but a city-bred-and-bound homicide cop seldom if ever saw any in person, and the cloak of snow spread atop ancient Ararat reminded him of a great shawl someone of giant size might have rested upon a pair of monumental maternal shoulders. *"And God said unto Noah,"* Erwin recalled from Genesis *6:13, "The end of all flesh is come before me; for the earth is filled with violence through them; and, behold, I will destroy them from the earth."*

Parrish's gaze slowly lowered to focus on his grudging host and the small party of professional archaeologists grouped at a roped-off area some three-hundred feet up the rocky slope. He began moving up to join them, awed as much by his thoughts as by the scene before him. *Just what, exactly,* Erwin pondered as he climbed, immediately obliged to breathe more self-consciously, was meant by *"I will destroy them?"* Them *who*? It sounded specific then, in that setting. True, if the story of the Flood—repeated in nearly every religion on earth—was true, he supposed the majority of life-forms (including human beings) had not survived. But almost everybody knew Noah had been told to take with him—

His step faltered, his chain of thought was broken. The five men and two women who were living the life Erwin Parrish had denied himself till that moment were instinctively opening a pathway for him as he drew near. For a moment it was quite like the mourners standing before a coffin in an American mortuary, thoughtfully making room for the newest arrival at the bier. Even small, dignified Dag, gently pulling at his beard, stepped away to admit Parrish.

What lay sprawled in stony rubble a dozen feet or so from Erwin looked at a glance like an ordinary middle-aged white male who'd been shot or stabbed to death—last week. Unlike the famous Iceman who was of enormous antiquity, this did not appear to be a leathery or mummified cadaver with most of the quickly-identified signs of common humanity weathered into the undisturbing, alien guise of a life-cessation dating to prehistory. This body, this *man,* did not oblige anyone by seeming as if his death and his life as well had transpired beyond modern-day kinship.

Even when Erwin went closer, this poor corpse somehow made the detective think of men he'd known, worked with, cared about. In a curious, vital way Parrish could not have put into words, the Mount Ararat Man was one of them. Of everyone.

Except, of course, that it was apparent he'd been frozen, and was no longer, that his partly-opened eyes—intact—lacked the consciousness of life, and the poor S.O.B. was every bit as dead as any man Erwin had found in abandoned warehouses, alleys, and the wrong women's apartments.

And those things were apparent because nothing that ever lived could still possess a living spirit with a good-sized hole where its heart belonged. When he automatically started to drop to his haunches and get a better look at the wound, a man with a days-old growth of yellow beard rested a fold of the tattered robe over it.

Preferring to think of the concealment as an act of sensitivity instead of an effort to hide something the younger man didn't want him to see ("There's more to this than they told the press," Gus had said), Parrish arose and stared down at the ordinary-looking dead man—who was from thirty-five hundred to five thousand years old or older. Then he glanced at the other people, expecting little Dag to introduce them. That would have been good manners anywhere on the planet.

So when the professor didn't do it, Erwin introduced himself, nodding his head at each man and the two women. None of them uttered a sound, though the yellow-bearded archaeologist and the marginally better-looking of the women nodded back.

There was a capacious tent a few yards away, smoke filtering through its top, an array of archaeological tools Parrish yearned to seize simply to look at them, and a couple of glittering machines he'd only read about in more recent journals. Feeling that he'd be damned if he let these strangers high-hat him and ruin the only such opportunity of his life, Erwin was thinking of taking matters into his own hands and starting to examine the robed corpse when the woman who had nodded decided to speak to him.

"Chief Ekin said you were of inestimable assistance in returning the serial killer to Turkey," she said. "He is Sherlock Holmes—or Sam Spade, maybe!—in this part of the world, so Dag permitted you to have a look." She had nice cheekbones and wide lips that looked as if they wanted to smile but had forgotten the formula. "You shouldn't expect him or the others to be very helpful. I'm Andrea Clayborne."

Erwin was so relieved that someone else spoke English she turned beautiful while he looked at her. "You're British, right?" He saw her nod. "Well, I've heard pros in this science can become a bit over-protective. Can you tell them I'm only here to observe?"

Dr. Clayborne wrinkled her nose. "Ekin told Dag that. But it doesn't matter, because they think all Americans know someone in the media and only want publicity—and money, of course."

She explained to him the site was being constantly guarded by members of their group until a decision was made about the proper disposition of the find, so she and the man with the stubble of yellow beard were assigned to stay at the site with Erwin that night. "Ordinarily we might all remain, but it gets pretty chilly on the slopes after dark, even in a heated tent. Tomorrow you can browse around to your heart's content."

Erwin thought of telling her that he was really somewhat more knowledgeable than a common browser, but didn't. "I take it the man who'll be with us isn't Turkish, either."

Andrea's pale brows rose. "How did you know that? His name is Erich Hoffmeister; he's German."

Parrish grinned tightly. "Just a good guess they'd stick two outsiders with the third one for tough duty—meaning we're men, and you're a woman. Who's the other woman married to?"

"Dag," Andrea Clayborne said, giving him a smile that succeeded radiantly in expressing her pleasure that he was astute enough to recognize the situation for what it was.

But what Parrish neither recognized nor understood when she, Hoffmeister and he were tucked in sleeping bags inside the tent for the night, was *why* Professor Dag, and his other Turkish colleagues were playing so cozy with an archaeological find that really wasn't exactly spectacular. It was a big deal to him, sure; just lying in the dark tent close to a genuine, active site was a moment he'd never forget.

Gus was right, there was more to this. And even after a cursory glance at the remains, Erwin was fairly sure Dag was either keeping something potentially earth-shaking to himself till he had the data to make a huge personal splash—

Or the problems the dating experts were having in establishing the dead man's age were exceptionally special. *"Giants in the earth . . ."*

Moving as soundlessly as possible, Parrish slipped out of his sleeping bag, groped in the dark for his parka. Before sundown he had sweated like a horse in it, finally removed it. Now, he would be glad he'd brought it. Obviously, he was meant simply to soak up atmosphere tonight, then be watched attentively by Dag and the others when daylight came.

Erwin didn't think he wanted to be a good little amateur anything anymore.

Edging toward the tent flap with Andrea Clayborne and Erich Hoffmeister just shadowy masses as he passed, Parrish realized this thing was a mystery as hard to crack as any he'd seen in detective work—and it might boil down to one question: *Who,* or maybe *what,* was their dead visitor from the past?

Once outside with the wind whistling down from the peaks surmounting Ararat, Erwin was eager to don the parka. The noise wasn't loud, merely steady, like that produced by a creature with gigantic lungs who had been summoning someone through the centuries. He found it necessary to watch his footing, after he nearly fell; the tent might have been pitched on fairly level ground, but this was still a mountainside. His friend Gus had told him last night that while this site was that of a volcano that was dormant, earthquakes occurred with terrifying frequency in Turkey. In all likelihood a quake had dislodged the boulders shielding the dead man's remains, then rolled him partway down the slope.

Reaching the site, noticing for the first time that Ararat Man had been provided with a framework of aluminum supports to prevent him from continuing his downhill descent, Parrish knelt and tried to make his vision adjust to the peculiar lighting. The moon was out and there was a mixture of reflection from the snow on the dual peaks and shifting shadows presumably formed from outcropping rock. He had never seen anything like it; the site was simultaneously adequately lit—even shockingly so, to his eyes—and so splotchy it was as if the entire slope was illuminated by something that kept shorting out.

Erwin supposed the impression he had that he was being watched was a neurotic commonplace for weirdly obsessive people like him who volunteered to work on the sides of mountains at night.

Using just his thumb and index finger, doing so as deftly as he had with any body he'd had to see, Parrish slowly brought the fold of the robe away from the awful wound in the chest. Then he leaned forward to examine the gaping hole with his naked eye.

"God saw that the wickedness of man was great in the earth . . ." No accident occurring when Ararat Man was being unceremoniously whipped this way and that had made this wound. No burrowing beast had made the aperture and devoured the heart, either.

Parrish was a good enough homicide detective to know that one or more persons had either dug into the fellow's flesh with a sharp instrument and cut his heart out or had driven something nice and round through the chest first, *then* removed the heart.

Rocking back on his heels, Erwin chewed on his drooping mustache and asked himself to theorize when the Mount Ararat Man had been killed, why, and by whom. Rumor had it that Chaldean priests of the 5th century BC had climbed Ararat and peeled away bituminous coating from Noah's ark. Maybe they also found this robe-wearing body, held some quaint superstitions, and excised the heart. But even the 5th century BC was more recent than he was supposed to be; such a theory amounted to suggesting he had been a *passenger* on the *Ark,* since most experts placed Noah's survival at approximately 3,500 BC!

Yet that *would* explain Professor Dag's secrecy. Human remains from Noah's ark would be priceless, even if it didn't explain how this body succeeded in looking like one that had been living and breathing a month ago.

Shivering, Parrish remembered the parts of *Genesis* concerning "sons of God," "daughters of men" and the distinction he himself had noticed regarding a time "when man began to multiply" and the daughters were then "born unto them." In hunting for an older definition of *giant,* he had wondered if men had even fathered daughters before the Flood. Perhaps the reason the "begats" tended to concentrate on men alone was because few females were born!

Erwin shivered. What if the male corpse so ingloriously sprawled at his feet was a "son of God" because, like Methusaleh, Lamech, and Noah, he had been a *giant of longevity*?

So one of the daughters of men, feeling her destiny was a short life of drudgery, had attempted to *reverse* the position she had with her mate—by taking and possibly devouring his all but immortal heart? Why, his own ex-wife Carmen had been jealous of his meaningful work! Imagining he wanted to "batter" her, she'd stolen everything he had but his career in law enforcement! Even Goodnight, the shrink, had said *he* had personal problems and couldn't enjoy a normal relationship with a living family—that was how pervasive the influence from the "daughters" had been on Carmen, his career—on *everything*!

He slid and scurried back to the tent to share his ideas with the professional archaeologists. "And of every living thing of all flesh," God had told Noah, "two of every sort shalt thou bring ... to keep them alive with thee; they shall be male and female." Suddenly it was clear to Parrish that the mate of Mount Ararat Man hadn't wished to settle for her paltry years, killed him during or after the voyage; he was probably one of *Noah's* sons—the greatest archaeological find in history!

Erwin threw back the tent flap as he entered and a pool of light spilled on Erich Hoffmeister where he still lay in his bag.

The sleeping bag was still zipped shut, but one end was soaked with blood.

Astounded, Parrish rushed over and yanked the zipper down from the young man's face with trembling fingers.

Herr Professor Hoffmeister's throat was torn open, his yellow beard had turned red, and his face was white as the snow atop Ararat.

There were no life signs. Erwin frowned; froze. This man's murder left one other, aside from himself, alive on the slope—and she was behind him. Clayborne must have killed the German, she probably cut out the heart of Ararat Man. She had either faked her credentials or just exploded like the powderkeg Erwin was supposed to have had inside him, raining her neurotic superstitions like shrapnel.

Waiting no longer, Parrish spun suddenly in the direction of the British woman's sleeping bag, prepared to subdue her any way he had to.

Except someone else already had subdued Andrea. Permanently.

He bent forward to peer down at her pale face and, below it, the rent in her throat. *An animal,* Erwin thought, *stalking us . . .*

But after he'd struck a match and looked more closely, he was able to detect the presence of what appeared to be bite marks, just under the ear, in her neck.

All right. Okay. It hadn't attacked him, so it must have come into the tent while Parrish was at the site.

Finding both that the tent held no additional surprises and a flashlight he had brought, Parrish took from the dead Hoffmeister the largest digging implement he could find, went slowly to the flap of the tent, and cautiously slithered outside.

Without thinking about it, he shone the flashlight on the roped-off site, and gasped.

Mount Ararat Man was gone!

Running then, rushing to where the remains had been restrained by supports, he found them kicked apart—

And an already-drying trail of snow-dampened sandaled feet leading up the slope toward the distant pair of peaks.

But nothing that ever lived could rise and walk without its *heart,* Erwin realized.

Then he used the beam from his flashlight to aid his vision in the odd, unnerving moonlight—sprayed it up the slope rising above him . . . and saw *her.*

Climbing at a rate of speed that seemed purposive but not hurried, clad in a robe similar to that which the long-dead man hanging limply in her arms wore but with no hood and a head of flaxen hair wafted behind her, she seemed almost to be drifting up Ararat. She looked to Erwin Parrish to stand six feet or more, and the thought seared through his mind that there was no logical reason why giants had to be male.

Without the slightest plan, he kept the beam centered on the amazing sight, tucked the shovel under one arm, and climbed after them. *Dag must've seen her,* he realized, panting after a matter of yards; *that's why he was so uncommunicative and maybe why he left three foreign outsiders on the mountain—as bait! He'd need proof that such a woman existed.*

Till Parrish was close enough to see the blonde woman clearly, she didn't pause in her effortless stride. Then, though—when he was within twenty yards or so and wondering how much farther he could climb—she turned, froze in place, and stared at him.

The Armenians' expression, "Mother of the World" vaulted into Erwin's mind. At a glance, she looked magnificent to him. Her robe prevented him from seeing any details of her figure, but her carriage was outstanding, her courage and sense of purpose obvious. She had wide-spaced eyes that could have been colorless, a widow's peak, and hair so tawny it might have belonged to a lioness.

But she opened her mouth in a snarl that exhibited blood still dripping from her generous lips and teeth, the latter long and jagged except for a tooth on either side that looked inches in length and came to points no larger in circumference than needles. *I have sought him for centuries, dwelling in the ark,* she said, *living on the blood of natives and those they said vanished because they could not draw breath.*

Erwin heard her speak with the voice of mountain wind, deep in his head. Thousands of years danced like motes, particles from elsewhere, between them. "Who *are* you?"

She said, *Noah, son of Lamech, chose to save my husband and me, two of all kinds, from the Flood. But our kind was not favored, so one was sent in the day when my husband slept to slay him. Though his heart was removed, I awakened in time to save it—as I have done for that moment when I might find him and put it back. For our eternal lives.*

Parrish was stunned. Her mate slept by day; his assassin had known he could only be killed then, by something carving into his heart. And *she,* the astounding woman of Ararat, had kept his heart for thousands of

years, believing she might reanimate him! Foolish to ask
her more about their kind, that which had slaughtered
Andrea and Hoffmeister the way she had, when he knew
then they were history's first vampires.

*Those with you kept me from reaching my husband
when his body was at last released,* she said as if reading
his thoughts, *so I waited longer, then bit them that I might
take him. Yet you are from another world; I need not
slay you. Leave us and you shall live.*

Erwin's brain spun. Then he shook his head. "You've
stolen from an archaeological site, and you're a suspect
in two murders." She began to climb; he lumbered after
her, weighted flashlight heavy, now, in his right hand.
He had to do this, but he couldn't make himself read
her her rights. She was mounting Ararat faster now,
scampering, putting distance between them. "I'll see to
it you're well-treated, get you a good—"

Parrish broke off because he heard the rumbling
sounds, both above and beneath him. He was drained
of breath and caught midway between the beginnings of
an avalanche and an earthquake! When rock slipped
from under his feet, he glanced down in mortal terror.

When he glanced up, the widow carrying her husband's remains had disappeared as if by magic.

But much farther up Ararat, fleetingly exposed when
lightning added to the uncanny illumination over the imposing mountain, Erwin saw the hull of an ancient ves-
sel—one that had easily been large enough to displace
43,000 tons and bring to safety the males and females of
every major species, including "every creeping thing of
the earth . . ."

Rock of every size poured down from the two peaks
of eternal Ararat even as Erwin, mortally wounded and
losing consciousness, believed he caught a glimpse of a
tall, magnificent blonde woman running like the wind in
an effort to save him.

He had time to feel glad that he himself could one
day be the focal point of a great archaeological discovery
and to whisper, too softly to be heard by any living
thing, "Mother."

FANGS
by
Douglas Borton

"Hey, look at this."

Litton beamed his flashlight at the girl's neck. Randall saw two puncture wounds oozing long streaks of blood.

"Hell," he muttered. "Syringe, you think?"

Litton shook his head. "Holes are too big. More like a stiletto—two quick jabs."

They knelt in a weedy lot on a side street off Mulholland Drive in the Hollywood Hills. Mist hazed the night air, sparkling with the red and blue glow of squad-car beacons.

The girl was young and scrawny and dead. She lay supine in a contorted pose, eyes wide and not yet glazed. Her skin was still warm.

"Think the incisions were the cause of death?" Randall asked.

"Could be. Something strange, though. There's not much blood. You'd expect ..." Litton's voice trailed off. "Shit."

"What?"

"See that moisture? Near the wounds?"

Randall leaned closer. "Saliva."

"He was licking her."

"Or sucking. Sucking blood from the holes."

Litton looked up from the body. "Dracula, huh? That what you're thinking?"

"There's no shortage of nuts in this town," Randall said, avoiding a direct answer. "Better collect that spit before it dries up. With luck, this asshole's a secretor."

He walked back to the street. Taylor, the shift commander, was just getting out of his car.

"Thought you were tied up with that bag-lady thing,"

Randall said. The lady had been knifed to death and left in a dumpster.

"I left Dickman in charge."

"Inspector Clouseau? He couldn't find a booger if it was hiding in his nose."

"This collar shouldn't be too tough. The perpetrator carved his gang monicker in the victim's chest."

They shared a laugh. Perps were so fucking stupid.

"What's the monicker?" Randall asked.

"Slikk. With two k's."

"Yeah, I know that fuckup." Randall spent a lot of time on the boulevards. "Real name is Julio Mendoza. He usually hangs at Benny's. You know, that burger place at Hollywood and Western."

"Dickman said the taco stand at Sunset and Wilton."

"Dickman should have the last three letters of his name removed for accuracy. It's Benny's. Trust me."

"I'll pass the word on. So what've you got here?"

"Female juvenile. Fifteen, sixteen. Black. Needle marks on her arms. Probably a hooker. Dressed like one."

"You don't know her?"

"No, but it's hard to keep up. The pimps are always recruiting."

"Yeah, well, they say the country's switching over to a service-oriented economy," Taylor said. "She raped?"

"No indication. Her clothes aren't torn."

"Cause of death?"

"Unknown. There's one funny thing." Randall told him about the puncture wounds. "Could be some freak who thinks he's a vampire."

"Great. How long does Litton think she's been there?"

"Oh, hell, she's not even cool yet. Somebody in that house"—he nodded at a silhouetted split-level next door to the vacant lot—"reported a scream at ten-forty-five."

"Half hour ago."

"Yeah. The beat cops found the body in the weeds. I was in the squad room when the call came in."

"Lucky you. CSU show up yet?"

"We're still waiting."

"They're gonna be thrilled you and Litton worked on the deceased before they bagged and tagged."

"We didn't touch anything. Except Litton got some saliva. Might be able to type the guy."

"That'll come in real handy at the trial. Won't help us catch him, though."

"That's what I like about you, Lieutenant." Randall jabbed a finger at him. "Your positive attitude."

The Crime Scene Unit arrived twenty minutes later. Randall supervised the collection of evidence. There wasn't much. A few scraps of cloth in the brush, a partial impression of a boot heel in some dirt near the curb. The CSU commander, Elkins, was snapping photos of the print when he saw the tread marks.

"You can barely make them out," he told Randall when the detective joined him at the curb. "A couple of feet from the shoe print."

"I see them. Can you make a cast?"

"Sure, no problem."

"Hmm. Do vampires drive cars, you think?"

Elkins looked at him blankly. He had examined the body, but had attached no significance to the puncture wounds. An unimaginative man.

"I mean," Randall added, "you'd think a vampire wouldn't need vehicular transportation. He could just turn into a bat and fly away."

"What the fuck are you talking about?"

"Might use a hearse, though. Yeah, I could see that. Big long hearse driven by a hunchback. Named Igor."

Elkins turned away and took more photos. He thought Randall was crazy, but that was nothing new. All homicide cops were crazy. They spent too much time with death.

Randall was nervous as he listened to the local news update on one of the morning shows. He stood in the kitchen, watching his black-and-white portable, a foamy toothbrush in his cheek. He always brushed his teeth in the kitchen because the tap water in the bathroom sink was rust-colored and speckled with small black things that worried him. Ought to have a plumber look at that, he often thought.

The news reader droned on. Overturned semi on the 405. Fire in a Compton warehouse. Gang drive-by in South-Central.

Nothing on the vampire. Randall relaxed. The TV clowns had probably dismissed the murder as just another hooker offed by her pimp. The possible implications of the puncture wounds must have eluded them; if they had tumbled to the Dracula angle, they would have played up the story big-time. Good. He didn't need a swarm of cameras in his face when he worked the streets.

At eight a.m. he witnessed the autopsy; his appearance was necessary to preserve the chain of evidence required by law. Litton got a shock when he cut the body open. The girl was nearly empty of blood.

"Looks like we've determined the cause of death," Litton remarked. "Crazy bastard sucked her dry."

"Christ Jesus." Randall felt a shiver move through him.

The post-mortem reduced the girl to a series of labeled bags, jars, and vials. When it was over, Randall checked in at the station house. A clerk in Communications had already faxed reports of the crime to law-enforcement agencies throughout California and out of state. "Notify the Feds?" Randall asked. The clerk nodded.

It was worth a shot. The perp had transportation; he might have crossed state lines. Lots of the crazies migrated west to the Golden State, killing as they went. And Randall was reasonably sure Dracula had killed before. The homicide just didn't have the feel of a first-time affair.

If he'd done it before, he would do it again. Perhaps soon.

By two P.M. Randall was on the street, showing a photo of the dead girl to the pimps and whores and dealers he knew. Nobody could I.D. her.

He warned the hookers to watch out for strange johns. "This nut thinks he's a vampire—you know, Count Dracula."

"So what we s'posed to do?" one of the girls asked. She called herself Pussy Tonite, though Randall doubted that her birth certificate carried that name. "Brush off every trick who acts weird? That's, like, *all* of 'em."

"The scuzzball offed her in a vacant lot up in the hills. He probably cruised the boulevard and picked her up, then drove up there. If you refuse to get in a john's car—"

"Lose half my bidness, man."

"Just for a couple of nights. Till things cool down. Look, I know you work out of the Starry Night motel."

"Never heard of it."

"Right. That dump's only a block and a half from your corner. You can walk there, can't you?"

"Sometimes they like to do it in the car."

"It's a bad idea right now."

She shrugged. Randall could see she wasn't buying it. The girl wasn't dumb; she was merely balancing the threat of Dracula, vague and speculative and remote, against the more immediate danger posed by her pimp, Johnny K. If she didn't bring in the cash, Johnny would take her smack away, maybe even work her over.

"All right," Randall said, "you handle it your way. Just tell me one thing. You carrying?"

" 'Course not. Got no permit to carry."

"Save it for the judge, for Christ's sakes."

He grabbed her purse, ignoring her yelp of protest, and looked inside. Pack of Trojans—he was glad to see that. Couple of sex toys for the customers. Kleenex. Keys. Cash. Pills; he didn't want to know what kind. At the bottom of the handbag, a small airweight .22. The clip was full: eight rounds.

"Smart," he said, handing it back. "I feel better. If this cretin does pick you up, plug him between his baby blues."

She would, too. She'd been on the street three years— a lifetime—and she knew how to take care of herself. It was the new girls he worried about, the ones who didn't know enough to pack a gun.

He called the crime lab in mid-afternoon.

"He's a secretor," the day-watch commander said. "We typed him from the saliva. O Positive. And there's news on the tire track."

"Yeah?" Randall was scribbling in his steno pad.

"They're Winston Truck Premiums. All-season steel-belted radials for four-by-fours, trucks, and vans."

"A van sounds right. These sickos always drive vans."

"Wait a minute, *I* drive a van."

"Yeah? What's your blood type?"

"Hey, fuck you, Randall—"

Randall cradled the receiver, smiling. Lab guys never could take a joke.

It took him two days to find the dead girl's pimp. A Haitian named Freddie Fire, strictly small-time. Freddie claimed he hadn't even known she was dead. "Thought she just run off somewhere. You know how these bitches are."

"What was her name?" Randall asked.

"Roberta something. I ain't sure, man. I picked her up at the bus station a couple weeks ago. She done run away from home, and she was real lonely, no money, nothin' to eat."

"So you helped her out. You're a real humanitarian, Freddie."

"Hey, man, I say you got to give something back, you know?"

"How long did it take you to get her hooked?"

"She didn't use."

"I saw the body, you dipshit. Needle marks all over her arms." Randall gentled his voice. "Look, forget that. What matters is, who wasted her? Did you see her pick up the trick? Did you help arrange it, maybe?"

"No, I was hanging at the steakhouse. She was on the corner, Hollywood and Normandie, smiling at the cars, like I taught her to do. Quick study, that girl."

"You didn't see the trick? His car? Anything?"

"I wasn't even around."

"You got witnesses that can place you at the steakhouse?"

"Sure." He rattled off a list of names, mostly street scum who might cover for him, but also the restaurant's manager, who was all right.

"Okay," Randall said. "I'll check. Meantime, you make no travel plans."

"Me? Leave town? Hey, baby, I love L.A."

The manager confirmed that Freddie had been in the steakhouse for most of the night. He was eliminated as a suspect. Randall worked the area around Hollywood and Normandie, hoping somebody had seen the girl picked up. Nobody had.

"Piece-of-shit case," he told Taylor. "Nothing to go on."

"Unless we get another body."

"Think we will?"

"Maybe. If he gets thirsty again."

Ten days passed. No more working girls turned up dead. Randall pushed the case to the bottom of the pile. He switched to the day shift, started sleeping at night again. Sometimes he wondered if the vampire perp slept at night. He doubted it.

At three o'clock on a Tuesday morning the phone rang, waking him.

"Yeah?"

"Randall? Aguilar." Desk sergeant on the morning watch. "Dracula tried putting the bite on another one."

Randall blinked awake. "Shit."

"He botched it, though."

"She's alive?"

"Sitting in the interview room right now."

Randall made it to Hollywood Division in six minutes. He recognized the girl immediately. A seventeen-year-old Filipina, street name Angel Sweet.

"Hey, Angel," he said with a nod. "I hear you had it pretty rough tonight."

She swallowed, head down. The left side of her neck was bandaged.

"Want to tell me about it?"

"Guess I don't got no choice," she said softly.

He led her though the story. She had been on Hollywood Boulevard, near Edgemont, looking for some action. Time: about eleven-thirty. A guy approached her on foot, flashed some bills, made a date. "I didn't think he was bad news. I'd heard the word you were puttin' out about the Dracula dude. But this john didn't look like no Dracula, and he didn't have no wheels either. The other girls said we was supposed to look out for a trick with wheels."

Randall nodded. "What did he look like?"

A vague description was all she could manage: young, about twenty or twenty-one. Blond. Tall. Thin.

"Accent?"

A shrug. "American."

They had walked two blocks to the motel she used, a dump called the Palms. In the room he got weird. Didn't want her to take off her clothes. Didn't want to fuck. Wanted to kiss. Which was okay, except all of a sudden his mouth moved down to her neck and there was pain, bright stabbing pain, and she tried to cry out and his hand was clapped over her mouth and he was holding her down on the bed, biting her neck, drinking her blood.

"Jesus," Randall said. "What the hell did you do?"

"Went for his eyes. With my nails."

"Get him?"

"No, but I scratched up his cheeks pretty good. He got off me for a second, and I could see his eyes. Scary eyes, devil eyes. Then I pulled this out."

She slipped her hand under her blouse and removed a small silver crucifix on a chain, worn around her neck. It flashed.

"I was raised Catholic in Manila," she said with a shrug. "I don't really believe. Or I didn't, till tonight. But I thought ... well, vampires, you know ..."

"It worked on him?"

She nodded eagerly. "The guy starts hissin' and growlin' and backin' away with his hands up, like I got a gun on him or something. Then I start sayin' the Lord's Prayer, you know, 'though I walk through the valley of the shadow of death.' And he takes off."

"Just ran away?"

"Right."

"What was he wearing?"

"I think some kind of leather jacket—one of those bomber jackets, it must've been. And corduroy pants or maybe black denim jeans. And boots. Big dark boots."

"Brown or black?"

"I don't know. Dark, is all. They went clomp-clomp-clomp on the floor."

"Shirt?"

"Might've been red. Can't remember."

He pressed her on details of the outfit and the perp's physical features.

"I don't remember," she kept saying, but then her eyes narrowed and she shivered. "One thing."

He waited.

"When I was using the cross on him, I could see . . . You're gonna say I'm fucked up."

"Tell me."

"Fangs."

He didn't say she was fucked up. He nodded slowly. It made sense. The puncture wounds in the neck of Freddie Fire's whore hadn't been made by regular teeth.

"What did they look like, exactly?" he asked.

"They were here . . . and here." She pointed at her upper canines. "I guess those teeth are always pointy, a little, but these were really fangs." She swallowed. "You think he's a for-real Dracula?"

Randall took her hand. "No way. He's just another nut."

"Then why'd the cross scare him off?"

"Because he thinks he's a vampire, and that's how vampires are supposed to react. He's playing a part, only he's playing it so well that he's even fooled himself."

"But the teeth . . ."

"Either the fangs are fake or he got his canines filed. Some dentists will do that, if you pay enough."

"I don't know, man." Fear was jumping in her voice. "Lots of strange shit goes down in Manila. They got witches there, who mix up these potions that can make you crazy. And spirits . . ."

"This ain't Manila."

"It's just as weird here, though. Just as fucking weird."

Randall could hardly argue with that.

The TV assholes were all over it now. Even the dumbest among them could hardly miss the vampire angle after Angel's story was leaked. Randall brushed his teeth in the kitchen and watched the earnest newscaster report darkly on the "Dracula killer" who was motivated, it seemed, "by a satanic appetite for human blood." The police, she added, had promised to release an IdentiKit portrait of "the vampire maniac" later today.

A copy of the sketch was on Randall's desk when he arrived in the squad room. He studied it. Lean face, short blondish hair, thin eyebrows, wide mouth, sharpened eyeteeth. A young man, maybe twenty or a little older.

After the day-watch muster, Taylor called Randall and

two other detectives into his office. "Juarez, Hart," he said briskly, "I'm assigning you to the vampire case. Juarez, you check out novelty shops, find out about recent purchases of fake fangs."

"Waste of time," Randall said. "Those holes weren't made by plastic teeth."

"Well, Christ." Taylor was tired and testy. "He's got fangs, so we look for fangs, right? Hart, I want you to contact local dentists, see if they know anything about a guy whose canines have been filed down. Randall, you're back on the street. Pass out those sketches. And don't talk to the fucking press."

Randall hadn't needed that advice. He went up and down the boulevards, handing out copies of the sketch like a Scientology shill distributing flyers, asking if anyone had seen the assailant last night. For the hell of it, he tossed in the idea that the perp probably drove a van. There was no proof the tires hadn't been put on a truck or a four-by-four; but somehow a van felt right. A person could do things in the back of a van that he couldn't do in the cab of a truck.

In early afternoon he got lucky.

"Yeah, I seen a guy run into a van and take off. You think it might've been him?"

Randall stood facing the man in an alley behind a bar on Bronson Avenue. A secluded place. Neither of them wanted to be seen together.

The man called himself Flash. His name was incomprehensible; nothing flashy about him. He was a squat, acne-scarred, generously tattooed Colombian who ran errands for dealers and pimps, probably pulled an occasional B & E, and earned extra income snitching for the cops.

"What time was this?" Randall asked.

"Midnight."

"Where?"

"In the alley behind the Palms."

The Palms Motel. It fit.

"You say he got into a van?"

"Yeah, and revved the engine and screamed out of there, man, like a fucking whatchacallit, bat outta hell."

"What kind of van?"

"I don't know, like, the make and model. Some crappy old van, is all."

"What color?"

"Maybe red. Or orange."

"Would you recognize that van if you saw it again?"

"I might."

Randall pressed a twenty into his hand. "Keep your eyes open. If you see it, call me immediately." Like all his snitches, Flash had both his home and office numbers.

"I got you." Flash eyed the crumpled bill. "Them phone calls can get kind of expensive."

"If it's a legit tip, I'll grease you again. Another twenty."

"Fifty."

"Twenty for the tip. Fifty if I collar the punk."

Flash considered the deal, then nodded. "Seems fair."

Randall was back in the squad room when his phone rang. The switchboard operator told him he had a long-distance call from Argentina.

"Argentina?"

"Hold, please."

He waited in a what-the-fuck-is-this mood.

"Detective Randall?" The voice was male and heavily accented. "I am Captain Vasquez of the Buenos Aires *policia*."

"What can I do for you, Captain?"

"You are investigating the, er, the Dracula killer, correct?" Drah-coo-lah.

"That's right."

"Yes, we have heard of this investigation today, on the television. On CNN, you see."

CNN was carrying the story? Jesus. "And?" he prompted.

"There were three similar murders in Buenos Aires in 1978. *Putas*—prostitutes—with two holes in their necks. In each case, much loss of blood. And there is more."

Randall was scribbling notes on his desk blotter, the only writing surface immediately available. "Go on."

"A fourth woman was attacked, but, like the young lady in your case, she wore a *crucifijo* and was able to frighten off the assailant. From her description we pre-

pared a sketch. The case was never closed; the drawing
is still on file."

"You have a fax machine there?"

"Of course." Vasquez sounded mildly offended.

"Do me a favor and fax that sketch to me right now."

Randall gave him the fax number. A few minutes later
a clerk carried the transmission sheet into the squad
room and handed it to Randall, still on the phone.

"I've got it," he said. He compared the two sketches.
"I think it's the same man."

"This was our conclusion, as well."

"Look, could you send me a copy of your report on
the case?"

"At once. And, Detective Randall, two more points I
should like to make."

"Yes."

"The victim who survived—she said the man was
americano. And he was twenty-one."

"That's what our girl says, too."

"Yes, but this was fourteen years ago. And the man
still looks twenty-one? His appearance is unchanged in
all that time?"

Randall frowned. "Yeah. Funny, huh?"

"It is, how you say, funny."

But both of them knew it wasn't funny at all.

The Argentina materials arrived via Federal Express
the next day. Taylor agreed that it was probably the
same perp. A bilingual cop was put in charge of con-
tacting police departments in major Latin American
cities with a request for a search of their files. The authorities in Santiago, Chile, promptly dug up a twenty-
year-old unsolved case with the same M.O. Two days
later La Paz, Bolivia, unearthed a vampire homicide
from 1964.

"Weirder and weirder," Taylor said. "If this guy's anywhere close to twenty-one, he wasn't even born in '64."

Randall pursed his lips and made no reply.

Juarez and Hart continued to work the teeth. The
novelty-store angle led nowhere, but Hart found a den-
tist who admitted to having filed down a male patient's
canines six month earlier. A surge of excitement gave

way to discouragement when the patient was interviewed and cleared.

"Guy's in a garage band," Hart reported with a frown of disgust. "Thinks the vampire gimmick is gonna make him a superstar. He's alibied for both nights, goddammit." His picture was shown to Angel Sweet anyway. She shook her head: "No, man, not him."

Randall showed Flash a photo array of vans. Flash thought the vehicle he'd seen was most likely a Dodge Ram. There were probably fifty thousand of them in the L.A. area. Still, Randall made a note to add the info to the computer database on the perp. And he told Flash to keep his eyes open. Especially on the next few nights.

"You think he'll try again soon?" Flash asked.

"Yeah. Because he fucked up the last time. Must have a powerful thirst by now."

"I'm feelin' a little thirsty, too."

Randall slipped him a ten. "Just don't get so drunk you can't see."

At four p.m. on Sunday, six days after the last attack, Randall and Taylor and the three other cops assigned full-time to the case had a meeting in the lieutenant's office. They reviewed their progress, which was minimal. Taylor was still mystified by the Argentina connection.

"If not for the physical resemblance," he said, pacing, "I'd assume they were two different perps. But the damn sketches are nearly identical. And if the earlier cases are also the work of the same guy, then, shit, he's got to be forty-seven, forty-eight years old."

"Angel said he was maybe twenty," Randall observed.

"That's what's so fucking crazy about it."

Hart suggested some kind of father-and-son weirdness. The idea was quickly rejected as too farfetched. Juarez said the guy might have had plastic surgery, facelifts and skin peels, to look younger. "He's forty-eight and he passes for twenty?" Taylor retorted. "Even Zsa Zsa couldn't pull that off."

"What if blood keeps him young?" a vice cop suggested in a half-joking voice. "Could be the secret of eternal youth. Might give him immortality."

"The only thing hookers' blood is gonna give him is AIDS," Taylor said harshly.

Randall looked around the room. "There's a possibility we're all ignoring."

Taylor met his gaze. "Which is?"

"Maybe he really is a vampire."

Groans and chuckles. A raspberry from the vice cop.

"I'm serious," Randall went on calmly. "Let's look at the facts. He's got fangs. He prowls at night. Preys on women. Bites their necks, drinks their blood. He hasn't aged in fifteen years or longer. A crucifix can drive him away."

"And he drives a van," Taylor said. "You think Count Dracula would drive a friggin' van?"

"Why not?"

"He could just turn into a bat and fly away."

"Maybe he can't do that. Suppose the vampire legend is rooted in fact, but a lot of the details are bullshit. You've got to separate the truth from the elaborations."

"And what is the truth, exactly?" the vice cop inquired with a shit-eating smile.

"That there are people who live on blood. Who stalk at night. And who don't grow old."

"How do they get that way?" Hart asked. "They extraterrestrials or something?"

"Maybe it's a disease—like AIDS," Randall said, with a nod at Taylor. "Spread via blood. You get bitten, and you're infected."

"Then Angel should be vamping it up by now," Hart countered. "He bit her good."

"But she scared him off before he'd drained her. That might've made the difference."

"So how about the other one? Freddie Fire's girl? Why didn't she get up off the autopsy table and do a suck job on you and Litton?"

Nervous laughter in the room.

Randall had already considered that question. "Maybe she would have, if not for the post-mortem. In the old days, bodies were buried in one piece. But after Litton got through with Freddie's doll, she was in a lot of little bags. Pretty hard to rise from the dead after a thorough dissection—"

"Enough of this crap," Taylor broke in. "You're jerking our chains."

"I used to think it was crazy, too," Randall said.

"Until that phone call from Buenos Aires. Now I'm not so sure."

"You've been working too hard. You need a rest."

Randall turned away without reply.

The meeting ended at five. Taylor took Randall aside while the others were filing out.

"I meant it about taking a rest," he said with gruff kindness. "Really."

"Right, Lieutenant. Right."

On his way home Randall stopped at a little store on Santa Monica Boulevard. He made a purchase for twelve dollars.

It was dark when he emerged from the store. The night was cool and blustery.

"Bad moon rising," he muttered as he headed back to his car.

A ringing telephone. Groping fingers fumbled the handset off the cradle.

"Hello?" Randall rasped as he climbed out of sleep.

"I seen it, man." Flash's voice. "The van. It's parked in an alley right now."

Alert now. Heart pounding. "Where?"

"Off Western, just south of Hollywood."

Randall threw on some clothes. Call for backup? No, Flash might be fucking with him, angling for some easy cash with a phony sighting. Better check it out first.

He reached Western in four minutes. Parked in a red zone and approached the alley on foot. His Beretta 9mm in his hand.

The black skeleton of an apartment house under construction loomed at the rear of the alley. Near it sat a rust-colored Dodge Ram, lights and motor off.

Randall squinted. The van was rocking slightly. Someone was in there. Maybe struggling. Maybe—

From inside the van, a gunshot.

He pounded down the alley. Reached the rear of the Dodge, grasped the door handle, cranked it down. The door flew open and Randall sprang into the doorway in the Weaver stance.

Pussy Tonite was curled up on the floor, breath jerking out of her in unrhythmic gasps. A gun, the little .22

Randall had seen in her purse, was clutched in both hands.

Beyond her lay the sprawled figure of a man.

"Pussy?" Randall whispered. "Baby, it's me."

She looked at him with dulled eyes. "Shot the mo'fucker."

"He dead?"

"Better be."

Randall climbed cautiously into the van and trained his pocket flash on the body. The man was young—twenty or twenty-one—and pale-skinned. He had been wearing a brown wig that had slipped off his head when he'd fallen, exposing the brush-cut blond hair beneath. His eyes were open, staring sightlessly. A lake of blood pasted his beige raincoat to his black shirt.

Randall kept his gun on the body as he scanned the interior of the van. The windows had been covered with the light-tight black paper used in darkrooms. A sleeping bag, not a coffin, lay on the floor. In a corner was a small steel box, padlocked.

"What happened?" he asked Pussy.

"Trick picked me up," she said tonelessly. "I didn't make him for Dracula. I mean, the vamp was s'posed to be a blond dude with, like, boots and shit."

"Yeah." Randall looked at the perp's feet and noted shiny new Reeboks. "He must've figured Angel would give us a description, so he put on the wig and changed his outfit."

"He said he wanted to do it in the motel down the street. We was walking there, and then he pulls me into the alley. I see the van, and all of a sudden I know what's going down. I start screamin', and he's draggin' me in here. Slams the fuckin' door and now it's dark as the inside of my cunt. Then I feel . . ." She hitched in a breath. "I feel his teeth on me."

She touched her neck. Randall saw two pinpoint punctures. "Go on."

"That's when I remember the heat I'm carryin'. I pull it out of my bag and pop him right in the chest from an inch away. Man, I could smell the powder." She frowned. "Hey, how'd you get here?"

"Just happened to be in the neighborhood." Randall

took a step closer to the body. "All right, Pussy, just sit tight."

"That's not my name, you know."

"No? No, I guess it's not. So what's your real name?"

"Connie Larkin."

"Connie, huh? Connie. I like it. Like it a lot."

"Maybe I'll start using it again." Connie Larkin shuddered. "After tonight, I don't think I want to be on the street no more."

"That's a good move. I know some people who can help you out. Things'll be better now. Everything's gonna be just fine."

Randall crouched by the perp and felt the carotid artery. No pulse. He beamed the flash into the eyes and saw no dilation of the pupils.

Dead, all right.

But if he was a vampire—a for-real Dracula, as Angel had said—then he'd been dead for years, hadn't he?

Suppose the perp was playing possum. Crazy, sure, but just suppose . . .

Blur of motion beneath him. A pale hand clamped on his wrist. Sudden squeezing pressure, shock of pain, crackle of bone. The Beretta dropped from his limp fingers.

"Oh, shit," Connie was screaming, "oh, shit, *oh, shit*!"

The vampire released his wrist. Randall stopped, groping for the Beretta on the floor. Dracula moved faster. Snatched the gun, crushed it like a tin-foil toy, tossed it away. The barrel had been bent sideways, the handle crumpled.

Christ, the guy did that with his hands, his bare *hands*.

The perp twisted into a kneeling pose, then swayed upright. Randall stared at him from a foot away and tried to think of something to do.

Behind him, the click of a hammer dropping. Instinctively he dropped to his knees, and the van rocked as Connie fired her .22.

A howl of animal pain. Blood splashed the walls. Dracula staggered backward, then steadied himself and advanced on the girl.

Randall reached out, grabbed his leg. A kick in the face sent him spinning into a corner of the van. His head struck the sharp edge of the padlocked metal box. Blinding pain. His awareness flickered, dimmed.

A vague nightmarish scene unreeled before him. He saw Connie squeeze off another shot, and then the monster wrenched the gun from her hand and hurled it through the rear doorway. Grunting, he fell on her and buried his fangs in her neck while her fists beat helplessly like trapped birds.

Randall shook himself alert. Dizziness and confusion receded. He remembered what he had bought earlier today. Fished it out of his pocket with his left hand. A small silver crucifix on a chain.

He lurched to his feet. Shoved the crucifix directly into the killer's face.

"Eat *this,* motherfucker."

The vampire recoiled, lips skinned back from fangs washed red with blood. Randall pushed the cross at him again. Hissing, the vampire scuttled out of the van into the alley and was gone.

Randall crouched by Connie. She was dazed but apparently okay. He became aware of a shooting pain in his right arm and realized his wrist was broken. Damn.

He pulled out his radio, thumbed the transmit button, called for backup. Code 20: officer in need of assistance. Then he climbed out of the van and retrieved Connie's pistol. Checked the clip. Five rounds.

Randall was pretty sure Dracula had fled west, toward the construction project. He looped the crucifix around his neck, then advanced down the alley holding the .22 in his good hand.

Ahead loomed the silhouette of the unfinished building, a modest three-story job. The foundation had been poured and the walls were going up in a latticework of wooden beams. A chicken-wire fence bordered the site, but the fence had been cut open, probably by vandals raiding supplies. On a barb of cut wire Randall found a scrap of beige vinyl that might have come from Dracula's raincoat.

He entered the shell of the structure. Chancy starlight filtered through the overhead beams. Randall studied every shadow, sniffed for scents, listened for alien breathing, all his senses alert.

His arms prickled with gooseflesh. The short hairs at

the nape of his neck twitched and stirred. Dracula was
here, all right. Very close. Watching him.

Slowly he turned in a wide circle. Rows of vertical
beams stood around him like the X-rays of walls. The
beams were too narrow to offer concealment.

Nobody in sight. Yet he couldn't shake the certainty
that he was being observed. He felt the vampire's gaze
as surely as the mouse senses the shadow of the hawk.
The hawk . . .

His head jerked up.

There.

Directly above him. Perched on an overhead beam
like a roosting bat. Raincoat billowing in the night
breeze. Eyes glowing like cat's eyes in the dark.

Randall lifted the gun, and the vampire swooped off
the beam, plunging toward him, hands extended, fingers
hooked like claws.

The gun bucked once. Randall caught a brief impression of the vampire shuddering in mid-descent as the
bullet ripped through him. He snap-rolled clear of the
falling body. Dracula hit the ground, writhing, then
flopped onto his side and prepared to rise.

Four bullets in him, and he wouldn't quit. God*damn.*

Randall took a breath, then squeezed off a point-blank
shot to the head. The vampire's face disappeared in a
cloud of blood. Agony warbled out of a straining throat.

That has to stop him, Randall thought desperately.
Has to.

It didn't. As he watched, the creature struggled blindly
to force itself upright.

How do you kill the undead? Sunlight, silver bullet,
stake through the heart . . .

A few yards away lay a pile of discarded two-by-fours.
Randall rummaged through the pile. Found a plank that
had been unevenly sawed, one end cut at a sharp angle.
Hoisted it in his left hand. Turned.

Dracula was on his feet now. Swaying, stumbling. And
his face—was it only imagination or were the pale features beginning to reassemble themselves like a filmstrip
run in reverse?

Randall pinched the plank under his right arm. Aimed
the pistol with his good hand. Three shots left.

He emptied the clip. Three echoing reports. The vampire danced drunkenly, then collapsed on his side, mewling. Randall kicked him in the face and the monster rolled onto his back.

Now. Do it *now*.

He grabbed hold of the plank with his left hand, braced it against the crook of his right arm, and delivered a quick downward thrust. The diagonal end slammed into the creature's chest with a splinter of ribs.

The vampire shrieked. A wild keening cry like the scream of a wounded animal.

Randall leaned on the beam, putting all of his weight behind it, forcing it in deeper while the monster thrashed and wailed. Somewhere a distant dog howled in instinctive response.

"Die, you bloodsucking freak," Randall muttered. "Goddamn you, *die*."

With a final effort he punched the beam through the creature's heart. The shriek was abruptly cut off, and only the dog's howling went on, pained and mournful, like the baying of a lonely wolf.

The vampire shuddered all over, then lay still.

Randall made his way back to the van just as squad cars were pulling into the alley in response to his Code 20, too late.

The crime scene was chaotic for hours. The media arrived but were held behind the cordons. Connie Larkin, formerly Pussy Tonite, was taken to Kaiser Hospital for treatment of what the paramedics described as minor injuries and traumatic shock. Elkins' CSU team searched the van, the alley, and the building site for expended shell casings and other evidence.

Randall stayed in the van, his wrist bandaged, refusing further medical care. He was looking through the contents of the steel box in the corner. The rusted padlock had yielded to a single strike from the butt of Connie's .22.

Inside the box were documents. Some were recent: papers concerning the purchase of a Dodge Ram, used, from an Inglewood dealer two months ago; a Mexicana ticket stub for a night flight from Mexico City to Los Angeles, dated a few days prior to the acquisition of the van.

Others were older. Yellowed newspaper clippings, in Spanish, covering the murders of prostitutes and other young women in Santiago, Buenos Airs, Rio de Janeiro, Caracas, Tegucigalpa, over a period of nearly forty years. Three-month single-entry tourist cards for various Latin American countries, along with stacks of ninety-day extensions, many with the dates left blank. Fakes, obviously. Easy enough to obtain on the black market. With them, an American could remain south of the border for years, for decades, passing as a tourist, avoiding suspicion wherever he went.

At the bottom of the box was a passport to Argentina, dated 1942. The face in the passport photo was that of the dead man. His name was William Ashton. Born in Columbus, Ohio, on November 6, 1921.

So, Randall mused, Ashton went to Latin America not long after Pearl Harbor. He was twenty-one then. Was he a vampire already? Or just a young man trying to escape the war?

The latter seemed more likely. If so, Ashton had found a worse fate in some sleepy village or teeming slum than he would have met on any battlefield.

"Randall." Taylor's voice.

"Yeah, Lieutenant?"

"Get out here."

Randall emerged into the pale gray dawn. "You're not starting the shooting-team investigation this soon, are you?" he asked with a tired smile.

"No. I just . . . want you to take a look at something. Hurry up."

Quickly he led Randall down the alley into the construction site. The Crime Scene Unit had already gone over the place; after that, Litton, the pathologist, had taken over, examining the deceased.

Randall stepped inside the building, then stopped. He stared past a ring of uniforms at the remains of William Ashton, lying on the cement floor in a pool of daylight.

"Jesus."

Litton met his eyes. "It started happening as soon as the sun came up."

The body was decomposing with impossible rapidity, flesh turning to powder, hair unraveling and flying away like puff balls strewn by the wind. The clothes remained, and the bloody stake, but other than that, there were only white bones.

"You were right," Taylor said quietly. "He really was Dracula."

One of the uniformed cops muttered agreement. But Randall shook his head.

"No," he whispered. "He was Bill Ashton of Columbus, Ohio. And he was probably a good kid ... once."

As they watched, the process of disintegration went on, until even the skeleton had vanished, dissolving into blowing whorls of dust.

THE NIGHT OF THEIR LIVES
by
Max Allan Collins

I spent the first week in the shantytown near the Thirty-first Street Bridge, nestled in Slaughter's Run. The Run was a non-sequitur in the city, a sooty, barren gully just northeast of downtown. For local merchants it was a festering eyesore—particularly the ramshackle Hoovervilles clustered here and there, mostly near the several bridges that allowed civilization passage over this sunken stretch of wilderness.

For men—and women—down on their luck, as so many were in these hard times, the Run was a godsend. Smack dab in the middle of the city, here were wide open spaces where you could hunt wild game—pigeons, squirrels, wild dogs, and the delicacy of the day: Hoover hog, also known as jack rabbit.

In the Thirty-first Street Jungle, a world of corrugated metal and tar paper and tin cans, I met "former" everythings: college professor, stock broker, haberdasher, and lots of steel mill workers, laid off in this "goddamn Depression." I don't know that I ever heard the latter word without the former attached.

Saddest to me were the families—particularly the women who were alone, their husbands having hopped the rails leaving them to raise a passel of dirty-faced, tattered kids. A ragamuffin-laden woman, even an attractive one, was unlikely to find a mate in this packing-crate purgatory.

Since Thursday of last week I'd been wandering the streets near the Central Market, where hobos haunted the rubbish bins. The weather was pleasant enough: a cool late April with occasional showers and lots of sunshine. I hadn't shaved the whole time; I wore a denim work shirt, brown raggedy cotton trousers and shoes with holes in the soles covered by cardboard insteps. My "home" was a discarded packing crate in an alley off Freemont Avenue, behind a warehouse, in the heart of the city's skid row district.

When I talked the chief into letting me take this undercover assignment, he'd suggested I take my .38 Police Special along. I said no. All I'd need was a few personal items, in my canvas kit bag. I never went anywhere without my kit bag.

"It's a good idea," the chief had said. He was a heavyset, bald, grizzled man who spoke around an ever-present stogie, frozen permanently in the left corner of his mouth. "As just another hobo, you can gain some trust ... we can't get this riff-raff to cooperate, when we haul 'em in on rousts. But they might talk to another bum."

"That's the theory," I said, nodding.

Of course, if I told the chief my *real* theory, he'd have fitted me for a suit that buttoned up the back—you know the kind: where you can't scratch yourself because your arms are strapped in?

It had been three weeks since the last body had been found. The total was at eleven—always men, dismembered "with surgical precision," whose limbs turned up here and there, washed up on a riverbank, floating in a sewage drainage pool, wrapped in newspaper in an alley, scattered in the weeds of the Run itself. Several heads were missing. So was damn near every drop of blood from each victim's jigsaw-puzzle corpse.

Because the butcher's prey was the faceless, homeless rabble washed up on the shores of this Depression, it took a long time for the city to give a damn. But the Slaughter Run Butcher was approaching an even dozen now, and that was enough to interest not just the police, but the press and the public.

The mission at Fourth and Freemont was always crowded—unlike a lot of soup kitchens, they didn't require you to pay for your supper by sitting through a hell-and-damnation sermon. In fact, I never saw anybody seated in the pews of the little chapel room off the dining hall, although occasionally you saw somebody sleeping it off in there; the minister was a mousy guy with white hair and a thin black mustache. He didn't seem to do much beside mill around, touching bums on the shoulder, saying, "Bless you my son."

The person who really seemed to be in charge was this dark-haired society dame—Rebecca Radclau. If the gossip columns were correct, Miss Radclau was funding the Fourth Street Mission. Though schooled in America, she was said to be of European blood—her late father was royalty, a count it was rumored—and the family fortune was made in munitions.

Or so the society sob sisters said. They also followed the movie-star lovely Miss Radclau to various social functions—balls, ballet, theater, opera, particularly fundraisers for the local Relief Association. She was the queen of local night life, on the weekends.

But on weeknights, this socially conscious socialite spent her time dressed in a gray nurse's-type uniform with a white apron, her long black hair up in a bun, standing behind the table ladling bowls of soup for the unfortunate faceless men who paraded before her.

Even in the dowdy, matronly attire, she was a knockout. The soup was good—tomato and rice, delicately spiced—but her slender, top-heavy shape, and her delicate, catlike features, were the draw. Men would hold out their soup bowls and stare at her pale face, hypnotized by its beauty, and grin like schoolboys when she bestowed her thin red smile like a blessing.

"I'd like a piece of *that*," the guy in front of me in line said. He was rail thin with a white stubbly beard and rheumy eyes.

"She seems friendly enough," I said. "Why not give it a try?"

"She don't fraternize," the guy behind me said. He was short, skinny, and bright-eyed, with a full beard.

"Bull," the first guy said, "shit." He lowered his voice to a whisper. "I seen her and Harry Toomis get in her fancy limo out back ... it comes and picks her up, you know, midnight on the dot, every night, uniformed driver and the works."

"Yeah?" I said.

"Yeah," he said. "Anyway, I seen the night Harry

Toomis got in the limo with her, and she was hanging on 'em like a cheap suit of clothes."

The other guy's expression turned puzzled in the maze of his beard. "Say—whatever *happened* to Harry? I ain't seen him in weeks!"

Somebody behind him said, "I heard he hopped the rails, over to Philly. Steel mills out there are hiring again, word is."

We were close to the food table, where I picked up a generous hunk of bread and took an empty wooden bowl; soon I was handing it toward the dark-haired vision in white apron and gray dress, and she smiled like a madonna as she filled it.

"You're the most beautiful woman I've ever seen," I said.

"Thank you," she said. Her voice was low, warm; no accent.

"I feel I've known you forever."

She looked at me hard; her almond-shaped eyes were a deep brown that approached black—it was as if she had only pupils, no irises.

"You seem familiar to me as well," she said melodically.

"Hey, come on!" the guy behind me said. "Other people want to eat, too, ya know!"

Others joined in. "Yeah! This goddamn Depression'll be over before we get fed!" I smiled at her and shrugged, and she smiled warmly and shrugged, too, and I moved on.

I sat at a bench at one of the long tables and sipped my soup. When I was finished, I waited until the food line had been shut down for the evening, then found my way back to her.

"Need some help in the kitchen?" I asked, helping her with one handle of the big metal soup basin.

"We have some volunteers already," she said. "Maybe tomorrow night?"

"Any night you like," I said, and tried to layer it with as much meaning as possible.

Then I touched her hand as it gripped the basin; hers was cool, mine was hot.

"I wasn't always a tramp," I said. "I was somebody you might have danced with, at a cotillion. Maybe we did dance. Under the stars one night? Maybe that's where I know you from."

"Please ..." she began. Her brow was knit. Confusion? Embarrassment?

Interest?

"I'm sorry to be so forward," I said. "It's just ... I haven't seen a woman so beautiful, so cultured, in a very long time. Forgive me."

And I silently helped her into the kitchen with the basin, turned, and went out of the mission.

The night sky was brilliant with stars; a full moon cast an ivory glow upon skid row, giving it an unreal beauty. An arty photograph, or perhaps a watercolor or an oil in a gallery, might have captured this landscape of abstract beauty and abject poverty. Rebecca Radclau might have admired such a work of art, on her social travels.

From around a corner, I watched as her dark-windowed limousine arrived at midnight, pulling into the alleyway where an impossibly tall, improbably burly chauffeur stepped out and opened the door for her. She was still wearing the dowdy gray uniform of her missionary duties. A sister of mercy.

She was alone.

She slipped into the back of the limo, her uniformed gorilla of a driver shut her inside, and they backed out into the street and glided away into the ivory-washed night.

Perhaps I'd misjudged her.

Or perhaps tonight she just wasn't thirsty ...

For the next two nights I worked in the kitchen, washing the wooden soup bowls the first night, drying them the next—and there were a lot of goddamn bowls to wash and dry. She would move through the small, steamy kitchen as if floating, attending to the next night's menu with the portly little man who was the cook for the mission, and in her employ.

Rumor had it he'd been the chef at a top local hotel that had gone under in '29. Certainly the delicately seasoned soups we'd been eating indicated a finer hand than you might expect at a skid-row soup kitchen.

I would catch her eye, if possible. She would hesitate,

our gazes would lock, and I would smile, just a little. She remained impassive. I didn't want to push it: I didn't repeat my soliloquy of the first night, nor did I add to it, or present a variation, either. I tried to talk to her with my eyes. That was a language I felt sure she was easily fluent in.

The next night, as I went through the soup line, she said, "We won't need you in the kitchen tonight," rather coldly I thought, and I went to one of the long tables, sat, sipped my soup, thinking. *Damn! I screwed up. Came on too strong. She needed to think she was selecting me.*

And just as this thought had passed, I felt a hand on my shoulder: hers.

I looked up and she was barely smiling; her catlike eyes sparkled.

"How was your soup?"

I turned sideways and she loomed over me. "Dandy," I said. "I never see *you* trying any. Don't you like the company?"

"I never eat . . . soup."

"It's pretty good, you know. Rich enough even for your blood, I'd think. Want to sit down?"

"No. No. I never fraternize."

"I've heard that."

"I just wanted to thank you for your help." And she smiled in a tight, businesslike way. Others were watching us, and when she extended her slender fingers toward me, and I took them, we seemed to be shaking hands in an equally businesslike way.

Nobody but me noticed the tiny slip of paper she'd passed me.

And I didn't look at it until I was outside, ducked into my alley home.

Midnight, it said.

Written in a flowing, lush hand. No further instructions. No signature.

But I knew where to be.

She stepped out of the back door of the alley, looking glamorous despite the dowdy uniform being damp with sweat and steam, black tendrils drifting down into her face from the pile of pinned-up hair. The whites of her eyes were large as she took in the alley, looking for me, I supposed. She seemed perplexed.

When the limousine glided into the alley next to the mission, and the tall burly chauffeur got out to let her in, I stepped from the recess of a doorway, kit bag in hand, and said, "You did mean midnight, tonight?"

She jumped as if I'd said "boo."

She touched her generous chest. "You startled me! When I didn't see you, I thought you'd misunderstood . . . or just stood me up."

I went to her; took her hand and bent from the waist and kissed her hand, saying archly, "Stand up a lovely lady like yourself? Pshaw."

I'd always wanted to say "Pshaw," but it never came up before.

She smiled slyly, a thin smile that settled in one pretty dimple of her high-cheekboned face. "Did you think this was a date?"

"I had hoped."

"Mister . . . what is your name?"

"Jones, or Smith, or something. Is it important?"

"Let's make it Smith-Jones, then."

"Sure! That's high-tone enough. And may I call you Rebecca?"

"I prefer Becky."

"All right."

The chauffeur was standing with the limo's rear door open. His face was shadowed by his visor, but I could make out a firm jaw and a bucketlike skull.

"Let's not stand out here talking," she said, suddenly glancing about, almost furtively.

"Why not? You're not mistaking a member of the Smith-Jones clan for the sort of riff-raff you don't care to be seen with?"

"Please get in. What is that you have there?"

"Just my old kit bag. I don't go anywhere without my old kit bag—it contains what few possessions I still have."

"Fine. But do please get in."

The chauffeur moved forward, and I had the feeling that if I didn't get in, he'd toss me there.

"Ladies first," I said, bowing, gesturing, and she quickly ducked in.

I followed. The leather seats smelled new; they were deep and comfortable—like living-room furniture, not the back seat of a car.

"Mr. Smith-Jones, I wanted to express my gratitude to you, this evening."

She was unpinning the black hair; it fell in cascades to her shoulders. She shook her head and it shimmered and brushed her shoulders, flipping up at the bottom.

"Gratitude?" I asked. "For what?"

"For your help, these last several days."

"In the kitchen? Jeez, lady ... Rebecca ... Becky ... it's only fair. You've been always good to guys like me, down on their luck, making sure we get a square meal once in a while."

"I've known adversity myself," she said solemnly. It sounded silly, but I managed not to laugh.

"So, uh ... how exactly do you intend to express your gratitude?"

She touched my hand; she looked at me with those iris-less dark eyes. She seemed about to say something provocative, something sensual, something seductive. What she said was: "Food."

"Food?"

"Food. Real food. A real meal. Prepared by a five-star chef."

"No kidding. I had something else in mind ..." I grinned at her lecherously, and she just smiled. "... but I'll settle."

She didn't let it go. "*What* else did you have in mind, Mr. Smith-Jones?"

I sighed. Looked down at my tattered clothes. Shook my head. "I shouldn't even kid about it. How can you look at somebody like me ... unshaven ... dirty clothes ... breath that would knock a buzzard off a dung wagon ... and think of me in any other way but one of pity?"

She patted my hand. "That's not necessarily true, Mr. Smith-Jones. I can look at you and see ... possibilities. I can see the man you were—the man you still are, underneath the bad luck and the hard times."

"That's kind of you to say."

Her cool hand grasped mine. "And I don't think your breath is bad at all ... I think it smells sweet ... like night-blooming jasmine ..."

She leaned forward; her thin but beautiful lips parted—they were scarlet, but I wasn't sure she was wearing lip rouge—and she touched her lips to mine, delicately. Then she touched my unshaven cheek with the slender, long-nailed fingers of one hand and stared soulfully at me.

"You're a fine man, Mr. Smith-Jones. We're going to clean you up ... a bath ... a shave ... an incredible meal. You're going to have the night of your life ..."

The Radclau mansion was a modern brick castle beyond a black wrought-iron gate; three massive stories, its turreted shape rose against the clear night sky in sharp silhouette, the moon poised above and to the right as if placed there for the sole purpose of lighting this imposing structure.

"This is really something," I said. "When was this built?"

"Just a few years ago," she said.

We were around the side of the building now, gliding into a garage which opened automatically for us—whether the chauffeur triggered it somehow, or someone inside saw us coming and lifted the drawbridge, I couldn't say.

"I recruited one of the top local architects to build something modern that would evoke my family home," she said.

"Where *was* the family home?"

"Europe."

"That doesn't narrow it down much."

"Just a little corner of eastern Europe. You probably wouldn't even have heard of it."

Maybe I would have.

We stepped from the cement cavern of the four-car garage into a wine cellar passageway that led to an elevator.

"I was never in a private home that had an elevator," I told her; the leather strap of my canvas kit bag was tight in my hand. The chauffeur—whose bucketlike skull turned out to have two dead eyes, a misshapen nose, and grim line of a mouth stuck on it—was playing elevator operator for us.

"Why, Mr. Smith-Jones," she said, looping her arm in

mine, smiling her wry one-sided dimpled smile again, "I find that difficult to believe."

The elevator, a silver-gray chamber, rose to the fourth floor and opened onto a red-painted door in a cream-colored plaster alcove.

"We're in one of the guest towers," she said. She stepped out into the alcove with me, still arm-in-arm. "These are your quarters ... you'll find everything you need, I think. I just guessed on your size. If I've got it wrong, just pick up the phone and ask for me. We can accommodate you. Then, let us know when you're ready to dine ..."

She smiled—both dimples this time—and ducked back into the elevator, whose doors slid shut, and she was gone.

"I'll be damned," I said, and in the little alcove, it echoed.

The red door was unlocked, and opened onto a vast modern living room—plush white carpet, round white leather sofa, deep white armchairs, sleek decorative figurines, black-and-white decorative framed prints, a fireplace, a complete bar, a radio console, you name it. Everything but the kitchen sink. Everything but mirrors.

Beyond the living room was a bedroom; it was another white room, with one exception: the round bed was covered with red silk sheets. On the wall, over the bed, was a huge, bamboo-framed, sleekly decorative watercolor of a black panther, about to strike.

In the closet hung a full-dress tux—white tie and tails, pip pip. And the size *was* right, down to the black size nine and a half shoes, so shiny I could see my face in 'em, but probably not hers ...

I tossed my kit bag on the bed, and checked out the bathroom; it was bigger than most apartments. On the white marble counter (and there *was* a mirror in here, at least) I found a straight razor, a brush and cup and shaving soap, and fancy French imported after-shave cologne. Also deodorant powder, and toothbrush and Pepsodent.

She apparently wanted me clean and smelling good, for dinner.

I made sure the guest-room door was locked, and stuck a chair under the knob to make double-sure, before stripping down to take a long, elaborate, very hot bubble bath. After two weeks of the hobo life, I was ready to take advantage of Miss Radclau's hospitality and soak off the slime.

Dressed to the nines, looking like neither a hobo nor an undercover cop in my white tie and tails, I picked up the phone and said, "Mr. Smith-Jones is ready to dine."

Within minutes, a knock at the door announced the chauffeur, who was serving as a room-service man this time; he wheeled in a cart with several covered dishes.

"Please wait for the lady, sir," the chauffeur said, in a voice as dead as his eyes. "Madam is still dressing."

"Sure," I said.

It was another ten minutes before another knock came, and I hadn't even peeked under the dull, nonreflective lids of the hot dishes. I didn't want to be an ungracious guest.

I answered the door, bowing, with an arch, "Enchanté."

But it almost caught in my throat, because as I was bowing I found myself staring into her round, ripe decolletage.

I backed up awkwardly. "You're sure a sight."

She floated inside. Madam still looked undressed: her astonishingly low-cut gown was a vivid dark red and clung to her as if wet. Her waist was tiny, her hips flaring, but she was too tall, too long-legged, to have an hour-glass shape; she was wearing open-toed heels that brought her to my eye level. Her toenails were the same bright red as the dress and her lips.

She gestured theatrically to herself, with both hands. "I trust this is better than the apron?"

"Than the apron and the gray uniform," I said. "Maybe not just the apron . . ."

Her laugh was long and sultry. She was draped in an exotic, incenselike perfume, which was making me feel woozy.

She gestured with a slender red-nailed hand toward the tray with the covered food.

"Please dine," she said.

I pulled up a comfy chair that was a little short for the tray; it made me feel like a child. Before I sat, I asked, "Aren't you joining me?"

"I've eaten."

I doubted that.

"Please," she said, "I take great pleasure from watching you enjoy yourself. The carnal pleasures are so . . ."

"Pleasurable?" I offered, lifting a round lid; the fragrance of prime rib rose to my nostrils like a cobra from a snake charmer's basket, only I was the one doing the biting, sinking my teeth into the tender, very rare, succulent meat.

"I know I promised you the work of a five-star chef," she said, perched nearby on the arm of the couch, legs crossed, giving me a generous view, hands clasped in her lap, "and that is the work of a master, but . . . I could tell that you had . . . *basic* appetites."

She rose and switched on the radio and drifted back to her perch on the couch arm. A dance band was playing "Where or When." She swayed gently to it, her black hair shimmying.

"This is swell," I said. The prime rib, Yorkshire pudding, and browned potatoes were, in fact, delicious. No salad, no vegetable. But what the hell—it was free. So far.

She watched me with what seemed to be genuine pleasure, eyebrows raising as she savored me savoring every bite, her thin, pretty mouth tied up in a cupid's bow of shared bliss. Why she was getting such a vicarious glow out of watching me dig into the rare roast beef, I couldn't say. But I had a pretty good hunch. . . .

I touched my napkin to my lips, sipped the red wine she had risen to pour for me, in a goblet-sized glass, and said, "This is a hell of a public service program you got here, lady."

"I don't single just *anyone* out, you know." She looked almost hurt by my remark. "Once in a while, working in that line, serving up soup . . . I see someone . . . special. Someone who shouldn't be there. Someone who . . . deserves better. Deserves more."

She leaned in and the incenselike smell of her was overwhelming; her mouth locked onto mine and her kiss was sweet, much sweeter than mere wine . . .

The lights were off, suddenly, as if she'd willed it, and she led me into the bedroom, where the red gown slipped off and confirmed my suspicion that there was nothing, not even the slightest, wispiest step-in, underneath. A window allowed some moonlight to filter in, and her slender, yet full-breasted, wide-hipped, long-limbed frame was like some artist's dream of female perfection. And a horny artist, at that.

She drew me onto her bed, and laid me down on the cool silk sheets, and climbed on top of me, to grant me yet another gift. The erect blood-red tips of her breasts were as hypnotic as the intoxicated and intoxicating almond eyes, as she rode me, and I kept waiting, lost in her as I was, with my left hand dropped down along the side of the bed, waiting for her head to dip toward my throat, but it didn't, and when her face lowered, it was merely to kiss me again, deeply, passionately, as we flew together to some high, fevered place . . .

Maybe she was just some rich-bitch society girl who felt sorry for (and had a yen for) poor down-and-out schmucks like me, or like the poor down-and-out schmuck I was supposed to be. Maybe the suspicions that had brought me here were unfounded. Maybe I was the only dishonest one in this bed.

It had seemed a reasonable theory—what better place for an ancient monster to hide than behind the mask of a modern monster? The mass murderer that the city took the Butcher of Slaughter Run for would be the perfect disguise for a demon of the night.

And how better for the beast to gather its victims than behind the mask of an angel of mercy?

She seemed to be sleeping; the perfect globes of her bosom rose and fell, heavily, gloriously, in what seemed to be slumber. But as I stared at her, leaning on one elbow, her eyes popped open, startling me.

"What's wrong?" she asked.

"Nothing," I said. "I was just . . . admiring you."

She smiled a little, a pursed-lipped, kiss of a smile. "In what way?"

"Physically. You're a handsome woman. The handsomest I've ever seen. But it's more than that."

"Oh?"

"I admire what you're trying to do. Helping guys like me out."

She laughed. "I told you—I don't make love to all of them."

I shook my head. "I didn't mean that. Not everyone who's ... advantaged ... takes the time to give a little back."

"I know. Please don't take this in a condescending manner, Mr. Smith-Jones, but the 'little people' of society, they're the life's blood of the 'advantaged.' It seems to me the least an advantaged person can do is, now and then, make life a little better for someone less fortunate."

"Well, you've certainly made my life better, tonight."

She smiled, and it seemed, suddenly, a sad, bittersweet kind of smile; the thin red lips looked black in the near dark. "Good. That was my desire."

She leaned forward and kissed me, gently, tenderly, then buried her face in my shoulder, and I had a sudden flash of what was about to happen, and pulled away.

Her fangs were distended; her eyes were wide and there was no longer any difficulty in telling the pupils from the irises, because the latter were a ghastly yellow.

Naked, I jumped out of the bed; she was poised there, on all fours, as if mimicking the panther on the wall looming over her.

"You are from a privileged, moneyed family, aren't you, Miss Radclau?"

Her response was a deep, throaty snarling sound; I wasn't sure she was capable of speech, at this point.

"You think just 'cause I'm a bum, I can't do a damn anagram?" I asked, and I swung viciously at her, and it landed.

A punch on the jaw, even with all my weight behind it, wouldn't be enough to knock her out—she had metamorphosed into something beyond human, stronger than a mere man—but it had surprised her, and threw her onto her back, which was where I wanted her.

The kit bag was out from under the bed in a flash and the pointed stake and the mallet were in my hands in another flash, and I drove my knee into her stomach, and the stake into her heart. She yowled with pain; it was a wolflike sound. Blood bubbled from around the stake, and I hammered it again, and it sunk deeper, and she yowled again, but her eyes weren't yellow anymore.

And they weren't savage, anymore, either.

Her expression was sad, and maybe even grateful.

She was still alive when I raised the machete—heaving under the pain, her hands clutching the stake but unable to remove it, slender fingers streaked with her own blood, a perfect match to her nail polish.

"I know you acted out of compassion," I said. "I know you gave me, and the other men, the best night of their lives, before taking those lives, when you wouldn't have had to. You could have just been a beast. Instead, you were a beauty."

She seemed to be smiling, a little, when the machete swung down and severed her head from pale, pale shoulders.

I had no trouble getting out of the place. I took the elevator down to the wine cellar passage to the garage, with the bloody machete in hand in case I had to ward off the gorillalike chauffeur or any other minions of the night who might appear.

But none did.

I found a button in the garage and pushed it and the door swung up and open and I ran out into a cool, clear night. At the first farmhouse, I called in to the station, and told them to wake the chief.

"He's not going to like it," the desk sergeant said.

"Just *do* it." I couldn't tell him I'd stopped the Slaughter Run Butcher or I'd be up to my eyeballs in reporters out here. "Understand, sergeant?"

I could hear the shrug in his voice: "If you say so, Lieutenant Van Helsing."

NIGHT TIDINGS
by
Gary Alan Ruse

Father Paul Mundy hesitated a long moment on the top step, pulling his overcoat tighter against the chill air. Behind him stood the modestly imposing structure of St. Jerome's, reaching up toward the darkened heavens like a beacon of hope, shelter, and warmth. Before him stretched the raw night, uncertain, sinister, dangerous. As parish priest, Father Mundy had frequently ventured out after dark, to call upon someone in need, to give comfort to a shut-in, or, sometimes, to administer last rites to a dying parishioner. But never had he felt quite the trepidation that he felt this night.

With a great, deep sigh, Mundy steeled himself to his task and strode down the steps of St. Jerome's to the street. Puddles from the rain that had quit an hour earlier glistened dully in the darkness, and a gray mist still hung in the air. He was not sure if he truly heard it or only imagined it, but he could swear he heard the strains of Johann Sebastian Bach's *Concerto No. 1 in D Minor* ebbing through the night, an eerie, lively counterpoint to his own regular footsteps.

His destination was not far. It was, in fact, only a few blocks from his church, which was why he was traversing the distance on foot. But in significant ways other than distance, it was very far indeed.

Father Mundy found himself looking up at the old three-story brownstone, a narrow, brooding structure that dated back to the late 1800s. His view of it was through an ornamental wrought-iron gate that reminded him unpleasantly of a graveyard closure, and the gate's protesting squawk as he slowly opened it made his flesh crawl. He quickly brought his own clammy hand to the back of his neck to suppress the shiver that danced along the muscles there, and remembered once again why this was not a place he cared to visit often.

He advanced along the short stone walk and up the steps to the massive wooden door, there to reach out with tentative fingers and grasp the heavy bronze door-knocker cast in the shape of a gargoyle. He knocked three times, then three times again, and waited. If his mission had been any less important, he would have gladly postponed his visit until daylight hours.

He was sure now he could hear the Bach concerto, emanating from a second-floor window. A moment later, the sound became louder, ebbing out through the front door as latches were released and it swung slowly inward.

"Yes . . . ?" inquired the bearded man who peered out from within, fixing him with a piercing stare. Mundy knew him. It was Sergei Volkov, the owner's servant and driver, dressed in a simple black suit, with white shirt and black tie.

"I, ah," stammered Father Mundy, normally at no loss for words. "If . . . if you would be so kind, I've come hoping to speak with Mr. Travanian."

"If it's about a donation, Father, I'll be glad to relay your request—"

"No, it's not a donation. I . . . I need his help in another way."

Volkov raised an eyebrow and considered it a moment. A long moment. "Wait here . . . please."

Travanian's manservant retreated within and was gone from sight for what seemed an eternity to Mundy. Then he abruptly reappeared and opened the door more fully. "He will see you."

Father Mundy swallowed hard and stepped cautiously into the vestibule. He said a quick, silent prayer that he had not made the wrong decision in coming here, even as he heard the sound of the heavy door closing behind him with a solid, all too permanent sounding *chunk*.

"Forgive the inconvenience, Father," Volkov told him as he began to pat the priest down. "House rules."

Mundy fought back a sense of outrage at being frisked. "Surely you don't think *I* would bring a weapon here?"

The bearded man continued his routine search dispassionately. "One can't be too careful. Besides, if I didn't do my job, the boss would have my neck." He stopped as he felt something in Mundy's inside coat pocket, reached in, and extracted a wooden pencil with the point sharpened. He held it dangling between his thumb and forefinger with a disapproving look, then placed it in a small basket on a stand near the door. "Okay—let's go."

Volkov led him from the entrance hall into a spacious room that appeared to be an office, simply but elegantly furnished. There was a large, ornate desk and chairs, tapestries hung on two of the walls, and authentic looking suits of armor stood guard on either side of the door. It had a decidedly European look to it.

A staircase with ebony steps and plush red carpeting took up most of the back wall, leading upstairs, and it was to this that Volkov now led the parish priest. The building's original gaslight fixtures had been retained, but refitted for electricity. Their soft glow provided light without glare.

The sound of the music grew louder with each step Father Mundy took up the stairs. With each step, a faintly musty odor grew more discernible. There were old things here. It reminded him a bit of a museum he had once visited. That, and of something else he could not quite put his finger on. Something vaguely unpleasant.

As he reached the top of the stairs, Father Mundy saw that the second-floor chamber was also quite large, and bathed in a weak glow more mellow, more golden than the ground floor office had been. Rows of tall bookcases were arranged along the side walls, almost in the fashion of a library, and a richly dark carpeting covered the floor. In the center of the room were a number of comfortable looking chairs and a massive oak table. Heavy velvet curtains framed the windows of the front wall. There were a number of curio cases filled with odd relics and antiques, and several cats lolled regally upon a chair and cabinet top.

It was now, also, that Father Mundy became aware of the room's occupant, and that occupant became aware of the good Father. Seated in a high-backed chair next to an end table upon which stereo equipment and a

handful of leatherbound books nestled was a man of
indeterminate age whose appearance was not only striking, but also startlingly commanding. His raven-black
hair was well-groomed and lustrous, his aristocratic features angular and strong. True, the complexion of his
face and hands seemed pale, even sickly, and yet there
was an odd vitality about him that spoke of quiet athleti-
cism and restrained strength. But the single most striking
feature were the eyes. Eyes that were obsidian disks with
odd golden glints. Eyes that caught and held your attention, and spoke volumes with but a single glance. Eyes
that were now fixed unblinkingly upon Father Mundy
with a look that might be curiosity, or might be something else. Whatever, it sent a chill down the parish
priest's spine.

Gregor Travanian switched off the music with a quick
tap of his elegantly long fingers, and rose from his chair
to greet his uninvited guest. His velvet and satin smoking
jacket threw reddish glints of light as he straightened,
and his unexpectedly tall form was as perfectly postured
as a Prussian military officer.

"So, Father Mundy," he said in a controlled, cultured
tone, "at last we meet."

He did not extend his hand in greeting, but rather
gestured gracefully toward a chair across from, but not
too close to, his own. He waited until the priest had
taken his seat before sitting back down again.

"I can offer you a fine Napoleon brandy to ward off
the chill ... ?"

"Thank you, but no," said Father Mundy. "I need a
clear head for this."

"As you wish. Then tell me what brings you here on
such a damp and dismal evening, since you say it is not
a donation."

"It's not," Mundy assured him. "Though I must say I
am grateful for your support these past years." He
glanced at several oil portraits on the wall, men whose
clothing styles spanned a century or more, but whose
family resemblance to one another was eerily strong.
"And I know your father and grandfather were also
very generous."

Gregor Travanian smiled an odd smile.

"But," Mundy continued, "I am here on quite another

matter of some urgency. I am asking your help in solving a murder."

Travanian's eyes narrowed a bit, but sparkled with interest. "My help ... solving a murder? My good Father, how can you suppose that I would be qualified to offer such assistance."

Mundy drew in a deep breath and let it out. "It ... it has come to my attention, in a way I would rather not discuss, that you have at times assisted the police here in solving particularly difficult cases."

"Ah ... I might have known." Travanian smiled wanly and brought a hand up to stroke his chin. "I should have realized that Captain O'Halloran, good Irish Catholic that he is, would have to confess sooner or later. No doubt he was feeling guilty about taking credit for work done by someone else?"

Father Mundy hesitated a moment. "What is told a priest in confessional is privileged information, and may not be divulged. However, in a hypothetical situation such as you describe, I would certainly assure such a person that all good police officers use informants and confidential advisors who, of necessity, must remain anonymous."

"Wise counsel," said Travanian. "Tell me, Father— just how much *do* you know about me, hypothetical or otherwise?"

Mundy squirmed uncomfortably in his seat. "Other than our indirect business through the church charity drives, very little. I know you are reclusive, and seem to be well off financially."

Travanian shrugged. "Old money, wisely invested."

"No doubt. But, I've also heard the rumors. Most of the adults in the parish think you must be some kind of gangster. And the children ... well, some of them say that you're a ... a vampire." Mundy gave a nervous chuckle, but it came out more like a dry cough. "Imagine."

Travanian's eyes twinkled. "Out of the mouths of babes. You must be very brave, Father. If either one of those rumors were true, your life could be in danger just by coming here."

Father Mundy leaned slightly forward in his seat. "Not

brave—desperate. Frankly, I have nowhere else to turn. I'd almost make a deal with the devil if I had to."

"I can assure you, I am not the devil, though in the past, I have done things that I am not proud of. Over the past . . . number of years . . . I have sought to make amends for those transgressions. Now—tell me of this murder case you wish me to solve."

Tears welled up in Father Mundy's eyes. He blinked them back and cleared his throat several times. "Forgive me. My professional composure has been sorely tested by this matter, and perhaps my faith as well. One of my parishioners, a young woman named Trish Dengler, was found two days ago, dead on the sidewalk beneath her twelfth floor apartment."

Gregor Travanian leaned forward slightly, seemingly intrigued as much by the parish priest's display of emotion as by the facts of the case. "Ah, yes . . . the apparent suicide. I read of it in the newspaper. A tragic waste."

"The police are wrong," said Mundy, with a trace of anger creeping into his voice.

"Was there not a suicide note found?"

"Yes . . . and it was her handwriting. I don't deny that." Mundy shook his head in exasperation. "And her apartment door was found locked and bolted from the inside, which further convinced the police, and the church hierarchy as well."

Trevanian arched an eyebrow. "But not you, Father?"

"No. Never! Trish was not only a parishioner, she was a friend and a volunteer at St. Jerome's, helping with the homeless and other unfortunate people. She was a sweet and innocent girl, barely twenty, with her whole life ahead of her. Always cheerful and willing to lend a hand. No one can make me believe she would ever kill herself. She just couldn't. I'd bet my life on it."

"One should never wager more than one can afford to lose," Travanian said in a cautionary tone. "However, the strength of your conviction leads me to believe you may be right. Men of the cloth tend to be keen observers of human nature, and I do not doubt you knew Miss Dengler's emotional makeup far better than the police."

Mundy seemed encouraged. "Then, you will help me? As I say, I have nowhere else to turn. I can't afford to hire a private detective, and although I will certainly do what I can myself, I know my limitations. I am no Father Brown or Father Dowling."

Gregor Travanian pushed out of his chair and stood tall and imposing before the parish priest. "Help you? Yes. Your plea, and this case, cannot be ignored. But I must make one demand in return. Just as you zealously guard the secrets of your confessional, you must swear to guard my own secrets, too. What I reveal to you about myself, and what you see me do, must never be spoken of to other ears. Do I have your word on that?"

Father Mundy swallowed hard. There was something about this man, his looks and his demeanor, the very tone of his deep and resonant voice, that though pleasant and compelling, still sent a chill down his spine. He hoped that his instincts had not been impaired by his desperation.

"I do so swear," Mundy told him, "to you, and before God, that I shall not violate your trust."

"Splendid. We should begin at once, before the trail grows any colder. Can you show me the girl's apartment?"

"Yes, of course. But I have no key."

"A minor inconvenience." Travanian's eyes twinkled oddly. Then, looking suddenly beyond Father Mundy, he said, "Sergei—bring the car around to the front."

"Yes, sir."

Father Mundy twisted around in time to see the grim-faced servant step forward from the shadows where he had apparently been standing. Mundy had completely forgotten about the presence of the odd fellow with his auburn hair and beard, and plain black suit, since first catching sight of Gregor Travanian. He watched as the man turned and disappeared through the doorway to another room.

"Come, Father," said Travanian smoothly. "We may wait downstairs. . . ."

The car that Volkov brought round proved to be a black Mercedes-Benz limo, about ten years old, but maintained in pristine condition and polished bright as a casket at a rich man's funeral. Volkov now wore a chauffeur's cap, and his master had left his smoking jacket behind in favor of a more suitable garment and topcoat. The ride across town to Trish Dengler's apartment building took only fifteen minutes, and the occupants of the limo maintained an uneasy silence for the duration of the trip. It was not until Travanian and Mundy left the elevator on the twelfth floor and neared one of the apartment doors that the silence was broken.

"This is it here," said Father Mundy. "But I suppose that must be obvious."

Travanian nodded as they came to a halt before the door. Two strips of yellow and black "Police Line" tape stretched from one side of the doorframe to the other, at shoulder and knee height. "They are keeping the area secure, even though they have not labeled it a crime scene."

Father Mundy reached out and tested the doorknob. "It's locked, of course. We could speak with the superintendent, but I doubt he would violate a police order—"

"No need to," said Travanian, with a glance up and down the hall. "Doors are no problem for me. We are safe, for the moment, from prying eyes. I trust, Father, that you do not frighten easily, and that you remember your oath to me?"

Mundy frowned quizzically, but nodded in agreement. If he was about to be a party to breaking and entering, he hoped the Lord would forgive him.

Gregor Travanian let his arms hang loose at his sides and cast his steady gaze down at the floor. Almost at once, the details of his face, his hands, his entire body, became indistinct and hazy. He melted into a cloud of gray mist that briefly swirled in the spot where last he stood, then that cloud swiftly flowed down and through the crack beneath the door, disappearing within the apartment.

Father Mundy's jaw dropped down to his clerical collar. In a cracking voice that was barely a whisper, he said, "Merciful heavens!"

In the next moment the latch clicked and the door before him swung open. Travanian stood there on the other side, beckoning him in. He guided the parish priest to step through the opening between the two strips of tape, then closed the door behind him and switched on the light.

Mundy regained his composure with a vengeance.

"My word, man! You went through there like ... like ... like a demon from Hell!"

Travanian bristled slightly. "I prefer to think of myself as supernaturally gifted."

"Then it's true ... you really are a —"

"Let's not quibble over labels, Father. If you want my help, then we had best get down to the work at hand." He started to explore the modestly furnished apartment. "Now, am I to understand that Miss Dengler lived here alone?"

Mundy followed after him, still trying to cope with the bizarre nature of his companion. "Ah ... yes, she did."

"Why not with her parents? If she was the innocent lamb you describe ..."

"There was a bit of a falling out," Mundy admitted. "Her father didn't approve of her volunteer work with the homeless and downtrodden. He called them the 'dregs of society,' and forbade her from further contact with them as long as she lived under his roof. So, she moved out."

"I see. Principled, if not practical." Travanian examined several framed snapshots standing on the desk. "Had she any boyfriends?"

"Yes, one." Mundy pointed to one of the photos. "That young man there. He's in the military, currently stationed in the Middle East."

"So he has an alibi, by virtue of distance."

Father Mundy nodded. "I'm not sure if they'll even let him come back for the funeral."

"When is it?"

"Two days from now ... Saturday." Mundy sighed inwardly. "I wasn't positive I would be able to give her a full Catholic service. The church is more lenient now about suicides than it once was, but there is still a stigma. In the past, they were not allowed burial in consecrated ground, but now we try to make allowance. Fortunately, the Bishop agreed that if Trish truly did take her own life, she must not have been in her right mind, and was not responsible for her actions."

Travanian was methodically examining the room. "But you still want to set the record straight—clear her name and see justice done."

"With every fiber of my being," replied Father Mundy.

There was a momentary pause as Travanian picked up a small piece of cardstock from the floor, just beneath the edge of the desk. He studied it briefly. "I presume Miss Dengler held a job, since she was estranged from her family and shows no signs from her lifestyle of being independently wealthy . . . ?"

"Yes. She worked in the display department at Compton's department store. She made barely enough to cover her own expenses. More often than not, what little extra she had, she gave away to the homeless people she worked with."

"Compton's?" Travanian gave a small shrug. "That hardly seems the type of position where she could make enemies who would be willing to murder her. Tell me, why didn't she have a car?"

"Sold it," said Mundy. "Right after she moved out of her family's house, so she could pay the deposit on this apartment. How did you know?"

Travanian held the card he found for the priest to see. "Last month's bus pass. There were several previous ones on her desk. Now, is this the balcony out here?"

"Yes." Mundy headed reluctantly for the sliding glass door. He unlatched it and slid it open. "When the police arrived here early in the morning, after they found her body, this door was open, of course."

The sounds and smells of the city intruded upon the apartment as a slight breeze wafted through the opening. Gregor Travanian stepped through onto the small balcony, and Father Mundy joined him there. There were a few potted plants, placed where their flowers could be seen through the sliding glass door. City lights twinkled in the murky night like prayer candles in a darkened church.

Gregor Travanian placed his hands upon the rail and looked over it to the pavement below. "It is a long drop, for mortal flesh," he said solemnly. Backing away, he studied the rest of the balcony, then cast his gaze up to the top of the building. "I suppose someone could have lowered themselves from the roof to gain entry to the apartment, and then returned that way so as to leave Miss Dengler's front door locked."

"The police looked into that," Father Mundy told him. "I brought up the question myself. They told me there was no sign on the roof of anything being disturbed recently. Besides, the access door to the roof is locked, and only the building superintendent has a key."

Mundy had to steel himself to look over the edge to the sidewalk and street below. Imagining poor Trish's lifeless form sprawled on the ground down there brought waves of sorrow and anger flooding through him. Then a slight sense of vertigo overwhelmed him and he retreated away from the railing.

Turning, he asked, "What else should we check . . . ?" Mundy found himself staring at nothingness. He quickly looked left and right, then did a complete turn-around, only to have his first impression confirmed—he was alone on the balcony. "Mr. Travanian?" he called out softly, then stepped through the open doorway and back into the apartment.

There was no sign of his unusual companion here, either. Mundy crossed to the apartment's bedroom and looked in there, also checking the small bath adjoining it. Still no luck. Mundy was uncertain which was worse— being *with* this frighteningly strange and sinister man, or suddenly being without him, alone in the dead girl's apartment.

"They were right," said Gregor Travanian abruptly. "No one used the roof to reach the balcony."

Father Mundy nearly jumped out of his skin. Wheeling around at the sound of Travanian's voice, he watched as the very man he had searched for in vain suddenly entered the apartment from the previously empty balcony, dusting his hands and smoothing his windblown hair.

"Good Lord, man! Where were you?"

"Why," said Travanian, "the roof, of course."

"But . . . how did you get up . . . no, never mind," Mundy said with a sudden change of heart, the color draining from his features. "I don't think I want to know."

Travanian's lips briefly twisted in a trace of an amused smile. "And the ends of the balcony are at least ten feet from the ends of the balconies on either side, making it unlikely anyone could have jumped across."

Mundy sighed as he digested the information. "So what are you saying? That you agree with the police? That Trish must have committed suicide?"

"Not at all," said Travanian, beginning to pace. "I am merely narrowing the possibilities, so that we may focus our attention upon the one correct path that will lead us to the killer. Now, as to motive. Who, in your estimation, might want to kill Miss Dengler?"

The parish priest threw up his hands in a helpless gesture. "I have agonized over this for two days. I can't think of anyone who knew her who would want her dead. Certainly not her family, friends, or coworkers. I can't even believe that any of the street people she worked with could be responsible. They all seemed to adore her for her kindness and her selflessness."

"Street people are not behind this," agreed Travanian. "They are too direct, and would not bother with anything so elaborate as a faked suicide." His pacing brought him to the table near the room's center. On it lay a pad of paper and a pen. "You say you saw the alleged suicide note?"

"Yes," replied Mundy. "The police showed it to me, to have me verify that it was Trish's handwriting."

Travanian indicated the pad on the table. "Did it look like it came from this pad?"

Mundy examined it. "Why, yes. I believe so."

"The exact words—can you recall them?"

"I almost wish I couldn't. It said, 'To all: I know now that things can't get any better for me. It's hopeless to think otherwise. There's only one way for me to set things right. Farewell'."

Travanian was silent a long moment as he held the pad in his hands and angled it vertically beneath the ceiling light. "Yes, I can still make out the impressions left on this top sheet. Yet here is something odd. Father Mundy—was the upper right hand corner of the sheet you saw intact, or was it torn?"

The priest had to think about it. The words written in Trish's feminine hand had been so traumatic that he had paid little attention to anything else at the time. But the image had been burned painfully into his memory. "Torn? Yes . . . it *was* torn. Is that piece still attached to the pad?"

"No," replied Travanian. "The sheet was cleanly removed in its entirety."

"How strange."

"Not so very strange, when you consider that the missing piece had the number 'two' written upon it."

Mundy took a step closer. "Then there was another page before it! But the police found only the one."

"That is all the killer wanted them to find. As further proof, the 't' in 'to all' is not capitalized, suggesting that it was not merely her way of addressing 'everyone', but rather part of a sentence continued over from the first page. I think once the police have given the page they already have in evidence an electrostatic detection test, they will be able to read the impressions left on it from the missing page. That may shed some light on this. At what time did they think the girl met her unfortunate end?"

"Her body was found at three in the morning," Mundy told him. "But they think she must have died sometime between midnight and one o'clock. She was dressed in her nightclothes. The building superintendent told the police she was connected with St. Jerome's, so they called me right away. I went with them when they notified her family. That was perhaps the hardest thing I've ever had to do."

Travanian bent to pick up a tiny, white fragment of something wedged in the carpeting. "You may yet have harder things to face before this is over, Father." He examined the fragment briefly before putting it in his overcoat pocket with the small stationery pad. "Come—I have seen all that I need to in here."

They left the apartment, careful not to disturb the police tape, and locked and reclosed the door behind them. Once in the hall, Travanian paused to ask the priest a question.

"Did the police inquire if the neighbors saw or heard anything that night?"

Mundy shook his head. "It wasn't possible. The neighbor on the left is on vacation, and the apartment on the right is unoccupied."

Travanian pointed at the door. "This one—unoccupied?"

"Yes." Mundy watched as his eerie companion walked

quickly to that door and tested the lock. "You're . . . not going to . . . do that again, are you?"

"You may look the other way, if you prefer."

Father Mundy averted his eyes briefly, but as frightening as the transformation he had witnessed earlier was, he could not resist looking now. Oddly, Travanian had already disappeared and the door was standing open, the lights on. Mundy looked both ways down the hall and quickly entered the apartment.

"Didn't I tell you?" said Travanian innocently as he closed the door behind him. "It was unlocked."

Mundy gave him his best *Shame on you for fooling the Father* frown, but his gaze soon shifted to take in the details of the vacant apartment.

It was identical in layout to Trish's, but it looked different since there was not a stick of furniture in the place. Painters' dropcloths covered the floor in several spots and a new door for the bedroom leaned against the wall. A damaged section of ceiling was under repair all along the opposite wall, with a long scaffolding plank raised upon two sawhorses to enable whoever was doing the work to reach it.

"How long has this apartment been vacant?" asked Travanian.

"About a month, I think," Mundy replied. "Trish told me last week that they'd been working on it earlier, and all the hammering had been knocking pictures off her walls. But she said there was some sort of dispute between the building's owner and the repair crew over money, and they hadn't worked on it at all in four or five days. It's sad there wasn't someone living here. They might have heard something."

"It's sadder than you know," observed Travanian, who at first appeared to be pacing, but who now clearly was stepping off a distance along the wall by which the sawhorses and scaffolding plank stood. "This apartment was the means by which the killer was able to exit Miss Dengler's locked apartment. Had it not been vacant, she might still be alive."

"My word!"

Travanian was moving now with unbridled energy, poking about the room, searching for something. He found it at last, beneath one of the canvas dropcloths.

A coil of rope reposed there, and, snatching it up, Travanian strode back to the sawhorses and proceeded to tie one end of the rope around one end of the heavy scaffolding plank.

Mundy watched in puzzlement. "What are you doing?"

"If you would be so good as to slide open the door to the balcony," replied Travanian, lifting the plank as if it were a feather, "I will show you."

Father Mundy hastened to do as instructed, stepping aside as his grim companion carried the long plank through the opening and out onto the balcony. He followed him out, to watch.

"Disregard my own strength," Travanian told him. "Even a man of moderate vigor could do this."

He stood the thick plank on end near the railing on the far side of the balcony, the rope tied to the top end and stretching down tautly to his firm grip. Bracing a foot against the bottom end of the plank, he allowed it to tip forward, gradually lowering the top end by letting out the rope until the plank came to a stop, resting level across the end rails of this balcony and that of Trish Dengler's apartment.

Turning to Mundy, he said, "There you have a bridge, by which the killer was able to return to this apartment and escape. His principal tool was hidden in plain sight."

Travanian now reeled in the rope, raising the plank like a narrow drawbridge until it was once more standing upright on the balcony of the vacant apartment. He returned it to the sawhorses and replaced the rope as well.

"You will inform Captain O'Halloran of this?" asked Father Mundy.

"You may count upon that, for I will also need his help with certain information. Now, let us lock up this place and leave it, for there is one more thing I must ask to see before we part company this night. . . ."

The big black limo was like a part of the night itself, speeding across town with a soft, throaty purr, catching glints of lights from its surroundings and throwing them back like cast-off stars. Safely ensconced within its well-upholstered interior, with Travanian and Mundy on opposite ends of the back seat and Volkov expertly driving, the passengers this time were not silent.

"This is the most encouraged I've felt in days," said Father Mundy. "I greatly appreciate what you've done."

Gregor Travanian raised a finger in a cautionary gesture. "We still have not a clue as to the killer's identity."

"No, but at least you've found evidence that should prove it *was* murder, not suicide, and shows how it was done." Mundy sighed, his brow furrowing. "It's frightening, to think of the trouble to which someone went to kill Trish. Do you think perhaps that in the course of her activities she saw something she shouldn't have, some illegal activity or whatever, and had to be silenced? Could organized crime be involved?"

"Those are possibilities that should be investigated," Travanian replied. "But I doubt that is the answer. We may have found how the killer *left* her apartment, but I do not think that is how the killer entered it. Remember—there was no sign of a struggle, and no sign of a break-in, save for the latch bolt the police no doubt broke when they had to force their way in."

Mundy nodded. "I see. Yes ... that means that Trish must have known the person who killed her, at least well enough to let him or her inside at a late hour." Mundy flashed a troubled glance toward the man seated next to him. "Unless, of course, it was another ... person ... with the same remarkable talents you have demonstrated tonight."

Travanian gave an irritated sigh. "I wondered how long it would be before you gave voice to that apprehension."

"I'm not accusing *you,* mind you. I'm certain you had nothing to do with Trish's death. But the events I have witnessed tonight have been quite startling, and I'm sure you can understand my having grave concerns about the manner in which you ... sustain yourself."

"You may put your fears to rest, if you are concerned about your own safety, or that of anyone else in this city. It may interest you to know that I own a controlling interest in the Fourth Street Clinic and Bloodbank. It is relatively easy for me to divert sufficient blood from those supplies to meet my needs. And as far as others of my kind being involved, I do not think that likely. Now, are there any other nagging doubts troubling you?"

Mundy shook his head. "No. But I am curious about something. Before tonight, you've always avoided direct contact with me, using an intermediary for your charitable donations. Does the fact that I'm a priest make you uncomfortable?"

Travanian arched an aristocratic eyebrow. "Not in the way you probably think. I suspect that most of what you know, or think you know, about my kind has come from lurid fiction and Hollywood movies. I can assure you that I will neither melt nor wither away if I touch you. My only discomfort comes from the fact that, in the past, when I have met a man of your profession, Father, he has more often than not been approaching me with a cross in one hand and a wooden stake in the other. That is not conducive to building a good relationship."

Father Mundy blushed slightly, then brought his hand up to his lips to conceal a small gasp. "Oh, my! Now I understand about the pencil. . . ."

The limo was soon parked outside the funeral home in which Trish Dengler lay in repose. Somber but comforting organ music played softly through the building's musical system. Father Mundy led the way, with Gregor Travanian close behind.

"Are you sure this is necessary?" whispered Mundy with a plaintive tone.

"Yes. I must see on whose behalf my efforts are spent. Besides, we may both learn something from this."

The two darkly clad men turned the corner down a hall and entered the second viewing room on the right. At the end of the room stood a silver-gray casket on a draped stand, the upper half of its lid raised. An employee was positioning torchiere lamps on either side of the casket, and looked up at the sound of the men's approach.

"Oh—good evening, Father Mundy. I'm sorry, I thought you knew the official viewing isn't until tomorrow."

"Yes, I know," Mundy told him. "My apologies for the inconvenience. I just . . . I just had to stop by."

The man nodded knowingly. "Of course. I understand. I'll just give you a few moments' privacy while I take a break, and finish my work later."

"Thank you."

There was a bit of a questioning look in the man's eyes as he passed Gregor Travanian, but as Travanian met that gaze the employee averted his eyes and continued on out of the room. The two men approached the casket, stopping directly in front of it.

The young woman at rest within showed remarkably little sign of injury at first glance, but her gown's long sleeves covered her arms, and the lower half of her body was hidden by the other half of the casket lid. Her long hair had been arranged artfully, and her lovely face had been spared damage.

"Her legs took the brunt of the impact," said Father Mundy. His face displayed a steely calm, but his eyes were moist. "She looks like an angel, doesn't she? An angel fallen from Heaven."

Gregor Travanian studied the mortal remains of Trish Dengler with the kind of quiet dismay of a museum curator confronted with a particularly fine work of art that had been destroyed by vandals. Oddly touched by the sight of her, he said, "Until now, she was merely a name and a description. Now I think I more fully understand your sense of outrage and sadness. You do realize," he added, lowering his voice, "that a mere prick of my finger . . . a drop of my blood against her lips . . . and she could rise and tell us who her killer is. But no, that is not the kind of eternal life you would wish for her. Nor would I."

After a long pause, Father Mundy asked, "So . . . what do we do now?"

Travanian placed a comforting hand upon the parish priest's shoulder and turned him toward the door. "First, I will drop you off at St. Jerome's. You have done all that you can do tonight and I must speak with Captain O'Halloran right away. I have already decided upon several areas of research to pursue, and once I have the information I need I must spend the rest of the evening mulling over this mystery."

"My prayers will be with you. You will call me as soon as you learn anything?"

"You may count on it. And I may yet need your help, in ways more tangible than prayers. . . ."

Father Mundy awoke the next morning after a troubled sleep. His dreams had been haunted by horrific images of Trish Dengler being thrown from her twelfth-floor balcony by an amorphous, faceless killer, and he had awakened several times in a cold sweat, thinking he had heard the peculiar sound of leathery wings beating the air nearby.

Only three cups of strong coffee and, he was sure, divine assistance had gotten him through his morning mass and communion calls. By lunch time he still had not heard anything from Travanian, and although he had no appetite he forced himself to eat something to keep his strength up.

By three in the afternoon, he was beside himself with agitation, and beginning to question his own sanity. Surely there could be no such things as vampires in the real world. Could he have imagined or dreamt the entire visit with Gregor Travanian?

By four-fifteen, the call came. "Father Mundy," said Travanian in his decidedly European and oddly compelling voice, "can you come at once? I have much to tell you."

Mundy heard himself answering as if it were someone else speaking. "Yes, of course. I'll be right there."

"Good. And you'd best make arrangements for someone else to handle the evening prayer. For if what I suspect is true, the two of us may be able to lay our hands upon Miss Dengler's killer this very night. . . ."

Mundy found the black limo waiting outside St. Jerome's as he left the church and went down the steps. Volkov drove him the short distance to Travanian's brownstone and dropped him off before parking the car in back.

Gregor Travanian, wearing a rich, brocaded robe, was waiting for him on the stairs as he came in. "Come join me in my study, Father. I had just arisen from my own sleep before calling you. I am not normally up at this hour, but we have no choice."

The parish priest followed him up the stairs and into the room where first they met. The curtains were drawn against the windows and there were other changes in the large, cluttered room. File folders and papers were scattered across the entire top of the massive table at the room's center, and a free-standing bulletin board had been rolled into place nearby, a city map affixed to its

surface and covered with a multitude of map pins with
brightly colored heads.

"What have you learned?" Mundy asked eagerly.

Travanian handed him a piece of paper that had a
smudged, almost ghostly image on it. "This is a copy of
what the police found on the alleged suicide note, using
an ESDA test. As I suspected, it revealed the existence
of a first page."

Father Mundy examined the copy with a puzzled look.
The oddly shadowed words, in Trish's own hand, said:

Attention Personnel Department,
I have been working for your company for three
years now, and have yet to receive a raise, even
though less deserving employees in my department
have. Also, you allow unsafe working conditions to
exist. I have just injured myself here today, due to
these conditions. I have contacted the appropriate
agencies, and am sending complete reports

There were no further words, and as Mundy looked up
from the page, he added, from memory, "—to all. I
know now that things can't get any better for me. It's
hopeless to think otherwise. There's only one way for
me to set things right. Farewell."

"See," said Travanian. "It wasn't a suicide note. It
was a letter of resignation, dictated to her by the person
who killed her. I am sure it was a man, someone she
was acquainted with, who went to her apartment late
that night. He was probably wearing a fake cast on his
hand and arm, claiming he had broken it in an accident
at work. He told her he was going to quit his job and
asked her help in writing the letter, since he could not
use his hand."

"And of course Trish helped," said Mundy with a
shake of his head.

"He waited until she got to the word 'reports,' and
then had her continue the rest on the next page. I suspect he then knocked her out with the hard plaster cast,
put the first page in his pocket, and made the period
after 'to all' on the second page look like a colon. Then,"
Travanian said with a somber tone, "he dropped Miss
Dengler from the balcony, and used the scaffolding

plank he had placed there earlier to reach the adjacent apartment, leaving a locked room behind. But I found a bit of plaster-impregnated gauze on the carpet, most likely broken loose by the blow he struck her, and the coroner's report states that traces of plaster were found on the back of her head. They assumed it was because she struck part of the building on the way down."

Father Mundy closed his eyes against the unpleasant images the words evoked, and wrung his hands. "So you think it was someone she knew?"

Travanian nodded. "She would not have opened her door to a stranger at that hour. I at first suspected the building superintendent, since he knew about the vacant apartment. But then I remembered that she had told you about it, and would likely have mentioned it in casual conversation with other friends and acquaintances as well."

"So, it could have been . . . *anyone* she knew. We are no closer now than before."

"Not just anyone," replied Gregor Travanian. "This was not a crime of passion. It was premeditated murder, cold-blooded and ruthless, and elaborately planned by someone who I suspect has done it before. And there was no apparent motive."

Mundy digested the information as he paced. "What you're suggesting sounds like some sort of serial killer."

Travanian indicated the stacks of papers and file folders weighing down his table. "Once I accepted the possibility this might not be an isolated case, I began to wonder if any other apparent suicides might be connected. Captain O'Halloran was kind enough to supply data on such deaths for the past three years. The color-coded pins you see there on the map show where those people lived and where they worked."

Mundy drew nearer the large city map, puzzled but clearly fascinated. "All those . . . suicides?"

"Yes, tragic, isn't it," replied Travanian. "Now, to make it easier for you to see the pattern that emerges, I shall remove the pins of those who do not fit the same characteristics of Miss Dengler . . . those who were old, those who were ill, those who had a history of mental illness. I shall leave only the pins representing young women."

Gregor Travanian's elegant hands virtually flew over the map, deftly plucking out pins here and there, until at last there were only the red pins left. There was an oval scattering of pins on the residential west side of town, and another oval scattering of pins along the downtown and east side business districts. Both ovals were roughly centered on a line that ran east and west.

"Thirteen young women," said Travanian, gesturing at the clusters of pins. "Thirteen young women who lived in *this* part of town, and worked in *that* part of town. Does that pattern suggest anything to you?"

After a moment of thought, Mundy responded, "Yes—the Fifth Avenue bus!"

Travanian had an exultant look, despite his apparent weariness. "Bravo, Father. I checked ... none of those women had cars. All were commuters on the same bus route."

"That has to be more than coincidence. And if their suicides were also faked, that suggests their killer found and targeted them by riding on the bus."

"Precisely."

"My word." Mundy's eyes widened. "That means ... the killer must ride that bus to work himself ... every day ... even today!"

"What time did Trish get off work at the department store?"

"Five or so," Mundy said. "I believe she caught the five-twenty bus most days."

"Then there is no time to lose. Sergei will take us to the bus stop near Compton's." Travanian slipped out of his robe as his servant came forward holding a nondescript coat.

Father Mundy could not help noticing that the bizarre detective's face looked even more ashen than usual. "It's still daylight out. Can you do this?"

"Oh, yes," Travanian said with determination. "I am greatly weakened during the day, but sunlight will not harm me. That is another Hollywood myth. . . ."

They arrived at the bus stop with barely a minute to spare before the arrival of the Fifth Avenue bus. Travanian had added a hat and dark glasses to his outfit, but Father Mundy had not altered his own clerical garb.

Boarding the bus, they moved to the center and grabbed onto the handrail for support.

As the city bus lurched along over the next few blocks, Father Mundy stole furtive glances at every passenger's face, and grew more and more concerned. "This is hopeless," he whispered. "We don't even know what we're looking for."

"I do," Gregor Travanian said softly. "His scent is here. I recognize it from Miss Dengler's apartment."

Mundy tensed. "Where?"

Travanian was silent a moment, until several passengers who had been standing near the rear of the bus disembarked, yielding a clear view of the seating beyond. "There. . . ."

The parish priest followed the direction of his gaze and saw a man in his late twenties or early thirties seated near the back of the bus. His hair was slightly long and his clothing was that of a blue collar worker. Though slender, his cheeks were chubby and his aspect pleasant enough. But there was an almost feral alertness to his eyes that Mundy had seen before in sociopathic criminals. The man had taken a seat next to that occupied by a young woman, and was even now attempting to engage her in conversation.

Mundy felt a chill go through him. "He's starting up again with another one."

"We must follow him when he leaves the bus."

"What about the police?"

"It will be taken care of," Travanian told him.

The bus was creeping through rush hour traffic, as usual, giving the young man plenty of time to ply his conversation in a casual, nonthreatening way. Father Mundy could well imagine the man playing the same deadly game with Trish during her daily rides to and from work, seeming to be pleasant, making small talk, gaining her confidence over a period of weeks or months until he could use her trust against her. It was all Mundy could do to keep from seizing the man and blurting out a warning to the young woman beside him. He prayed for strength and guidance, and struggled to keep his gaze from revealing the multitude of unchristian emotions welling up within him.

Some twenty blocks later, the young woman got off

the bus, giving Mundy some sense of relief, however
misplaced. Another seven blocks and the young man
himself got to his feet, pulled the signal cord, and waited
in the step well for the bus to halt and the exit door to
open. As soon as he was out the door, Travanian and
Mundy were moving to follow him, and were no more
than twenty paces behind him as they stepped down to
the sidewalk. Gregor Travanian threw a glance and a
quick nod to Volkov, who had been following the bus,
and the servant instantly reached for the limo's car
phone.

It was after six now and night was beginning to fall.
As the two men pursued their suspect down a side street
at a safe distance, Travanian seemed to lose his weariness and gain increasing energy. His features, though still
pale, appeared younger now. He put the dark glasses in
his pocket.

They tried to keep hidden behind other people walking down the street, but suddenly, whether through some
sixth sense or his own natural caution, the man they
followed abruptly glanced back over his shoulder and
made eye contact with them. It only lasted a moment,
but as he looked forward once more, his pace picked up.

"He knows we are following him," said Travanian rue-
fully. "We must try something different."

The slender suspect reached the end of the block and
glanced back again. He did not see the pair he had spotted earlier, but he assumed they might still be there
somewhere. He walked quickly past the run-down apartment building where his own lodgings were located and
went another two blocks to be sure. Then he ducked
down an alley and ran swiftly to the next street over,
doubling back and keeping to the shadows until he
reached his own building. Several times he glanced back,
yet he did not see any sign of the two men.

Once he had climbed the stairs to his own apartment,
he locked himself in and went to the rear window, peering out cautiously. He breathed a sigh of relief as he
saw that the only ones on the street behind him were a
blind man and his seeing eye dog.

Drawing the curtain, he began turning his lights on,
revealing a room cluttered with more than just the usual
furnishings. Nearly covering one wall were newspaper

clippings and candid photographs of the thirteen young women whose deaths had been classified as suicides. Trish Dengler's was the latest one added to the macabre collection.

The man read and reread the news article on Trish's death, then smiled as he contemplated his glory wall. It was an evil, leering smile, full of smug self-satisfaction.

The smile faded in the next moment as a scratching sound came at his door. He jerked around, listening, then got his gun from the desk drawer and stepped closer to the door.

The sound came again, louder this time. Keeping the gun ready, he reached out and unlatched the door, then jerked it open wide.

The blind man and his seeing eye dog faced him in the hall. The suspect was trying to grasp the meaning of this incongruity when he realized that the large dog was in reality a wolf. A wolf with raven-black fur. A wolf with unusually long fangs who was now snarling malevolently at him.

The gun swung in their direction. The wolf sprang, instantly metamorphosing into Gregor Travanian's lean, aristocratic form, knocking the killer over backward and forcing the gun from his hand. The man's head cracked against the floor with a resounding thump, knocking him senseless. Yet even unconscious, he still retained his wide-eyed look of terror and disbelief.

Father Paul Mundy removed the hat and dark glasses Travanian had given him to wear, and replaced his white clerical collar. He stared down at the killer with mingled contempt and sadness. "Maybe now Trish can rest in peace."

Sirens split the night, growing louder with each passing moment. Gregor Travanian got to his feet and dusted himself off. He said, "The police will be here any minute, and take this refuse into custody."

Father Mundy stepped forward and extended his hand. "I owe you a debt of gratitude I may never be able to repay."

Travanian studied the offered hand a moment, then clasped it with his own, watching Mundy wince a bit at its cold and clammy contact. "The debt is mine, Father. Mine and Captain O'Halloran's. He will be the toast of the city tomorrow for solving this one. Which, of course, means that you will very likely find him in the confessional again."

Both men chuckled, and Gregor Travanian's laughter lengthened and deepened, echoing eerily through the night . . .

The author wishes to thank Father James McDougall of St. Thomas University for information on church policy and the daily routine of a Catholic priest, and Linda Hart, handwriting expert, for information on ESDA tests.

GOD-LESS MEN
by
James Kisner

East Texas:

The people of Shannonbaugh, a dirtball little town on the outskirts of nowhere, had a problem.

Somebody was killing their young women in an unusual way—draining them of their blood through holes in their necks.

Like in the movies. Like when vampires did it.

Sheriff Lucas McIntyre didn't buy that vampire bullshit, but he did know one thing: people didn't keep running after they got hit with two or maybe three .357 Magnum slugs.

Not regular people anyhow. But the guy Lucas saw running away from the car with the dead young woman in it took the shots he fired at him—Lucas saw him jerk with the impact—but didn't stop for a second.

Lucas had tried to follow the trail of blood the guy left, but it went only a few feet then suddenly disappeared. As if the guy himself had somehow disappeared.

It didn't make a damn bit of sense.

Lucas had to tell the preacher, Reverend John Satchel, about the dead woman personally. She was the preacher's daughter.

Reverend Satchel was in his late fifties, a medium-sized man who generally wore a wide-brimmed black felt hat, a plaid shirt, and jeans when he wasn't in the pulpit. His face was craggy and weatherbeaten, the face of a man who had seen too much—even before this tragedy.

Rumor was that before he replaced the late Reverend Paige, Satchel was involved with snake-handling cults and other renegade Christian sects. He'd neither confirm

nor deny the rumors. But his visage bore the stamp of
having seen hellfire up close and personal, like no
other preacher.

His son had been in trouble with the law a couple of
times, mostly because of drinking and driving, and his
daughter had been his only solace in life. She was a
good Christian girl who made her father proud—who
would've made her mother proud, too, if Lona Satchel
hadn't passed on ten years before.

Satchel turned from the dead girl on the table in the
clinic, trembling and nodding his bald head.

"A God-less man did this," he muttered, wiping his
brow with an orange bandana. "God-less man took my
Beth."

"This is number six," Lucas said quietly. "It's more
than I can handle, Reverend. We need the Feds now, for
sure. I should've called them in sooner—before this. . . ."

"I know of a man," Satchel said, turning his bloodshot
eyes in Lucas' direction, his bushy eyebrows dripping
from the heat, "a man who is a specialist in these
matters."

"What in hell you mean, Reverend?"

"A tracker. A *real* detective who's dealt with this kind
of evil before. The *federals* will not take it seriously and
they will not catch our man."

"But, Reverend, don't you think we should . . . ?"

Satchel stood firm, staring up in Lucas' eyes with a
determination that scared the young man. "I know
what's right, by God. I'm a preacher." He lowered his
gravelly voice an octave. "And it takes a God-less man
to catch another one."

"I don't understand."

"You shot him. He kept on going. You're not dealing
with a normal man. Maybe not even a *mortal* man.
Maybe some kind of monster. Whatever he or it is, is
certainly not something of God."

Lucas realized Satchel was buying into the vampire
theory, though he didn't come right out and say it. What
kind of preacher would believe in vampires? And what
was this heavy talk about "God-less" men?

Lucas tried to argue, but the preacher wouldn't budge.
So the sheriff agreed to call in the specialist, the vampire hunter.

How could he deny Satchel when his *daughter* had been slain?

It was another hot day that July when the diminutive, bronze-skinned man appeared in Lucas' small office, but the man didn't remove his straw hat or wipe his brow, despite the lack of air conditioning. He wasn't even sweating.

Lucas, thirty-five, with thinning blond hair and azure blue eyes, remained behind his desk, staring up at the short Indian with ill-concealed disdain. His own shirt was soaked, and the fan buzzing in the corner offered little respite from the humidity.

"You don't look like a detective, Cochise," he said. He leaned back in his chair a bit to give his guest a look at his lanky, tall body and the gun at his side. He always greeted strangers in more a physical than a verbal way, figuring it was best to intimidate anyone who might cause trouble before they even thought about it.

"I'm not a detective. I just get paid for what I do, White Eyes." The man evidently wasn't impressed by Lucas' body language. "And my name is not 'Cochise.' "

Lucas relaxed a little. He'd had dealings with Indians before and knew some of them were hard-headed and easily offended. This one, though small, had an air of confidence about him, a no-bullshit stance that Lucas had to admire.

"Sit down, Mr. ... ?"

"Sundance. Joe Sundance."

"Right, Sundance." He watched as Sundance sat down rather stiffly in the folding chair at the corner of his desk. The Indian wore a denim shirt and jeans, with snakeskin boots. He made eye contact with Lucas without flinching, another admirable trait in the sheriff's book of reckoning.

"What's your problem?" Sundance asked.

Lucas looked away, out the window at the cracked pavement running through the center of town. Across the street he saw a rich local climbing into a red Cadillac after leaving the hardware store. A kid rode past on a small bicycle. Then a big red dog ambled by in the opposite direction, his nose to the ground, following some odd scent. Lucas suddenly felt foolish; Shannonbaugh was a small, *normal* town. Weird things just did not happen here. Six girls didn't get killed savagely. By a monster.

Yet he had invited a man who was known as a vampire hunter to come help him. As if that were normal police procedure. He hadn't anticipated how ridiculous and foolish he would feel when the time came to deal with the man.

Sundance waited patiently.

Damn him, Lucas thought, wishing he'd go away. Finally, he said, "Well, we've had a slew of killings lately, and the evidence points to something—well, maybe— I don't know—something unusual." He wondered how Satchel even *knew* about people like this Sundance guy. Maybe the old man had handled more than snakes in his time.

"You don't believe in Changers, do you?"

Lucas was caught off guard both by the question and the Indian's unaffected manner of speaking. "What the hell do you mean?"

"Changers. Vampires."

"Oh. Hell, no, I don't. Why should I?"

"Because that is what is killing women here, and that is what will continue to kill them until it is stopped."

"I think it's just some sick bastard."

"Could be. Some people like to think they are Changers, just like some people like to think they are God, or trees."

"Why would anyone like to think he was a damn tree?"

"Why would anyone like to think he was a damn vampire?"

"I don't know."

"Me, neither." Sundance almost smiled, but his rugged face wasn't built for handling that expression. His long black hair was streaked with gray, and Lucas guessed he was fifty or so, though it was hard to tell with Indians. He might be a hundred.

"Let's cut through all the crap, Sundance," Lucas bristled. "I was against calling you here, but you're here now, so maybe you can help me. I don't have but one deputy and he's part-time and dumber than owl shit to boot. You're probably a good tracker if nothing else, so, whether this character is a vampire or not, you're hired."

"Fine with me. You don't have to believe if you don't want to."

"So what do you normally do first?"

"I want to see his latest victim—if you haven't buried her yet."

"No problem. She's in cold storage over at the clinic, which serves as funeral home and morgue in this town."

"Let's go. We need to do much before nightfall."

"Why's that?"

"He will strike again tonight. I feel it."

Lucas said nothing. He realized he was going to be weirded out by the Indian no matter what he said or did and decided, grudgingly, to accept it. He grabbed his hat, motioned to the door, and followed Sundance out into the hot sun.

She was about nineteen, and even with most of the blood gone from her body, it was evident Beth was attractive, especially with that long blonde hair. It was a damn shame the killer was picking out the best local specimens of womanhood to prey on.

Why couldn't he attack nasty fat old women with bitchy attitudes that not many people would miss?

Lucas considered asking Sundance that, but the little man was busy studying the holes on Beth's neck.

"Judging from the space between the holes, I'd say this Changer is an adult."

"I could've told you that. I shot the son of a bitch."

"I know. Preacher Satchel told me. I was stating the fact for the record."

Lucas started to ask "What record?" but decided against it.

"So what else?"

"If a chemist took some blood from the wounds, he would find a substance there such as vampire bats secrete when they feed on animals—something in their saliva that keeps the blood from coagulating."

"Should I get someone to examine it?"

"If you want. Makes no difference now. Woman is dead."

"But that'd prove something, wouldn't it?"

"Proves your killer is a Changer and not a madman who only *thinks* he's one. But woman still is dead, and so will the next one be. Do what you want. Now take me to where she was found."

About two miles outside of town was a Lover's Lane, on an old gravel road that led up to a ridge overlooking a forest, where the preacher's daughter had been found in her car.

"Now Beth was a good girl," Lucas told Sundance, "but she wasn't perfect. The preacher knew she went out occasionally, though I doubt she let anyone go all the way with her. So I figure she was making out with the guy, then he kills her. The damnedest thing about it is there are no signs of struggle. How in hell could he do that to her without her fighting back?"

"Magic eyes."

"Say what?"

"Hypnotism. Changers are like snakes who hypnotize birds. The woman submitted without fighting. As I suspect the other victims apparently did."

"That's right," Lucas admitted.

"Bad sign."

"Why?"

"A lunatic may think he's a vampire, but he usually has to kill, then drink. Only a true Changer has the magic eyes to drink while the victim lives."

"Maybe not. Maybe he ..." Lucas had no "maybe" to apply now that he thought about it.

Sundance asked to see where the man had run to and Lucas showed him. There were still dark brown spots on the ground where the blood had leaked.

"And it stops here."

"Bad sign." Sundance was down on his haunches, dipping his finger in the browned dirt. He wet his finger so dirt would stick to it, then brought it up to his nose to sniff. "Bad sign."

"Now what?"

"Two possibilities, both bad. One is Changer has special blood that coagulates almost instantly. Ordinary bullets may make hole, but not for long. By now, he's probably healed."

"Bullshit."

"The universe is full of bullshit, Sheriff."

"What's the other possibility?"

"He took off like an eagle. Some Changers can become different animals, depending on the necessity of the moment."

"Now you *are* bullshitting me, Sherlock." Lucas removed his hat and wiped his forehead, marveling again at how the Indian didn't sweat.

"I don't make the rules," Sundance replied. "I only report the facts." A cool breeze came out of nowhere, and he shivered. "Tonight will be a good time for the Changer. It will rain. It will be hard to find him in time. He will not expect us."

"How the hell will we know where to look? He's killed in several different places."

"I have an idea where he will *come* from."

Lucas scratched his head in amazement. "How in blazes could you have an idea? We don't have a god-damn clue."

"There are no atheists in foxholes, Sheriff. Remember that when the time comes."

Lucas' mouth dropped open at the apparent non-sequitur. Was Sundance being inscrutable to irritate him, or did his words really mean something?

Or was it all a bunch of crap, a show for the gullible White Man resented by all Indians?

Lucas decided to wait and see. But if Sundance *was* jerking him around, he'd kick his ass from here to Houston.

An hour before sunset, after a quick dinner at Belle's Cafe and Service Station, Joe Sundance and Sheriff Lucas McIntyre went together to gather what Sundance called his "trapping apparatus," which he kept in a cloth bag behind the bench seat in the ancient Chevy pickup truck he drove.

Sundance struggled to unwedge the heavy bag from its hiding place. When he finally pulled it loose and set it on the ground, Lucas saw it was three feet long, about a foot and a half high, and another foot or so deep. A beaded figure was sewn on one side of the bag—some kind of bird as far as Lucas could make it out—and on the other side was a representation of a crucifix, not in beads, but in embroidery.

Lucas had to ask, "You a Christian?"

"I am a God-fearing man."

"But are you a Christian?"

"No. I worship my Gods."

"Then why the cross on the suitcase?"

"You never see a vampire movie?"

"Now, Sundance, don't try to tell me that even half the horsecrap in a movie is ..."

"... more than half is based on some legend which some people believe somewhere. In every part of the world there have been Changers, some say since the beginning of time. So every part of the world has a way of dealing with them. Myself, I am a pragmatist."

"A what?"

"A practical man. I don't have to believe in Jesus for Him—or in this case His symbol—to have power. I've got Holy Water, garlic, ten-inch spikes, a wooden stake and mallet, among other things in my bag, as well as a well-honed *kukri*—in short, my friend, all the necessities for killing Changers, vampires, or even mortal men."

"What the hell is a 'coo-kree'?"

Sundance almost smiled as a child might who wanted to show off his toys, then knelt, unzipped the bag, and pulled out a knife with a curved blade that was at least a foot long.

"This is a *kukri*, Sheriff. Ask a Vietnam vet. This weapon can behead a man with a single motion." Sundance demonstrated by slicing the air, and Lucas shuddered.

"Put that goddamn sickle away. I'm not going to let you go around chopping people's heads off."

"You may want me to when the time comes. Chop off Changer's head, destroy it, or stuff mouth with garlic, bury—Changer dead for good."

"You're a sick fuck," Lucas said solemnly. "I've half a mind to send you packing."

"Wait till after tonight, Sheriff. After I do my job."

Lucas watched Sundance drop the knife in the bag, then take out a small brass crucifix before zipping it shut. He tucked it in one of his shirt pockets and stood.

"All right, Sundance," Lucas said, "you get one chance."

"One is all I need." He cast his eyes to the sky. The

temperature had dropped ten degrees and dark clouds were forming overhead. "Here comes the rain. And night soon, too." He hefted the bag over his shoulder by its strap. "Come, it's time to go after the Changer. He should be stirring soon."

"But where the hell are we going?"

Sundance got into the sheriff's car, tossing the bag in the back seat and closing the door on the passenger side. "You're driving."

Lucas got in and slammed his door shut. "Where, for God's sake?"

"The good preacher's house—drive there."

"Now, wait a minute . . ."

"We have no time for argument, Sheriff. Besides, what have you got to lose?"

"Just my badge."

"Better than losing your ass, Sheriff. Take it from one who knows."

Lucas grumbled, then started the engine as the first big drops of rain pelted the windshield. He switched on the wipers, put the car in drive, then drove slowly to the edge of town, while Sundance sat and watched quietly.

By the time they reached Satchel's home, the rain was a dense sheet before them, and the sky had darkened.

It was night at last, and Sundance finally showed some fear. The little man was sweating like a pig as Lucas turned off the engine. Lucas rested his hand casually on his .357, determined to be ready for something, even if he wasn't sure what it was.

They sat and watched and waited while the rain fell and it grew darker and darker.

The reverend's house was a small old frame structure, one story high, with a pointed roof. There was a porch out front on which sat a rusty swing glider, which the wind was causing to sway back and forth, making it emit tiny shrieks.

"Somebody ought to oil that thing," Lucas whispered.

Sundance said nothing. They were parked off the road on the edge of the woods that circled part of the town. They could see both the front and back door of the house. Sundance watched intently, barely breathing it seemed to Lucas, as if he were a cat and not a man.

After an hour of sitting in the rain, listening to the porch glider squeak and seeing nothing, Lucas spoke up.

"Why are we here?"

"You will see."

"You know, Reverend Satchel recommended you, though I don't know how the hell he would know about a guy like you."

"People who need me find me," Sundance said simply.

"What I'm getting at—well, if Satchel called you, why are we watching him?" Lucas cast an uneasy glance at Sundance. "Damn, you don't think *he*'s the killer?"

"No, I don't."

"Then who . . . ?"

Sundance stared out into the rain. It seemed a couple of minutes before he answered.

"He has a son, doesn't he?"

Lucas didn't know what to say. Maybe Sundance was the lunatic in this situation. Maybe Satchel himself. Maybe Satchel was crazy enough to think his son would kill his own baby sister. Which would make Jeremy Satchel crazy, too.

Hell, maybe *he'd* be screwy before this was over.

Lucas awoke with a start, then realized he had been jabbed in the ribs and yelped.

"What the hell?"

"He preys." Sundance pointed toward the back of the house, where a figure draped in a dark plastic rain poncho was departing.

"That's Jeremy . . ."

". . . the reverend's son," Sundance finished. "Follow him. Slowly. At a distance. But do not lose him."

Lucas started the car and edged out on the road. "Why doesn't he take the old man's Buick?"

"It would raise suspicion. He doesn't need it, anyhow. He is fleet of foot. See how he moves. Like a wraith. Like a low cloud."

Lucas watched and had to confirm what Sundance observed. Jeremy Satchel seemed almost to float along the shoulder of the road as he headed into town. "I'll be damned."

The rain had slackened somewhat, so visibility was

much improved and they could follow Jeremy at a safe
distance and still see him clearly enough not to lose him.

"You have any idea where he's going?"

Sundance shook his head. "This is your town, Sheriff.
Who is close by?"

Lucas thought a moment. "Two possibilities. A couple
of blocks down, Linda Stumpf. Twentyish. Works at the
restaurant. What the hell time is it?"

"After midnight."

"She'd be home then on a weeknight."

"And the other?"

"A nurse. Thirty or so. Lives in the trailer park. The
only single woman there."

"Which is closer?"

"About the same from here, depending on whether
you go north or east."

"He turns east."

"Linda."

"Hurry, Sheriff. We need to get there ahead of him
if we can."

"I can go in from the back."

"Do it!"

They parked in the alley behind a small duplex in
one half of which Linda Stumpf lived. Sundance dragged
the bag from the back seat and they approached
cautiously.

The rain was coming down hard again by the time
they reached the back door.

"I hope you're right," Lucas said, rapping on the door.

"A hungry man goes for the quickest meal. He has
not fed since the preacher's daughter. He is no doubt
famished and crazy with the great thirst that drives his
kind."

"Quit that vampire talk for a while, Sundance. It's
getting on my nerves. We have to *prove* Jeremy's the
killer, you know. We can't just assume . . ."

The door opened and an attractive brunette woman
with a full bosom, barely covered by a robe, greeted
them.

"Why, Sheriff, what y'all doin' at my door this time
of night?"

"Saving your life, I hope."

Linda blanched. "You mean . . . ?"

"We think he's picked you next."

"Come on in out of the rain, then, Lucas." She ushered the sheriff and Sundance into her kitchen. "Who's this?"

"Special deputy," Lucas said quickly. Then he glared at Sundance. "Well, hot shot, what now?"

"Turn out the light. Lady, go back in your bed."

"Whatever for? I was going to make some coffee for you and ..."

"Do it," Lucas said. "No time to explain anything."

Linda nodded nervously and switched off the kitchen light. She led the sheriff and Sundance down a hall which was dimly-lit by a night light in an outlet near the bedroom. "I leave that on in case I have to go tinkle in the middle of the night," Linda said. "Y'all know what I mean?"

"Hurry," Sundance whispered.

Linda hesitated at her bedroom door. "Are you coming in my bedroom, too?"

"Yes," Sundance said. "We'll hide by the bed."

"Can I trust this Indian?"

"Yeah, sure. He won't molest you. Just get in the bed and pretend you're asleep."

"I don't know if I can."

"Hurry. He comes!" Sundance pushed her toward the bed, which was barely illuminated by a street lamp shining in through the curtained windows, then pulled Lucas down with him as he dropped to the floor.

"How do you know ... ?"

"Listen."

Lucas heard the sound of rain hitting something soft. "What is it?"

"The poncho. He may walk in silence like the night, but the rain cannot be hushed as it hits his cloak."

As the sheriff and Sundance huddled on the floor next to the bed, Linda drew the covers up around her neck.

"Keep your eyes shut," Sundance ordered. "He must not suspect."

The sound of wood resisting pressure squeaked in the room. There was a shadow at the window of a man trying to pull it open.

"That window won't open," Linda whispered. "Painted shut."

"Shush!"

"He'll give up," Lucas said.

"No," Sundance muttered. He unzipped the bag.

Lucas could hear him pulling something out.

The shadow stopped tugging on the window abruptly.

"Damn!" Lucas said.

"Oh, my God, I peed my pants!" Linda gasped.

"No time . . ." Sundance said.

Then there was an explosion of glass and splintered wood as the shadow hurled itself through the window, hit the floor with a roll, and sprang up on the bed, immediately pinning Linda's arms down.

She screamed.

Lucas stood up and drew his pistol.

The shadow hissed.

Sundance turned a bright flashlight on the shadow, revealing the snarling features of Jeremy Satchel, whose mouth was gaping open. Sharp fangs jutted from his teeth. His eyes were yellowish and bloodshot, his brown hair matted to his head from rain and sweat. He looked much older than his twenty-five years—*much*, much older.

"Stop, Jeremy!" Lucas yelled.

"He will not," Sundance said.

"Do something," Linda said, beginning to thrash under Jeremy.

Jeremy let go of one of her wrists and swung at Lucas. When he connected, the sheriff was jolted half way across the room. Then Jeremy grabbed Linda's wrist again and started to press down on her, his lips quivering as he sought her neck.

He had apparently forgotten about Sundance.

Sundance had the small crucifix in his hand now. He thrust it under Jeremy's face.

Jeremy growled and swatted the offensive symbol away.

"So you do not believe in this God," Sundance said.

A God-less man, Lucas thought.

Jeremy paused to laugh. "If there is a God, why would he allow *things*—creatures—like me to exist?"

Lucas had recovered enough to throw on the overhead light. Somehow he had managed to hold on to his pistol, so he lifted it and aimed for Jeremy's shoulder.

"I'll stop him!" He pulled the trigger and part of Jeremy peeled off and splattered both Sundance and the girl. Linda screamed louder than ever when the blood hit her face. Jeremy shuddered but quickly regained his hold on the woman and resumed his attack.

Sundance tossed the crucifix on the floor, then ducked down to get something else from the bag.

"If you do not believe in one God," he said, rising with the curved knife in one hand and something wooden in the other, "other gods will find you. *My* Gods will do." He brandished a carved eagle in Jeremy's direction and the young man found himself unable to move. "This God condemns you! This God that *I* believe in!"

"No!" Jeremy squealed, obviously shocked by the eagle's effect on him—so much so that he let go of the woman to cover his face.

Sundance took advantage of Jeremy's reaction quickly. He wielded the knife and with a single swift motion neatly lopped off the vampire's head and the hands covering the face.

The beheaded body, gushing dark blood from the neck, pitched forward on Linda, who emitted sounds that might have caused earthquakes in less sturdy surroundings.

Jeremy's head bounced across the floor, landing at Lucas' feet; the eyes seemed to be staring in amazement. The two severed hands flew into the corner.

Lucas' stomach heaved. He thought the eyes blinked. Reflexively, he shot the head, blowing a good third of it away.

"Good," Sundance said. "You have saved me having to destroy it." He pushed the body away from Linda, and tried to calm her. "It is over."

It was many hours before she calmed down, and many more hours before Lucas was able to explain what happened without choking on his own words.

Sundance remained inscrutable throughout it all.

The next day, Sundance was waiting for Lucas in his office when he finally arrived, around noon.

Lucas' face was ashen and there were dark circles under his eyes. "It was the damnedest thing," he said quietly to Sundance as he sat behind his desk. "The reverend didn't get that upset. He even insisted I tell him *every* detail of what happened. The only thing he wanted was for me not to mention anything about the vampire part. As if I would."

"It is to be expected."

"He even seemed relieved."

"That, too, is to be expected."

"I don't get it," Lucas said. "None of it. Why *Jeremy*?"

"He didn't believe in God. Someone—some *thing*—another Changer, perhaps, took advantage of that to make him into one of their kind."

"But surely he didn't believe in the eagle thing you had."

"But *I* did, my friend. That is why there are no atheists in foxholes. Every soldier believes in a god, and the enemy that doesn't is easier to overcome."

"It's too simple."

"Not simple at all. I make it simple so I don't have to talk about it for three hours."

"But Satchel—he said you were a 'God-less' man."

Sundance nodded gravely. "To him, yes. To him there's but one God. No sweat. My faith is as strong as his. We both end up in paradise or . . ." He paused and his eyes almost twinkled. ". . . in hell."

"You're a strange bird, Sundance."

Sundance nodded imperceptibly, then started toward the door. "My work here is finished. My bill will go to the reverend—by his request. I am tired and the journey back home is long."

"Wait a minute. Since you know everything, maybe you can tell me why Satchel wasn't so upset today."

"Another simple thing. He summoned me. He *knew*."

"He *wanted* you to destroy his son?"

"It is always a loved one who calls to put them out of their misery. The preacher's son was suffering torments I hope neither you nor I will ever endure. And the preacher was suffering too, knowing his son had forsaken *his* God. He tried to live with it, the horror of his son, but when Jeremy killed his sister, Satchel could no longer protect him."

"So you suspected him from the beginning."

"Yes."

"Then why go through all the rigmarole of inspecting the body and staking out the place?"

"I had to be sure. It was possible the preacher was mistaken, too."

"Sounds reasonable and damned logical. I guess I underestimated you."

"People often do." Sundance pulled the door open.

Lucas stood. "I'll walk you out."

Outside, before Sundance got into his truck, he stopped and confronted Lucas.

"Tell me, Sheriff, do you believe in vampires now?"

Lucas' brow wrinkled as he considered all he had seen in the last twenty-four hours.

"I'm damned if I know," he said finally. "Cutting anybody's head off is going to stop them."

"Sounds reasonable," Sundance replied. He shook hands with Lucas and climbed up into the truck. "Good knowing you, Sheriff."

"What now, Chief?" Lucas asked.

"People who need me find me," he said, starting the engine. "You'd be surprised how much business I get."

NO BLOOD FOR A VAMPIRE
by
Edward D. Hoch

I'd found myself in many strange places with my friend
Simon Ark, but none quite so strange as this. Crowded
in among spectators of every possible skin pigment, we
were watching a staged combat between a pair of large
warthogs, each weighing more than two hundred pounds.
The corrugated metal warehouse into which a hundred
or more spectators had jammed was steaming with foul,
humid air that no one else seemed to notice. Even after
the fight started and the beasts had locked tusks for the
first time, an Arab with a canvas purse tied around his
waist still moved among the spectators, taking bets on
the outcome.

"It is a bit close in here," Simon Ark admitted when
I expressed my discomfort. "Perhaps we could stand
nearer the door if we return tomorrow evening."

"Tomorrow!" I was aghast at the thought of it.

The two ugly warthogs came apart, circled, and then
charged again, this time butting heads as they attempted
to jab each other with their incurving tusks. The large
facial warts that gave the beasts their name served as
some protection, and they soon broke off the encounter
as the partisan roaring of the crowd increased. I tried to
block out the sight of it and recall what had brought
me here to a humid, stinking warehouse on the coast
of Madagascar.

It had been a warm August afternoon in Manhattan
when my secretary at Neptune Books had buzzed me to
announce quietly, "Mr. Simon Ark—a tall old man in a

black suit. He has no appointment. Is he one of our authors?"

She'd been with me only a few months, and anyone's first encounter with Simon could be a bit unnerving. "He did a book on Satanism some years back," I explained. "Send him in."

Simon's vigor was undiminished since I'd last seen him six months earlier. As soon as he'd greeted me, he unfolded a map of Africa and pointed to the large island of Madagascar off the eastern coast. "Vampires," he announced dramatically in the harsh voice I'd grown to know so well.

Like most people I was vaguely aware of Madagascar's existence, but it wasn't high on my tourist agenda. "I didn't think you believed in vampires, Simon."

"I believe in them only as a manifestation of a greater evil. Men do not turn into bats and flit through the night air, but they do indeed commit murder and drink the blood of their victims upon occasion. There are many well-documented cases, as you know. A person named Mano Ratki believes such a killer is loose in Madagascar."

"Surely it's a matter for the local police."

"They scoff at the very idea, because no blood has been spilled. The victims have all been strangled. Ratki has read that old book of mine and thinks I can help."

"How could you find what the police can't?"

"He says only that he recognized this person from another country, where the person was forced to leave because of charges of vampirism. My correspondent knows the same thing is happening again, even if he doesn't know how. Madagascar is a strange country in many ways. The people open the tombs of the dead, and sometimes dance with the corpses of departed relatives."

"What? Can such things be, Simon? This is practically the twenty-first century!"

"Come with me, my friend, and see for yourself."

So I had come, risking yet another scene with my wife Shelly, who'd never quite approved of Simon Ark. In her younger days she could joke about his claim of wandering the earth for two thousand years seeking battle with Satan. Now, with both of us well into middle age and Simon looking much the same, the jokes had grown tired.

It was Simon's correspondent, Mano Ratki, who met us at the airport in Madagascar's centrally located capital city of Antananarivo. He was a small brown-skinned man of uncertain ancestry, but I judged him to be mainly Malayan-Indonesian like the bulk of the nation's population. "I thank you for coming this distance," he said, speaking English with a trace of French accent. Madagascar had been a French colony until its independence in 1960.

"I have read your letters with interest," Simon told him. "Are we to see the person you claim is a vampire?"

"All in good time," the small man told us, smiling to reveal a gap-toothed grin. "First we will drive to the coastal town of Brickaville, about a hundred miles from here. There is a warthog fight tonight which you may find interesting."

"Warthogs?" I repeated, catching Simon's eye to signal my distaste.

We stowed our luggage in the back of his battered Land Rover and set off down the highway. The temperature in the low eighties was quite pleasant and Simon remarked on it, trying to encourage conversation with this man who'd summoned us nearly halfway around the world.

"I fear it will be more humid on the coast," Mano Ratki said, keeping his eyes on the road.

"Are there a great many warthogs in Madagascar?" I asked finally.

Ratki gave a snort. "There are no warthogs on the entire island! They are imported from Mozambique on the African mainland. Our poor country has only second-best—a similar animal called a bushpig. They fight head-to-head, much like the warthogs, but they lack those impressive tusks. People come to Nafud's fights to see those tusks in action."

"Who is Nafud?" Simon asked.

"An Arab trader. He runs the fights and takes bets on the outcome."

"And the vampire?"

"Ah! You shall see!"

Later, as we maneuvered a steep jungle road, I asked, "Is the entire country as hilly as this?"

"There is a flat plain to the west on the Mozambique Channel. The rest is rough, but hardly impassable."

Presently we drove down onto a narrow coastal plain near the village of Brickaville. A decidedly European influence was visible here, and I assumed that the docking facilities and warehousing had been left by the French when they departed. A small hotel called the Seaman's Rest could be seen a bit farther along the shore.

We made at once for one of the corrugated metal warehouses, joining a crowd that was already gathering. Here, on the shore of the Indian Ocean, the diversity of race and ethnic origin seemed even greater than I'd observed during our overland journey. Some, like our companion, seemed to have Far Eastern roots, but Arabs and Africans were present, too. There was even a Frenchman named Dr. Creux who might have remained as a child when his countrymen pulled out in 1960.

I asked him about this, when Ratki had introduced us, but he smiled and shook his head. "No, I was born and educated in France. But French doctors remained here after the country gained its independence, and there was always a need for more. A great many French-speaking people remain, though Malagasy is the official language."

He was a man in his forties, graying at the temples, who seemed somehow at home among this mixture of races and nationalities. "Do you actually come here to see the warthog fights?" I asked.

Dr. Creux smiled. "This is not an exciting place. We must make the best of the few amusements available. If Nafud wants to hold warthog fights, I will come and watch."

Simon Ark let his gaze sweep over the spectators as they filled the place. "Which one is Nafud?"

"The Arab with the canvas purse," Ratki replied. "You'll meet him later. We'd better get inside."

I noticed the French doctor pause to speak with a strikingly handsome young woman with a camera around her neck. It was an expensive camera and I suspected she was more than a tourist. As the crush of spectators increased, I lost sight of them and we were pressed against a cage full of noisy lemurs awaiting shipment.

The warthog duel ended after some fifteen minutes when one of the animals drew blood. It was none too soon for me. Both animals were taken away while the Arab with the canvas purse paid off the winners.

Ratki led us through the crowd to Nafud's side. When he'd finished his gambling transactions we were introduced. "I welcome visitors from America," he said formally, shaking our hands. Then he peered more closely at Simon's chiseled features. "You have some Hamite or Berber ancestry in your blood, Mr. Ark. I see it in the lines of your face."

"I trace my lineage back to Egypt some two millennia ago," Simon answered a bit vaguely. Then, changing the subject, he gestured back toward the lemur cages where we'd been standing. "Are you responsible for those creatures?"

"They are awaiting shipment to zoos."

"Lemurs are nocturnal. Their cages should be covered."

"In this hot place it is better they get some air. And lemurs are evolving into daytime creatures anyway, Mr. Ark."

"It is a profitable export," Mano Raki explained. "Lemurs are found nowhere else on earth."

A late bettor came up to claim his winnings and we continued outside. I realized we hadn't eaten since a meager snack on the plane some hours earlier and Mano Ratki apologized for his neglect. He led us through the gathering darkness to a cafe in the small hotel I'd noticed earlier. "It is not very good," he cautioned, "but it is the best we can offer."

The spicy East Indian food was filling, at least for the moment, and that was all we asked. After dinner, relaxing with an American soft drink, I saw Dr. Creux enter with the attractive brunette woman I'd observed earlier. "Enjoying our local cuisine?" the doctor asked with a smile. "May I present Madame Desladas, a visitor to our shores."

"Carla Desladas," she corrected with a smile, extending a hand to Simon and me. She was a tall, slender woman in her thirties, and her jet-black hair was loose to her shoulders. The expensive Japanese camera still hung from her neck by a strap. She was wearing an old plaid shirt and tapered jeans, for which she immediately apologized. "After all, what do you wear to a warthog fight?"

"It is a man's sport," Ratki admitted. "Here, join us for a drink."

He pulled up extra chairs to our table and Dr. Creux and the woman sat down. "Only for a moment," the doctor said. "I must get back to my clinic."

"It's here, in Brickaville?" Simon asked.

"Just a mile up the coast. We are well equipped for all the usual ills and even some unusual ones. The clinic has the only kidney dialysis machine in this part of the country, and full surgical facilities as well. This evening, as we do once a week, we are offering free tests for AIDS."

"It's a problem in Madagascar, too?" Carla Desladas asked.

The doctor nodded. "On the African mainland it is very serious. We try to keep it from our island, but that is impossible."

Before long Simon had struck up a conversation with the Frenchwoman. "I'm a journalist," she was explaining. "I've been here on the coast for a few weeks and tomorrow I head inland for the season of famadihana."

Simon Ark nodded. "The turning of the bones."

She seemed surprised. "You are familiar with the local custom?"

"I know that ancestor worship here is as strong today as it was hundreds of years ago. Even the Catholic Church has come to terms with it."

"You'd better explain it," I said.

"In August and September, when the crops are in and the weather begins to cool, the people feast and often bring the dead from their tombs to be wrapped in new shrouds."

"All this and warthogs, too!" Madagascar seemed farther from Manhattan with each new revelation.

Dr. Creux dismissed that with a wave of his hand. "The warthogs are strictly Nafud's scheme to make a little money. They have nothing to do with the reality of life in this country. Up in the hills, at villages like Imerina where men dance with the dead one last time—that is reality here."

"I will take you there tomorrow morning," Mano Ratki promised Simon and me.

"You're actually going there?" Carla asked. "Would you have room for an extra passenger?"

Ratki eyed her for a moment before responding. "I suppose so," he agreed. "If you don't have luggage."

"Only me. And my camera."

"We leave promptly at nine, from the hotel."

I'd been hoping that we'd be spending the night back in the capital, where a few modern buildings seen from the air had led me to imagine a first-class hotel. Instead we ended up at the Seaman's Rest, upstairs over the cafe. "Merchant seamen often like a night ashore," Ratki explained, "with a woman. This fills a need."

I could hear comings and goings in the hall half the night, before finally drifting into a restless sleep in the lumpy bed. I awakened shortly after six to find Simon standing by the shutters, fully dressed, observing the street below. "You're up early," I muttered before burying my face in the pillow.

"Get dressed, my friend. There seems to be an altercation in front of the hotel, between Mano Ratki and a police officer."

"All right," I gave in, knowing that further sleep was impossible. "I want to shower first. I'll meet you downstairs."

He hadn't told me that the trickle from the shower head was lukewarm at best. I dressed quickly and joined Simon on the street. The dark-skinned police officer, Captain Billy Lightly, wore a braided shirt and a large gold badge. He was questioning them about a murder that had occurred during the night, down by the docks. "You are always on the scene when there is a killing, Mano," he told our friend. "I have my eye on you." Finally he turned and crossed the street to a waiting police car, removing his sun helmet to wipe his forehead.

"What happened?" I asked Ratki.

The small man wrinkled his brow, seeming genuinely

concerned. "Another man strangled with a cord, down by the dock."

"A seaman?" I asked.

"No, one of the workmen at Nafud's warehouse. They are never seamen."

Simon raised his eyes. "The victims of your so-called vampire? They are never seamen?"

"That is correct."

"Interesting. Why does the captain think you are involved?"

"He looks for a scapegoat. I am on the scene because of my suspicions, but he scoffs when I mention vampires. There is no blood for vampires, he says. There are no teeth marks on the throat. But he sees too many films."

"What do the autopsies show?"

"No noticeable blood loss. But that is why I summoned you, Mr. Ark. You must find out how it is being done."

I wondered whether the heat of this place had gotten to Ratki, obsessing him with visions of black-caped stalkers. "What does it matter to you?" I asked. "Why do you care so much?"

He led the way to his Land Rover and opened the door. "I care because the first victim was my brother," he said. "Far away, in a different country. I have followed his killer here."

"Name him for me," Simon urged.

"In due time."

Later that morning, after a breakfast of native fruit, we set off for the interior, first stopping to pick up Carla Desladas as promised. She was dressed today in a khaki bush jacket with matching shirt and pants, her long black hair pulled into a bun in back. She carried a camera bag in one hand.

Carla joined me in the back seat for our journey, and as we drove past the warehouse we saw Nafud and two of his helpers lugging a large burlap sack. "Looks as if he has a body in there," Carla joked.

"Stranger things have happened here," Ratki said from behind the wheel.

I knew Simon was as frustrated as I was by the man's frequent hints of dark doings, never once naming the person he suspected. At one point on the journey I re-

membered the lemurs and said, "With all the odd animals in Madagascar, surely you have vampire bats."

"No, true vampire bats are found only in Central and
South America. Here there is only the false vampire bat.
Like the bushpig, we are second best." He lapsed again
into silence.

"Have you done much African photography?" I asked
Carla after another few miles of driving.

"Some. My ex-husband and I used to shoot large animals—elephants, giraffes, hippos."

"What happened to him?"

"We split up, and after that he got involved in some
nasty business. Poachers were killing elephants for their
ivory tusks. Ron photographed them, but they bought
him off. He was always something of a weakling. The
last I heard he was serving a short prison sentence."

"Is ivory poaching still a problem?"

"Your country and some others now ban the importa-
tion of African elephant ivory. That has helped a great
deal. Of course there are no elephants in Madagascar so
it has never been a problem here."

Suddenly we topped a rise in the road and came upon
a small village surrounded by rice fields. "This is our
destination," Ratki told us. "A festival is in progress.
They will open the tomb later today."

He'd barely parked the Land Rover when a black man
wearing a jacket and headband approached us. He was
a member of the village council named Ramajiso and he
greeted Ratki warmly. "You arrive in good time for the
feast," he told us. "We will open the tomb soon and
later the council will read out the names of the dead to
be brought up."

"Is this a family tomb?" Simon Ark asked.

"Yes, my family is there—nearly two hundred of
them, stretching back for generations."

"I would like to see it. Your customs here are strange
to us."

"But first you must eat," Ramajiso insisted.

The feast was indeed under way, and we gorged our-
selves on helpings of beef, pork, and rice, washing it
down with a locally brewed alcohol. "I won't want to
eat for a week," Carla announced when we'd consumed

all that we could. I glanced around for Mano Ratki, but he seemed to have disappeared.

"If you wish to see the tomb," Ramajiso told Simon, "I will take you now. Once the names are read out, the male relatives will enter immediately to bring forth the bodies."

Though I was included in the invitation, it was explained that women never entered the tomb. Carla reluctantly stayed behind, clicking off shots of the tomb entrance as the heavy granite door was opened for us. It was built into the side of a grassy knoll some distance from the center of the village, and the door was not locked now, if it ever was. Ramajiso handed us candles and lit them, revealing a flight of wooden stairs leading to the underground tomb. "This is my family resting place," he said with quiet dignity.

I had expected a typical mausoleum with rows of coffins in niches. Instead we found slabs of granite upon which rested some two hundred bodies wrapped in white cloth and sheathed in straw mats. "You don't use coffins?" I asked.

"Only to carry the body to the tomb. Then it is removed and borne inside. This has been so in my family for one hundred fifty years."

"Some of these will be removed today?" Simon asked.

"Eleven names will be read, and we will bring the bodies up. My family will dance and there will be more feasting. The dead will be rewrapped in fresh white cloths before being returned here."

The odor of the place was beginning to reach me, and I was grateful when we were back above ground. Already we could see the villagers gathering for the reading of names. Carla Desladas stood near the fringe of the crowd, her camera humming with each click of the shutter.

As Ramajiso had predicted, all eleven names were members of his extended family who had died during the past decade. The wrapped bodies were carried from the tomb by celebrating male relatives who might have been enjoying a Mardi Gras. In most cases the dried dead skin had separated from the bones and the effect was gruesome in the extreme. The dancing, singing family members seemed not to notice.

Then it happened without warning. As Carla edged closer with her camera, one of the straw mats was unrolled, revealing a white cloth that seemed cleaner and fresher than the others. Ramajiso himself bent to uncover the body, then leaped back with a gasp of horror. This was not one of his family.

It was the body of Mano Ratki, and he'd been strangled like the other victims.

When the village police arrived to investigate the killing, Simon Ark and I stood off to one side. "I couldn't have known," he said quietly, staring down at the body under its white covering.

"Of course not," I agreed. "Don't blame yourself. Anyway, this can't be the work of any vampire. There's not a drop of blood anywhere. That white cloth is spotless." We both saw that it wasn't completely true, and Simon bent to examine a dark brown smudge in one corner. He rubbed a bit and most of it came off on his hand.

"Interesting," he said.

"What is it? Not blood, certainly."

He sniffed his fingers. "It appears to be greasepaint."

"But why—?"

We were interrupted by a native police officer in charge of the investigation. He bore little resemblance to the dapper figure of Captain Lightly back in Brickaville. "Which of you is Simon Ark?"

"I am."

"I have communicated by telephone with Billy Lightly. He encountered you this morning while investigating another murder. This dead man, Mano Ratki, was also questioned about it."

"That's correct," Simon agreed.

"Murder seems to follow you around, Mr. Ark. May I ask what you are doing here?"

"The dead man, Mr. Ratki, brought us to witness the festival."

Carla was standing nearby, holding her camera, but she'd made no effort to take a picture since the arrival of the police. The officer asked why she was there. "I'm a news photographer," she answered, not altogether truthfully. It seemed to satisfy him.

The villagers had been in a turmoil since the uncovering of the unwelcome body, and I couldn't blame them. Ramajiso and his brothers had immediately searched the tomb by candlelight, taking inventory of the bodies. All were accounted for. Ratki's corpse had merely been added to the collection, shoved onto a slab near the tomb entrance. If it had not been found before the tomb was closed again, it might have gone undiscovered for a decade.

"A perfect hiding place," Simon observed. "Down among the dead men and women."

"Why did no one see it happen?" I asked.

"The tomb is some distance from the village center, hidden by that knoll. Someone could easily have lured Ratki away during the feast and strangled him. The fresh winding sheets and mats are laid out nearby. And he was a small man, easily carried."

"Who were his enemies here?" the officer asked.

"There were none," Ramajiso insisted. "He came here occasionally, but I knew him best from my own trips into Brickaville for supplies."

"Have there been any other murders or unexplained deaths recently?" Simon asked.

"Not a one!" Ramajiso insisted. "We are a peaceful people."

Carla agreed to drive Ratki's Land Rover back to Brickaville. On the way, I could see Simon was deep in thought, puzzling over events of the past twenty-four hours. Mano Ratki had summoned him because he suspected a vampire killer had come to Madagascar. There were mysterious deaths, but none seemed to involve the spilling of blood. The only blood I'd seen had been spilled by that warthog's gouging tusks, and even vampires didn't resort to warthog blood.

Simon broke the silence only once. "Ratki would have introduced us to the person he suspected. I feel certain we have met the killer."

Captain Lightly was waiting for us back at the docks in Brickaville. He wore a fresh, neatly pressed uniform, but was without his sun helmet. "You are a great detective, Mr. Ark," he said by way of greeting. "Do you know who strangled our good friend Ratki?"

He hadn't seemed so friendly with Ratki earlier that

day, but I didn't bother to remind him. The question
had been directed to Simon and he answered it. "Not
yet, but I will know in time. Has the autopsy been completed on last night's victim?"

"The body was sent to the capital. The preliminary
report gives strangulation as the cause of death."

"No wounds of any sort?"

Captain Lightly smiled slightly, revealing teeth stained
with betel juice. "Nothing unusual. Men who work in
the warehouse always have a few cuts and scrapes on
their arms."

"What about his blood?"

Billy Lightly sighed. "The medical authorities in An-
ananarivo are not bothered by fine points. This man, like
the others, had the proper volume of blood in his body.
That is all I can tell you. The body has been released
for embalming."

Simon had a sudden thought. "Embalming? He's not
one of those to be buried in a native village like Imerina,
his body wrapped in a mat and placed in a family
tomb?"

The captain smiled again. "Once people leave their
native villages they rarely return. The dead are usually
buried where they die. Ratki was born here but he has
lived in Marseille and Rome." He eyed Simon and
asked, "Will you be returning to America soon?"

"Perhaps tomorrow."

"Ah, then I may see you at Nafud's warehouse
tonight."

"Tonight?"

"There is to be another of his warthog fights."

Carla went off to take a bath, claiming the odor of
death still clung to her. I felt like doing the same thing,
but Simon insisted we visit the dock area while it was
still daylight. "After the fight it will be getting dark," he
said, remembering the previous evening.

I followed him out to the docks, past bags of coffee,
rice, and peanuts waiting to be loaded onto the next
ship. A few workmen turned to stare as Simon's tall,
black-garbed figure moved among them, but most ignored him. Finally he found what he was seeking—the
burlap sack we'd seen Nafud and his men carrying earlier in the day. "Do you have a knife?" he asked me.

I unfolded a penknife and handed it to him. He made a quick cut in the burlap and we stood back. On the shore people were beginning to gather at Nafud's warehouse. It was almost time for the match to begin.

"It's as I thought," Simon told me.

I stared into the burlap sack. "A dead warthog. Probably the loser in last night's battle. What was he going to do, heave it into the ocean?"

"The cargo ship would dump it for him, well offshore." He used my penknife to poke at the head. "Notice that the tusks are missing."

"The tusks?"

"Ivory, my friend. Not as large as elephant tusks, but better than nothing."

"My God! Is that why Nafud imports them from the mainland?"

"It seems so."

I bent to examine the wounds where the tusks had been cut out. "I'm surprised there aren't more bloodstains," I commented.

Simon felt of the dead animal and made another incision on its underside, where the force of gravity should have drawn the blood after death. "There is no blood," he said quietly.

"Simon—!"

He glanced quickly toward shore. "Come my friend. We have not a moment to lose!"

I followed him off the dock and into the milling crowd. The first person we recognized was Captain Lightly, busily conversing with a couple of sailors off one of the freighters. But Simon didn't stop to speak until we encountered Carla, looking fresh and cool in a clean shirt and jeans. "Have you seen Nafud?" Simon asked.

She nodded. "He's taking bets over on the other side. His men are bringing in the animals now. You'd better sit down."

I could read the anxiety on Simon's face as he struggled to break free of the press of spectators and reach Nafud. We saw the Arab now, moving among the late arrivals near the big warehouse doors, accepting currency in return for betting slips. But it was useless. I placed a hand on his shoulder and cautioned, "You'll be trampled in this crowd. Wait till it's over. He's not going anywhere."

He settled down reluctantly between Carla and me as the warthogs were brought in. I could see that the crowd was larger than the previous evening, possibly because there was one more freighter in port. But it seemed that some of the natives from nearby villages had made the trip in, too. "Isn't that Ramajiso?" I pointed out to Simon. "What's he doing here?"

The council member from Imerina was easily recognizable by his jacket and colored headband. "I've seen him in Brickaville before," Carla said. "He told us he came here for supplies."

"On the day of their festival?"

"Ratki's murder and the desecration of the family tomb may have put a damper on the festival," Simon Ark suggested.

There was a roar from the crowd as the warthogs faced each other and were released by their handlers. I spotted Dr. Creux at ringside, forced backward into the crowd as the animals locked tusks virtually in his lap. The battle dragged on longer than the previous night's fray, indicating the large animals were more evenly matched. Watching two ugly creatures batter and slam at one another was not my idea of a sport or prize contest, and I was relieved when one of them finally toppled over from exhaustion. Nafud stepped forward to declare a winner, amidst cheers and boos.

"At least it's not quite as humid as last evening," I said as the crowd began to flow toward the door.

But Simon had other things on his mind. "We must reach Nafud at once. Follow me," he urged.

Carla started to trail along, but we were separated by the warthog handlers. I was about to return and try to rescue her when I saw Dr. Creux reach out and offer his hand as she stepped around the collapsed animal. I noticed what looked like a brown birthmark on his arm.

Apparently the favorite had lost and there were few bettors to be paid off. The Arab finished with them, closed the purse at his waist and beat a hasty retreat toward the rear of the warehouse. "This way!" Simon urged, trying to head him off.

If Nafud saw us, he wasn't about to stop. A rear door

stood open and he was nowhere to be seen. "Nafud!" Simon shouted, but there was no reply.

"I guess he doesn't want to see us," I suggested.

"We must find him before there is another murder."

"You mean Nafud is the vam—?"

"Quiet!" He stood by the door with one foot outside. There was a movement nearby, in the darkness. No one had come out the door with us, but almost anyone could have slipped around from the dispersing crowd at the front of the building.

There was a sudden gasp, and the sound of a tussle. My fingers, running down the door frame, found a light switch and I snapped it on. The sudden overhead light spilled out into the tall grass behind the building, revealing two men locked in a struggle. Simon and I sprang forward together to pull them apart.

"Thank heaven you were there!" Dr. Creux gasped. "Nafud was trying to strangle me."

I had the Arab in my grasp, but it was Simon Ark who loosened my grip and turned to Dr. Creux instead. "You've killed your last man, Doctor. And drunk your last beaker of blood."

Doctor Creux protested his innocence right up until the moment Captain Lightly opened the locked refrigerator at the clinic and discovered three and a half gallons of human blood in carefully labeled jugs. Then he fell silent and refused to speak at all.

"He was drinking human blood?" Billy Lightly asked, still unable to believe the evidence before him. "You mean like a vampire?"

"Exactly like a vampire," Simon Ark confirmed. The doctor had been taken away, but we were still at his clinic listening to Simon explain it all. "His criminal madness manifested itself in a craving for human blood—large quantities of human blood. His problem was in obtaining the blood from his victims in a manner that would not be discovered. He succeeded in this quite well. I believe Mano Ratki knew the doctor back in Marseille where his brother was killed. When Creux fled here to Madagascar, Ratki followed him. He became aware of the mysterious stranglings, and summoned me to investigate. Unfortunately, Dr. Creux decided he had to die before he could voice his suspicions."

"How could he have killed Ratki?" I asked. "He wasn't even at the village."

"Ah, but he was, my friend. The smear of brown greasepaint on that white winding sheet hinted that the killer might have darkened his skin color to pass as a native."

"I noticed the same sort of brown mark on Creux's arm this evening," I admitted. "I thought it was a birthmark."

"He simply hadn't had time to wash it all off. He probably parked his car some distance away, mingled with the villagers and got Ratki aside to kill him, hiding his body in that tomb. He was unlucky that it was discovered before the tomb was sealed again."

Captain Lightly gestured toward the gallon jugs of dark red liquid. "If we are to believe the labels, there is none of Ratki's blood here."

"Of course not. Creux had neither the time nor the equipment to extract it, away from his clinic."

"But the others died away from the clinic," the officer protested.

"They died here. Nafud was to be another exception tonight. Dr. Creux saw us on the pier earlier, examining the body of a dead warthog. He knew he had to kill the Arab before we questioned him."

"What could Nafud tell you?"

"He was bringing the warthogs over for the gambling matches, then killing them for their ivory tusks."

Captain Lightly shrugged. "It's not illegal. Only elephant ivory is protected."

"I know that," Simon replied. "But Creux cut out the tusks for him, to obtain the maximum amount of ivory. And while he was at it he drained the warthog's blood."

"What? Why would he do that?"

Suddenly I realized the horror of it before Simon Ark uttered the words. "Don't you see, Captain? The doctor replaced his victims' blood with that of a warthog."

Lightly's reaction at his words was a disbelieving snort. "That's impossible!"

"Is it? The warthogs weigh around two hundred pounds, so their bodies would have roughly the same amount of blood as an adult human. You'll remember that the doctor offered free AIDS testing here one night a week. When the patients returned for the results, he chose one who was free of AIDS and other diseases, strangled him, and immediately hooked up his body to the kidney dialysis machine he mentioned to us. The dead man's blood supply was removed and replaced with warthog blood. The needle marks on the body passed unnoticed on a dark-skinned workman whose arms already had a number of cuts and scrapes."

"An autopsy would certainly reveal that it was animal blood," I argued.

"It probably would if anyone suspected. The test is a simple one. But why would they test? The victims were strangled, remember, without a drop of blood being spilled. It may be that Creux came to Madagascar for the very reason that autopsies here might be less thorough than back in France, and animal blood was more readily available."

Captain Lightly examined the labels on the jugs. "How much from each victim?"

"Probably about six quarts," Simon answered, "depending upon the body weight."

"It's a strange world."

"It is indeed."

We flew home the following day, shortly after learning that Dr. Creux had committed suicide in his cell by biting through his wrists and bleeding to death.

THE COUNT'S MAILBOX
by
William Sanders

Dear Vlad:

Bad news, I'm afraid; our first response and it's a bounce. Don't worry. In all the years I've been an agent I've never handled a manuscript that didn't get at least a few turndowns at first.

As I told you, I don't usually like to send actual rejection letters to the client, because authors—especially first-timers—often get discouraged when they read them. However, since you were insistent on this point, enclosed is a copy of the letter from Delbert Cassidy at Wedgewood & Culpepper.

Sorry,
Nate

Dear Mr. Aronson:

Thanks for the chance to read Vlad Dracul's *MEMOIRS OF THE UNDEAD*. It has its moments, but I'm afraid it's not right for our list in its present form. The horror market, as you know, is very weak right now.

A suggestion: the story has all the basic elements—old castle, aristocratic European family, ancient curse, etc.—of a pretty good romance. If your client would consider rewriting the whole thing from the viewpoint of a *female* character, and using a feminine pen name, you might have better luck placing it.

Best,
Delbert

Dear Mr. Vladr:

Are you satisfied with your present life insurance coverage? Fill out the enclosed postpaid card for no-obligation information about policies tailored to fit *your* needs. No salesman will call.

> Cordially,
> J.C. Grimshaw Associates

Dear Vlad:

This is one of the reasons I don't like to do multiple simultaneous submissions—sometimes this means you also get multiple simultaneous rejections, and the effect can be pretty grim. Actually these didn't come in a bunch; I was gone for a couple of weeks, and when I came back they were all on my desk.

Hang in there—

> Nate

Dear Nate,

I *loved* this story! Vlad Dracul is obviously a *tremendously* talented new voice and I'll *certainly* want to see more work by him.

However, I've got to pass on the present submission. It's just not our cup of tea—too *gloomy* and *negative,* lacking in that *joy of life* that a Climax book must have. Sorry!

> Betsy Wetzl
> Senior Assistant Editor

Dear Mr. Aronson:

I'm returning Mr. Dracul's manuscript herewith. An interesting and unusual read, but not, I'm afraid, for Raintree Press.

The basic narrative device—telling a fictional story as if it were an actual memoir—is pretty much a cliché by now. Almost equally trite is the old trick of giving the narrator the same name as the author, The story itself seemed improbable and scientifically dubious, and I don't believe the historical background is factually accurate.

Good luck in placing MEMOIRS OF THE UN-DEAD elsewhere.

> Joseph Foley
> Executive Editor

Dear Mr. Arronsen:

Enclosed please find herewith MEMORIES OF THE DEAD by Val Drexel. We regret to report that we can not consider making an offer, as, by long standing policy, Apex Books does not publish science fiction.

Morton P. Lindblad
Assistant to the Associate
Editor

Dear Vlad:

Your letter cracked me up. I have to tell you that up till now I've had an impression of you as a pretty serious, even humorless guy—maybe because of your writing style. Boy, did I have you wrong! What an outrageous gag—asking me to cosign for a loan at the blood bank! Vlad, you're too much.

With a sense of humor like that, I know you won't let the enclosed couple of notes get you depressed. Be of courage; I'm working on something.

Nate

Dear Nathan,

Frankly, I don't see it. The basic story has possibilities, maybe as one of those psycho-serial-killer splatter books. But it would take a complete rewrite, and I wonder whether your client could bring it off. His narrator rambles on and on in this heavy-handed, old-fashioned prose—God, he sounds like Bela Lugosi or somebody!

Sorry I can't be more encouraging—

Jack Bernard
Editor

Nate—

What can I say? The guy sucks.

Marvin

Dear Mr. Dracul:

As per your inquiry: this company offers no policy specifically insuring against the eventuality you describe. However, "a wooden stake through the heart" would definitely fall within the category of fatal accidents, or else that of unlawful homicide, depending on the circumstances. Either of these would be fully covered under our basic comprehensive policy.

Feel free to call if you have further inquiries.

Bob Mizell

J.C. Grimshaw Associates

Dear Nate:

Sorry to have to return Vlad Dracul's *Memoirs Of The Undead*. As I told you at the HWA convention, horror is selling poorly and anything with a historical background is all but doomed. Tell your client not to take it personally; everyone's in the same boat. Only last week I had to turn down another good manuscript, from a doctor named Von Helsing. What can you do?

Barry

P.S. I really liked the way Dracul writes, though. Would he be interested in taking over the LEATHERSLAP-PER adult-Western series?

Vlad:

Hang onto your cape, big guy, we got an offer!

Rodney Duval of Grommet House loved *Memoirs* and wants it for their list. Between you and me, the advance isn't great, but I think you ought to go for it. Advances are never high for first-timers and the important thing is to get your work out there where it will be read and get some good critical ink. Next time for the big bucks.

I'll get back to you with the full details in a day or so. Meanwhile, congratulations!

Nate

Vlad:

Enclosed are the contracts, as amended. Please sign them and initial all changes, and get them back to me ASAP.

As to the other matter you brought up in your letter: no, Vlad, there's no way in hell you can sue the *Batman* people on any conceivable grounds. The concept was around in comic book form probably before you were born.

Nate

Dear Vlad:

Just a note to introduce myself. I'll be your editor on MEMOIRS OF THE UNDEAD—and, I hope, many more fine stories to come.

I can't tell you how excited we all are here at Grommet House to have the chance to publish such an original and brilliant work. My assistant, Marge Stansfield, was so taken by your manuscript that she made a copy to take home for her own reading.

I'll be getting back to you on various points. Right now, just one small problem area. Don't be offended, Vlad, but the consensus here is that your title just doesn't make it. We need something punchy, a title that grabs the attention and makes a statement.

We've tentatively settled on THE BLEEDING. However, if you've got any suggestions of your own, we'll certainly consider them.

Glad to have you on board—

Rodney Duval

P.S. Any chance you'll be in the city soon? How about doing lunch?

Vlad:

Just to keep you happy, I checked with the agency's lawyers. You *don't* have grounds for a lawsuit, Goddamn it, even if the Batman logo *does* look like your mother. Let it rest.

If I sound a little impatient, I just got off the phone with Rodney Duval and he told me about last night. You know, Vlad, I went to some trouble to set it up for you to have dinner with him. It's pretty rare for an editor to meet with an author outside the usual lunch-hours setting, but I explained to him that you don't get out much during daytime hours, and he was nice about it. Said he was used to writers who work all night and sleep all day.

So he took you to a nice Italian restaurant and—Jesus Christ, Vlad, so they put a lot of garlic in your pasta, so you've got some kind of allergy to garlic, what the hell? You could have just sent it back instead of making a big scene. Throwing the plate at the waiter, stalking out of the place with that damn cape wrapped over your face, listen, Vlad, you really made one hell of a bad impression there.

I'll tell you straight out: you pull something like that on the Letterman show, I won't answer for the consequences.

Nate

Dear Vlad:

Sorry to say none of your alternate title choices struck any sparks with the publishing committee. You'll be happy to know, though, that we've dropped THE BLEEDING which you disliked so much. Instead we're presently considering either TRANSYLVANIAN TROLLOPS or BITE ME, MY DARLING. Any preferences?

Rodney

Dear Mr. Dracul:

Please fill out the enclosed Author Information Form and return it. Also, we need a good clear eight-by-ten portrait of you for the dust jacket.

Derek Wilde
Publicity & Promo

Dear Mr. Dracul,

This is a private rather than official letter and I hope you won't say anything about it to Mr. Duval.

I am Mr. Duval's assistant at Grommet House and I've been reading your novel every night. I stayed up all last night finishing the last chapters and I plan to start all over again from Chapter One tonight. I can't tell you how powerfully your story has touched me. Somehow you seem to speak directly to something inside me that I never knew was there.

I know it's unprofessional to engage in private correspondence with an author like this, but I felt I had to tell you my feelings.

Faithfully,
Marge Stansfield

Vlad:

There's not much I can do about the title changes. The people who make those decisions are well above me in the corporate pecking order. The actual suggestion for the final approved title—RED FANGS, WHITE SKIN—was made by Bruce Sirius of the Art Department, who feels he can design a really dynamite foil-embossed cover around the concept. Everyone on the committee agreed immediately and enthusiastically.

The text itself is just fine. Nobody wants to change a thing. Just a few little details that I think need a bit of fine-tuning:

(1) The lead character's name is going to be very hard for most US readers to pronounce or even remember. It really needs to be changed to something like "Victor Dorian"—of course, then it wouldn't be the same as yours, but hey, don't you think that's kind of a corny gimmick anyway? I know Kinky Friedman gets away with it, but. . . .

(2) Consider moving the whole story to a more modern setting, and preferably in the USA. A castle in Transylvania (wherever that is—couldn't find it in my Funk & Wagnalls) makes the book resemble a Gothic and that might cause problems with the booksellers, who get nervous about crossing category lines.

How about setting it in a small New England town? You might be able to develop a good subplot: make this Doctor Von Helsing a dedicated local *cop,* and introduce this town council that doesn't want word of the killings to get out because it might hurt the tourist trade.

(3) The whole idea of this guy killing people by biting them on the neck sounds pretty implausible. Wouldn't it work better to have him use a machete or something?

(4) This kinky little bit where he bites women and they promptly become his devoted slaves—listen, Vlad, the feminists would *crucify* us on that one. You've got to change all the victims to men, and make sure they're white and *straight,* if you know what I mean. These days you can't be too careful.

Looking forward to reading your rewrite—
Rodney

Dear Mr. Dracul:

Obviously I didn't make myself clear about the portrait, but I never *dreamed* . . . Look, the standard size is eight by ten *inches,* and we normally prefer photos, though a top-quality line drawing might be acceptable.

Please tell me what I am to do with this enormous framed oil painting those men delivered. It's taking up half my office.

When you do get a proper photo taken, I'd suggest a more casual look—and for God's sake *lose the cape,* okay?
                                    Derek Wilde

Dear Vlad:

I hear what you're saying, but there's damn little I can do to help. The stuff you're talking about is pretty much par for the course in this business. I could tell you some real horror stories.

But I assure you, things would have been no different at any other house. Some of those guys would have ripped you off, too. Believe me, Vlad, there are some genuine bloodsuckers around.
                                    Nate
P.S. I called Rodney as you requested, and he assures me the check is in the mail.

Dear Mr. Dracul:

Thank you *so* much for your warm and gracious letter. I hadn't dared hope that you would even respond to my little note.

And yes, yes, *yes,* I'd *love* to come to your place for dinner some night. *Any* night. Just say when.
                                    Devotedly,
                                    Marge

Dear Mr. Vladracul:

Congratulations! You are one of the lucky winners in our contest! Come by the Goldentone studio nearest you to collect your prize: a FREE introductory session in our safe, scientific tanning rooms. Get that glowing California-look tan you've always wanted! Offer expires in 30 days, so HURRY!

Vlad:

Have you heard anything from Rodney Duval in the last few days? I can't seem to raise him on the phone; he's never in his office and he doesn't return my calls. Not unusual for Rodney of course (or any other editor) but I'm starting to wonder. Let me know if you hear from him, will you?

Nate

Dear Mr. Dracul:

   This is a difficult and awkward letter to have to write.

   Rodney Duval will no longer be your editor here at Grommet House.

   To be perfectly candid—and I rely on your discretion—Mr. Duval has simply disappeared. He has not shown up for work for days and he doesn't answer his home phone. We actually went so far as to check with the police, but no accident or crime victim answering his description has turned up in the Manhattan area.

   Rodney's duties will be taken over by his assistant, Ms. Margery Stansfield. I hope you will be able to work with her in the remaining parts of the editorial process. If you have problems, please call on me.

Sincerely,
Sylvia Ritter
Senior Managing Editor

My Darling Master,

   Rodney Duval will never again put his insolent paws on your splendid words. It was even easier than you promised. The fool never heard me behind him until the last second, and even then he didn't look around. His last words were, "Better make another pot of coffee, Marge, it's going to be a long night—"

   Never fear, they will not find him. I hid the body where it will be safe from any chance of detection—in the mailroom, under a pile of incoming manuscripts. Just to make sure it would rest undisturbed, I stacked a few months' worth of royalty statements and advance checks on top.

   And Bruce Sirius—he of the tacky title changes—is to meet me this evening for an unscheduled after-hours conference in Rodney's office. (Pardon me, in *my* office, aha!) He will be even easier, believe me—although that stupid paisley scarf he always wears may pose a minor problem.

   Every hour will be an eternity until I see you again, my love—but then we *have* eternity now, don't we?

Obediently,
Marge

TOM RUDOLPH'S LAST TAPE
by
John Maclay

My name's Tom Rudolph, and I'm a private eye. That's how I usually begin the stories I tell. Then I fill in my background: pushing forty, thinning dark hair, cheap suit, and a hat. A stint in the Marines, office in an old building downtown, oak desk, worn leather couch that doubles as my bed. Partiality to bourbon, .38 in a shoulder holster. My world, a two-block stretch of cheap hotels, pool halls, pinball arcades, lunch counters, and nude bars. A part of town that's a throwback to the 1950s: as, of course, am I.

Next, on the reel-to-reel tape deck I use, I go into the case. Like the one about the slasher I caught, and the brave young woman who decoyed for me. Or the work I did for a guy who had mob ties but a heart of gold. Or how I caught the book thief, or crashed a car on purpose to kill a crook as a favor for my girl. Or the one about Monique, the woman in blue. . . .

Yeah, that's how I begin. But, though the reels are turning, the wheels in my head aren't, not tonight. Because there's something wrong with old Tom, and it's not too much bourbon. You ever have a time, maybe in February, when you go on day after gray day, not realizing that you're not yourself? Then something wakes you up, and your real life seems like a history that belongs to somebody else? "In a real dark night of the soul, it's always three o'clock in the morning, day after day." Yeah, I had some college, too. But this time, maybe you won't come out of it.

I get up from my desk, out from under the circle of

light from the forty-watt bulb, and walk to my fifth-floor window. The city's still there; cold rain, lights reflected by the slick asphalt. That's a start. And I must still be here to see it: a start, as well. I stretch, flop down on the worn leather cushions. What you do, then, is trace it back. Yeah, you trace it back. . . .

Monique was a nude dancer—okay, a hooker—who made good. Long blonde hair, beautiful face, smooth creamy skin, body more like a model's than a B-girl's. Wore blue dresses all the time, cut low above, high below. I'd had her twice, and both were milestones in my life; she made love with a fineness I still could hardly believe. What do you say about breasts like hers, legs like hers, a place like hers . . . damn.

Anyway, Monique hooked up with a guy named Kelty, a rich contractor in his fifties. Even stole him away from his wife, married him; I was a party to that. Saw her ride off into the sunset, wished her all the best, thought I'd never see her again. And didn't . . . until a week ago.

When it all started—yes. When Kelty turned up killed.

My old friend Sergeant Crandall called me over. He was a throwback like me: trench coat, hat, even a little cigar. Met him standing in a puddle of water at one of Kelty's building sites. Nodded a greeting, followed his stare to the bottom of the excavation. Where a guy a lot like us was lying. Except he was dead.

But it was the way he was dead; I saw it right off. Face and hands white as fish, even the eyes sort of drained. It wasn't that cold, either. Something was wrong.

"You did some work for this stiff, didn't you, Tom," Crandall stated.

"Nope, for his bride. He almost killed me for boffing her in the process, but since I helped her into his arms, he let it go."

"Whatever. But what we've got here, Rudolph, is motive—his dough, for Chrissake—opportunity—his wife—all of it, but no cause of death." Crandall shrugged. "Or I oughta say, a cause so weird it makes me want to retire at last."

I shifted my feet out of the puddle; the police department wouldn't buy me new shoes. And I let it ride that he thought Monique did it. "So tell me," I said.

He rattled it off. "No heart attack. No fall into this big hole. No gunshot wound. No knife. Doc says no poison.

"Nope, this Kelty had every drop of blood drained out of him instead. And we still can't figure how."

The coroner's men were bringing the body up now, slipping in the mud, and I couldn't see how, either. Nothing visible on the neck, like with a stuck pig. Nothing on the backs of the wrists; only fools thought you cut the fronts. And no blood anywhere: he must have been dumped, or staggered in.

I looked at Crandall. "So what the hell do you want me to do about it, Sarge?"

He put a hand on my shoulder. "Simple, Tom. You know the merry widow. Get close to her again. See what you can find."

Without mentioning money, he walked away. But he must have known Monique well enough to figure I'd be drawn into the web.

I found her early that evening, in a big house in the suburbs. Red brick Tudor, circular driveway, old trees, the whole ball of wax. My '79 Toyota sputtered to a stop, eyed condescendingly by the butler at the door. Monique was in a huge room with a fireplace, sheets of rain hitting the leaded windows. She wasn't wearing black, but her dress was a darker shade of blue.

"You've done pretty well for yourself," I said, settling into a chair. I took a pull on the straight Wild Turkey she poured me.

"Yes, Tom," her low voice answered. And that voice, plus the way she looked, hit me right between the legs.

If Monique had been nineteen or so when I first saw her, and the best-looking B-girl in the world, now her twenty-three and her new life made her the best in the world, period. She was centerfold, movie star, Society woman, all in one. Her classy yet sensual face, breasts, tail, those long legs ... oh, hell.

"They think I did it, don't they?" she sighed, arranging herself across from me.

"You always were up front," I said. "Yeah, they do."

She fixed me with her blue eyes. "Well, then it's up to me to put you right. I've been thinking about it myself." She paused. "Maybe if we think like the killer, if

I can get you thinking like the killer ... isn't that how it's done?"

I didn't really know what she meant, not then. But I didn't care.

Because she was rising like a goddess, pulling me up ... leading my hard-used body to the hallway, to some wide, winding stairs. To a room that was all blue ruffles, and a bed the size of a football field.

Where, with a smile, she got naked as the day I'd first seen her dancing, and took me to heaven again.

"Damn, your husband just died this morning," I said afterward, stroking her spun-gold mound.

Monique shrugged, playing with her long blonde hair. "You know me well enough, Tom. I hooked, I even had a guy or two die in the saddle. No point not letting life go on."

"Right," I answered. When I was lying with her, everything was all right with me.

We got dressed, and she saw me downstairs to the door. We hadn't done much "thinking" together, just boffing, but already I was feeling sort of different. If Monique had killed Kelty, if I could find out the all-important "how", I wasn't in as big a hurry to do it now. Hell, I wasn't in much of a hurry to do anything; I drove back to the city feeling a bit drowsy, drained. That was when I should have known what was happening; thinking back on it, that was when the change began.

When I got to my office, Sergeant Crandall was waiting. He was sprawled in my swivel chair, muddy feet propped up on my oak desk.

"How the hell did you get in here?" I grunted.

"Credit card. You really oughta get a better lock, Rudolph."

I poured us both an Early Times, sat down on the couch across from him. "You find out anything more from the body?"

"Naw. Not a mark on him. 'Cept for a couple of shaving cuts, guy was clean as a whistle." He took a sip. "You?"

"Nope. If the merry widow did it, she's cool as ice." I paused. "Like she was our age or older, not a creamy-skinned twenty-three."

Crandall eyed me, got up to go. "You be careful, Tom.

Wouldn't want it said I got you back into something, if you know what I mean."

I smiled weakly. "Yeah. Okay."

I went down and got a bite at one of the lunch counters, then shot a little pool. But I felt tireder than I had in years, so I hit the couch at ten p.m. Must have slept like a baby, too, because the next thing I knew it was daylight, at least nine. There was traffic in the street, and my phone was ringing.

I stumbled over. "Tom Rudolph Investigations."

"Hello, Tom? It's Monique. I wondered if we might get together for some more thinking tonight."

Even over the phone, that low voice had me. But I knew I literally wouldn't be up for her again, not that soon. I felt half unconscious already, without her making me that way in her arms.

"Listen," I wheezed. "Give me a couple of days. Got some work to do."

"Well, all right, Tom. I want you, but with Kelty gone, I do have all the time in the world."

So I spent those days around the office, clearing up some paperwork on other cases. But I still felt a little detached. It was small things: dropping a pencil, nicking myself while shaving and not even noticing it until later. When the night rolled around, though, I went to the woman in blue.

This time the butler was gone, and she opened the door in her underwear. I couldn't believe how great she looked: blonde hair over one eye like Veronica Lake, the tiniest powder-blue bra and panties. Her high round breasts, flat belly, exposed behind, barely-hidden mound made me rise like gangbusters, despite my tiredness.

We did it on a soft couch in the paneled library. I was aware of some ancient leather books, but not much else: she seemed to carry me far off into space and time; like they said in the 1960s, to put me through changes. I didn't even know when it was over; I must have gone on to sleep. Woke up with a stiff neck, still lying there, and Monique sitting nude in a chair opposite.

"I think you're beginning to know something, Tom," she said mysteriously.

She was right. If I didn't know it, I sensed it, and that

was good enough for me. Maybe later I'd have doubts, but then. . . .

So I spent the rest of the night with her, then ran the Toyota back downtown. And, in the predawn weirdness, the patches of gray fog I met on the road, I decided a couple of things. One, that I'd tell Crandall I couldn't find out anything; get him once and for all off Monique's case.

And two, that I'd see her, like a charm, for another, a third time.

I slept the next day away. Didn't feel hungry somehow, not even thirsty for bourbon. Did go out about twilight for a game of pinball, a rare steak, and some fries. Wandered down to a nude bar; sat and nursed a red wine, unusual for me. Watched the naked flesh onstage, was surprised to find my mouth was watering. Thought I was too old, too hardened for that.

Then I walked wearily back to the office, pulled my swivel chair over to the window, turned out the lights and sat watching the city. It was still raining, and the gray soup matched the inside of my mind.

But I wasn't sleepy. No, all night, I wasn't sleepy.

A couple of days passed that way. Crandall did phone, and I got rid of him. Then Monique called, and, like a lamb to the slaughter, I went out there one more time.

She met me wearing a long, flowing robe, so dark blue it at first looked black. Her creamy skin, what I could see of it, had an unaccustomed pallor. I reached out, thinking to lead her up to the bedroom or at least to the library couch. But she shook her blonde head no. With a mysterious smile, an upraised finger, she had me follow her someplace else.

To a plain door beneath the winding main staircase, and down some plain wooden steps. To the cool, stone basement, lit by a few hanging bulbs.

To the corner where it was hidden, behind some old trunks. The coffin, that looked old as time itself.

I must have shrunk back; I even reached for my .38. But Monique took it out of my hand, flipped open the cylinder, let the bullets fall to the packed-earth floor. Then, with a graceful motion to her throat, she cast aside her robe and stood before me in all her beautiful, unabashed nudity. And smiled again, wider than I'd ever seen her smile before.

Though I'd try to deny it later, that was when I really knew. Knew that Kelty must have known eventually, too. No wonder she'd been working in a nude bar, where there were endless men to almost casually ... kiss. No wonder, in the cold, modern city, she'd soon hooked up with one who'd been able to support her in the style to which she'd been long accustomed.

"But why ...?" I gasped. My bowels were loose, knees weakening, yet not from desire.

Now Monique did put her hands on my shoulder; I inhaled a strange perfume. "It's simple, Tom," she replied. "He was no good, only a means to an end. When he found out after a while, I made his second time ... his last." She paused. "My, did I have a feast that night; I was sick all the next day, before you came to me! Then I just had the butler—one like me—help me put the body in the Rolls and dump it where it was found."

She threw back her classy head, laughed. There they were, fully revealed in all their sharp, twin glory, and any doubt was gone.

"But don't worry, Mr. Tom Rudolph," Monique concluded, her low voice full of the allure of a thousand years. "You see, I've always liked you. Maybe it's because you're a throwback to the past; I know a lot about that. So when I saw you were on my case, I decided to give you something, something precious. To let you live, instead. To get you to think like me, and then...."

"To make me like you are," I replied flatly. And, for the life of me, I knew I could never resist the woman in blue.

I was dimly conscious of a ceremony, there in the dim cellar, in the bed of the silk-lined coffin. It involved a coupling below, one even more fantastic, mind-altering, than what I'd had before with her perfect body. But what took place above was even more important. As, with a third and final set of "shaving cuts," Monique not only took, but gave.

Then I slept. And woke, but didn't wake. The butler must have driven my car and me back to the city, because I found myself on my worn leather couch, the dawn coming in the dirty window. With a preternatural quickness, I got up, pulled the shade down.

And remembered my lover's half-humorous parting words. "Never go out in the daylight, Tom. But that shouldn't bother you. You always were a *noir* type, anyway."

. . . So I lie here, listening to the run-out tape flap, flap, flap on the reel. This part won't be recorded, nor the other cases—damn, how many thousands will there be?—that I solve in the years ahead. Like the man said, it wouldn't be prudent. The cases I solve, as I go around the night city with my thinning hair, my cheap suit and hat . . . my close-mouthed smile. In the purgatory of my neighborhood, with its cheap hotels, pool halls, pinball arcades, lunch counters . . . and nude bars. Stopping, when I hunger, to kiss a hooker on the neck. A true existential hero, goddamn.

Yeah, there are times when you go on day after gray day, not realizing that you're not yourself. And maybe you won't come out of it, one of those times. Even if you can trace it back, find out what happened.

But there's nothing really wrong with you; suddenly you feel stronger than the ages. So you don't trace it back anymore, don't deny it anymore.

You've got a new self now.

You go on.

THE TURNING
by
Jack Ketchum

In three years the City had changed again.

You could almost smell the blood in the air.

Bad blood.

He walked down Riverside from 82nd. For six blocks no one had passed him. The cool night breeze drifted off the Hudson. Across the street the park was gray and empty in the moonlight.

This area was one of the loveliest in New York. It still was. Old, newly-renovated townhouses along one side, the park along the other. The residents, who were extremely well-off, saw to it that the sidewalks were kept mostly clean. At night there was little traffic.

But look. Here.

He had to walk around her. Her filthy skirt hitched up to her fat pasty thighs. Cap pulled down over dull brown matted hair. She lay asleep, her toothless mouth wide open—a foul, black hole beneath the streetlight.

He walked by.

It occurred to him that this had been coming for a very long time. The wealthy—or almost wealthy—and the poor living in wholly separate camps, paths barely intersecting. The middle class, such as they were, little more than badly disguised servants to the rich. Insulated by the same cloak of privilege that draped the shoulders of their masters.

You could no longer refer to the "growing numbers" of the poor. The poor were multitudes.

Even here. On this quiet street.

And not surprisingly, he heard them before he saw them.

Ahead of him. Not far.

He walked slowly, with a measured stride. He was in no hurry to see.

They were across the street in the park at 78th Street, the old man helpless against a tree, the four boys going at him with fists and stones. The homeless man pleading, the sense of his words lost in broken teeth and blood and bone because the tall boy was shoving a rock into his mouth at the same time—no, a piece of jagged macadam from the street—while two others hooted their encouragement and the smallest of the boys, thin and blonde and wiry, twelve maybe, crushed his left kneecap with three rapid blows from a metal bat. The bat gleamed in the moonlight. The man collapsed, shrieking, the chunk of macadam tumbling from his mouth out onto the grass.

He did not need to watch more.

There were many of these groups now.

Not all of them children.

At 72nd Street he turned East toward Broadway. As always in the City, a single turn, a different block, and you were in another world entirely.

Here there was plenty of traffic. Horns blared. Fire engines sudden in the distance. People passed by without a glance. While he studied faces. Hard young women, soft young men. Both with money. Barely able to conceal their fury that they did not have more. Shopowners stern and forbidding standing in doorways, defending their mercantile fortresses. And the elderly. Barely hanging on, having lived too long. Fear etched deep into pale brows and faces.

As though they knew. Knew in their ancient bones.

What was coming.

And knew they had helped create it.

And everywhere the homeless. Standing at banks like hopeless sentries, on streetcorners like whores, sprawled, squatting, kneeling on broken limbs and no limbs at all, strong and crippled and drunk and crazy, young and old and impossible to guess how old.

Too cowed, most of them, even to beg anymore.

He felt the turning.

There. That one.

He crossed Broadway, walking toward Columbus.

That one, yes, but not this.

She was beautiful. Perhaps that was why the owner of
the bar allowed her to sit there. Perhaps her beauty off-
set her situation and could be counted upon to not
overly offend the owner's patrons. Perhaps the man retained a shred of pity.

There was a dirty white cast on her right leg. A taped
wooden crutch across her lap. Her clothes were too small
but they were relatively clean. An empty fast-food coffee
cup stood on the sidewalk beside her.

She could not have been more than twenty. Her skin
was the deep rich black of the islands, tight and soft-
looking over her whippet-thin frame. Her eyes were
wide, brown and luminous. The eyes of a doe trapped
in headlights. Permanently startled, and fearful.

They looked fearfully at him now as he stopped beside her.

He saw that she was afraid to speak. Knew she would
not speak. That it was necessary for her to be careful.
He could already feel the stares of passersby, their disgust with him for stopping. He crouched down.

"Are you hungry?"

"Yes, sir. I am."

Her voice was soft and tired. It reminded him of the
voice of someone who has just lost a loved one and now,
finally, has no more tears left, who has been crying for
days and who is now exhausted.

"Your leg. What happened to it?"

She almost smiled. She didn't quite dare.

"Stupid thing. I fell right off that curb here."

She pointed.

"Right into ... whaddya call it? The bars. Over the ... ?"

"The grate? Over the sewer?"

"That's right. I guess I wasn't looking. Fixed me up
at Emergency. But they wouldn't let me stay."

"You have no place to stay?"

"No, sir. There's a place down on West End will keep
me for a week, but you need twenty dollars for that and
I ain't got twenty dollars. If I had a place, even for a
week, then I got an address. Can't nobody get a job
without an address. Me, I got nothin'."

He reached for his wallet.

He was certain. Not her.

Maybe she'd even survive this. Maybe. Who knew.

"Here's twenty."

Her smile alone was worth the twenty. He thought, what beautiful teeth.

She squealed over the twenty like a little girl. It was as though he'd given her a hundred.

"Thank you! God, thank you!"

She leaned over and wrapped her arms around him, hugged him, and kissed him on the cheek.

Behind him a woman's eyes stabbed hard at them both. They ignored her.

"Bet you never been kissed by a black girl before," she laughed.

"You'd be wrong," he said. "Now I want you to get out of here, all right? Go to that place you were talking about. I don't want to see you out here again. You understand?"

"Yes, sir. You know I will. God! Thank you, sir, thank you."

He helped her up. Stood watching her hobble toward West End Avenue. She didn't look back.

"Asshole," someone muttered behind him.

The man walked by and shot him an angry glance over his shoulder.

Not even a man yet, he thought. *A boy. A boy who thinks he's a man because his job pays him $100,000 a year plus bonuses.*

The boy would be lucky to survive exactly what and who he was about to pass, there on the corner of Columbus.

That one.

He lay up against the streetlight. Babbling madly to whatever voices babbled back inside him.

He was already changing.

There were more and more who were changing now. And not just the crazy ones.

He had seen it happen once before. A long, long time ago. When the collective will and consciousness of an entire people had grown intense enough, black enough, angry enough, fearful enough and focused enough to rend deep into the nature of human life as it had existed up till then, all that dark cruel energy focused like a laser on an entire class, transforming them in reality into how they were perceived and imagined to be almost metaphorically.

In the past it had been the rich—the ruling class who were perceived as vampires. Feeding off the poor and destitute.

Now it was the poor themselves.

And it wouldn't be long at all before everyone in the City and in half the world for that matter would be seeing what he'd been seeing for quite a while from his own unique perspective, recognizing exactly what was happening because it had happened to him.

Because last time it had *been* him. Him and a handful of others. Nobles, kings, princes.

This time, of course, they would not be merely a handful.

This time they would be legion.

He could see them everywhere.

Turning.

Changing.

He hoped the girl with the beautiful smile and the fine, warm skin would not be one of them.

He had always enjoyed walking New York. He would have continued walking, but it was late by now and he was hungry. At Columbus he hailed a taxi.

A taxi was safer than a limousine.

Limousine drivers always felt the need to be ingratiating. To talk to you.

Whereas cabbies almost never bothered to glance back at anything other than traffic through their rear-view mirrors—and that was important.

You almost weren't there.

"The Four Seasons," he said.

He had a reservation.

To dine with a beautiful recently-divorced real-estate heiress and then return to her East Side penthouse apartment filled with drawings by Vlaminck, Emile Nolde, and Gauguin, originals, all of them, twenty-one stories above the East River, with a built-in steambath and sauna.

Unlike most of the world, he preferred to feed upon his own.

YOU'LL CATCH YOUR DEATH
by
P.N. Elrod

The wind tearing off the lake was a vindictive blast of pure misery that should have stayed at the pole where it belonged. Black water lapped restlessly at the shore, merged with the sand, and turned to ice as I watched. The place was as bleak and lonely as they come, but I didn't mind and was well past the point of having second thoughts about being here. I'd returned to face whatever demons it had to offer, except they'd all gone home by now, and the ones in my head were slowly fading with each day's dose of oblivion. The solitude felt good.

Things had been rough for the last few nights. I had killed, again, and had come close to being killed, again, and in that damned lake, again. And though my partner, Escott, seemed to thrive on that kind of action, I still wasn't recovered enough to be normal yet.

Bullshit.

The fact was that I was all too normal. I was glad to be alive and not a bit sorry the other man was dead. He could stay at the bottom of the lake forever with the rest of the slime and good riddance. The water splashed at my feet, a vast and ignorant ally, enemy, murderer, and midwife, and a great keeper of secrets. It was welcome to mine.

I drank in a breath of damp air sharp enough to cut iron and held it in until the edge was gone. Releasing it slowly, the wind whisked it straight from my lips into the endless sky to mix and travel and grow clean and cold once more. Perhaps I could do the same by spreading my arms and gradually becoming transparent until the wind swept me away to God knows where.

Ah, nuts. I'd probably just soar up the bluff to the road like a lost balloon and smash into my car where it sat parked on the shoulder. That would send me solid again fast enough. I didn't quite laugh at the idea, but managed a smile, and that felt good, too. Time to go back home and tell Escott he could take what was becoming a chronic worried look off his face. I was going to be all right.

Ready to leave, I glanced up and down the beach one last time as though crossing a street. It didn't seem so bleak now and the high clouds reflected back plenty of light from the city, not that I needed much to see well at night. My changed condition had its compensations, otherwise I would have completely missed the figure struggling along the shoreline from the east.

Fisherman? Not at one in the morning and in this weather. Fresh air fiend out for a walk? Then he was bug-eyed crazy.

The figure came closer. It was a woman, on the small side, and looking pretty done in as she stumbled over the slick rocks and sand. She wore a simple dark dress and light shoes and nothing more. No coat, hat, or gloves. She was all hunched over, arms folded tight, hands clutching her bare elbows to hoard any warmth coming from her slight body. Thinking that she'd been in some kind of an accident, I started toward her.

"Hey, lady, you need some help?"

Not the best of introductions, and not much good since she didn't seem to hear any of it. The wind and water noises had drowned out my voice. Stepping up my pace, I yelled another question at her. She stopped, swaying a little, and looked behind her. The wind grabbed her wild brown hair and plastered it over her face as she turned, creating a vertical part along the back of her unprotected head.

"Over here," I shouted.

She snapped around, clawing hair from her eyes. Uncertain for a second, she stiffened when she caught sight of me emerging from the general darkness. I glimpsed a very young face burned dead white from the cold. Terror and torment flashed over it like a bolt of lightning, then she whirled to her left, away from the lake, toward the road, and tried to run. She didn't get far; the sand and uneven clumps of dead grass slowed her too much. I caught up easily enough, but kept a couple yards distance between us so as not to spook her any more.

I called at her again, and she stopped as abruptly as she'd started, gaping at me. She looked like a crazy woman, all right, but fear can do that to you.

"Who . . . ?" was all she gasped out. She didn't have enough breath left to finish the question.

"My name's Fleming. You need some help?" I spread my empty hands, trying to look earnest, harmless, and honest all at the same time. It seemed to work; she took a half-step toward me with an expression on her face like a lost soul who'd just gotten a last-second reprieve from hell. Then a kind of small shriek came out of her that twisted her mouth and made it ugly. In sudden silence, she and the rest of the universe flashed up into a blaze of silver light. The earth bucked once as though to get rid of me and damn near succeeded. I sprawled over its lurching surface. Sand grated against my teeth and tongue.

She screamed again. This one had more throat to it and a double dose of anguish. Nice of her to be concerned. Behind and above me, a man snarled at her to shut up. She did. Then he called her an obscene name and told her to get out of the way. There was a lot of raw venom in his tone. She whipped off without another word.

He turned me over, cursing under his breath the way other people nervously whistle. He had a tough jaw in a lean, prematurely jaded face. He wore an old red plaid hunting jacket and hat that weren't really enough to protect him from this kind of cold, but it was more than the girl had had on.

The silver light focused down to a single excruciating spot of pain on the back of my skull. Jesus, what had I done to deserve this? It had been wood, of course. I recognized its particular agony all too well. If he'd hit me with something metal or a rock, I wouldn't be lying paralyzed at his feet, but he'd used wood—probably the stock of the rifle he carried. While I'd been concentrating on the girl, he'd slipped up behind and. . . .

Not a hard hit, just enough to knock an ordinary man unconscious, but he didn't know that I was different and my fixed and staring eyes alarmed him. With his teeth, he tore off a glove to feel for a pulse in my neck and swore again when he couldn't find one. Had I been able to speak, I'd have joined him in the chorus because my head hurt like hell and pain always seems worse when you can't give it verbal expression. Well, in a few minutes he was in for the surprise of his life, if he hung around that long.

He didn't. The bastard took off. Not after the girl, but up toward the road. I moaned inwardly with disgust and tried to move.

Too soon for that. Much too soon. Take it easy, Jack, there's not much you can do about it until the shock passes away.

The wind rolled over me, plucking random grains of sand from my cheeks. Some flew to lodge right in my eyes. I couldn't move to rub them clean. I couldn't even blink. Shit . . . that *hurt*. Tears welled, clouding my vision. They helped a little. The excess water leaked from my eyes, traced past my temples and into my hair, leaving behind threads of chill. Soon I might end up with tiny icicles clinging to the skin.

The man was returning. I heard the air rasping in and out of his throat first, then the awkward, irregular tread of his feet as he came down the rise from the road. He probably still had the rifle, and its weight would throw off his balance. I picked up the sound of another person following him.

"Here," he said. "He's right there." His voice was high and taut with near-panic now that he had someone with whom to share his fear. They reached the bottom, stopping just a few paces out of my field of vision. The bright beam of a flashlight played over my face, my body.

"Give me that thing," ordered the newcomer. A woman. She had a deeper, more mature voice than the girl I'd encountered, and it was rough with impatience and raw nerve. The light jumped as it was transferred to another hand.

"I think he's dead," the man told her unhappily.

"Shut up, Lloyd, and cover him," she said, and I heard him unsling the rifle from his shoulder.

The woman came closer cautiously, as though my utter, and apparently final, stillness might somehow contaminate her. After a moment she knelt within my sight, though I couldn't focus on her because of the sand and tears. From what I could see, she looked as tough as the man. The hard jaw was slightly softened on her, but just as distinctive. She wore a cheap cloth coat with a shabby fur collar; a heavy scarf was wrapped around her head and tied firmly under her chin, completely covering her hair. Her expression was as cold as the wind booming over us.

She stretched out a gloved hand as though to caress the side of my face. Her fingertips brushed at the tear tracks from my smarting eyes. She aimed the beam into them again, blinding me for a few seconds.

"Ellie?" His voice was thin. "Is he ... ?"

Ellie removed one glove as Lloyd had done before and sought out the big vein in my throat, pressing hard. She withdrew her hand after a few seconds, then started undoing the buttons of my overcoat.

"What're you doing?" Lloyd demanded.

A question I might reasonably ask myself if I hadn't already guessed the answer. She opened the coat wide and pawed at the clothes beneath. Her head ducked from view and lay heavily on my chest, ear flat over my heart. She listened for a long time before straightening.

"You killed him," she concluded matter-of-factly.

Lloyd was anything but contrite about it, to judge by his language. "What'll we do with him?"

"We don't have to do anything."

"But he's *dead*."

"So? You wanta call a cop?"

"You know what I mean," he snarled.

"Yeah, so think about it, then. That's probably his car up there off the road. When someone finds him, they'll figure he stopped to take a pee, slipped on something, and cracked his head open. There's nothing to tie him to what we're doing."

"But what about Susan?"

"Nothing's changed. We go on as before. You think she'll talk after tonight?"

"Suppose the cops—"   •

"Lloyd, shut the hell up. There's *nothing* between us and this guy. He's a total stranger who had the bad luck to slip on a rock in the wrong place. You did us all a favor when you hit him."

Like hell you did, I thought through the pain.

"If you want to do something," she continued, "go find that idiot wife of yours before she runs into somebody else and really spoils things."

"What?"

"She ran off over there. Go get her!"

Probably better at action than thought, Lloyd obeyed, loping away in the indicated direction. Ellie frowned after him, then looked at me with equal displeasure.

Or so I assumed.

Ellie snapped off the flashlight. She waited a moment, probably to get used to the dark, then leaned closer. I took in more of her face this time: the wide-set eyes, narrow nose, broad, sensual mouth, the lips parted just enough to show the edges of her teeth. The image writhed in and out of my swimming vision.

Her fingers touched my face again, cold, tickling a little because of their lightness. She brushed at the sand on my cheeks, carefully sweeping away each grain.

What are you up to, lady? I wondered uncomfortably.

As if she'd heard my thought, she paused, her head coming up for a furtive look in Lloyd's direction. She stood, going out of range, pacing one way, another, as though searching. Over the wind, I could hear her breath begin to quicken. Out of fear? Maybe a car was coming. Maybe even a cop. A cop would come in very handy about now.

No such luck. She came back, kneeling very close by my side, taking one more look around. The clean line of her neck escaped the collar of her coat; I was abruptly aware of the blood pounding within her, the suppressed excitement that drove it.

Hers was not a frown of displeasure, but quite the opposite, coupled with intense concentration.

Her eyes dropped to me again. They were bright with ... anticipation? Greed? Either way, I didn't like what was there.

One more flick of her nail on my skin. Deliberate.

She licked her lips, wetting them thoroughly. Then she lowered her head. Our lips touched, sliding over one another, cold as shards of ice on the lake. Her tongue eased into my mouth and leisurely churned against mine. It probed and curled along the roof of my mouth and raked over my teeth. It forced itself deeper until I should have gagged, only I couldn't. I was inert flesh. Dead flesh, to her. Safe to play with, safe to. . . .

The probing turned to suction. She drew hard on my tongue, taking it into her own mouth, sucking on it like a piece of sweet fruit. She teased and nipped and pulled it out as far as she could before releasing it at last. It dropped free, bulging from my mouth as if I'd been strangled. She settled heavily on my chest, head erect, and muscles stiff with inner tension for several crucial seconds. Her hands, like claws, dug into my shoulders as she failed to hold back a soft moan escaping from her open lips. Her teeth clamped together, turning the moan to a sharp sibilant. Then, like an exaggerated sigh, she emptied her lungs completely.

Her returning breath was uneven, but I sensed that she was done with me. Or herself. After a few long moments, she was under control once more, her eyes still bright, but calm. With an icy fingertip, she pressed my tongue back where it belonged and sealed my lips shut. Our Secret.

She pulled my clothes together and buttoned my coat back up to make things look right to whoever found the body. Finished, she rose and brushed sand from her knees, peering down the beach where Lloyd had gone.

"Find her?" she yelled at him. I didn't catch the reply, but she did, and must have found it pretty exasperating. With language similar in ripeness to Lloyd's, she went after him. Just like that.

She'd gotten what she'd wanted. In times to come, she would return to this beach again and again to remember how she'd shared a kiss with death and walked away in hidden triumph.

I wanted to vomit.

Tears still seeped from my eyes. Ellie might have at least closed them up along with everything else. The clouds and stars swam in and out of focus like fish in dark water. The stinging from the sand lessened somewhat. Maybe it was finally washing away. A minute or two later and I was able to blink again. It was incredibly sweet and soothing to blot out the sand and wind and other, less pleasant things. I would never take that often ignored reflex action for granted ever again.

Willfully distracted by eye problems, I was taken by surprise when my fingers suddenly twitched with returning life. Good and better. Muscles in my legs began to flex, a promise of full recovery to come, but like any healing, the process was taking too long. I knew for certain that the girl, Susan, had no time to spare. On the drive out here I'd listened to the weather on the radio. The temperature was a lethal fourteen degrees. Couple that with the high wind. . . .

I lurched over on my belly. Long after I'd stopped, my head still felt as if it was turning. Big silver balls danced behind my eyes, interfering with my view of the beach. I tried to blink them away like the sand, but it didn't work as well.

Blood would have helped. It always did when I was hurt. Why the hell hadn't I stopped at the Stockyards earlier? With a body flushed full of hot red life, the sock I'd taken from Lloyd might not have affected me as much. On the other hand, I'd have missed Susan completely.

I crawled messily forward through the damp sand, moving toward the lake. It was instinctual, I think. I've heard that wounded animals are drawn to water. Halfway there, I'd progressed to a stagger, but collapsed to my knees just at the shore's edge. Like Lloyd and Ellie before me, I fumbled off a glove with my teeth. I dipped into the searing cold water and gently slopped some against the swelling lump on the back of my head.

That woke me up completely—like a five alarm fire between my ears with all the bells going off at once. I hissed at the jolt and swore with quiet sincerity. It was a toss-up whether the cure was worse than the injury, but the overall pain abated . . . in microscopic increments. When the ringing toned down, I dipped into the water again to clean the last of the sand from my eyes.

Lloyd was due for a big payback. In an amazingly short time I planned out a number of destructive things I'd do once I got my hands on him. Topping the list was

a new use for that damned wooden rifle stock in relation
to his rectal opening. After that, I could toss him in the
lake to find out if he knew how to swim.

As for Ellie ... well, I wasn't responsible for her kinks,
but she sure as hell could have kept them to herself.
Though absolutely unable to drink anything but blood,
I stooped and pulled in a huge gulp of lake water and
rinsed it through my mouth. Impulsively, I swallowed,
knowing what would happen.

The stuff struck the bottom of my stomach like a
sword of frost. I took in another gulp and got it down.
The sword twisted as though alive. Another drink, and
it started cutting at me. I closed my throat off to keep
the stuff down as long as possible.

Not long, though. The sword cut deeply, doubling me
over with cramp and then everything came spewing out.
I'd wanted to vomit, this was the only way. It was this
or carry along the slick touch of Ellie's lips forever. I
needed this cleansing, this symbolic rejection of what
she'd done to me.

I spat the last drops into the lake. It accepted the
bubbly spittle with hardly a murmur. I rubbed my mouth
on my sleeve, wiping away the last trace of Ellie's touch.
Clean. With some help. I regarded the endless stretch
of shifting shadows with something like wonder. Sky,
earth, and especially water, ancient, but alive. A different kind of life to be sure, but wise and tolerant of one
man's little troubles.

Clean. Time to go to work.

I got to my feet, still woozy, but wanting a good look
around. Lloyd was now an indistinct figure far down on
the beach. He moved fast, but erratically, circling and
doubling in his tracks. Ellie stood on the road in a spot
where she could overlook most of the area. She had the
flashlight on and helpfully stabbed its pale beam in
Lloyd's direction. Susan was nowhere in sight, which was
just as well for her. Then the sickening thought washed
over me that she'd dropped in her tracks someplace to
curl up for a last, freezing sleep.

And I'd offered to help. Pulling the glove back on, I
plodded unsteadily back to where I'd fallen. My crumpled and forgotten hat marked the spot. Punching out
the dents, I got the idea of putting myself in the girl's

place to try and guess where she might have gone while Ellie and Lloyd had been busy with me. How much time had they taken? Had it been enough for her to get back up to the road? It's something I might have tried in hope of flagging down a car or finding better cover on the other side.

The light reflecting back from the clouds was enough for Ellie to spot me crossing the road. Vanishing was out of the question for the present; my head was buzzing so much that any attempt to do so would only make things worse. Have to try it the regular way, then, and wait for the right opportunity.

Lloyd was an unintentional help as his own search for Susan took him farther along the beach. Ellie kept even with him, playing the light around. I waited until her back was turned, then quickly topped the rise and slipped across the wide band of concrete. The land dipped down again where it ended, but not by much. Aside from the road bank, there was no shelter, just dead grass, gravel, and some snow that hadn't melted off before the latest cold front had blown in. A few hundred yards ahead in the middle of a flat, exposed field was a stand of trees. Would she have tried for it? I was acutely conscious of the wasted time if I'd guessed wrong.

My doubts dropped away when I found a single footstep left in a patch of snow. The toe of her light shoe pointed right at the trees.

While Ellie faced the beach, I sprinted over the open ground, but kept glancing over my shoulder. It slowed me down and threatened to put a crick in my neck, but I needed to know if she moved. The least swing in my direction and I'd have to drop flat. At night she'd see a moving object more easily than a still one.

I made the trees, ducking gratefully under their boughs. Evergreens, thank God, with lovely, dark, obscuring clusters of needles between me and Ellie's flashlight. Their piney scent stung my nose pleasantly as I blundered through them, looking for the girl.

She was curled up all right, just as I'd envisioned, but not asleep yet. Her legs were drawn tight to her chest and she was shivering like a dozen earthquakes. When she heard me coming, her breath stopped halfway between a sob and a moan.

"It's all right," I told her, making sure she could hear my voice clearly. It was too dark here for her to see me. "I'm the man you saw by the lake. Will you let me help you?" I was afraid she might bolt off again. A needless fear, now; she looked too cold to do much of anything.

She nodded, her face marred with pain. I moved closer until she could see me better and began unbuttoning my coat as fast as I could. Not fast enough. I yanked off my gloves and threw them at her. They landed by her feet and she stared at them, unable to understand.

"Put 'em on, honey," I said. "You don't want to lose any fingers."

Another nod and she stiffly obeyed. With my hands unencumbered I made better time with the buttons and shrugged the coat off and got it around her shoulders. She didn't say a thing when I rocked her back and swept it under her feet to put the cloth between herself and the ground. It was like hugging a block of living ice; I could feel her goose bumps right through the fabric. I had a wool neck scarf as well and wrapped it all around her head, tucking in the ends, and topped things off with my hat. By the time I'd finished, she was bundled up like a postal package and only lacked some string and an address.

"Better," she whispered, the word coming out with difficulty, but laced with gratitude.

"That's good. You're Susan, aren't you?"

Another nod.

"I heard them mention your name. Lloyd's your husband?"

"Yes."

"Who's Ellie?"

"His sister."

Nice couple. "They want to kill you?"

She moaned again, an affirmative as far as I could tell. "You know why?"

"Money for me," she murmured cryptically. Then like a child, added, "I want to go home."

"As soon as possible. I have to take care of Lloyd and Ellie before I can get to my car."

"I can walk."

"It's too far."

"Won't there be a house or something?"

"I didn't see any driving out here. You just sit tight
and I'll get us a ride. On second thought, maybe you'd
better move around. Can you do that?"

"Think so."

There was a liquor smell on her breath. Whatever
false warmth an earlier drink might have given her
would have worn off by now. The alcohol in her body
would do her more harm than good in this cold.

"They try and get you drunk?" I asked, helping her
up. She was so small, the hem of my coat dragged on
the ground.

"Yeah. We went out. Said it was a party for me. Made
me drink, but I got sick." She was as rocky on her feet
as I had been. She couldn't have been much more than
twenty, probably younger.

"They wanted you to conk out, huh?" I took a few
steps with her.

"Guess so. I got sleepy. Didn't wanta drink any more.
Kept telling Lloyd I wanted to go home. He wouldn't
listen, just laughed."

"What about Ellie?"

"She laughed with him, but said we should leave. People were staring."

"Then they drove out here?"

"Don't remember the drive. Then Ellie said I had to
get ready for bed and to take my coat off. But I was in
the truck, not in bed. Woke up some, then, and knew
something was wrong."

That's for damn sure. We paced and turned, paced
and turned. Even cut by the trees and the improvements
my condition gave my body, the icy wind was starting
to get to me. "Then you got away from them?"

"Pretended to be worse than I was. Told 'em I had to
go to the bathroom. They took me out of the truck. I asked
Lloyd for my coat, but he said I'd just mess it up and to
hurry. Didn't know where I was, just somewhere by the
lake. Somewhere quiet. No lights. No people."

So convenient for Lloyd and Ellie. Get the girl drunk,
let her pass out, and eventually she'll freeze to death.
Tragic, but understandable in this weather. I could have
almost thrown up again.

"That's when I ran away. Lost 'em in the dark for a while. It was so cold."

"I saw you on the beach."

"Thought you were Lloyd at first, then I knew better, and then he came up behind you."

"Yeah, I know all about that part."

"You hurt bad?"

"I'll get by. You said they'd get money for you?"

"Insurance. Lloyd has a two thousand dollar policy on me."

"Two thousand? He's trying to kill you for—" I bit the rest off. As though a larger amount of money involved would have justified a murder. Two thousand or two million, it didn't matter. Death was death.

"Mister, that's all the money in the world," she told me with awed conviction.

To people like Lloyd and Ellie, that was probably true. Last summer Roosevelt had assured us that the depression was over. Maybe it was for him, but the rest of us weren't seeing much evidence of it.

"Wish he hadn't done it," she continued, talking now more to herself than to me. "Things were getting better for us. Lots better. He hadn't hit me for the longest time; I thought that he'd really changed. Even Ellie was being nice to me. They were going to buy a store, they said, set up a real business. I'd ask where they were going to get the money and they'd just laugh, funnin' me. Then Ellie'd say, 'We're laughing with you, not at you, Susie.' I didn't know what the joke was. I do now. Wish he hadn't done it."

He was going to wish he hadn't, too, after I got through with him. I didn't have to think about it, either. My gut said that this girl was okay and I'd already received solid proof that the other two weren't. My head was still ready to float off and explode.

"Susan . . . has Lloyd ever been married before?" The question popped out of nowhere. Some part of my mind was busy turning things over, making patterns out of the brief, but intense, impressions gained from contact with Lloyd and Ellie. That or I was just guessing.

It surprised her enough to make her stop her pacing. "Yeah. He didn't talk about her much. He only said . . .

said . . . she drowned. A stupid accident when they went fishing. How'd you know?"

Or another murder. Or perhaps a real accident that inspired him to try repeating it for profit. Had there been other wives?

Susan looked up at me. "How'd you . . . ?"

Then she realized why I'd asked in the first place and the realization was the same as if I'd smacked her between the eyes with a brick. Why hadn't I kicked myself, instead?

"Oh, God," she groaned. "Oh, God."

I pulled her tight. She shuddered, went still, and shuddered some more. No tears. She was too shocked for those to flow, yet.

"You going to be all right here for a while?" I asked when she finally pushed away.

"Can't we just walk back to town?" Her voice was dull, thick.

"It's too far."

"But he's got his gun."

That wouldn't help him against me. "Where's this truck of theirs?" I hadn't noticed it anywhere on the road.

"Some place off the beach a ways. Don't know how far."

Possibly too far for us to make use of it. The car was our best chance. "I don't know how long this'll take, so you keep walking around. Keep yourself moving and don't stop. I'll come back as soon as I can." Real soon. The wind was biting like a rabid animal.

She nodded numbly and was obediently pacing again as I slipped off.

I stopped at the edge of the trees to check ahead. Ellie was no longer watching the beach; she was nowhere in sight at all. Hmm. She could be with her brother, helping him search, or maybe sitting in my car, taking advantage of its shelter. I hadn't locked it. Because of the reflections off the windows, I couldn't see to tell. On the other hand, she had only to glance at the field at the wrong time to see me coming. Damn the lack of cover. All I had to work with were the trees, car, and a line of telephone poles marching grimly out from the city. Those were much too thin to hide behind, even if I managed to get to them without being spotted. I tried to vanish, just as an experiment. Still too soon, though I felt a faint encouraging flutter from within. The hell with it; I didn't have time to wait for my recovering body to catch up with the situation. Besides, I was really *cold*, now.

The run over the field was slightly warming. I dashed straight for my Buick like a ball player for home base. It wasn't really safe, though; I felt terribly exposed. Bobbing up, I checked through the windows, but it was happily empty of lurking killers. I punched the door latch with my thumb and winced at the clunk and squeak it made opening.

Motion. Brightness. Corner of my eye. Headlights. Some kind of noisy vehicle coming up fast from the east.

Decision: stay or run? Flag down possible help or duck away from a possible threat?

The lights separated as they drew closer. They were mounted to an old, rusty, open-bed truck. No rescue this time, the driver was Ellie. Above the glare, I recognized the sleek shape of her scarf-covered head.

I stayed. I'd have to confront them sooner or later.

Though she must have seen me right away, she didn't slow until the last second, bringing the truck to a long, sliding halt on its bald tires. The brakes squealed like dying pigs. Leaving the lights on and the engine running, she thrust out the door and came around the front bumper, her expression all grim curiosity.

She honestly didn't know me at first. I was without my bulky overcoat and standing up, after all.

And I was alive.

It was a pleasure to watch the changes flow through her brain and emerge onto her face. The grimness melted off first, leaving behind an ingrained layer of suspicion, the sort you reserve for any unexpected stranger. It fought with leftover curiosity for dominance, until both were replaced by sick doubt. Then came the slow dawning that something was really, *really* wrong with the world.

She backed off a step in reflex, then held her ground. She wasn't quite ready to accept that final connection to ... whatever it was I represented to her. I was a stranger come out of the darkness, probably a tramp, someone inconvenient who needed to leave. Quickly.

She yelled Lloyd's name into the air, her voice strange and high with imperfectly suppressed fear. She yelled again. No answer. She gave a little jump when I straightened and slammed my half-opened door, not once taking my eyes from her.

Ellie pulled a little revolver from her coat pocket. Her hand shook. A lot. She steadied it with her other hand and held it on me. Wish I'd thought to bring a gun, but I hadn't anticipated the need for one just for a walk on the beach. In the future, I'd make a habit of it. There are far too many bad guys out there.

"Who are you?" she asked, the words dribbling out shaky and not at all what she wanted to say. I don't think there are any words for this kind of a situation.

I gave a short laugh. "What's the matter, Ellie? Don't you want another kiss?"

She shrieked . . . internally. Nothing audible came out of her, and that made it seem more awful. I could feel it, though, running straight through me like glass scraping against glass.

I'd said the wrong thing. On purpose, of course, which made it all right. But I'd expected her to cut and run and she did not. She wasn't about to let me go with my half of Our Secret.

The gun flared and jumped in her hand. The explosion was almost too loud to hear, and registered more like a shockwave than a shot. Astonishingly, I felt nothing. Ellie was so spooked that from six feet away, she'd completely missed.

She wasn't getting a second chance to correct her aim. I ducked around the front of the car, keeping low. None of this was helping my tender head. I wanted someplace warm and quiet, and a long, red drink, not this kind of nonsense.

Ellie followed, but I kept the car between us, preventing her from getting a clear shot. It made for another frigging decision: charge her and risk catching a bullet or play squirrel tag until I got frostbite. I'd already lost feeling in my ears. Damn, if I could just vanish.

She wasn't wasting bullets, unfortunately. Five more misses and I could cut all this short. It'd likely be cut short, anyway, but not in my favor. Lloyd would certainly have heard something and be on his way from

whatever rock he'd crawled under. I didn't have time to
spend all night playing death games with his crazy sister.

Okay, I'd try for a frontal attack and hope for the
best.

Then Lloyd changed my mind. Skulking around the
rear bumper, I glanced across the field. Lloyd was sham-
bling toward us as fast as he could. In one hand was his
rifle, the other had Susan by the scruff of the neck. She
stumbled along, her feet tangling in the flapping hem of
my coat. Whenever she fell, Lloyd dragged her up again,
hardly slowing his pace, like an adult impatiently dealing
with a balky child. Her cries sliced the air like a thin-
bladed knife.

He'd given up on the beach and decided to investigate
the trees, probably sneaking up while I'd been talking
with Susan.

Ellie, from her cover behind the front fender of the
car, yelled at him. He sprinted forward. The headlights
were still on; he noticed me right away. Like Ellie, he
saw me only as a new threat to be neutralized; not the
corpse he'd left on the beach.

Ellie screamed at him to shoot me.

That made him pause, but he was too used to doing
what she told him to ask questions. He closed up the
distance to only ten yards, released Susan—who immediately scrambled off—and brought up the rifle. I was
looking straight down the gun barrel. Free of the agitation I'd inspired in Ellie, his shooting would be steady.

I dropped back to get away from the truck's lights and
to put the car in the way, remembering about Ellie a
fraction too late.

I dodged, but not quickly enough.

Her shot slams into my ribs like a runaway train.

I stagger once from the impact, arms flying. Dimly, I
hear Ellie's crow of victory as she sees me falter. The
graveled shoulder of the road rushes up to me, but I
miss hitting it in the sudden gray fog that sweeps over
my sight.

Scissors cut paper. Paper wraps stone. Stone breaks
scissors. The child's game whips into my head and out
again, inspiring a personal variation.

Metal overcomes wood.

With a wrench like I'm being turned inside out, I vanish.

It's never before been painful. Never. Too close onto the head injury. No screaming allowed. Haven't got a mouth anymore.

Ellie's voice fails her. As Lloyd comes up, neither can answer the other's question of what has happened. Their fear pushes at me like the pressure of a sea wave. The wind threatens to carry me off like a crumpled scrap of paper. I reach out with a pseudopod of something that should be my hand and wrap it around the car's bumper to hold myself in place. I need weight, solidity, but I'm afraid to re-form, fearful of again being seized by that sawing, grating tug of nerve from muscle from bone until nothing is left but a sharp memory writhing unseen in the air.

Lloyd and Ellie begin arguing, somehow talking themselves back into the comfortable world they're used to, the one where men don't return to life after they're dead, where men don't disappear into the air when they're shot, where it's perfectly okay to collect money on a young girl's death.

Finally and firmly dismissing the impossibility of what they'd seen, Ellie urges Lloyd to go after Susan. The girl's headed for the trees. False safety there for her. Better cover for them. If they think of it, see the advantages, they can finish their work in that spot. Somewhere quiet. No lights. No people. Like skinning a rabbit, they'll strip my coat from Susan's small body and begin the process of killing once more. Pain or no pain, I have to come back.

But it's easy. The wall I expect to strike isn't in the way. I pour back into myself. Cautiously.

Bit by bit, the grayness resolves into the recognizable shapes of normal reality. Sky, earth, and water mix with the hard lines of human artifacts ... and the humans, too.

There is no resumption of the pain until the metal of the car's bumper starts freezing my hand. Dematerialized, I'd forgotten the cold; now it works its way from hand to arm, fresh and cutting, as though I'd just emerged from a warm house. I pause in the process, holding in a halfway state until I can get my bearings.

Lying on the pavement, just about to sit up, only the hand gripping the bumper is solid. The rest of me trails off from it, ghostlike; I can see through myself.

So can Ellie and Lloyd.

Their bloodless faces stare down at me like the world's about to end. It has, for them. Dead men *can* return.

Ellie's not ready to give up her illusions. She brings her gun to bear on me and fires. But I'm semitransparent and the bullet has no effect. I feel nothing this time, but do have to fight the wind. Unlike the bullet, which spears through only one small spot, the wind hits me all over, like the sail on a ship.

Ellie shoots again. All she gets in response is a grin, then a laugh, a silent one to be sure, but she hears it, if only in her mind. There, it takes on a greater voice and volume than any I could put to it. She falls back against Lloyd, who's been unable to move. Her touch hits him like an electric shock and now they're both unable to get out of there fast enough. I'm still laughing as they scramble around and pile into the truck.

I look behind me, across the field for Susan, but the headlights spoil the view. She'll have to wait a little longer.

Lloyd drives, or tries to; he torturously shifts the gears and the truck rolls forward, passing my car. I vanish and let the wind take me for a single second. Slamming into the hard metal of the truck's sides, I slide up and in. I'm rolling over in its narrow bed behind the cab. The wind takes a different direction, artificially altered by the speeding truck.

The gears growl and grind; I plummet forward, coming to the back of the cab. There's nothing to hold on to there. It's all pitted metal with a small rectangle of smooth glass in the middle. With invisible fingers I claw at the window. More permeable than the rest of the truck's body, I'm able to slip through it.

The opening is small. I don't like small spaces or sieving through glass. It always seems about to break and then doesn't. Then I'm beyond its bitter barrier. I tumble like an invisible ball in the little cab, then settle into an upright posture on the creaking seat.

There are bodies on either side of me; Lloyd driving on my left, Ellie tense and trapped on my right. She

urges him to go faster. As always, he obeys, struggling
with the sluggish gears. They haven't noticed the increased chill, which is a side effect I have in this form.

"You *bitch*! You told me he was dead." Lloyd was
close to tears.

"He *was* dead. I know he was dead."

"So what is he now? You tell me that. Oh, God. Oh,
God*damn* it."

"Just shut up!"

"Shut up yourself. What about Susan? What'll we do
about her?"

"Leave her."

"But she'll—"

"It don't matter. We'll be gone. The hell with her."

"Oh, God*damn* it. Oh, shit. What *was* he?"

A maniac's grin sprouts on my invisible face.

I'm still grinning when I materialize between them.
Their reaction is immediate, and loud. Their yells in the
tight space of the cab are deafening, the fight fast and
ineffective. Lloyd's grip on the wheel loosens as he tries
to hit me with a frantic, poorly aimed fist. Ellie tries to
use her gun. Lloyd shrieks at her not to; Lloyd fights
the steering; I fight Ellie, the truck goes into a long skid
as Lloyd hits the brakes.

Bald tires useless and screaming against the slick road,
we charge ahead, hitting a sudden patch of silence: a bit
of leftover ice that slews us around like a circus ride.
The slender black shape of a telephone pole comes flying
toward us out of the night.

I don't want to be there. Instinct obliges me. Half a
second, half a heartbeat, I'm gone. There, but not there
as everything comes slamming to an inarguable stop.
Distantly, I feel the impact as we strike the pole. Lloyd's
body flies into mine . . . or where mine should have been
had I remained solid. I hear heavy, meaty thumps, the
tear and crimp of steel, the crunch and crack of wood
and bone. The truck motor grunts and dies.

Silence.

The wind tunneling in my ears is like an echo from
a seashell.

It's cold.

I'm solid again, staring at the wreckage. The truck is

folded around the stump of the broken pole. Some of its lines have snapped and trail on the ground. There's shattered glass all over, grinding and breaking into smaller pieces as I pace the area.

I don't have to breathe to get a whiff of it, the blood-smell. It's all over, sickeningly mixed with the stink of gasoline, which is also all over. I keep a prudent distance, in case there's a spark.

Through the twisted frame of the back window I see the shape of a head. Or it could be part of a shoulder. No need to check, I really don't want to know.

It's moving. Someone inside moans and chokes and gives a short cough. I don't want to go closer, but do so, walking around to the front of the truck.

I hate what I see through the spiderweb cracks of the windshield.

Ellie is smashed against the passenger door. Her scarf is pushed back. I notice for the first and last time that she has black hair. One of her eyes looks normal, quite alive and aware. The other is lost in a pulpy mess that went through the window when we hit the pole.

She moves a little and the hair goes up on my neck for an instant until I realize the motion is not her own, but another's. Lloyd is trying to pry himself free. He gets to the driver's door but can't open it. He doesn't see me, his mind is focused solely on escape. Desperation gives him inspiration. He bring up a leg and kicks at the windshield.

Shards fly, strike the hood, and skitter off. He makes a hole big enough to use and hunches forward. He's got blood all over him and adds to it as he crawls out. His breathing is difficult, perhaps from damaged ribs. He wheezes and cries and clutches his left arm. The sleeve from his woolen hunting jacket is badly torn. Most of the blood comes from there.

He worms over the hood, loses his balance, and rolls off, hitting the ground like a bag heavy with sand. When his breath returns, he starts whimpering for help.

I can't bring myself to move toward him.

Footsteps. Another set of lungs. Susan came up. She'd lost my hat, but she still wore the coat. Some of her hair had escaped from the scarf and she had to brush it from her eyes.

"No need to see this," I said, stepping between her and horror.

She ran forward, anyway, not to her husband lying in the gravel on the shoulder of the road, but to me. I put my arm around her, selfishly glad of her company.

"Are they dead?" she asked in a clear and quiet voice.

"Ellie's dead. Lloyd needs help. He's cut pretty bad." The bloodsmell teases at me. "Without a tourniquet or at least some pressure on the wound, he'll bleed to death."

"No," she said hollowly.

The belt on my pants would do. I gently shrugged away from her and started to unbuckle it. Susan's hands fell strongly onto mine.

"I said no, mister."

"But we need to . . ." Then I saw the look on her face. I read the bitter and bright hatred there, the crystalline awareness transmitting belated realization to me.

"No, we don't," she told me. Her eyes darted from me to the weakly shivering figure of the husband who had betrayed her and no telling how many others. "No. We don't need to do anything."

I sighed. "You sure?"

"Aren't you?" She read my face in turn and was satisfied with the answer. She walked over to her husband, just close enough so he could see her, know her. "Wish you hadn't done it, Lloyd," she said, then walked back. "Can we go home, now?"

In answer, I took her arm, the two of us heading quickly for my car. I planned to have the engine going and the heater at its highest setting in record time. My ears were going numb again. I got the door open and hustled her inside. The air was cold, but still, and the car smelled comfortably of stale tobacco smoke and damp leather. Susan huddled deep in my coat, looking justifiably tired but peaceful.

"The keys are in the right pocket," I said, almost apologetically.

"Oh." She sat up a little, dug for them, and gave them over. My gloves looked comical on her small hands, but I didn't laugh.

"Last chance," I said, starting up the car. Its headlights flooded the wreck, making it look like some terrible set piece for a play. Lloyd's insignificant figure hardly stirred, now.

She only shook her head, her whitened lips compressed. "You know something? When Lloyd took out that insurance policy on me, he took one out on himself. I guess it was so's it wouldn't look funny later on."

"Guess so," I agreed.

"You know something else? He tol' me that if one of us died in a' accident, the insurance would be twice as much."

"Well," I said, hauling the wheel around to make a U-turn back to the city, "accidents happen."

SHELL GAME
by
John Lutz

The lowering sun was like a red eye peering over the
pine trees on Gray Mountain, into the quiet band room.
Hans Jorgan had been the music teacher and band director at Allville High School for ten years. He was forty-
three and had given up his aspirations to compose
Broadway musicals. It was, he often told his colleague
and lover Ella Smith, a time in life for reality. Usually
Ella would misinterpret his statement and turn the conversation in the direction of marriage—her notion of de-
sired reality.

Willy Kruger, sitting among the swirling dust motes in
a slanted beam of evening sunlight, wasn't adding to the
sense of reality Jorgan was seeking to make the new
basis of his life. Willy was a pudgy sophomore who
played second tuba in the band. He had a round face,
and a fold of flesh beneath his chin that would become
more defined and then duplicate itself as he grew older
and heavier, tiny blue eyes that could only bring to mind
the hogs his father Zeb raised out on Route 13 near the
edge of town. Jorgan often thought that as a tuba player,
Willy had a future as a hog farmer.

Now here, in the warm band room that smelled of
stale sweat and sticky varnish from the rows of wooden
bench seats, beneath the portrait of John Philip Sousa,
near Visit, the tiger-striped cat that had strayed in last
month and become the band mascot, in this setting of
small town normality, even suffocating mundaneness,
Willy was stating the remarkable: "I mean it, Mr. Jorgan! Old Miss Kraft's a vampire!"

Jorgan sighed and put away the last of the clarinets,

snapping the worn black case shut. "Why are you telling me this, Willy? Why not your mom and dad?"

"Told 'em," Willy said. "They don't believe me."

Jorgan could imagine mean and dumb Zeb Kruger's reaction to his son's vampire story. "What makes you think I'll believe you?"

"You're a man of music. You believe in the romantic and obscene. You said that once to the band, remember."

"That's 'obscure,' Willy, not 'obscene.' "

"Whatever," Willy said. "I s'pose this is something of both those things."

Jorgan sat down, crossed his legs, and tried to look like a wise uncle. After all, Willy was placing faith in him. Maybe it was part of a teacher's job to try to justify that faith. It shouldn't be difficult to talk Willy out of the idea that old Miss Kraft, a weathered woman probably really only in her fifties, was a vampire.

Jorgan watched a hawk circle high up near the top of Gray Mountain, which was more a hill than an actual mountain. Allville residents tilted toward the grandiose sometimes when describing their town and its surroundings. Miss Kraft had a ramshackle old cottage up there among the pines. Natural that some of the kids figured her for a witch, and now, apparently, a vampire. Jorgan said, "Vampires are usually men, Willy. Haven't you ever seen *Dracula*?"

"Sure. Read the book, too." He scratched his pudgy cheek with a dirty fingernail. "Read lotsa books about vampires. Truth is, they can become most anything they wanna be, when they're looking for blood. It's like they're wearing a shell. That's part of the magic of 'em. An' they can be all-fire tricky. If it was dark enough, Miss Kraft could even be that there hawk."

Jorgan laughed. "I'll be honest, Willy, you'll have a difficult time talking me into the idea that poor Miss Kraft's a vampire. She's an unfortunate woman who lives a frugal but decent hard life struggling to get by in the world."

"That's what she was till she got bit," Willy said. "That's how it works, vampires create other vampires. Been times whole towns were taken over."

"That's not likely to happen to Allville," Jorgan said.

"Well, it's something I'd sure like not to be here and see it happen," Willy said.

"Have you been cutting third hour English?"

"No, sir. Anyways, I don't reckon all the English in the world'd get you to believing me. That's why I waited around till near sundown to talk to you. What I wanna do is *show* you Miss Kraft's a vampire."

A breeze pushed in through the open window. Visit wandered over and jumped up on Jorgan's lap. Jorgan stroked the calico cat and listened to it purr. Like a small motor running. "Is Miss Kraft going to rise up from a coffin at sunset?" Jorgan asked.

"Might," Willy said with all seriousness. "I seen her do that once. And once she was a bat. And once—"

"Really, Willy. A bat—a genuine bat—is hardly large enough to cause anyone a great deal of trouble."

"But size is something a vampire can change. She was a bat even taller than you, Mr. Jorgan, with wings that dragged on the ground when she walked. You shoulda seen it!"

"Shoulda," Jorgan agreed, wondering again about third hour English.

"So you gonna?"

"Gonna— Going to what?"

"Gonna hike up on Gray Mountain with me and watch through Miss Kraft's window when the sun goes down?"

"Willy, I'm not a peeping Tom, and I'd strongly advise you not to sneak looks through people's windows."

"We won't have to get too close. It's not like she's got shades or anything."

"Willy—"

"Tell you what, we can just stand outa sight in the woods and watch her front porch. She'll come out right after dusk. She's gotta search for food."

"How would we know she's a vampire?"

Willy suddenly looked years older. He said, "When you see her, you'll know. She'll have changed some. She'll be out after animals and other creatures for blood."

Jorgan felt a chill. The boy was certainly convincing.

"You scared to go up on the mountain, Mr. Jorgan?"

"Of course not."

"Well, I sure am. That's why I came here. Ain't nobody else I could tell this to. Nobody who'd help me."

The boy was unquestionably frightened, and about to break out in the kind of repetitive gasping sobs Jorgan had seen when Willy was informed he wasn't first tuba. Jorgan didn't want that to happen, not ever again.

"I'll go," he said quickly. "It's less than an hour until sundown, and I've got a little time to spare. You'll have to wait while I finish cleaning the band room, though."

"I don't mind, Mr. Jorgan. Really." His fleshy cheeks quivered. He swallowed. "I—I guess, thanks."

Jorgan had to smile. "It's okay, Willy."

"I'll help you put things away."

"Fine." Jorgan glanced at his watch. "In a little less than an hour, we should be able to put an end to your bad dreams about vampires."

Jorgan stood up and Visit dropped from his lap and curled into a soft, tight lump of fur on the floor.

Willy said, "You won't think that after you see Miss Kraft. She looks pale and . . . I dunno, hungry, desperate."

And I must be desperate for something to do, Jorgan thought, to have agreed to this.

When the band room was in order and securely locked, he and Willy left the red brick building and trudged toward the gathering gloom on Gray Mountain.

It was almost dusk when they stood at the edge of the woods and watched the tilted front porch of Miss Kraft's decrepit cottage. Guttering dangled from one corner of the roof, and a shutter lay on the ground beneath one of the front windows. Imagining what it must be like to live in such desolation, Jorgan felt sorry for Miss Kraft. And more than a little guilty for spying on her from the shadows of the trees.

Willy peered skyward. "Gonna be a full moon," he said.

"You're thinking of werewolves," Jorgan told him. "Don't get your tall tales confused."

"I just meant we'd be able to see her okay," Willy said.

"And she might be able to see us," Jorgan told him. He gripped Willy's shoulder and backed a step into deeper shadow. Visit had tagged along up the mountain;

Jorgan hoped the cat wouldn't wander away from where it lay and reveal their presence.

Crickets screamed, small creatures stirred behind them in the woods, and Jorgan asked himself why he wasn't in town calling to see if Ella wanted to drive out to the roadhouse for supper. After supper—

Despite the warm night, a chill wind passed through the dark pines, at exactly the time the cottage door swung open, squealing shrilly on its hinges.

Jorgan felt something—a tiny insect or his hair—stir on the back of his neck.

"Vampires gotta feed," Willy said, "so they use tricks to get people, pets, whatever, away from other folks and the towns so's they can get at them."

Jorgan stared hard at the black rectangle that was the cottage doorway. He edged forward, bending a supple tree limb to keep it before him for concealment.

"If Miss Kraft's a vampire," he whispered to Willy, "how'd she get that way? I mean, she wasn't always a—"

His words lodged like something square in his throat as he looked at Willy. The boy's chubby features had somehow taken on a gaunt, aged appearance, as if he'd gained fifty years and lost fifty pounds. He smiled, and Jorgan saw Willy's teeth and heard his own harsh intake of breath. He remembered what Willy had said about vampires maneuvering people into isolated situations, then making them victims. Miss Kraft had used Willy, or vice versa, to lure Jorgan to the mountain. Jorgan knew it was true; how could he not believe, staring at Willy, smelling the sudden stench that wafted from the boy who was no longer a boy.

Jorgan let the branch beneath his arm spring backward into Willy's face, and in the same motion whirled and began to run. He almost tripped over Visit, instinctively stooped, and scooped up the cat rather than leave it with Willy or Miss Kraft, and ran with all his might toward the shelter of the deep woods farther down the mountain.

He didn't dare look back. Branches scratched his face and arms, underbrush tugged at his ankles, like grasping hands trying to trip him. He was making so much noise crashing through the woods that he couldn't be sure if Willy was following.

Of course, Willy might not have to run after him. If all of the madness was true, he might be a bat flying effortlessly behind him above tree level. Jorgan glanced up, tripped and almost fell, ran on.

But he couldn't outrun his terror. Exhausted, pain ripping through his lungs with each ragged breath, he finally slowed down, dropped Visit, and slouched with his back against a tree, peering fearfully into the night sky.

He could see nothing but darkness. The branch he'd let snap into Willy's face had startled the student, who despite his vampirism was still a short-legged, overweight boy.

All right, he thought, I've lost him for now, but if he ever catches up with me here in the deep woods, there'll be nowhere to run for help, no one to hear my screams.

Jorgan felt anything but secure. The darkness, the foliage, was a shelter only if Willy, or for that matter Miss Kraft, didn't know his whereabouts.

Alarmed at the force of his heart bashing against his ribs, he made himself think clearly and decided what to do. Though he was protected by the cover of the deep woods, he was also isolated. He couldn't remain hidden here forever, but they'd expect him to try. The smart thing would be to maintain the element of surprise, the advantage of suddenness, and run hard down the mountain toward town as soon as he caught his breath.

No, he shouldn't even wait that long! Now was the time!

He pushed himself away from the tree, sucked cool night air and the scent of pine needles into his lungs, *life!*, and started to run toward where the full moon revealed a narrow path through the trees.

The five words spoken behind him froze him.

"Not so fast, Mr. Jorgan."

And Jorgan knew how he'd been tricked to come to this forlorn place where he would die but not die. Knew who had manipulated him.

Paralyzed with terror, he could hear the cat's breathing, like a huge brush stroking harshly across velvet. He could sense its new immensity.

He turned around to look.

Wished he hadn't.

THE SECRET
by
Barbara Paul

It was a rich man's ego that turned us into secret-keepers. Wilson Pritchard was never satisfied with his arduously accumulated totems of potency, instead forever seeking the untoppable win in the I'm-bigger-than-you-are sweepstakes. No mere Trump Tower or Portmeirion would do. A sports arena named after himself? Too ordinary. TBS, TNT? Better, but Pritchard wanted a more tangibly permanent memorial than colorized images on a screen. Oddly, it was London Bridge straddling an inlet of Lake Havasu in our neighboring state that caught Pritchard's fancy. He liked the idea of importing European cul-chah wholesale. So he bought a town. He bought the *whole* town.

It took him a while to find what he was looking for. Pritchard had in mind something vaguely medieval; thus no highrises, no autobahns, no métros. Villages aplenty met his criteria, but Wilson Pritchard wasn't about to settle for anything as paltry as a mere village. Finally he found a once-prosperous market town in Romania that had fallen on hard times. Like, three hundred years ago it fell on hard times. No growth, not much in the way of change or betterment since then. Not quite medieval, but close enough. Pritchard pulled out his checkbook.

A castle came with the town, which may have been the deciding factor for Pritchard; he liked playing lord of the manor. But even as Romanian workmen were dismantling the castle for shipment to the stretch of ranchland Pritchard had set aside for his "little bit of Europe" in New Mexico, the local paper was already printing vampire jokes, suggesting we exercise a little discretion as to exactly which European traditions we

262

were willing to import. The town of El Secreto went along with the gag; for instance, a drugstore held a contest, offering a year's supply of dental floss for the best list of problems facing vampires with toothaches. The reason behind all this jollity was that Pritchard City, as it was now called (originally it was something unpronounceable ending in -*jiu*), had been located in the section of Romania called Valachia or Wallachia, depending on which atlas you consult. And Valachia, not Transylvania, had been the old stomping grounds of the original, the historic, the one-and-only—ta da!—Vlad the Impaler, dubbed Dracula ("son of the devil") by his peers. Impressed? We were. Kind of.

Virtually overnight a vampire industry sprang up in downtown El Secreto—vampire costumes and makeup, vampire comic books, charms against vampirism. An outright boom in crucifixes, and our only bookstore quickly sold out of Bram Stoker. Our one-half-watt TV station held a Bela Lugosi film festival. I felt responsible for this flurry of opportunistic goings on, because I'm the one who tipped off the editor of our local rag that Valachia was Dracula's true home. In my innocence I even told him how Vlad the Impaler did his impaling— from the bottom up. The sonuvabitch printed every gory detail.

"Nice going, Fritz," Ellen said dryly. "Don't you know by now that every word you say to Mike Johnson is going to end up in print?"

Just what I needed to hear. "He's always going on about how he puts out a nice family newspaper," I grumbled. "I didn't think he'd actually print the stuff."

She laughed. "He's always hungry for news—nothing ever happens in El Secreto. If Wilson Pritchard is seen sneezing, Mike'll write a story about it."

"Um, yeah, but I wonder what Pritchard's going to think when he learns everybody's saying he bought a vampire town."

As it turned out, he loved it. Pritchard had big plans for his relocated town. After restoring it, he intended to run it as a resort. He hired some historian from the East Coast to come in and oversee the authenticity of the place—authentic food and clothing, authentic living conditions, authentic work. If you were willing to pay an

arm and a leg, you could go to Pritchard City and live
for a week or two exactly the way Romanians lived three
hundred years ago. That's what you've always wanted to
do, isn't it? So the rumor of a vampire or two in residence was bound to be good for business.

And business was booming. Pritchard City needed a
big work force, people to impersonate townspeople and
even more people to run things behind the scenes. Since
Pritchard's new toy was going up right down the highway
from El Secreto, our town supplied the first of the labor.
But we didn't have enough manpower to handle the entire job; soon strangers began moving in, technicians and
actors and cooks and accountants ... and El Secreto was
expected to accommodate them all. New motels and res-
taurants and even an apartment building went up, all
built by Pritchard's own construction company. He made
money, the town made money, the influx of new employees made money. Everybody was happy.

Everybody except me. Pritchard City, unfortunately,
would lie completely this side of the county line, and
that put it in my jurisdiction. El Secreto had been a one-
peace-officer town for as long as anybody could remember; but with all these new people moving in, I was going
to need a deputy. And whenever El Secreto needed
something, you went to see Wilson Pritchard.

So one Friday morning I set out to do just that. Ellen
was at home, sleeping the sleep of the dead. She was on
duty at the hospital when the Highway Patrol brought
in the victims of a four-car pile-up, so she'd been up all
night stitching the hapless drivers and their passengers
back together. I was backing the sheriff's car out of the
driveway when Mike Johnson pulled up in his Buick,
waving at me to stop.

I was still a little ticked off at him for publishing all
that vampire crap, so I said, "Can it wait, Mike? I'm on
my way to see Pritchard."

"I'll go with you." He left his car and climbed into
mine. I said nothing, just turned the car toward Pritchard
City and stepped on the gas pedal.

"My dog was killed last night, Fritz," Mike said without preamble. "We found her this morning, in the front
yard." He paused. "She'd been ripped to shreds."

At first I thought it was a tasteless joke, still working

the vampire gag. But when I saw it wasn't, I hit the brake. "I'm sorry, Mike ... poor old LouLou! God. Ripped to shreds? Show me."

He shook his head. "We buried her, fast—before the kids could see. There ... there wasn't much left." He started to gag at the memory. "Sorry."

I put a hand on his shoulder, not knowing what to say. I really needed to take a look at the dog if I was going to figure out what was behind the killing, but asking Mike to watch me dig LouLou back up right now seemed cruel. Another couple of hours wouldn't change anything. "Do the kids know?"

"Not yet. We couldn't tell them and then send them off to school as if nothing had happened." He stared absently out the side window. "Today's Friday."

"Yeah." Give them the weekend to get used to the idea that old LouLou was gone. I started the car rolling again and asked what questions I could. When was the last time he'd seen the dog? Was it usual for her to stay out all night? Mike said she'd taken to sleeping on the side porch on hot nights; one of the kids had made a bed for her there. Last night they'd fed her, and she'd curled up and watched television with them for a while before pawing the door to be let out. Same as every night. Neither Mike nor I mentioned vampires.

No automobiles were allowed inside Pritchard City; Pritchard didn't want his almost-medieval town stinking of exhaust fumes. Besides, most of the reconstructed cobblestone streets were too narrow to accommodate anything wider than a peddler's cart. As it turned out, Pritchard wasn't there; a man overseeing the erection of a stone wall said it was the first day he'd been late.

So I headed the car back the way we'd come; we'd passed the turnoff to Pritchard's mansion on the way. He'd built the place out in the New Mexico desert when he was going through his Howard Hughes phase, theatrically seeking to sever all contact with the human race. That passed, in time; I guess being alone didn't turn out to be the kick he'd expected. But he'd kept the mansion as his main residence, the place he always returned to from the places he had been. Why not? He was God here. El Secreto had started life as a hideout camp for bandits, the site chosen for its isolation. Now the town's only secret was why anybody stayed there. El Secreto was dying when Pritchard came along and bought all those undeveloped acres claimed by the town council back in more optimistic days, when expansion seemed an inevitable next step instead of the pipe dream it had become. Pritchard's money had saved us, and he never quite let us forget that. But at least he was a benevolent despot.

We'd been riding only five or ten minutes when the car phone buzzed. "Sheriff Brubaker? This is Wilson Pritchard. I need you here at my place. Immediately."

"I'm on my way there right now, Mr. Pritchard. What's wrong?"

"My dog has been slaughtered. Viciously, wantonly slaughtered."

I shot a quick look at Mike Johnson. "Don't touch a thing," I told Pritchard. "And don't let anybody else touch anything. I'll be there in fifteen minutes." I broke the connection and hit the gas.

Pritchard's desert mansion was walled off from the rest of the world; we had to wait while the gate was electronically opened from someplace inside. I took the camera from the car and we went in search of Pritchard; we found him sitting on a patio, quietly breathing fire. Standing unobtrusively behind him was a heavily muscled man in tennis shorts and shirt—a bodyguard, I assumed. Sitting next to Pritchard was a square-jawed blonde wearing a lot of makeup and very little else.

"Mr. Pritchard," I said. "Mrs. Pritchard." She nodded. Pritchard sometimes married his ladies, sometimes not. We called them all Mrs. Pritchard.

Pritchard looked at Mike. "Johnson. Well, here's something for that paper of yours."

"Where's the dog?" I asked.

Pritchard got up heavily and led the way, followed by the bodyguard; Mrs. Pritchard stayed where she was. The dog was around back, what remained of him. His face and four paws were intact; every other part of his body looked as if it had been put through a shredder. White intestines, blue veins, yellowish parts I couldn't identify—all rent into wet little ribbons.

"A mastiff?" I asked.

Pritchard grunted yes. "A big, strong, courageous animal . . . and they had to kill him. Why do they hate me so? I pump life back into that fetid little town, and this is how they repay me."

Just like the man; the attack *had* to be against him. "Mike's dog was killed last night, too," I said.

That caught him by surprise. Mike himself was trying not to gag; he pointed to the mastiff's remains and said, "That's exactly what my dog looked like."

At least now I wouldn't have to dig up old LouLou. I asked Pritchard where his dog usually slept. In a kennel, he said, but the mastiff had the run of the grounds at night. The gate was kept locked all the time. The surrounding wall was twelve feet high and smooth as glass. There were no trees out here to help an intruder climb up. "The only way to get over that wall is to fly," Pritchard said. He glanced at the bodyguard. "And don't go thinking any of the staff did this—they didn't." He snorted. "They wouldn't dare."

I believed him. "Did you touch anything?"

"You said not to."

"The dog wasn't moved from another place?"

"No!" Irritated.

I took a deep breath. "Then where's the blood?" The other three stared at me. "The blood," I repeated slowly. "This animal has been disemboweled—yet there's very little blood here. What happened to it?"

Pritchard's mouth dropped open when it hit him. "That's absurd! All that vampire stuff—that's just a publicity gag!"

"Mike? What about LouLou?"

He'd turned white. "I, I didn't think of it at the time . . . but you're right! There was almost no blood!"

Pritchard exploded. "A vampire? You're saying this was done by a goddamned bloody *vampire*?"

"I'm saying someone could have gotten the idea from the vampire stories. Copycat stuff, some sicko's idea of a good joke. Mike, don't print anything more about vampires. Mr. Pritchard, order your publicity people to knock it off."

They both nodded, stunned.

The bodyguard was looking queasy, so I took the camera and started snapping pictures of the dog's carcass.

When I'd finished, Pritchard said, "Sheriff, you were already on your way here when I called? Why?"

I'd forgotten. I told him about the need for a deputy, in view of the increase in El Secreto's population. He said he'd make a few phone calls. That meant it was as good as done.

One other dog had been killed that night, a mongrel that didn't seem to belong to anybody. But when a week passed with no more mutilations, we began to breathe a bit easier. I still didn't know who the perpetrator was or how he got over Wilson Pritchard's wall, but perhaps he was having second thoughts about killing dogs and siphoning off their blood just to give people a scare. Mike Johnson wrote a strong editorial to that effect and announced there'd be no more Dracula jokes in the paper. He also printed one of the pictures I took of Pritchard's mastiff; vampires stopped being funny *real* fast.

My new deputy was a part-Navajo from Socorro named Hatch, a young fellow just starting out, on his first assignment and eager to make good. His paychecks came from the county, just like mine; Pritchard's Rolodex held the solutions to bigger problems than mine. I filled Hatch in on the vampire gag gone sour; he thought the idea of vampires in El Secreto, New Mexico, was hilarious. I cut that short and instructed him to inform me immediately if he got any reports of animal deaths. But no such reports came in; I think he was disappointed.

On the second Monday after the dog slayings I'd taken the sheriff's car to the garage for a tune-up, so Ellen came by to pick me up on her way home from the hospital. Hatch had just gotten back from checking out a complaint about trespassing cattle and was riding a high; authority was new to him. "Just a little misunderstanding, Sheriff Brubaker," he announced importantly. "I took care of it."

Ellen leaned against the door frame, waiting while I finished up something at my desk. "I think I've found your next vampire victim," she said casually. "New patient. Worst case of anemia I've ever seen. I actually had to give him a transfusion."

Hatch couldn't resist. "Did you check for puncture wounds?"

Ellen grinned. "Not a mark on him. Smoothest, whitest skin I've ever seen. He must never go out in the sun."

"Aha! Never goes out in the sun. Does he speag mit ein aggzent?"

"Yes, but it's British. He's one of the actors Pritchard hired for his imported town."

Hatch was not fazed. "Dracula left a lot of bitten folks behind in England, didn't he? One of them could have been an actor who took a night flight to Hollywood and—"

I thrust one of the photos of Pritchard's dog into his hands. "I want you to study that picture, Hatch," I said. "I want you to study it real good." I took Ellen's arm and steered her outside.

"You were a little rough on him, weren't you?" she asked as we got into her car.

"Maybe. But I don't want him making jokes about vampires."

"Oh, Fritz! The sick person who killed those dogs would have found an excuse even without the vampire jokes."

"Maybe," I said again. "But there's no harm in being careful."

Nothing more was said about it that evening, but at two in the morning the hospital called. Ellen's anemia patient was hallucinating and "acting wild."

"That's a good medical diagnosis," she said dryly as she got dressed. "I prescribed a sedative, but he hasn't been to sleep at all."

Normally when Ellen's called out in the middle of the night, I just roll over and go back to sleep. But this time I got up and went with her.

We could hear him before we got to his room. Hysterical laughter followed by deep moans, both interspersed with a rapid babbling of unintelligible words. "He's been like that for an hour, Dr. Brubaker," the nurse said. "I didn't know what to do."

In the room, an abnormally pale, frighteningly thin man of thirty or less was pacing and ranting. His dark hair stood up in spikes and his eyes were, well, wild.

The voice that gurgled out of his throat was raspy and his hands were shaking. He seemed to be seeing things that the rest of us couldn't see.

"Now, Mr. Michaels," Ellen said soothingly. "Wouldn't you feel better back in bed? Come along now."

He whirled toward her and screamed, "My bed is gone! My bed is gone!"

"No, it isn't—it's right here. See? Come lie down, now."

He started babbling something again, but with the help of the nurse, Ellen got him back into bed. "He won't stay," the nurse panted.

Ellen stood frowning down at him a moment. "This looks like an extreme case of sleep deprivation—the hallucinations, the wild mood swings . . . first thing, we have to calm him down."

Under Ellen's directions, the nurse hooked up an IV. Whatever Ellen gave him, it did calm him some. The state he went into wasn't exactly what you'd call sleep, but it was more restful than the wild ranting that had been going on before. When Ellen was satisfied he was settled for the night, we left.

"His name's Michaels?" I asked on the way back to the car.

"John Michaels. A worker at Pritchard City found him collapsed in one of the streets there. He was able to tell us his name and that he was an actor before he lost consciousness, but that's all. No I.D., nothing in his pockets except a rolled-up copy of the newspaper. He was in pretty bad shape. Malnutrition, anemia, and now sleeplessness. No wonder he was hallucinating."

"John Michaels," I repeated. "And the only thing in his possession was a newspaper?"

"Yes."

"And what's the name of the editor of that newspaper?"

Ellen's head jerked around. "Mike Johnson."

I nodded. "Mike Johnson, John Michaels. Tomorrow I think I'll ask a few questions about your Mr. Michaels."

The next morning I parked outside Pritchard City and walked inside. The reconstruction was coming along nicely; already Pritchard's Romanian town was generating an atmosphere of its own—dark, otherworldly, and most of all, old. The stones in the buildings gave off a damp chill that was the accumulation of centuries. Many of the buildings met over the streets, so the streets themselves were little more than tunnels where New Mexico's hot sun would never penetrate. The place made me uncomfortable; I couldn't imagine people spending their lives in a place with no sunlight.

Pritchard City's operating offices were skillfully concealed inside the town's agricultural exchange building, like one of our old granges. But inside was all modern efficiency; the personnel director was able to tap a few computer keys and tell me Pritchard City employed no one named John Michaels, either as an actor or in any other capacity. When I described him, she just shook her head; didn't know him. I thanked her and headed for the castle.

El Secreto was laid out on a 180-degree plane, so Pritchard had had a little hill built up to hold his castle. Only the first floor had been completed; the place looked as if the top stories had been sliced off with a giant knife. A number of workmen were visible on the exposed second floor, guiding the blocks of stone a crane was lifting up to them. Wilson Pritchard was standing by the entrance to the castle, and so was Mike Johnson—getting his daily Pritchard story, I supposed. They both greeted me with unfriendly looks; after all, I'd failed to catch the nut who'd killed their dogs. After a few amenities, I asked Pritchard if his purchase of the castle included any underground areas—basement, dungeons, a torture chamber or two.

"I got everything," he growled. "Even a couple of crypts."

"May I see them?"

"What're you looking for, Sheriff? Real vampires?" When I didn't say anything, he shrugged. "All right—come on. I'll show you myself. I've been down there only once, and I'm not all too sure what's there. Storage crates, mostly."

"Have you opened them?" Mike Johnson asked.

"Not yet. I was kind of saving them for dessert."

The three of us went inside. If I'd thought the streets

were damp and chill, this place was an icebox. Pritchard gestured toward high casement windows, all of them shuttered. "Nobody's lived here for over two hundred years. The place hadn't seen sunlight in that long. This way." He led us to an ornately carved wooden door toward the rear of the place; the thing was so heavy Mike and I had to help him open it. Inside the door were half a dozen lantern-type flashlights; we needed them to see our way down the steps.

"Do you feel as if you're caught in a B movie?" Mike muttered in my ear.

There was only one underground area, divided into two unequal alcoves. The smaller and less cluttered section held two stone crypts. The workmen had cleaned up after themselves; no undisturbed dust of centuries or unbroken spiderwebs to tell me what I wanted to know. I hated to say it, but I did. "We're going to have to open them."

"What?" Mike practically yelled the word.

I told them about Ellen's patient, the condition he was in, his need for blood. "You know what that sounds like, don't you?" I said. "The only thing he had on him was a copy of the newspaper. That's how he learned his town had been moved and what you were planning for it, Mr. Pritchard. He even took Mike's name and reversed it, calling himself John Michaels. He told Ellen he's an actor employed by Pritchard City, but he's not. No one of that name or description is on the payroll. I checked."

Their faces were hidden in shadow, so I couldn't tell how they were taking it. Then Mike exploded, "This is insane!"

"I couldn't agree more," I said.

"You really think that guy in the hospital is a vampire! Fritz, have you gone completely nuts?"

"There's one more thing. Mike, LouLou was an old dog and couldn't have put up much of a fight. But Mr. Pritchard, you described your mastiff as strong and courageous. Would an ordinary man be able to do that to him? Would your dog *let* him? I don't think so. But vampires are supposed to have superhuman strength, aren't they?" Silence. "I just want to take a look."

Pritchard made up his mind. "We'll open the crypts," he announced in his not-to-be-argued-with voice.

We put down the flashlights and struggled to move the heavy stone lids. Inside each crypt we found one mummified body.

"That's not it, then," I said. "Let's look at those crates on the other side. We need one large enough to hold a man."

"If he is a man," Pritchard muttered.

The crates were stacked so as to leave a series of narrow aisles; even so, it was hard to make out the exact size and shape of each crate in such poor light. I was beginning to feel like a fool when Pritchard's voice said, "Over here, Sheriff."

The crate he'd found had a big split along one side and one corner was crushed. The lid was jammed in at an odd angle, and it took Mike and me both to wrestle it loose. The crate was empty.

Almost. A dark clod of something was caught in the corner that had been crushed. I picked it up and shined the light on my hand. "Soil."

I could hear them breathing in the darkness. "Oh, my God," Mike said. "Oh, my God!"

"Mr. Pritchard, can you find out what happened to this crate? I think we'd better hurry." Ellen was by no means alone in that hospital, and her patient hadn't looked dangerous, but . . .

"Right," Pritchard said hoarsely. "Let's get out of here."

Outside, he used a walkie-talkie to summon the fore-man of the crew that had moved crates and crypts both to their new resting places. A man I didn't know showed up; in response to Pritchard's questions, he told us all the crates had been stacked outside for over a week while the ground was being excavated and the stones relaid. The crate with the crushed corner? Real sorry about that, Mr. Pritchard, but it just got away from the boys while they were lifting it. Wasn't nothin' in it but dirt anyway. What happened to the dirt? Wind blew it away.

My bed is gone! Ellen's patient had cried.

I headed back to the car at a trot, followed by Pritch-ard and Mike. The phone was buzzing. "Yeah?"

It was Hatch. "Sheriff Brubaker? Your wife called. She said that John Michaels is missing—just walked out of the hospital when no one was looking. Dr. Brubaker seemed to think it was important."

I groaned. "Damn right it's important. Listen, Hatch, I want you to go look for him. Start at the hospital, check the neighborhood—somebody had to have seen him." I gave him a description of "John Michaels" and added, "And Hatch, if you find him, don't approach him. Do you understand? *Do not approach.* Call me—I'm on my way back."

He'd caught the urgency in my voice and didn't waste time asking questions. "Right, Sheriff. I'm on my way."

Mike and Pritchard piled into the car; I drove back toward El Secreto as fast as the engine could take us. "So I guess we know what happened," I said. "He got out of his box to explore his new surroundings, and while he was gone the workmen dropped the crate and his native soil was scattered by the wind. When he came back and found his 'bed' no longer existed, he must have panicked. Hid out, until hunger sent him looking for fresh blood. He got hold of a newspaper, so he knows where he is and *when* he is—no telling how long he'd been sleeping."

"Swing by my place, Sheriff," Pritchard said. "I want to pick up my Browning auto."

"Whoa, now. He hasn't hurt anyone yet. He killed the dogs, yeah, but we don't shoot people for that."

"You're going to wait until he kills somebody before you do anything?"

Mike said, "Would a rifle bullet stop him? Don't you have to drive a stake through his heart or burn him alive or something equally grisly? Your Browning automatic wouldn't be any help."

Pritchard grunted. "Maybe you're right. What you got in mind, Sheriff?"

"Find him, first. Then we see what condition he's in— he wasn't rational the one time I saw him. I think we'd better talk to Ellen."

The hospital parking lot was a paved-over square of dirt in the rear. Ellen was in her office, waiting; she'd been expecting me. She barely looked at Pritchard and Mike before she said, "We tried feeding him intravenously, but his body suffered such a violent reaction that we had to stop. I ordered another blood transfusion, but when the nurse went in to give it to him, he was gone. He must have been afraid of what else we'd do to him."

"Ellen, this is important," I said. "Did he know you were going to give him more blood?"

She thought back. "No, I gave the nurse her instructions out in the hallway."

Both Pritchard and Mike groaned. The latter said, "If he'd just waited a few more minutes...."

"What?" Ellen looked from them back to me. "What's happened?"

I told her what we'd found at the castle, and what had happened to the soil John Michaels had been sleeping on. "I can't explain it, Ellen," I said, "but it looks as if we've got a live one here."

"That's impossible," she said automatically, but her face told me she wasn't convinced that was true. "Nothing is conclusive—it can all be explained away."

"Even 'My bed is gone!'?"

She was silent a moment, and then nodded. "It could be delusional, you know. But that doesn't make it any the less real for him."

Pritchard lumbered over to her. "It's real for all of us, Doctor. This John Michaels is a vampire. Don't tell me that hadn't already occurred to you."

She admitted it had. "There's a germ of truth at the center of every myth. But how much of the myth is fantasy, embellishment—"

"For God's sake, woman, you're a scientist!" Pritchard interrupted vehemently. "You should know what to do!"

"Allow me to introduce myself," my wife said dryly. "My name is Dr. Brubaker, not Dr. Von Helsing. I'm afraid the only thing I can suggest is to isolate John Michaels. If he's what you think he is, then he's a carrier of disease. Unless you want more vampires in El Secreto, he must be put in quarantine. Then we'll try to figure out what to do."

"Maybe he'll tell us what to do," I said. "If he's coherent."

"Hmm," Ellen said. "If all he needs is blood, that's something I *can* take care of. I'll need a portable refrigerated pack...." She reached for her phone.

"Will that do it?" Mike asked. "We keep him supplied with blood and he leaves us alone?"

No one knew. It took Ellen about fifteen minutes to assemble the gear she needed, and then we all left to search for our missing vampire.

Night was coming on and we were getting discouraged; John Michaels had spent the day hiding in dark places and he was hiding still. We'd all regrouped, trying to think of a new approach, when the car phone buzzed.

It was Hatch. "I don't have John Michaels, but I got somebody here who talked to him. We're at the station."

"We'll be right there."

No one said a word during the short drive. We hurried into the station, where Hatch was waiting with a boy of ten or eleven.

"This is Dwight McCullough," my deputy said. "Dwight, you tell Sheriff Brubaker what you told me. Go on, tell him."

The kid shrugged and said, "It was this real weirdo dude, you know? He wanted me to tie him up."

"Tie him up?"

"Yeah, but I know all about them guys. My mom warned me about *them*."

"Hmm. Dwight, tell me what he looked like."

"Oh, you know—*weird*. He had this funny hair sticking out, and his skin was this real dead white, ugh. I don't think he was from around here. And he had these really strange eyes ... I think he was trying to hypnotize me, but I wouldn't look straight at 'im, y'know?"

"Smart move. And he asked you to tie him up? Did he say why?"

"Oh, you know why!"

"But did he *say*?"

"Naw."

"Where did this happen, Dwight?"

"Well, he was in that alley right by the video store. I stayed out on the street."

"On Valencia," Hatch said. "Between Sixth and Seventh."

"He kept callin' me to come in," Dwight went on. "He kept sayin', like, 'You wanna tie me up? Come on and tie me up!' But I ain't about to go in no dark alley with no stranger. My mom told me all about that!"

"Your mom told you right," I said. "Where was this weird dude the last time you saw him?"

"Still in the alley, I guess. I ran away."

"I checked," Hatch said over the kid's head. "Long gone."

"Can I go now?" Dwight asked. "I'm already late for dinner, and I'm gonna get killed."

"Yes, you can go, and thanks for your help. Where do you live?"

"'Bout three blocks from here."

"Deputy Hatch will walk you home. And thanks again." The kid looked scornful at being treated like a baby. I said, "The deputy can explain to your folks why you're so late." His face lit up; he hadn't thought of that. I waved them out, not telling young Dwight that there really are things that go bump in the night.

They were no sooner out the door than Pritchard burst out, "He wanted the kid to tie him up? But why? With all that vampire strength, he could just bust the ropes."

"Maybe he had chains in mind," Mike suggested.

"The point is," I said, "he feels the need to feed again coming on, and he's trying to stop himself. This vampire doesn't want to hurt anybody."

"What about your deputy, Fritz?" Ellen asked. "Are you going to tell him what's going on?"

I hesitated. "Let's hold off on that. Maybe this won't have to go any farther than us four, but if—" The phone ringing interrupted me. I took the call. "Someone's just broken into the butcher shop on Costilla Street," I said as I hung up.

It took a second to register—then all four of us were running toward the car. John Michaels, in his desperate search for blood, was trying everything he could think of. Ellen checked her equipment as I drove.

I pulled up in front of the shop and gestured *Stay inside* to the neighbor who'd called in the break-in. Now that we were close, we all lost some of our eagerness. I took out my revolver. Just in case.

We found him in the freezer. He was collapsed on the floor, wild eyes staring up at the sides of beef hung on the movable rack over his head—all of them frozen solid. No supper here. When we went to move him to a warmer part of the shop, he fought back, screaming, not really seeing us. It took all four of us to get him moved. Malnourished, anemic, skeleton-thin ... but he was still stronger than any one of us individually.

Eventually he seemed to pass out; his eyes closed and his body went limp. We got him stretched out on the floor in front of the meat counters, and Ellen started feeding him blood. "It'll take a while," she said. "We'll have to wait."

Pritchard was bent over the object of our search, studying him as if trying to memorize what a vampire looks like. Mike and I leaned against the counter and waited.

John Michaels was almost through his second pint of blood before he began to stir. When Ellen hooked up the third bottle, he opened his eyes. "The lady physician," he rasped faintly. "You give me blood?"

"As much as you need."

The vampire managed to smile.

I went over and hunkered down beside him. "My name's Fritz Brubaker," I said. "I'm the sheriff here. That's Wilson Pritchard, and this is Mike Johnson. I'm sure you know both those names." He did. "Now, Mr. Michaels, we all know what your problem is." Ellen shot me a funny look. "I mean, we know about your native soil getting lost and how you can't sleep without it. We can take care of the eating part, but we're going to need some help with the sleeping. I want you to tell me the truth—don't make up any more stories about being an actor or the like. Let's start with your name."

He swallowed painfully and said. "Antonescu. My name is Miron Antonescu, and I do not belong in your world."

"Yeah, well, we kind of figured that out. You were born in Romania?" He nodded.

Pritchard barked out a question. "Can you fly?" Thinking of the wall around his place, I suppose.

Antonescu looked startled but said, "I can levitate, yes."

"Where did you learn to speak such good English?" Ellen asked.

"I was educated in England. In fact, I had been offered a position as tutor at Purling Lock in East Anglia, when I returned home for a brief visit before assuming my duties ... and there fell victim to *vàmpīr*."

Mike came over and looked down at him. "You're the one who killed LouLou?"

"No!" Antonescu cried, horrified. "I kill no one! Animals—only animals!"

"LouLou was his dog," I said.

Antonescu closed his eyes. "I am sorry. When the hunger comes...." He trailed off, and after a moment opened his eyes again. "Your time is so strange. Whole towns moved from one place to another, machines that float in the sky ... and never have I seen so bright a sun. Even when I conceal myself in deepest shadow, your sun drains me. Mr. Mike Johnson, your newspaper says this place is called *New* Mexico. Is there an Old Mexico?"

Mike grinned sourly. "Man, you have been asleep a long time. There's a country just south of here named Mexico. New Mexico is part of the United States."

"United ... States?"

"Of America."

"America, ah, I know of—" He broke off and his face crumpled. "Then I am truly doomed! Damned to wander without rest, so far from the soil of my homeland!"

Pritchard spoke up. "No, you're not. We buy you a ticket, put you on a plane—"

"You do not understand!" Antonescu cried. "Between your country and mine lies an ocean. I cannot cross water ... *except in a bed of my homeland soil*. And my bed is gone."

We were all silent. Then Pritchard said, "Well, that tears it."

Eventually the whole story came out. Antonescu was a distant relative of the family that originally occupied the castle now being rebuilt in Pritchard City. Unwilling to put a family member to death using any of the accepted vampire-killing methods, they agreed on a compromise. It seems a vampire can be bound, in a certain explicit way, and placed facedown in a bed of soil. In such a position, he sleeps without ever waking ... *unless his position is changed*. Only then can he awake.

"That's what happened, then," Pritchard said. "That

crate got flipped over somehow during the move. Christ."

"But now I cannot be rebound," our vampire said. "I thought perhaps I could, but that was a delusion born of desperation. Without the soil, the bindings are useless." He swallowed a couple of times and said, "You must kill me. That is the only solution. I cannot control the hunger. Without sleep, the day will come when small animals no longer satisfy. You must kill me."

We all looked at each other uneasily. "Can you live without sleep?" I asked. "We can keep you supplied with blood—"

"Not even that, I'm afraid," Ellen said. "In two days, he's just about depleted our blood supply. We'll get more, of course, but not enough to keep him fed. There's just not that much blood available. No, we'll have to find a way to put him back to sleep." She turned back to Antonescu. "You don't really want to die."

He looked her straight in the eye. "Death is preferable to the only alternative available to me."

"The only alternative *now*. You know, the end result of what you're suffering is a physical disorder—science ought to be able to find an answer. From what I've read about vampirism, the only studies of the subject have been psychological or historic ... they've all tried to explain it away by linking it to outbreaks of cholera or the like. No one has ever studied it as a *disease*."

"Ellen," I said.

"I know—where'll I get the funding? But damn it, Fritz, I have to try."

Of course she did. "There's something else." I turned to Mike Johnson. "Mike—"

"You don't have to say it." He sighed. "The biggest story of my life ... and I have to sit on it."

"Your word?"

"My word."

That was good enough for me.

"But the soil!" Antonescu whispered. "We can do nothing without the soil!"

Pritchard smiled, the first time that day. "Now you stop fretting, son. We can handle that, too."

It was Mike Johnson who made the trip. He came

back with three big crates of good Romanian topsoil, erring on the side of caution. Antonescu now lies in the alcove next to the crypts in Pritchard's castle; a state-of-the-art security system makes sure he'll remain undisturbed.

Ellen took tissue samples and works daily to find a medical solution. But we've had to face the possibility that the answer might not come in our lifetimes, so we've made arrangements for the secret to be kept after we're gone. Pritchard's children are grown and living in other parts of the country, and Ellen and I don't have any kids. So Pritchard has made a new will, leaving the castle and its contents—that's *all* its contents—to Mike's two children. We haven't told Hatch yet, waiting to see if he's here for the long haul or just using El Secreto as a stepping stone.

So we've done the best we can for Antonescu. But one thing bothers me. Is El Secreto unique? Or are there other places, all over the world, each one guarding its own sleeping vampire? Try as I will, I cannot convince myself that ours is the only secret.

BLIND PIG ON NORTH HALSTED
by
Wayne Allen Sallee

The murders started up again the autumn after those dismemberment killings in Milwaukee. Our Body Founds certainly couldn't be considered copycat, even though all the victims were gay and most were killed in the same block of North Halsted.

Some of the more sensationalistic true crime books likened the Milwaukee killer to a cannibalistic psychiatrist in a recent Hollywood film. The guy here in Chicago simply drained their blood.

My name is Dunleavy, and I'm a street cop in the New Town District. Street cops get all the scut work; by the time the primary detective shows, the case is often open and shut as a gang drive-by shooting or a domestic quarrel gone into the twilight zone.

These days, with the murders hitting three a day in Cook County, it seems like all there is.

Until the vampire hit the night scene. Let me fill you in before you herniate, okay? At least I wouldn't have walked away from a bleeding Laotian boy because his companion says it's all a lover's quarrel. Sure, cops can be jaded by the homosexual community. Part of it lies in their promiscuousness, even since the advent of HIV. Deep down, myself, I feel like a gay man is just asking for the worst the same way I would if I had a fifteen-year-old daughter who stayed out all hours.

The clues were there almost from the beginning. The first call came from the back door of a blind pig south of Armitage. The Handyman. A juice bar, I had to laugh about it later. Used to be, when North Clark between

Kinzie and Ontario was The Strip, most every bar had a blind pig. Not the old-fashioned prohibition kind. These were places set off in the back where a man could go and, under secrecy of the minimalist black-lighting, have several variations of sex. Ever hear of a circle jerk? I'll tell you about it another time.

The stiff was in his thirties; at least it wasn't a runaway or transient. Guys like Gacy zoned in on the former like a fly on shit, I tell you. Thing was, on this particular Body Found, there was no fucking way of telling how long the deceased had been that way.

Bervid, the M.E., confirmed our conundrum. There was no lividity to the corpse. Rigor mortis had set in, the eyes were no longer moist, but there should have been a reddening of the skin.

Back at the Harrison Street morgue, it was proven that John Doe #91-44 had less than a half-pint of blood in him. There were two small wounds behind his right ear.

That was the second of October. On the eighth, we caught the squeal on a blind pig off Cambridge. Cock Robin's was the name of the place. The back room was a series of stairwells that went nowhere. Reminded me of The Grab Bag, back of the defunct Gold Coast in the aforementioned Strip. I've seen it all, been a cop now seven years. All rookies in New Town are queered—pun intended by the superiors—into finding out about these back room beauties on their lonesome.

The guy in the bar, they first noticed him when the lights came on. Ass to Jesus, the biggest look of contentment on his face. Puncture wounds on the right thigh, I saw right off. I asked a few questions that I probably should have known just from watching Geraldo.

One of the guys in the bar then was a local actor named Ben Murdy. Mostly commercials, but he had a short-lived series on Fox, "Just Like A Romeo In Joliet." Meaning the prison. Murdy enjoyed cop work, liked to help out. Made him feel like he had gotten his big break into film.

Murdy told me that two highly erogenous zones, for him, were behind the earlobe and the inside of his right thigh. Now I knew that there was nothing on the John Doe's skull wound in the papers; crazy as it was, there was a *blood*sucker out there when there should have been a, well, you get the thrust.

What am I going to do, tell my squad commander that I think there is a lunatic who thinks he's a vampire out there? After the bad press the coppers got in Milwaukee and the L.A. videotape, shit. Squad CQ would have me dust my ass for fingerprints.

But he did okay me an undercover, let me use Murdy the way I would a snitch on a wire. Three weeks now, we've been hitting the blind pigs. I shaved my head (no hard deal with my balding scalp), got used to wearing leather chaps. I pretty much stay on the sidelines, the only wallflower not wearing a zipper-mask, it seems.

Murdy goes in with a wire, one of those I've Fallen and I Can't Get Up things. I'll be right in there, if the guy shows. We've been everywhere. The Viking Pontiac. Hungry-Boy. The Glory Hole. Places even less obvious.

I run into Bervid now and then. Big tall guy, I went to high school with him. Damn intimidating medical examiner.

I saw him outside the Rock 'n Roll McDonalds on Clark, he was pronouncing a Mad Dog veteran at the scene. An alley behind a record shop. I went up to the Berv, burger and fries already wolfed while crossing the street.

"Haven't seen you in a while," he said while signing the tags.

"You'll never guess what I've been up to the past month or so," I told him, looking deadpan as possible, because he knew what went on in New Town, pronouncing his share of flames with hep or HIV.

Bervid mulled it over a bit, then he stared me down.

"I'll bite," he grinned.

PHIL THE VAMPIRE
by
Richard Laymon

"It's my husband," she said.

"I see."

"I don't think so."

"Tell me about it, then."

"He's . . . seeing other women."

I nodded. It was what I'd figured.

The gal's name was Traci Darnell. She looked too young, too sweet, too terrific to have a husband stepping out on her. But all that doesn't matter if you're hooked with the wrong kind of guy. Some fellows don't care how good they've got it at home.

I'd seen it plenty of times before.

It never made much sense. It always made me a little sad, and more than a little disgusted.

"I'm sorry," I told Traci.

"Well." Her shoulders gave a quick, nervous hop. The rest of her didn't move at all, just sat rigid in the chair across from my desk, leaning forward slightly, hands folded on her lap. "It's not as if . . . I mean, I knew what I was getting into."

"What do you mean?"

"I knew there would be other women. A lot of them. I knew that going in. But . . ." She pinched her lower lip between her teeth. Her shoulders hopped again. "I thought I could handle it. I thought it wouldn't matter. But it does." Her eyes met mine. They were blue, intelligent, the sort of eyes that should gleam with fun. But they were grim. They made me want to hurt the guy responsible. "I love him," she said. "I love him so much. It just . . . rips me apart. I can't stand it anymore." Her eyes brimmed.

"Are you sure he's seeing other women?" I asked.

She sniffed. "Oh, he's never made any secret of it."

"He admits it?"

"Admits? He doesn't *admit* anything, he *shares his experiences* with me. He tells me every detail of every conquest. Her name, what she looked like, what she was wearing—or not wearing—exactly where he had her. He tells me everything that was said. What she did, what he did. The feel of her, the smell of her, the taste."

Leaning forward, I shoved a box of tissues closer to the edge of my desk. Traci plucked one out and blew her nose.

"Why did he tell you those things?" I asked. "To rub it in? To make you squirm?"

"Oh, no. It wasn't anything like that. It was like I said, his way of sharing. He wanted me to know what was going on in his life, that's all. It was never meant to hurt me. He thought it would bring us closer."

"Bring you *closer*? Telling you about the women he's . . ." I hesitated, reluctant to use any graphic terms in front of a gal who seemed so innocent and vulnerable.

"Sucked?" she suggested.

For a second there, I wondered if Traci had a lisp. "Did you say 'sucked'?" I asked.

"Sucked."

"Sucked or fucked?"

Her face blushed scarlet. "Ssssucked."

"Oh. Sorry." I felt my own face get hot. "He told you about *sucking* these other women?"

"That's right. And he . . . he certainly didn't do that *other* thing."

I couldn't see one whole hell of a lot of difference, myself. It seemed to me that Traci was splitting hairs.

Indignant, she said, "He's never been unfaithful. He's not a lech, he's a vampire."

I didn't miss a beat. "Ah," I said. "I see."

"Do you?" She looked hopeful.

"Sure. He's a vampire. He isn't having affairs with any of these women, he's just sucking their blood."

"You really *do* understand?"

"Sure. *Dracula, Salem's Lot,* Lugosi and Christopher Lee, Barnabus Collins—you'd have to be culturally illiterate not to know a thing or two vampires. And your husband's a vampire. What's his name, by the way?"

"Phillip."

"Phil the vampire."

I wished I hadn't said that. Traci looked betrayed.

"You think this is all a great big joke."

"No. I really don't. Whatever's going on, it's obvious that you're ..."

"I *told* you what's going on."

"Well, not exactly."

"Every night, he leaves me alone and goes off stalking victims. He drinks their blood. Then he comes home and *tells* me all about it. I hate it that he's seeing these other women ... that he *needs* them. It makes me feel so ... inadequate. You know, that *I'm* not enough for him."

"No woman would be enough for his kind," I said.

"Is that another wisecrack? Because if it is, I'm going to waltz right out that door and ..."

"I was being entirely serious," I explained. "As a vampire, he couldn't possibly subsist on your blood alone. You'd be depleted in no time flat. You'd be dead. Phil *has* to play the field. He would kill you otherwise. His roaming, actually, might be viewed as an act of love. Love for you."

"I know that." She looked ready to start weeping again. "But that doesn't make it any easier ... to live with."

"You're jealous of these women he sucks?"

"Of course I am."

"Does he ever suck you?"

"Sometimes." She dipped her fingers under the collar of her blouse and pulled it aside. Her top button came undone, but she didn't seem to notice. The side of her neck had a pair of wounds just where you'd expect to find them in a Dracula movie. Healed, though. Scar tissue that looked like small, pink craters.

Real or makeup? I wondered.

Only one way to find out. I knocked my chair back on its rollers, stepped around my desk, and crouched in front of Traci. Close up, the scars looked pretty authentic.

"Do they hurt?" I asked.

"No. They never did hurt. Not even when he had his teeth in me."

"Getting bit like that didn't hurt?"

"Oh, no." With a dreamy look on her face, she fingered the tiny remains of the punctures. "It felt . . . incredible."

I raised my index finger. "Do you mind?"

Shaking her head, she moved her hand out of the way. I gently probed both the scars. They felt real, all right. "Phil actually made these with his teeth? He actually sucked blood out of your neck?"

"Yes."

While Traci straightened her collar, I stood up and sat on the front edge of my desk. She didn't fasten the button that had come undone.

"And you're here because you don't like him doing it to other women?"

"That's right."

"Has Phil killed any of these women?"

"No. Oh, no, I'm sure he hasn't. He's not at all like—you know, Dracula. He's a kind, gentle man. He respects life."

"Wouldn't harm a fly, huh?"

"Oh, he sometimes eats them. But he doesn't have a malicious bone in his body. He wouldn't kill a *person*. He's very careful never to harm anyone."

"Is he taking their blood by force?"

She looked confused. "Well, he's sucking it out."

"But with their permission? Are they willing partners?"

"Oh, of course. Who wouldn't be? Phil's . . . a hunk, you know? And smart and witty. I think most women find him irresistible. But he also has his powers."

"Powers?"

"What I mean is, he can pretty much zap the mind of anyone he meets. He has this hypnotic thing he can do. Puts them under." Traci snapped her fingers. "Just like that, they're zombies. Not *literally* zombies. You know what I mean."

"He can put them in a trance, and they'll comply with whatever he wants."

"Right. But also, the main thing is they can't remember anything afterward."

"And Phil uses this power on his victims?"

"I don't know if I'd call them victims."

"Whatever. The women he sucks. He zaps them?"

"All the time. Not me, though."

"Why's that?"

Her look suggested it was a dumb question. "Because I'm his wife, of course."

"Ah. All right. But here's the thing. If your husband is putting these women under—by hypnosis or whatever—he's compromising their ability to consent. In other words, he does not legally have their permission. If he was having sex with them . . ."

"He's not."

"But if he *was* having sex with them, it would be rape. So I'm pretty sure he's violating some sort of law by biting them and taking their blood without permission. That would make it a police matter. I'm just a private investigator, and don't have the authority to . . ."

"I don't want Phil *arrested*!" Traci blurted, shaking her head. "That's not why I came here. I don't want anything like that."

"What exactly *do* you want?"

"I want him to stop. I want him all to myself. I want him to quit using all those others!"

The way she looked made me want to take her into my arms. To comfort her. To make her hurts go away. But I knew better. My self-control isn't always terrific when it comes to gals, especially the pretty, vulnerable ones. So I kept to my perch.

She gazed up at me with shiny, imploring eyes. "Will you help me?" she asked.

"I'd like very much to help you," I said. "But maybe what you need is a shrink or . . ."

"A shrink? Are you saying I'm crazy?"

"Nothing of the sort. You obviously didn't put those bite marks on your own neck." A moment after I'd said that, I wondered how she *might've* gone about putting them there.

Self-inflicted wounds are a fairly common trick. Perps think them a very clever way to deceive cops, lawyers, doctors, insurance companies, and even PIs like me.

Traci might have made the punctures herself. Physical evidence to back up her weird tale. If she'd made them, though, she'd done some major advance planning. From the appearance of the scars, the injuries must've been inflicted at least a month ago.

Either she was a major-league schemer, or she was telling the truth—the truth as she saw it, anyway.

"The thing is," I explained, "a therapist might be better equipped to help you confront your problem."

She studied me with narrowed eyes. "My problem?"

"I want to help you, Traci. I honestly do. You wouldn't believe the creeps and losers and slimes that I have to deal with all the time—mostly attorneys. My clients. So I tell you, it really brightened my afternoon when you showed up. You seem to be a very nice young lady. Easy on the eyes, to boot," I added.

She gave me a smirk for that one. And blushed as she smirked. And kind of rolled her eyes toward the ceiling in a way that said, *Boy, what a line.*

"I'll do what I can for you, Traci. But we won't do each other any good unless we're honest about the situation. I intend to be honest with you. It might not be pleasant, but it's how I work. Okay?"

"Okay."

"Your problem. You come in here and tell me your husband's a vampire. Now, we all know about vampires. The living dead. They sleep in coffins during the day, prowl at night, suck the blood out of people. They've got magical powers. They can control people's minds, turn themselves into bats, wolves, fog, pretty much anything that suits their fancy. They're immortal—or as good as. Live hundreds of years, who knows? They're afraid of the cross, find garlic disagreeable. Their reflections don't show up in mirrors. They can't cross moving water. They can't be killed by ordinary means, you've gotta nail them with a wooden shaft. Or trick them into the sunlight. Probably other ways, but I'm no expert. I just know what every red-blooded American guy knows on the subject. Which includes that such things just don't exist."

"That's what you think."

"It's what I know, Traci. It's what everyone knows. I'm not saying there aren't weirdos who *think* they're vampires and maybe even act accordingly. But the actual supernatural-Dracula-immortal-batman-vampire is nothing but fiction. You just aren't gonna meet one, not in this life. That means Phil isn't one. That's for starters."

"So, you are saying I'm crazy."

"I told you. I'm not a shrink. I'm just a gumshoe, the poor man's Spade. What I'm doing here with you is trying to apply some tricks of my trade, and the best tricks I've got are my instincts and common sense."

"So what do they tell you?"

"First, I don't think you're crazy. Second, I'm pretty sure you aren't trying to put one over on me. So I'm forced to conclude that Phil has convinced you he's a vampire."

"He *is* a vampire."

"He bit your neck and sucked your blood."

She nodded. "Many times."

"He goes off by himself every night and comes back with stories of his conquests. Of women he entranced and sucked."

"Yes."

"And you believe him." I gave one of my bushy eyebrows a meaningful hoist. "Have you ever followed him during one of his nightly prowls?"

She frowned. "You're saying it might all be a lie?"

"Do you have any proof that it isn't?"

"He sometimes comes home with blood on his clothes."

"A *lot* of blood, or . . ."

"No, just a few little spots or smudges."

I fished my Swiss Army knife out of my pants pocket, opened the main blade, and nicked the back of my hand. A dot of blood bloomed out. I blotted it on the front of my white shirt. "Now I'm a vampire, too," I said.

And Traci smiled. It was the first time I'd seen her smile. It looked great. "You've ruined your shirt."

"Hire me, and I can afford a new one."

"Hire you?"

"That's why you came in here, right?"

"Well. Yes. I guess so."

"We were exploring the nature of your problem, right? Your husband has convinced you he's a vampire. As a vampire, he needs to drink human blood. So he goes out and sucks women, and you're jealous. You want it stopped. You want him to devote all his attention on you, not spread it around among strangers."

"That's pretty much it, I guess."

"That's your problem. But here's the question: what's Phil *really* up to? You can bet it's not sucking necks."

"You're saying ... it might all be like a cover while he's doing something he doesn't want me to know about?"

"I say you can bet on it. He might just be boozing with his buddies, something as innocent as that. Or maybe he's into some kind of criminal activity. Could be anything. But I've got to warn you, the most likely thing is that he's seeing another woman."

"That's what I *told* you. He's seeing another woman every night."

"But not to suck blood. To have sex."

"No."

"I realize it's a painful ..."

"It's not painful because I know he doesn't mess around with anyone." Though she spoke calmly, her face was bright red. "He *tells* me what he does to those women. Everything. Every small, intimate detail. And he ... we ... make out while he talks. We, you know, get naked. And then we fool around while he tells me all about the woman he'd been with that night, and when it comes to the part where he sinks his teeth into her, that's when he ... sinks his, uh ... that's when he enters me."

She wasn't so much red, really, as pink. Her face, her ears, her throat, the smooth skin that showed between the edges of her blouse where the button was undone.

I had a bulge in my lap. I folded my hands down there to hide it.

Dry-mouthed, I said, "So, he uses his stories to excite you. As a form of foreplay?"

"Something like that."

"And the story always finishes with ... intercourse?"

"Not always." She gazed down at her own folded hands. "Sometimes he ... we ... use our mouths. You know."

"Oh."

She raised her eyes. "Anyway, so I guess you can see how come I know he's not having any affairs."

"It may very well be that he's not. I hope he isn't, but obviously he's up to something. Something he means to keep secret from you, so he fabricated the vampire story."

"I don't think it's a fabrication."

"Does Phil have a job?"

"He doesn't need one. He's very rich."

"What does he do during the day?"

"He sleeps. In his coffin. In the basement."

That shouldn't have surprised me, but it did. Obviously, Phil was carrying his act to some rather major extremes.

"Have you ever seen him go outside in the sunlight?"

Traci shook her head. "He never leaves his coffin from dawn till after sunset."

"As far as you know."

"Well, I don't stand guard, if that's what you mean."

"What do *you* do during the day?"

"Sleep, do the shopping." She shrugged. "Different chores."

"Do you look in on him often?"

"At first I did. I couldn't ... you know, believe he'd stay down there so long. But he always did. It was a waste of time, checking on him. So I don't do it much anymore."

"So you can't say for sure whether he stays in the coffin."

"Not absolutely for sure," she admitted. "But pretty sure. What's the big deal?"

"No big deal. Just curious. Have you ever seen Phil turn into a bat or anything"

"He knows I can't stand bats."

"Have you ever seen him change into ... ?"

"He changed into a dog once. A big black Lab."

Right, I thought. But I kept the opinion to myself and asked, "He changed into it before your eyes?"

"Look, if you don't want to believe any of this ..."

"I just want to get at the truth, that's all. If you actually watched Phil turn himself into a dog, I guess I'd have to believe he's got supernatural powers."

"You wouldn't have to believe any such thing. You'd figure I was either lying or hallucinating, or that Phil had fooled me with some kind of magic trick."

"Is Phil a magician?"

"He's a vampire."

"Did you watch him turn into the dog?"

"No."

"Then what makes you think . . . ?"

"The dog was Phil." She turned pink again. "I know it was him."

"How do you know?"

"Never mind. Can we change the subject?"

"All right. Let's change it to mirrors. Does Phil show up in mirrors?"

"Yes."

I managed not to blurt, *Ah-ha!* But I couldn't help smiling. "You've seen his reflection in mirrors."

"Yes."

"Well, doesn't that suggest a hole in his vampire story?"

"I asked him about it."

"And?"

"He told me that mirrors aren't the same as they were in the old days. A lot of them used to be backed with silver, but that's pretty rare now. He said he wouldn't show up in a mirror that has a real silver backing. I don't have one like that, so I don't know."

"Convenient for Phil."

She frowned. "You know, I've never felt any great need to *prove* he's a vampire. I know what he is. So I haven't gone around *testing* him."

"If he's not a vampire, Traci, he has no excuse to go roaming at night."

"I know that. I know that better than anyone."

"If he's not a vampire, then he's not sucking those women you're so jealous of."

"I know. But he *is* one."

I let out a sigh. "Then how do you expect me to stop him from seeing those other gals? He *needs* blood, right? If he doesn't take it from strangers, where's he supposed to get it? He can't rely only on you. It'd kill you. Is that what you want?"

"No."

"What *do* you want?"

Traci bent down and reached for her handbag. She had placed it on the floor beside her chair immediately after sitting down. It was a large leather bag with a shoulder strap. As she took hold of the bag, I glanced down the front of her blouse. She wore a pale blue bra that was too skimpy to cover much. What it did cover, it was too transparent to hide. What I could see was her entire right breast.

My view went away when Traci sat up, lifting the handbag onto her lap. She slipped her hand inside the top and came out with a wooden stake.

It looked like a foot-long section of broom handle that had been whittled with a knife until it tapered down to a point.

"You're kidding me," I said.

She stared into my eyes.

"You want me to kill Phil?"

"It's the only way to stop him."

"Terrific," I muttered.

She handed the stake to me. I looked it over, thumbed its point. The point was very sharp.

"You said you wanted to help," she reminded me.

"You've got the wrong guy."

"I don't think so."

"I don't do murder."

"It wouldn't be murder."

"No, sure, of course not. He's a vampire. Right."

"It's the truth."

"Yeah, and I'm Tinkerbell."

"You've *got* to do this for me. Please. I'll pay you whatever ... How much do you want? Five thousand? Ten?"

"I don't get it. Why do you want him dead? I thought you loved him?"

"I do."

"You're just so jealous of these other gals?"

"Yes!" Her eyes flashed. "Is that so hard to understand? Every night—every night he leaves me alone and goes to someone else. I can't stand it!"

"But he always comes home to you," I said. "Those others are nothing to him except ... nourishment? It's you he loves. It's you he *makes* love to. And it sounds pretty damn passionate, if you ask me."

Lowering her head, she murmured, "It is. But ... *they're* the ones he sucks."

"You'd *rather* be sucked?"

"It's so much more ... more everything. Than sex. There's no comparison. It's a kind of rapture that you ... you just can't imagine."

"Does Phil know how you feel about this?"

"Of course he does. But he won't give in. He says that he likes me the way I am, that if he sucks me too often, I'll lose my spark. My spark. That's a laugh."

"It sounds as if he cares a lot about you."

"Well, he does. But not enough to stay home and bite *my* neck. That's all I want."

"And since he won't do it, you want me to kill him? That doesn't make any sense at all."

Her eyes darkened. "If I can't have him, nobody else will. You know what I mean? I'm sick to death of it."

All of a sudden, I believed her.

I didn't believe the part about Phil being a vampire. I knew she believed it, though, and I knew she wasn't kidding that she wanted him dead.

If I can't have him, nobody else will.

The magic words.

Graveyards are full of people who died because someone loved them—loved them too much, would rather see them dead than lose them to another person.

"I'm not a killer," I explained again.

"It's not as if you'd be killing a man."

"He *is* a man. You may think he's a vampire, but he's flesh and blood. If I took your money and whammed that stake through his heart, it'd be murder. In this state, it'd be first degree murder with special circumstances. That'd make it a capital crime. Not me, lady."

"How much?" she asked.

"Uncle Sam doesn't print enough."

"What if I can prove to you that Phil's a vampire?"

"Ain't gonna happen."

"But just suppose. How would you feel about killing a real ... what did you call it? A real, supernatural-immortal-batman-Dracula-vampire? There's no law against *that*, is there?"

"Of course not. But ..."

"*Would* you be willing to kill an actual vampire? For ten thousand dollars? And for me?"

I didn't miss a beat. What was to think about?

"Sure I'd do it," I told Traci. "But it won't happen. There's no way, not a chance in hell, you could ever prove to me that Phil's a vampire."

For the second time that afternoon, Traci smiled. "Want to bet?" she asked.

She glanced past me at the office window, then checked her wristwatch. "Sunset isn't till 6:25. That gives us almost an hour and a half."

I suddenly got an ucky feeling in my gut. "You want to do this now? Today?"

She nodded. "Before Phil wakes up."

Traci drove. I rode with her in the passenger seat of her Porsche. Normally, I would've driven my own car. There wasn't much normal about this trip, though. No telling what I might be getting into. If it got messy, I didn't want some neighbor or passerby giving the cops a description of my vehicle.

Besides, riding with Traci gave me more time to enjoy her. She didn't talk much. She smelled good, and had a fine profile. Her black leather skirt was very short, her legs long and smooth.

I thought a lot about how Phil told his stories every night while they worked on each other. How he timed things. *When it comes to the part where he sinks his teeth into her, that's when he sinks his . . .* That's when he put it to her.

Lucky stiff.

The whole vampire thing seemed to be a huge turn-on for both of them.

Assuming, of course, that Traci'd been telling me the truth.

I didn't like to think that she'd been lying about any of it. Lying would mean I'd signed on for a whole different ballgame. Maybe not even a ballgame, at all.

There wasn't much traffic, so we made good time. We left the city behind. Traci sped us through the woods on narrow roads shrouded with shadows.

It took us nearly an hour to reach the house.

A nicely kept two-story colonial. Normal looking. Nothing creepy about it, if you don't count finding it all by itself at the end of a half-mile of unpaved road.

"Where does Phil find all these gals he sucks?" I asked as Traci stopped the car.

"In the city, mostly."

"A commuter vampire."

"We'd better hurry."

As I followed her toward the front door, I checked my wristwatch. Five-fifty. If Traci was right about the sunset, Phil would be rousing himself in thirty-five minutes.

Not much time.

Not much, right. I felt like a dope for letting myself worry about it. Who cares when the sun goes down? It would only matter if Phil was a vampire, and I knew better.

I had better things to worry about.

What's really going on? for instance.

Traci entered the house first. I stepped in behind her. Even though the sun hadn't gone down yet, the house was pretty dark and gloomy inside. She didn't turn on any lights. Not till we stood at the top of the basement stairs. The basement was very dark. She flipped a switch. Lights came on. They made it a little better, but not much.

"He's down there?" I whispered.

Traci nodded. She removed the stake from her handbag and offered it to me.

I shook my head. I reached under my jacket and unlimbered my 45. It was a big heavy Colt, Army model. Out of fashion, I know. These days, it's all 9 mm Berettas and such. But the Colt auto was good enough for my old man in the Pacific. You remember the Pacific? That's when the Japs were too busy killing us to buy the country out from under our sorry butts.

I jacked a round into the chamber.

"That won't do you any good against Phil," Traci warned.

"Let's go," I said.

No reason to waste time explaining that vampires were the least of my worries.

For all I knew, this whole bit might've been a trap they'd laid for *me*. Maybe Phil was a guy I'd pissed off, one time or another. Maybe Traci was his cute little helper.

As Yogi Bera might've said, *You never know till you know.*

Traci kept hold of the stake, and started down. I let her get a few stairs below me, then followed. The stairway was wood. It creaked and moaned. It had open spaces between the treads, spaces that somebody could reach through and grab your ankle. I tried to brace myself for something like that.

The basement air was cool. It had the normal basement smell of dank concrete.

The walls and floor were concrete.

Phil's coffin was on the floor just beyond the foot of the stairs, just beneath a glaring, bare lightbulb.

He was inside. Stretched out on a lining that looked like red satin. Eyes shut. Hands folded on his belly. Dressed to the hilt in a vampire garb that looked like it might've been filched from the Universal Studios wardrobe department.

He looked a lot younger than Lugosi'd been back in those days. He had sort of a clean-cut, boyish appearance. Long, blond hair. He might've looked like a Santa Monica surfer if he'd had a good tan. But his face was pale, pasty. And his lips were bright red.

I stopped beside Traci. We both stood over the coffin, staring down at Phil.

"Now do you believe me?" she asked. She spoke in a normal tone, and her voice resounded through the basement, damn near echoed.

"Shhh."

"It's all right," she said. "We won't disturb him. He's totally out of it till the sun goes down." She checked her watch. "That's almost half an hour from now."

"Sure," I said.

Five minutes ago, the guy probably had his face pressed to the living room window. Saw us coming and hightailed for the basement, his black cloak flapping.

If that's how it had gone, though, he hadn't winded himself.

From where I stood, I couldn't tell whether he was breathing at all.

"Will you do it now?" Traci asked. She held the stake out for me. Again.

"No such thing as vampires," I said.

I gave the side of the coffin a good, rough kick. It gave the box a jolt. It shook Phil. But it didn't wake him up.

"Just take it." Traci pressed the stake into my hand. Then she hurried across the basement, heels clacking, rump flexing nicely against the seat of her skirt. She snatched something off a workbench near the wall. When she turned around, I saw it was a claw hammer. She gave it a little shake. "You'll need this."

"Not likely."

She stopped in front of me. She held out the hammer. "Please. Take it."

"My hands are full," I muttered.

"The gun won't do you any good, anyway. Here."

"No thanks."

"You *said* you'd do it."

"Yeah. And I will. If you can prove he's a vampire."

"Just look at him."

"That's no proof. That's a guy in a coffin and an outfit."

"I mean *look* at him. He's not alive."

He's not alive.

Holy shit!

I suddenly knew the score.

I jammed the muzzle of my .45 into Traci's gut. Her mouth sprang open. "Lose the hammer, honey," I said.

She dropped it. The steel head struck the concrete with a clank.

"Put your hands on top of your head and interlace your fingers."

She blinked at me. "What's . . . ?"

"Do it."

She did it.

"Stay put."

"What's *wrong*?" she blurted. "Why are you *doing* this?"

I didn't answer. I dropped the stake, shifted the Colt to my left hand, and crouched beside the coffin. Keeping the pistol aimed at Traci, I reached into the coffin with my right hand and found Phil's neck.

Its skin felt cold.

I fingered around, searching for the pulse. From the

temperature of the skin, though, I knew I wouldn't find one. And I didn't.

"He's dead, all right," I said.

"That's what I *told* you. He's not a man, he's a vampire."

"He's dead."

"He's *un*dead."

"Right. Where'd you get the idea I'm an idiot, lady?"

"What are you *talking* about."

"This." I stood up and stepped toward her. "Keep your hands on your head and turn around."

She turned around.

I stepped in close behind her. I started patting her down. "You murdered him. You put together this vampire story, got him into the outfit and coffin, checked your phone book for a likely . . ."

"You're crazy!"

"Not crazy enough to fall for your game." She was clean. I holstered my piece, brought her arms down behind her back, and cuffed them.

I go plenty of places without my Colt. I never leave home without my handcuffs.

They come in useful when I need to keep someone in custody. And they're a turn-on for a lot of my lady friends.

Traci fell into the former category.

Too bad. I'd liked her. I'd wanted her. Beautiful, sexy, innocent and vulnerable.

Cancel those last two.

Still beautiful and sexy, but about as innocent and vulnerable as a sidewinder.

A sidewinder. Rattlesnake or missile, take your pick.

After she was cuffed, I let go of her. She turned around and gazed at me with wide, stunned eyes.

"You had me going," I said. "Thing is, I'm an open-minded sort of guy. You tell me far-out stuff, I'll listen to reason. You had me about eighty percent convinced Phil might really *be* a vampire. But you fell a little short. Short to the tune of a murder rap."

Traci shook her head.

"If you'd just been a little more convincing, I might've given Phil the stake treatment and taken you off the hook."

"It's not too late," she said. "There's ten thousand in my handbag. Cash. Just kill him and . . ."

"And take the fall for you. Right. 'Fraid not."

"I've seen how you look at me."

"You're a good-looking woman."

"I'll be yours."

"Nope. I'll be in prison. Either that, or dead. More than likely dead. Otherwise, I might explain your little vampire fairy tale, and the cops might buy it. You planned to kill me, didn't you? I guess you'd claim you caught me in the act of staking your hubby. How were you going to explain his getup?"

"Please!" She started to weep.

"Forget it. I'm no one's patsy."

Cuffed and all, she made a break for the stairs. I grabbed for her but missed, so she got a short lead. I raced after her. She was partway up the stairs before I got hold of her. Just reached up, caught the hem of her skirt, and gave it a tug.

I meant to yank it down around her ankles, hobble her, trip her up.

But the skirt didn't pull down. When I gave it that tug, I plucked Traci backward off the stairs and she came falling at me. I had time to dodge her. But I stayed my ground. It was either catch her, or let her crash to the concrete floor. I couldn't allow her to crash, not with her arms cuffed behind her back. Even a gal who'd tried to frame me for murder deserved better than that. So I braced myself and spread my arms.

I almost stayed on my feet.

But not quite.

Her weight hit me. I grabbed her, stumbled back, and fell. She pounded down on top of me. The cuffs got me in the nuts. The back of her head clopped my chin, and the impact of that bashed my head against the concrete.

I went out.

When I came to, Traci wasn't on top of me anymore. But I spotted her easily enough. Opened my eyes, and there she was. Didn't even need to raise my head off the floor.

She was hanging from a ceiling girder. Dangling by her tied ankles. She was naked. Her skin was the color of a gloomy, overcast morning. Except where it was smudged with red handprints and lip marks, and where it trickled blood from punctures.

The punctures were bite marks like those she'd shown me on her neck. But these were fresh. Open, raw. And they were all over her, as if her attacker had been a connoisseur sampling tastes from her different regions—her thighs, her groin, her navel, her breasts, her face and the undersides of her drooping arms.

She still wore my cuffs. They were no longer connected, though. With the links between them broken, they encircled Traci's wrists like quirky silver bracelets.

I had reasons of my own for feeling miserable. But the way Traci looked made me feel a lot worse. She'd been broken. Used and trashed. And I was to blame.

I'd fucked up.

And she'd paid for it.

Without moving, I could feel the weight of my Colt in my shoulder holster. I snatched it out, tossed myself sideways, and rolled fast, ready to blast trouble.

What I saw while I rolled was Phil.

I came to a squat, facing him, taking aim.

He was sitting on the basement stairs, watching me. Second stair from the bottom, feet on the concrete floor, elbows resting on his knees, hands folded. He didn't have his outfit on. He had nothing on, at all. Except a lot of Traci's blood.

Sighing, he shook his head. "Women," he muttered. "You know what I mean?"

I put two slugs in his chest and one in his forehead.

They went through him like he was jelly. The holes flowed shut, and he was good as new before the bullets had time to quit ricocheting around the basement.

"Oh, shit," I muttered.

He acted like it hadn't happened. "You know what I mean?" he asked again.

I just gaped at him.

"You know?" he said. "I mean, what'd I ever do to Traci? I loved her. I treated her great. And what does she do? She brings you over to put a hit on me. Jesus H. Christ on a rubber crutch."

"She was jealous," I said.

"Jealous? Shit. I screwed her head off, man. Every single night . . ."

"She didn't want that," I explained. "She wanted you to suck her."

"Figures. They never listen. I told her over and over again, 'Traci,' I said, 'I'd *love* to suck you every night. You *know* that. But it'd *kill* you.' That's what I told her. But does she listen? Shit."

"Looks like she finally got her wish."

Phil gave me a weary smirk. "Well, she died happy."

"Will she become a vampire now?"

Phil huffed. "No way. I'm leaving her dead, man. She tried to have me snuffed. Good riddance." He shook his head again. He backhanded some blood off his lips. "Broads," he muttered. "You can't live with 'em, you can't live without 'em."

"Know what you mean," I said.

"What's your name?" he asked.

"Matthews. Cliff Matthews."

"Go on home, Cliff. I got no beef with you."

UNDERCOVER
by
Nancy Holder

It was a November night in Chicago, and the sleet stabbed Stan's shoulders like daggers—or in his case, incisors—as he ducked into the station house and crammed his umbrella into a stand inside a wire cage.

"Hey, Detective Stepanek," the desk sergeant greeted him. "Man, what a night, eh? It's enough to ... kill ... you." His voice trailed off and he went back to his paperwork. His face was a purple blush of embarrassment.

Stan sighed and began peeling off his gloves. Yeah, well, some guys never got used to him.

Neither did some women.

He scowled at everyone and no one as he unbuttoned his coat. Twelve months now since his Change. And Leslie wouldn't come near him. Some day he would find the fiend who'd done this to him and pay him back in spades.

Or stakes.

Man.

He ran a hand through his hair and pushed through the double doors past the sergeant's desk, and strode down the hall. A couple of beat cops, clad in dripping rain gear, saw him and nodded, but shifted their gazes as soon as they politely could. Fragging cowards.

His teeth hurt. He was hungry.

The black letters on the glass door read, "JACK ZIRES." That was his boss. He rapped hard, waited for the grunt, got it, and went into the small cubbyhole jammed with file cabinets and paper.

Tall and bald, Jack was eating a salad out of a Styrofoam container. Six months ago, he had become a vegetarian and ever since then, his cholesterol tapdanced near the danger zone and he couldn't bring it back down. It made him cranky.

"Hey." Jack gestured to a seat. He had heavy black eyebrows and a perpetual five o'clock shadow; was bitter about the lack of hair on his head. Took a lot of ribbing for it. Before he became a vegetarian.

"How you tonight " he asked between bites of salad. Stan had forgotten what lettuce tasted like. Not, he recalled, that it had ever tasted like much. Steak, he missed. Chocolate. Pizza. Not lettuce.

"I'm okay," Stan muttered, straddling the chair.

"Leslie again?" They were close enough to talk about things like that.

"Is it ever anything else?" Stan wiped the raindrops off his head and straightened out his legs. His shoes were soaked.

"Well, yeah, sometimes it is." Jack stabbed a carrot, picked it off the fork, and ate it with his fingers. "Sometimes it's your kids. Sometimes it's your parents. Sometimes it's your fellow detectives and other persons in uniform." As Jack, an unreconstructed chauvinist, referred to the women on the force.

"Jeez, Jack, I'm not a complainer."

"I know." Jack patted Stan's forearm. He was one of the few people Stan knew who would actually touch him. "Listen. Listen hard. I've got something for you, and I'm going to give it to you and you alone. Okay?" He nudged something in his salad, sneered at it, and put down his fork. "Some of these vegetables. I don't know." He touched a paper napkin to his lips and dropped it onto his cluttered desk.

"Okay," he said, and opened a drawer. He reached in and withdrew a plastic bag that contained the remains of a lady's black wallet.

He dropped the bag in front of Stan. Nodded at it.

"Check it out."

Stan eyed him, dropped his gaze. Opened the bag and fished out the wallet. "So?" he said, and then saw the fragment of a picture in the inside window, where ordinarily you might slip a driver's license. He gasped and almost dropped the wallet, then held it close and leaned into the beam of light from the crookneck lamp on Jack's desk.

It was part of a face, but it was a face he suddenly remembered with the force of a roundhouse right. Huge brown eyes, a long thin nose, and a beautiful red mouth that hid her cruel surprise. Yes, he knew it now: it'd been a woman, or something pretending to be one. Dear God.

"How—how did you get this?" He could barely speak.

"Stoolie Bob brought it in. Said he found some broad lying dead on the street. Or so he thought. Took her purse and he was going through it when she stood up and tried to kill him. That's all he said, but he hasn't been himself since. I thought of you." Jack winced. "No offense."

"None taken." Stan hadn't been the same since. "Why'd he bring it to you?"

"Wanted me to lock him up for theft."

Stan's hear beat faster. "Got anything else?"

"Put that new guy on finding out where the purse was bought, if possible. I dunno. It's a long shot. Could be somebody else's purse. I mean, does your wife carry pictures of herself in her own handbag?"

"I don't remember," Stan said morosely.

"Aw, man. Women can be so cold." Jack stared down at the remains of his salad and shut the Styrofoam container. "I need a hamburger injection, damn it."

"So," Stan pressed.

"So. I didn't hold Stoolie Bob, and he's waiting for you at The Old Same Place. Wants to talk."

Stan inclined his head. "Thanks, Jack."

"I ain't telling anybody else about this. You got enough problems. Anybody asks you what you're working on, tell 'em special detail, and if they have any more questions to come to me."

Stan reverently put the wallet back in the bag and slipped the whole thing into the pocket of his jacket. "Thank you. If I ever crack this, Jack, I'm buying you a steak."

Jack regarded Stan with sad eyes. "Wish you could eat one with me, buddy."

Stan said nothing.

There was nothing to say.

He took his own car to the South Side. The windshield wipers sluiced the gray rain away just in time for more gray rain to take its place. There was hardly anyone on the street; steam rose from the grates. Electric lights were muted, as if the bulbs had filled up with water.

It was not a fit night for man, beast, or those stuck somewhere in between.

But there was one highlight. He pulled into an alley, turned off the engine, and got out, rapped twice on a bright blue door. It opened and a handsome Hispanic woman appeared on the threshold. She was wearing a large, ornate crucifix that bothered Stan not at all.

"Buenas noches." He handed her a twenty.

"A usted," she replied. She was a nurse, worked for the university. She left for a moment, returned with something in a brown paper bag.

"O positive."

He took it. *"Gracias."*

With a barely suppressed shudder, she shut the door.

He ripped open the plastic container and scarfed down dinner.

About twenty minutes later, he parked in another alley, behind a Harley, and turned off the engine. Sat for a moment behind the wheel and calmed himself. Stoolie Bob was a real squirrel. He didn't want to spook him, have him clam up. Anything he could tell him about the woman, anything at all, would be the best news he'd had in a year.

He got out and walked around the corner. The Old Same Place was such a dive it didn't even have a nicely hand-lettered sign, much less an electric one. Its clientele consisted of those a buck or two away from homelessness, and looking to make that buck inside The Old Same Place by peddling drugs or other assorted good times, or hustling pool.

Used to be it was okay he went in there. But now, as he pushed open the wooden door, conversation died away for a moment before it resumed at a higher, more nervous pitch.

He wished he knew what he looked like. But of course, he cast no reflection in the mirror behind the bar.

The floor was cracked linoleum and the barstools and booths were covered in extremely distressed burgundy. Smoke that cast purple cobwebs hung motionless in the air. The place reeked of old cigarettes, mildew, sweat, and cheap perfume.

"G'evenin'," he said, and bellied up to the bar.

John Joseph, the grizzled old black proprietor, was washing a glass. A cigar hung out of his mouth. He nodded his reply.

"Stoolie Bob in?"

John Joseph jerked his head toward the back corner booth. Sure enough, Bob's signature navy-blue watch cap bobbed up and down like a puppet on *Sesame Street*.

The bartender poured Stan a drink, any drink; it was nice of him to do it when he knew Stan couldn't properly exploit it. Still, Stan blended in better with a fistful to carry around. He guessed. He took the glass and ambled over to Stoolie Bob's booth and stood there.

Stoolie Bob was talking to a young man with scars on his face and neck. Especially his neck. They both saw Stan and the young man whistled through his broken, brown teeth.

"It's true," he murmured, awed.

"You mind?" Stan asked harshly.

The man glanced at Stoolie Bob. "Later," he said, scooted to the end of the booth, hesitated, then got up and around Stan as fast as he could.

"I knew you'd come," Stoolie Bob gushed. He made to reach for Stan's hand, stopped himself. "Ya gotta help me. I'm marked now. She'll come back for me."

Stan slid back in his seat and feigned nonchalance. You got more out of Bob if he figured he wasn't going to get much out of you.

"She's like you, Mr. Detective!"

"Oh?" Stan yawned.

"Yeah! She's all white, and she's got these teeth!" Stoolie Bob lowered his voice. A vein pulsed below his jaw line like it was sending out a distress call. "I need your help. You gotta tell her to leave me alone. Tell her I'm your friend. That I help you solve cases, alla time. Please." Now Stoolie Bob did grab Stan's hands. His fingers were dry and papery.

"That so."

"Yeah!" Stoolie Bob gripped his fingers.

"And you made her acquaintance at?"

"I was down to the Loop. I was near the Hyatt. I

know I'm not supposed to be there, Mr. Detective. But I was hungry."

And the pickpocket pickings were pretty good down in yuppieland, Stan finished silently.

"And she was wearing?"

"I thought she was dead! I wasn't stealing from her!"

"And she was wearing?" Stan repeated.

"Black. All black. Black sweater. Black pants. Black coat." He paused. "Black boots."

Stan sighed. "Where's the rest of her purse? Was her wallet just lying beside her? Was it in her pocket?"

Stoolie Bob hesitated. He let go of Stan and dropped his hands under the table. Stared at the Formica.

"Bo-ob, yoo-hoo."

"I thought she was dead." He thrust out his lower lip.

"I'm not going to bust you." Stan folded his hands and leaned forward. "I want to help you. 'Cause you're right, Bob. She'll come back for you unless I can talk her out of it." A damn lie—well, maybe, how the hell should he know?—but what did it matter?

"Okay, okay." Stoolie Bob squared his shoulders. "It was in her pocket."

"Okay, Bob. That's okay. Now, this is important. Was there anything else in her pocket? Think about it. Anything else?"

Bob nodded. "Yeah. Yeah, there was. Book of matches."

Stan's eyes flickered. "Did you keep them? Do you have them?"

Stoolie Bob shook his head. "No. But I read 'em," he said hopefully. "They was from a restaurant. Called something funny. The Zigooner, something like that."

Zigooner. Stan thought. He called to John Joseph, "You got a Yellow Pages?"

John Joseph ducked his head under the bar, straightened, and showed him the phone book. Brought it over to the table.

"Thanks." Stan began to flip through it to the restaurant section. Zigooner. Zig.

Zigeuner. Bingo. Had to be.

Stan flipped the book shut. He rose, took out his wallet, and gave Stoolie Bob his usual fee of ten bucks.

"Night," John Joseph called, but Stan was already out the door.

"Tell her I'm your partner!" Stoolie Bob called out desperately.

Someone else muttered, "J.J. why you let that pasteface in here? He make me sick."

Pasteface. Damn.

The Zigeuner was a Rumanian restaurant near the Hyatt.

Bingo. Oh, yes, double bingo and it was all on red, baby.

Blood red.

Stan showed the photo to the waiters in white, open-throated Gypsy shirts, trying to keep his voice below the violin music, and they all acted so blind, deaf, and orally challenged that he knew he had the right place. Oh, he'd had people freeze up around him—such as his wife—but this was different; this was freezing with a purpose. This was freezing because they knew something.

But they sure didn't want to tell him what it was.

"Listen, I'll leave my card," he told a dark, husky man who kept opening the cash register, counting the money, and shutting it again. "I can be reached here on the night shift." He thought for a moment. "Here's my home phone, too. It's very urgent. If anyone remembers seeing this woman"—and here he held out her picture again, and the man flinched again—"I would really appreciate hearing about it. Really, I would."

He left, more hopeful than frustrated. And praying she wouldn't, or hadn't, left town.

Leslie was asleep when he got home. He tried not to wake her, but she had become a light sleeper since his Change.

He hadn't touched her in a year. Not even a kiss.

"Hi," she said, as he made sure the curtains were drawn against the windows. "How'd it go?"

"I have a lead." Her expression said she understood what he meant.

"Good."

"Maybe she . . . maybe I can be . . ." Changed back, he wanted to say, but he was afraid to.

Leslie took a deep breath. "Stan, I filed the papers today. This isn't fair to the kids. I . . ." She looked away.

"I love you," he whispered. "I would do anything . . ."

"You can't."

"I have a lead."

She wiped a tear from her eye. Her Adams apple bobbed. "It's just that, I, Stan . . ." She looked at him full on. "I can't help thinking about what you are. What you do to stay . . . alive." Her voice broke on that last word.

"Please sleep on the couch from now on." She looked away.

Why tonight? he thought. Why, when he finally had a clue?

"I haven't hurt anybody," he said.

"You might." She pulled the covers over herself.

He started to say more, sensed the futility of it.

Grabbing a pillow and a blanket, he trudged into the living room. Considered. The kids would try to wake him up. She hadn't thought of that. They would see him lying there, staring up at the ceiling like a zombie. Or like what he was.

He got back in his car and drove to a motel. Which was, he suspected, what she wanted all along.

He hoped no one at the restaurant called his home phone. Because all of a sudden, it wasn't home any more.

Sundown, and his eyes popped open.

He called Leslie when he woke up, and a man answered the phone. Depressed, he paid a visit to the owner of a pretty shady mortuary and had a snack. So let the guy overcharge on embalming, cut a few other funeral corners.

Man, police work was a dirty job sometimes. Or make that survival. But he had never hurt a soul; Leslie knew that. He had never touched a single living being in the entire hellish year.

He showed up for work at ten, as always. Jack had bent a lot of arms to keep him from rotating shifts; hell, he *had* broken some arms to keep Stan on the force.

The desk sergeant said, "Some woman called you. Wouldn't leave her name. Did leave a number."

Stan grabbed the slip of paper and ran to his office. Slammed the door. Yes, yes. He screwed up the number and had to punch it in again. Yes, baby, yes.

Jack ducked his head in, brows raised, with a look of eagerness of his sallow, underfed face. Evidently he knew about the call.

Stan looked up at him while the phone rang. Jack was a good friend.

"Hello?" Yes. It was a woman's voice, deep and sexy, very nervous. Stan hunched forward. Jack shut the door, leaving Stan in privacy.

"It's Stan Stepanek."

"Ah." A sigh of relief. "Ah, yes. Meet me now. Please, meet me. Alone. Tell no one."

Jeesh, so she could finish the job? He said, "Where are you?"

"No, not here. I can't trust . . ." She caught her breath. "Meet me in front of the aquarium in twenty minutes."

Dial tone.

Stan closed his eyes for a second. The room was whirling. He licked his lips and rose.

The door opened. Jack poked his head in.

"You got any silver bullets?" It was supposed to be a joke, but it fell flat.

Jack replied, very soberly, "No, but I was thinking you could use the tip of your umbrella, if you pushed hard enough. Was it her?"

"Maybe." Better have been.

"What's she want?"

"I don't know." But he knew what *he* wanted: revenge, an explanation, some help.

"You want backup?" Jack smiled grimly. "Guess not."

Without thinking, Stan checked the revolver in his shoulder, felt for his badge. What, was he going to Mirandize her? Bring her in for violating the laws of nature?

"Well," he said, and Jack shook his head. Swallowed hard.

"Good luck, buddy."

Stan nodded, said nothing. Left.

The moon hung low in the sky, casting a silvery glow over the river, and beyond, the vast expanse of Lake

Michigan. Over the tall figure who stood on the knoll, watching him advance.

Her face was cast in darkness. He tensed, wishing he had some protection. None of that Bela Lugosi stuff worked—crosses and holy water, no help at all. And he knew what he was talking about.

"Detective Stepanek?" she asked, in that deep, rich voice. It was heavily accented, some kind of East-Europe thing.

"Yes. And you?"

She came forward, into the soft fuzz of a streetlamp. He was taken aback. Despite the fact that she was white as chalk, she was the most beautiful woman he had ever seen in his life. Her eyes were huge and deep velvet brown; her cheekbones, her nose, her large red lips blended into a dream that just couldn't be real. Her hair tumbled around her shoulders in soft curls that kissed her neck. Her long, pale, slender neck.

Her photo had not done her justice.

"And you?" he repeated, his voice shaking, maybe not so much with terror as he had expected it to. Maybe with . . . wow, with he didn't know what—

She jerked. "I'm . . ." She looked away. "I was Natasha Boranova." When she looked back, tears glittered on her cheeks. "I'm sorry. I didn't know what I was doing. I'm . . . I'm a stranger here." The tears came in earnest now. They made her look so helpless, so vulnerable.

"Hey," he said softly, walking closer. She was shaking, probably just as . . . scared . . . as he was.

"We were here illegally."

"Yeah, I'll bet," he tried to joke. "I don't think Immigration has a quota on—"

"No, *before*." She cocked her head. "You don't know who I am, do you?"

"Besides Countess Dracula?" he retorted, and was immediately sorry. She jerked as if he'd hit her.

"I was a tennis player. I was here with my coach, Ivan Mazarek? We sought asylum."

Where had he been? Wrapped up in his Big Problem. He shrugged.

"Sorry. I don't know anything about that. But, ah,

aren't we all one big happy New World Order now anyway?"

"So they would all have us think." She threw back her head and raised her fists to her chest. "I'm so sorry. I didn't mean to leave you alive."

Whoah. His hand slipped into his jacket and touched his revolver. Futile, Stan. Futile. He cracked his knuckles and made a fist in his trouser pocket.

The moonlight drained even her lips of color. Even then, she was exquisite. "If you're left alive, you become . . . what you are now."

"Oh?" he rasped. "I thought it was the other way around."

"No." The beautiful hair waved back and forth, back and forth, as she shook her head in misery. "No, and they knew it, too."

She held out her hands. "Please, help me find the people did this to me. To us!"

And then she ran to him and threw her arms around him. Her lips sought, found his, and she kissed him so hard he staggered backward. It was heaven, pure and simple, especially when you have lived in hell for a year. He felt as if he were floating; he couldn't believe the sensations coursing through him. It was like . . . it was the way he imagined he would feel if he actually bit someone.

"Oh! I haven't touched another person in five years," she moaned, clinging to him. "Well, except . . . you know. I've been so lonely, so very lonely. The people at the Zigeuner, they try. But they could never really accept me."

"Yeah," he breathed. They kissed again. And again. They ran their hands along each other, starved, filling up. He tasted her blood on his lips. "You're so lovely."

"Am I?" She beamed at him. "I kept a picture of myself so I could remember what I looked like."

"You look swell. You're even more gorgeous than when you were . . . the other way."

"Human," she said wistfully, then glanced up at him through her lashes. His knees went weak. Her mouth was swollen and dotted with red, where his teeth had done a little damage.

"But do you know, if we are . . . together, for that

time we *are* human again." She nodded. "That much
they told me. They laughed at me and said I should go
make myself an 'Adam.' When they threw me out of the
car. After they murdered Ivan."

"Threw you ..." But his mind ran back to what she'd
said before that. "You mean, if we, um, get intimate, we
change back?"

"For a little time only." She saw something on his
face, and actually smiled. Her long, sharp canines glittered in the light.

"I understand, however, that you are married."

"What?"

"The desk sergeant told me. We had a chat. I had to
make sure you were the right one."

"I am the right one. My wife ..." And as sudden as
a gunshot, he knew he was leaving all that behind. Wife,
job, sunlight, the whole ball of wax, meant nothing while
he was in her arms. With her, he could be what he was
... and what he used to be.

As sure as he stood there, he finally, fully Changed.

"I'm a detective," he said. "I know how to find people." He held her tightly, so tightly.

"And when we find them, we'll rip their throats out."

"Oh, yes," she said breathlessly, her face buried
against his neck. "Yes, my darling, yes, we will."

FANTASY ANTHOLOGIES

Tanya Huff

☐ **SING THE FOUR QUARTERS** UE2628—$4.99
For Princess Annice, who could bring forth the elemental spirits from each of the four quarters, the call of magic was too strong to be denied, even if it meant renouncing her royal blood and becoming a fugitive in her own land.

VICTORY NELSON, INVESTIGATOR:
Otherworldly Crimes A Specialty
☐ **BLOOD PRICE: Book 1**	UE2471—$4.99
☐ **BLOOD TRAIL: Book 2**	UE2502—$4.50
☐ **BLOOD LINES: Book 3**	UE2530—$4.99
☐ **BLOOD PACT: Book 4**	UE2582—$4.99

THE NOVELS OF CRYSTAL
☐ **CHILD OF THE GROVE: Book 1**	UE2432—$4.50
☐ **THE LAST WIZARD: Book 2**	UE2331—$4.50

OTHER NOVELS
☐ **GATE OF DARKNESS, CIRCLE OF LIGHT**	UE2386—$4.50
☐ **THE FIRE'S STONE**	UE2445—$3.95

Elizabeth Forrest

☐ **PHOENIX FIRE**   UE2515—$4.99

As the legendary Phoenix awoke, so too did an ancient Chinese demon—and Los Angeles was destined to become the final battleground in their millenia-old war.

☐ **DARK TIDE**   UE2560—$4.99

In 1968, a freak accident at an amusement pier saw three boys drowned, and the only survivor pulled from the ocean in a near catatonic state. Years later, the survivor is forced to return to the town where it happened. And slowly, long buried memories start to resurface, and all his nightmares begin to come true . . .

☐ **DEATH WATCH**   UE2648—$5.99

For McKenzie Smith, a deadly legacy of fear and bloodshed will soon become all too real as she is targeted as the perfect victim by a mastermind of evil who can make virtual reality into the ultimate tool of destructive power. Stalked in both the real and virtual worlds, and with only herself to depend upon, can McKenzie defeat a deadly assassin who can strike out anywhere, at any time?
